TIA452346

Also by James Barclay from Gollancz:

CHRONICLES OF THE RAVEN

Dawnthief
Noonshade
Nightchild

LEGENDS OF THE RAVEN

Elfsorrow
Shadowheart
Demonstorm
Ravensoul

THE ASCENDANTS OF ESTOREA

Cry of the Newborn
Shout for the Dead

ELVES

Elves: Once Walked with Gods
Elves: Rise of the TaiGethen
Elves: Beyond the Mists of Katura

HEART OF GRANITE

JAMES BARCLAY

GOLLANCZ
LONDON

First published in Great Britain in 2016
by Gollancz
An imprint of the Orion Publishing Group
Carmelite House, 50 Victoria Embankment,
London EC4Y 0DZ
An Hachette UK Company

A CIP catalogue record for this book
is available from the British Library

ISBN 978 1 473 20243 6

1 3 5 7 9 10 8 6 4 2

Typeset at The Spartan Press Ltd,
Lymington, Hants

Printed and bound by CPI Group (UK) Ltd,
Croydon, CR0 4YY

www.jamesbarclay.com
www.orionbooks.co.uk
www.gollancz.co.uk

For my mother, Thea, whose love
and strength sustain and inspire me

'History will record that the discovery of alien technology and DNA on asteroid X345-102-401 brought us to a predictable catastrophe. Governments perverted our greatest gift to synthesise vehicles of destruction. Global conflict was inevitable.'

DOCTOR DAVID WONG,
THE DESTRUCTION OF HUMANITY

CHAPTER 1

> I don't remember getting the tap on the shoulder at school or the walk to the principal's office alongside the recruitment agents in their ERC uniforms. But I do remember the dripping jealousy on the faces of everyone I passed and I will never forget how cool that was.
>
> MAXIMUS HALLORAN

Max was woken by an insistent nagging at the back of his mind.

It probably wasn't important.

He let his head drop back to the pillow and stared at the ceiling where the dim ridge lights flickered in time with the whirr of the increasingly inefficient air-circulation system. Outside his pod, the squad rack was quiet. No one else was even awake, let alone up.

'Not like me to wake up early,' muttered Max.

'Don't you read your pings?'

Anna-Beth was lying on her stomach with her head turned away and the sheet clinging to the lines of her body. Max drew a finger down her spine and she rose on her elbows, her long black hair falling either side of her face. He grinned, sliding down next to her and leaning in for a kiss.

'Not if I can avoid it.'

'Are you kidding me?' Anna-Beth put a hand on his face and

pushed him away. 'You were *at* the briefing last night, right? I wondered why you were still here.'

'Because—'

'You know, the amount of shit you're in makes you completely undesirable right now,' she said, with a twinkle in her eye.

'Oh, really?' he said and began to push the sheet down, his fingertips tracing her silky skin.

'Really.' Anna-Beth slid a little closer to him, enjoying herself. Her hand cupped his balls. 'You really don't know why you're in the shit?'

'Don't know, don't care.'

'You're not bothered about skippering the escort for the marshal general's cortege, then?'

Max froze, colour draining from his face.

'That's tomorrow,' he said, stomach lurching.

'Uh-uh. Today.' She leaned into his ear and whispered. 'Right now.'

'Shit,' said Max, scrambling out of bed. 'Shitshitshit. Why didn't they wake me? What happened to—?'

His sweats struck him in the face. He grabbed for them, missed, stumbled against the door and trod on the corner of a belt buckle.

'Ow, bloodyfuckbollocks! Thanks a lot.'

'Any time,' said Anna-Beth, following up with some well-aimed boots.

Max pulled his joggers on and jammed his feet into his boots. He gave Anna-Beth a lopsided smile.

'Be here when I get back.'

'In your dreams, drake bitch.'

Anna-Beth's delicate blown kiss chased him from his room. He paused in the act of sprinting past the squad rec to take in the absurdly neat arrangement of sofas, chairs, screens and consoles. Every coffee- and teacup had been washed, dried and stacked by the gleamingly clean beverage machines – to which a note was attached. Max ran over and read it.

Did your chores for you. We heard it was a late one last night and didn't want to wake you. Set the alarm to give you just enough time to get to the most important flight of your so-far worthless life. But only just. Love, Inferno-X

'Very bloody funny. Bastards.' An alarm began to sound and he glanced up at the mission countdown timer. Lots of red numbers there. 'Shit.'

Max burst out of the squad dorm and powered along the spine, dodging from side to side to evade the masses dawdling to wherever it was they had loads of time to get. He sprinted through the echoing 'tenways' spine-link space that would become Gargan's bar later, wrinkling his nose at the stale smells of alcohol and sweat that clung to every surface.

He hurdled an auto-vac and raced off to the right down an access corridor, battering open the 'Emergency Access Only' door at the end. It stank of burnt toast out here within the flank armour. Water poured down the inside, catching a joint above his head and covering the ringing metal stairway, and him, in its fetid warmth.

Max grabbed the rail and swung over, letting go and turning in the air before catching the rails a storey below. He pushed himself back with his feet and dropped again, grabbing the base of the rail and swinging to land on his feet on the walkway.

'Nailed it,' he grinned and ran.

Outside the open door to the vast retractable flight deck, he could hear the competing cries and roars of drakes, geckos, chameleons, basilisks and komodos. Once inside, he slowed to a saunter and fought to control his breathing. He had to walk past the cages holding the ground-based lizards on the way to the drake pens, so he made sure he caught the eye of a jockey. He sniffed extravagantly.

'Wow, that's some powerful stench you're developing. New aftershave is it? Eau de Slime-Sucker; for the face-down, sand-eating, lizard-jock in your life.'

'Drop dead, dragon-shagger.' A gecko driver made a move towards him. 'Hey, let's compare IQs in a year's time, slop-head.'

Max blew a kiss and walked away. 'I'm going to look for you out there today. Gonna need a target for my drake to shit on.'

The drakes were calling, the sound echoing from the walls, drowning out the Flight Com orders coming over the PA. The beautiful white Inferno-X drakes were already moving onto the runway. Max broke into a run again, aching to be with them.

'Halloran!'

Thirty metres of drake moved serenely out of its pen and blocked his way. For about the millionth time, Max wondered why they didn't just call them dragons because that was sure as shit what they looked like. The drake's eyes were on him, and so were those of its pilot, Squadron Leader Valera Orin, going through her preflight routine.

The drake's mouth yawned to reveal its rows of bone-crushing teeth. Its five-metre neck flexed, the scales meshing and moving in a sinuous dance. Along its broad back, bone spurs rotated out to defensive position and then back flush to the armoured scales. And the tail, fully six metres long and run with thorns, whipped up into the scorpion position, its needle-sharp tip glistening.

'Skipper?'

'What time do you call this?'

'Why didn't anyone wake me? Too busy tidying up really quietly and leaving sarcastic notes?'

'That was Stepanek's idea. Good one, eh? It's almost a shame you've just squeaked in this time. But you'd better run and you'd better learn to take responsibility. There's two minutes on the countdown then I'm giving Stepanek the escort lead honour cap just to piss you off.'

'You'd give it to *Stepanek*?'

The drake's wings twitched in a shrug.

'Clock's ticking. Grim's got your suit already.'

Max ran down the line of drake pens, hearing catcalls and jibes all the way. He played up to it as he went, even taking a bow as he slid to a halt by his pen and Grimaldi, his flight tech.

'Ah, it's call sign dickhead. Hardly worth *almost* getting dressed, was it?'

'Very funny, Grim.'

Max stripped off his joggers. Grimaldi glowered at him with her trademark disdain and held out his suit, her hands filthy with drake dirt, her face and yellow overalls freckled with soot and dust.

Every time he forced his body into the rubberised, bio-plastic body sheath he wished there was a way to link with his drake without the clumsy mass of neuro-organic receptors. The suit squeezed his body like a too-tight wetsuit and itched like a bastard until it warmed up and expanded a fraction. He dragged it up his legs, over his torso and chest, and forced his arms into the sleeves.

Grimaldi zipped it up as he hauled the hood over his head, and felt the tightness around the sides of his face and the back of his skull. He pushed gently at his throat with forefinger and thumb, positioning the com controls to pick up his subvocalised commands. Moments later, he felt the warmth he longed for through his body and mind.

'There you are, gorgeous,' he said. 'Ready to play?'

Taloned feet slammed against the drake pen and an armoured head reared up. Hawk-keen reptilian eyes stared through the broad window at him and the drake's mouth opened in what Max maintained was a smile – a hideously toothy smile but a smile nonetheless – despite the Tweakers' denials that drakes experienced emotion.

'How's she doing?' asked Max, reaching to slap the warm glass by the drake's muzzle. The creature shook her head and spittle flew in all directions. 'Good to see you too, Martha.'

'One day,' said Grimaldi, 'I will beat out of you why you gave her that name. Anyway, she's peak, of course. Take a look.'

Grimaldi unlatched the pen door and slid it back. A wash

of warm air rushed out of the enclosure, which was lit with hot lamps and backed by infrared heat and light. Max's smile broadened and the warmth in his mind and body intensified.

Max held up a hand and Martha dipped her head so he could run his fingers over her fangs and the eight fuel ducts pulsating at the sides of her mouth. They were full and healthy, the openings pink and clear.

There was a rustling sensation in Max's left ear.

'This is *Heart of Granite* Flight Commander Moeller. Call sign Hal-X, confirm reception.'

'Loud and clear, sir. Good to hear you.'

'Nice of you to join us. Slime up. Sky-high in sixty seconds.'

'Copy, sir.'

'Right, close your eyes,' said Grimaldi. She was holding a thin hosepipe. Barely waiting for him to comply, she pulled the trigger. A fine spray misted out, smelling of oil and sweat. Max held his arms out and turned slowly, letting the liquid settle on every stitch of his suit. 'All done. Should stop you getting stuck halfway in.'

'Always the same joke,' said Max.

'Gets funnier each time I tell it.'

'In your flawed opinion.' Max cocked his head then turned to the faulty fan that wobbled in its brackets up in the roof structure, venting condensation inefficiently. 'Can you get on to those lazy arses in maintenance? That thing'll fall on Martha's head one day. Tell them when it does, I'll point them out to her.'

'Sure thing, Max,' said Grim.

Max raised his hands in front of Martha and the stunning white drake rose up to sit on her powerful hind legs. The front of her chest opened to reveal the receptor pouch within. The lubricant on Max's suit would mix with the pouch's secretions to ensure maximum connectivity.

Max climbed quickly up the chest scales, turned and slid into the bespoke pouch, feeling the mind-touch of the drake intensify and a soul-deep thrill course through him. He moved his feet into their bays and his arms into the receptor sleeves, keeping them close to his sides. He stretched out his gloved fingers.

Martha's chest closed and Max felt a gentle pressure across his body and thick, shock-absorbent fluid fill the pouch, expelling any air within. A layer of skin moved to cover his scalp and he placed his chin on the moulded rest, feeling the pouch tighten minutely against his throat and com controls. His visor, with heads-up display, slid down over his face. The drake shuddered, opened her mouth and roared her pleasure or, as the Tweakers who made her would have it, confirmed her state of readiness.

'You and me, baby,' he said. 'Let's walk.'

Max curled his toes and the drake rattled her rear talons on the bone floor. The rush of the receptors picking up and relaying his movements to Martha never lessened. He directed her to surge upright, move out of the pen and onto the runway. It was a gloomy day outside. The air was thick with dust and the *Heart of Granite* had thrown up huge clouds in her wake.

Max looked to his left to where Grimaldi stood proffering a water bottle with a long straw. He took a sip.

'Don't Fall.'

'Not today, not ever,' said Max, reciting the drake pilot mantra.

'Look after my Risa.'

'Always.'

Max looked forwards. He moved his leg again and Martha walked past the twenty-three waiting drakes and their pilots that made up Squadron Inferno-X. Radio chatter filled his ears and he laughed.

'Hal-X on the stand, Flight Command,' he said. 'Requesting permission to run.'

'Stand by, Hal-X.' A pause. 'Skin of your teeth, boy. Report to me on landing. You don't get off that easily.'

Hoots and howls ricocheted over the open com link. 'Copy, sir.'

'Depart left, climb to circle above flak range. Hal-X, you are clear to run.'

'Tail up, Martha, let's fly.'

Max nodded his head. Martha opened her mouth and bellowed. She stamped her feet and powered down the runway and Max's mind was filled with the promise of imminent freedom. Every footfall reverberated through the pouch, shock-absorbent fluid reducing the shuddering impacts to gentle ripples.

Max opened his mouth and breathed in the acceleration. His arms were tight to his sides, keeping Martha's wings folded hard against her body while she gathered pace, rocking gently from side to side, tail balancing her lateral movement. Flight crews and ground jocks turned to watch. Strip lights flashed, red pulsing bulbs blurred and alarms Dopplered as he sped by.

In front, the distance markings on the pitted runway began to merge. The retractor stays at the end of the sprint zone glared yellow. Max moved his arms away from his body exactly thirty centimetres. Martha snapped her wings out and with a gasp from Max they were airborne, shooting out of the flight deck and sweeping left. He turned his wrists out a fraction as he cleared the tail. Martha flared her wings and swept into a steep climb, high into the early morning skies of the Mid-Af warzone.

'This is Hal-X clear of the flight deck, the *HoG* in my wake and up-wings skywards. Not a cloud up here so it's gonna be a hot one later. Who'd be a grunt in a dust cloud?'

'Copy, Hal-X, circle on station,' said Moeller. 'And cut the chatter.'

Martha climbed hard and fast, lazy sweeps of her wings driving her on. Their current air speed and altitude were displayed above Max's right eye. He flattened his hands and canted his body slightly left. Martha cruised in a wide circle, levelling out and giving him a breathtaking view of the *Heart of Granite*.

'Look, Martha, there's your mum.'

And damn him if Martha's body didn't ripple in response. Max wondered if it was laughter or love.

CHAPTER 2

Who the hell comes up with ideas like growing battle lizards in big tanks anyway? MAXIMUS HALLORAN

Max cruised the length of the *HoG*, banked above her head and returned aft, four hundred metres above her. Martha was calm, her heartbeat measured and her wings barely beating, enjoying the thermals rising from the desert floor. Below them he could see Inferno-X streaking out of the flight deck and climbing through the dust clouds to circle on station with him.

'I-X, this is Hal-X moving to lead position.'

Max urged Martha to greater speed, dipping her into a shallow dive to get below the squad before swooping up in a perfect barrel roll through the middle of their spiral. He climbed into the pristine sky and rolled to take in the vast desert and ruined lands in the *HoG*'s wake.

'Typically understated,' muttered Valera.

Max opened his com again. 'You wouldn't have it any other way, Skipper.'

'The sad thing is you really believe that,' said Abraham, his gentle tone warming the airwaves.

'That roll will save your life one day, Abe. You should learn it.'

'You offering nightly tutorials in bed again, Max?' said Jak-X.

'Funny, Jaks. I'll check with the boss but I think those days are gone now.'

'Flight Com incoming,' said Valera. 'Go ahead, Flight Com.'

'Inferno-X, Flight Com. Marshal General Solomon is one hundred and seven klicks due north of your location. Make best speed. You will be relieving Squadron Lumière-C from the *Steelback*. The cortege is ground-bound. You know how active the Mafs and Sambas are right now, so this is not a procession. And it is not an excuse to show off your acrobatic skills. Are we clear, Inferno-X?'

A chorus of understanding crammed the coms.

'Do you understand, Hal-X?'

'I'm hurt, Flight Com. Do I have the cap?'

'Confirmed, Hal-X. Flight Com out.'

'Inferno-X, Hal-X flying skipper for the inbound cortege escort mission. Yes, kids, I have the honour cap. Orders, orders. Triple height staggered chevron. Val-X and Chevron-One at a thousand; Step-X and C-Three at fifteen hundred; Hal-X and C-Two at two thousand. Form up, I-X, let's show them what the best drake squad in the world looks like.'

Max rose to two thousand and watched Inferno-X form up. Valera and C-One peeled off left, diving in a long shallow circle. C-Three mirrored the move, climbing right and up. Both chevrons moved into perfect position simultaneously. It was simple and beautiful; not a wingbeat was wasted. White scales glittered in the bright sun, drake roars and calls filled the sky and Martha returned the cry. His private com clicked open.

'Good work, Hal-X. Keep it tight. I'm here if you need me.'

'Copy, Skipper.'

Max relaxed into the flight, feeling the rush of air as Martha powered forwards, and the vibrations of her wingbeats massaging his body through the modulations in the pouch. Martha's mind-touch was like a comfort blanket, reading and reacting to his micro-movements. Using her senses meant opening his mind to her a fraction, and it was seductive; she was always there wanting more, tempting him with images of freedom and power. One day she'd get what she wanted, and he'd Fall. Martha grumbled, sensing his briefly sombre mood.

Max used Martha's eyes to glance left and right at his eight-strong chevron, using his mind to suggest the movement and seeing what she saw projected in his visor. He remembered the first time he'd done that, back in the training days. He'd been so confused by what he was seeing that he'd all but flown the poor drake into the ground. Now it was easy, filtering Martha's view and adding his own to give him all-round vision.

'Inferno-X, Hal-X. We're in the cruise. Maintain formation and course. You all look beautiful.'

'Aw, shucks, Max,' said Borini. 'Makes me go all gooey inside.'

'"Shucks", Bor-X? Really? Holy Mother, where did you dredge that up?' asked Jes-X.

'I have depths of linguistic skill others only dream about, Jessy,' said Borini.

'Keep it well hidden, don't you?' said Nuge-X.

'All right, all right,' said Max. 'Let's focus.'

Max relaxed further, letting Martha ride the thermals and keeping her dead-on north. The next battlefront, where the behemoths of United Europa and Mid-Af would clash, was a hundred and fifty klicks south, just a couple of days' standard march for a behemoth. More land to slash, burn, and then own – and turn into vast, fertile croplands – if you cared about that. Max supposed he did, but mostly he cared about the next fight: lighting up enemy drakes, toasting enemy grunts and later, leading the celebrations at the victory party.

Ahead it was all blown sand, dust and scorched earth. But there was brightness on the northern horizon: water glittering under the sun. It was probably still dyed red from the blood washing off the Mediterranean beaches. That had been some battle.

Max and Martha looked around; Inferno-X was still alone in

the sky. He had half-expected them to be shadowed by now, most likely by forces from the Samba bloc. They had the impressive Águila and Relámpago squadrons but there was no evidence of them so far.

'Inferno-X is approaching the target zone,' said Max. 'Orders, orders. C-Three, three-sixty sky-watch for enemy specks. C-Two, we're on friendly drake watch. C-One, eyes open for vortices in the dust. Hal-X out.'

Max was enjoying the minimal stresses on the pouch, just the gentle push from the wings. This was as close to weightless as a drake pilot could get. Martha cruised above the sand and dust, and the moment's relative quiet was wonderful. Then his earpiece, set into the hood of his suit, crackled.

'Vortices ahead, bearing three-five-five,' said Valera. 'Big enough to be our target. Anything from Flight Com, Hal-X?'

Max couldn't see anything in the dust from his height, but on the horizon he could just see three black dots: the Lumière-Cs. They were flying a wide holding pattern, definitely a guard formation.

'Nothing yet, Skipper. I've got spots ahead.' Max opened his squad com. 'Inferno-X, we have vortices ahead at three-five-five and closing, specks in guard formation above them. Val-X, stay in formation and descend into the cloud; confirm target by sight. Hal-X out.'

'Copy, Hal-X,' said Valera. 'Leading descent.'

Max watched C-One disappear into the murk, following the vortices in the cloud formed by sprinting ground lizards, and the more confused eddies associated with the lumbering pace of larger, multi-legged constructs.

'Step-X, maintain course, eyes open for incoming targets.'

'Copy, Hal-X,' said Stepanek.

'C-Two, follow my lead and keep the chevron tight. We're going to relieve Lumière-C the way only I-X can.'

Max angled Martha into a climb to get himself and C-Three

two hundred metres above the Lumières. Martha's senses confirmed his chevron were in perfect form behind him. He cruised in a wider circle directly above the three dull brown Lumières who were flying a standard sentry formation, a hundred metres above the sand cloud. No doubt they'd seen the incoming Infernos and were off guard. They really should have known better.

'C-Three, we're going straight through their formation, pull a loop and settle in their wake. Easy stuff. On me, let's go in three.'

Max imagined noise and Martha bellowed, her jaws dripping saliva, some of which blew back across his visor and was whipped away by the wind. Max leaned forwards, his arms tight, and straightened his body head to toe. Martha dived, her form arrow-straight and her wings tight to her sides. Her speed was incredible and the air screamed past, whistling through her furled wings and singing along her tail.

Max trimmed his direction as he closed on the Lumière drakes, his smile broadening with every heartbeat. He'd calculated it perfectly, of course. Martha was on collision course with his target and the Lumière would be unable to evade him. Max laughed, pulse racing.

'You're coming in too close, Max,' said Kullani. 'Ease down.'

'I've got this, Kul-X. You've all got clear air, that's what matters.'

'It's gonna cost you if you hit.'

'I'm not hitting anyone.'

With the Lumière's scales large in his vision, Max twisted his body and Martha barrel-rolled past, missing the brown drake by a hair. Max and Martha roared with delight.

C-Three screamed through in his wake and he led them into a tight loop that finished with them right on station.

'Oh, we are on *rails* today,' purred Max. He opened his com. 'Lumière-C, you are officially relieved. Inferno-X has the reins.'

The coms lit up with furious shouts and threats.

'Hey, that's how the greatest squadron in the world flies. Lessons offered. Spaces still available.'

The Lumière drakes peeled away, heading west towards the *Steelback*. Max could still hear them muttering their threats, their drakes taut in the glide.

'Holy Mother, Max,' said Losano.

'I know. Perfect, weren't we? Orders, orders. Mont-X, Nuge-X, Red-X, take sentry. The rest of you with me.'

Max dived through the dust cloud, levelling out sharply at fifty. Ahead he could see the marshal gen's cortege and it was properly impressive; a Komodo One, surrounded by iguanas, geckos and basilisks. The chatter on the waves was still hot and his earpiece crackled insistently.

For the moment, he ignored it, choosing to bring his chevron in close to the Komodo One.

'C-Three is sky-high on lookout, C-Two on mid-sentry, C-One on close quarters patrol. Inferno-X has arrived,' said Max. 'Skipper, I think we've introduced ourselves.'

'You're an idiot, Max. I've got Moeller in one ear and the marshal gen in the other and neither is impressed.'

Max sighed. 'Copy, Val-X. My holy arse, but there's no sense of humour or style any more, is there?'

'You do remember who we're guarding here? Val-X out.'

Martha's warmth filled his mind. At least she'd enjoyed it. Below Max, the cortege spread across two kilometres of Nor-Af desert. It looked more like a relief force than a guard. Perhaps it was.

Max stared at it, trying to work out where Marshal General Solomon would be riding. Right in the centre was the Komodo Class One. It was about a quarter the size of a behemoth like the *Heart of Granite* and was designed as a troop carrier, or as a stupidly slow and vulnerable mobile hospital. It was lumbering along on its twelve pairs of legs, leaving Max wondering why any patient in their right mind would take a bed there. Better to die in the sand than puke your last in that thing.

The chances of the marshal gen being on it were minimal. It was escorted by half a dozen Geckos, the standard ground assault lizard. It was probably full of her luggage or something.

Four iguana support carriers were travelling at the major compass points around the komodo. They looked like miniature behemoths with their similar shape, and ability to carry two hundred people in their spine and bone pods either side of the gut. The marshal gen was most likely in one of them – unless she was riding a Basilisk. He had to suppress a chuckle at the thought. There were about fifty of the supremely fast runners though, unlike their mythological namesake, they couldn't turn anything to stone. Max felt that was a genuine omission. Tweakers always missed out the really important stuff.

Nope, it had to be an Iguana. His money was on the one to the north.

Max brought C-Two into a low pass across the Geckos, each of which was carrying around thirty elite fighters. Max shuddered seeing the pilot's pouch. The poor slime-suckers who drove them were face-down in lubricant, breathing through tubes and with their eyes wired into the lizard's via a sensory mask. They lay at the base of the neck, the pouch protected by thick, armoured scales.

'Inferno-X, Hal-X. Maintain your chevrons. C-One, maintain proximity to the cortege. C-Three, remain sky-high at a thousand. Give me a four-klick diameter, I want early warnings of any incoming Sambas and Mafs. C-Two, we're reforming on point above the dust cloud, sweeping east and west. We're the eyes, nothing gets past us. Let's fly.'

Max brought his chevron in a tight circle above the cortege, and then shot high and steep back through the cloud and into clear air.

'Hal-X, Flight Com.'

'Go ahead, Flight Com.'

'Patching the marshal general through. Flight Com out.'

Max had time to blow out his cheeks and feel his nerves echoed in the tremor that ran through Martha's body.

'Hal-X, this is Solomon.'

'Ma'am. It is an honour to fly your guard.'

'We are aware of your talents without the need for demonstrations. A word of warning: arrogance in pilots is only tolerable because your lives are short and violent. Foolishness is absolutely unacceptable when it risks expensive equipment. Do anything like that again and I'll ground you.'

'With respect, Marshal General, I was in total control of my drake at all times.'

There was an icy silence that shredded Max's good humour. He bit his lip harder with every passing moment.

'You may be in control of your drake. Do not assume everyone else is.'

'Understood, ma'am.'

'Report to me when we reach the *Granite*.'

'Yes, ma'am. Before or after I see the flight commander?'

'Even you can work out the chain of command, Hal-X. Solomon out.'

It was a huge honour to have the cap, recognising his talent and standing in the kill tables, and he had a brief moment of worry he might have blown it with his stunt. He quashed it though because no matter what she'd said, Solomon was impressed and you don't bench your best pilots.

'Inferno-X, this is Hal-X. We have the honour. Maintain your altitudes and circle on station. The cortege is making best speed to the *HoG*, let's try to be patient.'

Max heard some muttering.

'Come again, Kul-X?'

'Nothing,' said Kullani. 'Pots, kettles, that sort of thing.'

'Stay focused,' said Max.

It took every scrap of willpower Max possessed to take his own advice. The cortege was so slow he wondered how the squadron stayed in the air. Fighting the twin enemies of boredom and stalling was no easy task.

Max shrugged his shoulders and Martha rippled her wings.

'Sorry, Martha, didn't mean that one.'

Martha's warmth suffused him as if she understood and they turned a lazy circle to bring the chevron back into position, his movements echoed by C-One and C-Three. Time and again they repeated the manoeuvre while the ground lizards crept along beneath the cloud.

Max took C-Two on another sweep west where the dust was even denser than over the cortege, caught in a trap of thermal activity. Martha's neck tautened but Max had already seen what she was stretching towards. Away to the west, perhaps three klicks distant, there were vortices in the dust cloud. They were violent and spread over an area of some four hundred metres, approaching at pace: incoming drakes.

'Flight Com, Hal-X. Confirm position of Lumière-C.'

'Lumière-C is south east of your position, Hal-X.'

'Well, we've got vortices approaching fast from the west. Val-X, do you copy?'

'Copy that. I have the cap, Hal-X. C-Two, angle down and intercept. Let's see what we've got. C-One, C-Three, maintain formation.'

'Copy, Val-X,' said Max. 'Chevron Two on my tail. Eyes open.'

Max tipped his body forwards and Martha swept into a dive.

CHAPTER 3

At its height in 2247, the global conflict consumed the combined resources of seven power blocs on no less than fifteen different battlefronts. Where the majority fought themselves to a total standstill or negotiated local land split deals, the fronts in the mountains of Eastern UE and Mid-Af went on burning.

JANETH KARUPU – GREED, PRIDE AND GLOBAL CONFLICT.

Vortices in the dust: an angry storm born of beating drake wings and the swift passage of sleek reptilian bodies. There were at least thirty drakes approaching, their signatures boiling together, creating a confusing mass of false images and trails in the dust.

'Dense down there,' said Schmidt-X.

'Copy that, Schmiddy,' said Max. 'Break in pairs. Let's drive them down into C-One's flames. Close coms, shout your problems and don't Fall. Let's take them out.'

Max switched to personal com. 'You with me, buddy?'

'In your slipstream, Max,' replied Kullani, her tone as hard and cold as her drake.

'I'll go high. Feel me in there. Vision's going to be awful.'

'I hear you.'

They dropped into the dust cloud and with it came their only moment of vulnerability. Martha's senses dulled while she adjusted to the atmosphere. Max concentrated on focus and calm, and Martha's wings didn't miss a beat as they ploughed deeper.

Visibility was down to a handful of metres with dust and sand rattling on Max's visor and hissing against Martha's scales. Max could barely see anything beyond a confusion of eddies and pools in the sunlit grey. Luckily Martha wasn't reliant on her vision; she could smell her prey too.

Max felt her testing and sampling the air as they powered through the dust, searching for enemies. He saw her head twitch and steady just to her left and Max turned with her.

'We've got a lock,' he said.

'I'm with you,' said Kullani.

The dust was lit up by a bright yellow flare below them to the left. Max could feel the warmth and he heard the scream of an injured drake. He smiled; one enemy down.

In the after-glare, smeared silhouettes of drakes were stamped on the dust like charcoal on paper and gone the next instant. Max's mind-link fed him data via Martha's keen senses, allowing him to assess each drake's attitude, trim, distance and speed. Flare after flare shattered the gloom around them, their afterglows ricocheting across the dust cloud.

'One at twenty metres and closing hard on our twelve,' said Max.

'Copy,' said Kullani.

Max let his mind drift fractionally further into Martha's. He felt her primal urge to hunt and felt her strength of will too, just tamed, just under control. The enemy drake was fifty metres away now. Through Martha he could sense its shape. It was an Águila. Good skills.

'Split,' ordered Max.

He drove for the enemy's neck and suggested fine fire. Martha blew twin beams of tight blue flame. The Águila saw it coming and plunged downwards, where Kullani was waiting. Her drake, flying belly up, grabbed the Águila in its huge hind claws, the great jaws biting down hard on the back of its neck, just below the skull. Its tail fouled an enemy wing, the sharp tip jabbing and tearing.

The Águila shrieked with pain, its pilot losing control and the extra weight of Kullani dragging it down. Flame shot from its jaws, singeing dust and air in a spiral as Kullani pulled it around and around while Max got into position.

'Now, Kul-X.'

'Copy that.'

Kullani powered her drake upwards, dragging the helpless Águila with her. As soon as she achieved vertical, she let go, rolling away to the left, leaving Martha right in front of the Águila. Her head was level with the pilot's pouch and Max was so close he could see his enemy's eyes widen.

Max suggested wide-angle fire and a wash of deep orange flame enveloped the pilot's head, the pouch and the base of the Águila's neck. The enemy drake dropped screeching from the sky, fire raging in its chest cavity.

Max swept past Kullani, who was already hunting for a new target. Flare after flare, blue and yellow and red, added to the confusion in the dust cloud.

'All chevrons check in,' said Max. 'C-Two, report kills. C-One, confirm cortege still secure. C-Three, you are free to engage below the cloud.'

While the messages and confirmations came in, Max scoured the dust cloud ahead, seeking modulations within it, anything to give him an edge. He ducked forwards reflexively, making a half-turn left, and felt the beat of wings as an Águila swept overhead. Kullani was turning hard right and up, settling into its wake.

'I'll go low,' said Max.

'Am closing fast. I have the scent.'

Max turned hard and Martha heaved into the roll, the shock-absorbing pouch undulating with the forces exerted on it and the wind whistling about her wings. Max brought her head up and rolled his shoulders, levelling them out and accelerating hard.

'Kul-X, I'm behind and below you at a hundred and closing.'

'Copy, Hal-X. Enemy level... Strike that, he's diving hard... and he's got company.'

'Stay on his tail,' said Max. He switched to the C-Two com. 'C-Two, Hal-X. Get below the dust and form up if you're not already engaged. Águilas ahead of us. Out.'

Max tipped his body forwards and angled into a steep dive. Around him, he could sense his chevron coming into formation, drakes following Martha's scent. Kullani was next to him, blood on her drake's claws. They burst into clear air beneath the dust cloud together; seventy-five metres above the ground in a sky full of drakes. The Águilas split to his left, fleeing towards their comrades, engaged with Inferno-X drakes half a klick away.

'C-Two, go open com.'

Max's ears filled with Valera's calm command.

'—clear above the cortege. Kan-X, Xav-X, keep them moving west. New contacts south and east... C-Three, move to engage. Hal-X, C-Two, good of you to join us. I see five hulks burning in the sand. Good work. How was it in there?'

'Foggy, Skipper.'

Max looked at the tableau laid out for him as Inferno-X levelled out and headed after the Águilas, keeping close form and holding their distance at about eighty metres. Chevron Three was ahead, taking the mass of the Águilas – probably another eighteen of them – head-on and flying rings round them.

The cortege was plodding on, Chevron One still holding station above them. A few of the basilisks were on sprint patrol on the flanks guarding against new assault, and the turrets on the Iguanas were tracking but not firing. They wouldn't need to; Inferno-X was in town. Below him, he could see nine downed Águilas in total, many of them on fire, others still twitching through their death throes.

Ahead, four of the Águilas peeled away, heading off easterly at a sprint.

'I've got runners,' said Max. 'A quad heading east, possibly lining up a ground run. Orders, Val-X?'

'You know what to do, Hal-X. Take what you need.' Max followed them, signalling Kullani to match him.

'Copy, Val-X.' Max increased speed. 'Los-X, Schmidt-X, Nuge-X, Mont-X, on me for decoy on possible ground runs.'

'Copy, Hal-X,' came the chorus.

'They're turning,' said Kullani.

'Be ready,' said Max. 'Up we go, Kul-X.'

'Right with you, boss.'

Max and Kullani shot into the dust cloud, banking and turning immediately. It was all educated guesswork now. Course, speed, height… Max didn't want to leave the cloud cover too soon. He pushed Martha hard, hearing the sweep of her wings and feeling a rush of pleasure. He angled down very slightly, moving to the base of the dust cloud.

'Now, Max,' said Kullani, feathering her drake alongside Martha. 'They'll be on the cortege in less than thirty seconds.'

Max looked across at her. 'Take a breath, Kul-X.'

'Smug bastard.'

'With good reason. Dive!'

Max steeped his body forwards and drew his arms tight to his sides. Martha stretched her neck and tail, switched her wings back and screamed out of the cloud.

'Waaaaa hooooo!'

Right below them, the quartet of Águilas flashed across the ground, sending up whorls of sand in their wake. And buzzing them in front and behind the four Inferno-X drakes twisted and turned. Fire splashed across the backs of the enemy, reflected by armoured scales. The distracted Águilas snapped at empty space while their pilots fought to keep their beasts on target.

'Perfect,' said Max. 'C-Two, Kul-X and I will take the central pair. Kul-X, break right after impact and take out the flanker.'

'Copy that, Hal-X.'

Max and Kullani dropped out of the sky towards the fast-moving Águilas, their descent just shy of vertical and their targets never more than ten metres from the ground, following the undulations and staying below the ground lizards' guns. The decoy drakes remained close, their proximity obscuring Max's approach.

'C-Two decoys, stand by to clear,' said Max.

He was fifty metres from the ground in little more than a heartbeat and his vision was full of the Águila below him.

'Clear!' ordered Max.

The decoys split and Max drove in, the margin for error vanishingly small. He flared his arms and jerked his legs straight, timing perfect. Martha's massive clawed feet slammed into the Águila's back, shrieking against its scales and smashing it down. Martha sprang back into the air, forcing the Águila lower still. Its wing drove into the sand, dug deep and cartwheeled the drake into the ground.

It roared as it ploughed into the sand, smashing its shoulder. It collided with a dune and was flung back into the air before falling again, snapping its neck and flipping end over end. Way too close for comfort, Max jerked left, avoiding the dead bounce by a hair and climbing to see it slither to a halt in a cloud of sand, twitching its last.

Max drove Martha up after one of the surviving Águilas. The rest of C-Two was closing in.

'Report, Kul-X.'

'My Águila's down,' said Kullani. 'After my flanker now.'

'Missing you already,' said Max.

'Bollocks you are.'

His target was tired and Max moved into its wake as it climbed, obviously monitoring the two Inferno drakes closing on the flanks. It was Monteith and Nugent on the hunt.

'Mont-X, Nuge-X, he's going to break for the dust cloud. Blocking formation.'

'Copy that, Hal-X,' said Nugent.

Max urged Martha to beat her wings hard into the last of the climb, coming right up behind the enemy Águila as his chevron came in from the sides.

'Stand by,' said Max. 'Stand by . . . Drop out.'

Monteith and Nugent peeled away, dropping down out of sight as Martha opened her mouth and emitted twin streams of tight blue flame. They seared up the Águila's back, blackening scales, fusing ridges and driving heat into the drake's flesh. It wasn't a killing strike – just enough to force the Águila to twist and dive, away from the flames.

Max watched it drop straight into Monteith and Nugent's path, and their fire engulfed its head, neck and chest pouch as they flew past, one either side. The Águila fell from the sky, dead before it hit the ground.

'Good shooting,' said Max. 'Form up on me. C-Two, report.'

'Schmidt-X still flying. Slight damage. Águilas fleeing north. Fifteen down.'

'Mont-X, still flying, beauty scorch on the belly.'

'Nuge-X running pure.'

'Red-X is peak.'

'Cal-X boasting a minor wing tear. Still combat-ready.'

'Los-X running pure.'

'Kul-X never better.'

'We rule,' said Max. 'Val-X, orders?'

'Get your chevron back up to a thousand. Let's get Solomon home without any more excitement. The cap is yours again.'

'Copy, Val-X. C-Two, on me, let's get some sun. C-One, maintain close patrol over the cortege, C-Three, go on point at three hundred.'

'I need the sun,' said Kullani.

'There's nothing like it, buddy.'

'My blood is cold.'

Max's heart missed a beat. 'Say again, Kul-X?'

'Say what again?'

Kullani's voice was shaky, though. Max could hear her gasping. He switched to their private com.

'What can you see, Kullani?'

'There's dust and fire in my eyes.'

'Stay with me, buddy. Can you see me?'

'Of course I can, Max, what's up?'

'Nothing, Risa, nothing. Just do me a favour, okay?'

'Anything, any time.'

'Keep com silence to the end of the flight. Let's see if we can fly on feel, just for skills, eh?'

'I can feel my blood rushing inside me. It's so cold.'

'I hear you. Let's fly close, side-by-side like in training. Com silence, Kul-X. Hang on, land soft and stay in your drake till I come get you.'

'Copy, Hal-X.'

'Hal-X out.' Max bit his lip, hard, and Martha swam in the air, her neck snaking and her nostrils flaring as she sampled the distress of Kullani's drake. 'I know, Martha, I know.'

Her drake was flying level and true. No outward signs, so far. Max sighed and opened a channel to Valera.

'Val-X, Hal-X. One-to-one?'

'Go ahead, Hal-X. Wondering what to say to Solomon when we get home?'

'Negative, Val-X. We've got a code double zero.' There was silence. 'Skipper?'

'Copy that, Hal-X.' Max heard her clear her throat. 'Trust the squad, Max.'

CHAPTER 4

Flying a drake is *exactly* like drug addiction. An overdose'll kill you... prolonged flying'll make you sick... but no way in hell will you ever give it up because the absence is more terrifying than the inevitability of an early death.

MAX HALLORAN

It was interminable. The marshal gen's cortege crawled across the sand and dirt to rendezvous with the *Granite*. Max was wired, desperate for Kullani to get home safely. He was keeping his eyes on her drake while attempting to tune in to all the com chatter, trying to work out whether anyone else had twigged something was wrong. If they had, they were keeping it to themselves. Valera's voice in his ear every now and again was nothing but gentle support, as it would be in Kullani's. And she was flying as beautifully as ever. Perhaps even better.

'Talk to her, Max. Never mind her trim; you've stared at it long enough to know she's still in control. But she's alone in there. Don't let her disappear inside her fears.'

'Copy, Val-X. And thank you.'

'You're welcome, Hal-X. We've got the pair of you covered when you land. Trust the squad; once I-X, always I-X.'

'Kul-X, Hal-X on one-to-one. Hey...'

He'd meant to go on, say something sharp and funny but his mind turned up blank. Martha sensed it and her body rippled with brief anxiety. She continued her slow circle high above the cortege in a beautiful clear sky. Beyond the *Heart of Granite* and the *Steelback,* beyond the southern borders of the desert, the world was green and lush and soon to be churned to mud and blood by the forces of UE and Mid-Af. How peaceful it was up here now, and how extraordinary the noise would be when battle was joined.

'Yes? Fallen asleep on me, Max?'

'Very funny. I was just, y'know...' What the hell could he say to her?

'I may be going insane but I am currently able to respond to coherent sentences. If you could say some...'

'Just tell me what you see, smart arse.'

There was a pause and Max could all but hear her brain changing gear.

'It's stopped burning.'

'What has?'

'Everything.'

'OK... So how does "it" look now?' Whatever 'it' was.

'Cool.'

'Like me, then,' said Max, a little confused.

'Your capacity for narcissism is forever undiminished.'

That was more like it. 'I meant—'

'We know what you meant.'

'We?'

A hideous pause. 'I. I said, "I".'

'So you did.'

'And you really think you're cool?'

'I hate to fly in the face of public opinion,' said Max.

'Did you hear that?'

'What?'

'It was the sound of me vomiting into my pouch.' Kullani made the sound again.

'Messy.'

'You're on cleaning duty.'

Max managed a chuckle at last. 'I'd do it, if I didn't have to see Solomon and Moeller *immediately* on landing.'

'Damn.'

'I wish it wasn't the case, really I do.'

'No, not that. I need to get home and wash the blood off. We're all drowning in blood.'

'Hang on, Kul-X. We'll be home soon.'

Her com quietened and Max swore. He heard the quiet bleep of another incoming voice.

'Good job,' said Valera, her voice a little thick. 'Hope you didn't mind me listening in.'

'You're the boss.' Max felt like he'd lost a skirmish.

'We'll fix her,' said Valera.

'For now.'

'It's all any of us can hope for when our time comes.'

The dust cloud surrounding the *Heart of Granite* had largely dissipated under strengthening winds at a thousand and above. Max could see her flight deck fully lowered from her belly, bone ramps deployed, and her tail up in readiness for the embarkation of the cortege. The glare from the *Granite*'s solar arrays forced the Inferno-X drakes low on approach. The late afternoon sun was hot and strong and the arrays would harvest enough energy to keep the generators going for another night. This close to a regeneration cycle it was a mere fistful of sand in the desert, but anything that held off the tedium of a big swim was worth it.

Down on the sand, the cortege was approaching the tail. The *Granite*'s ground forces were providing security on the approach to the ramps, allowing tired geckos and basilisks to tuck into the flanks of the larger lizards and reduce their pace to a gentle walk.

'Come on, Flight Com, don't keep us waiting...' muttered Max.

He shuffled in his pouch and Martha shook herself from head to tail tip. 'Almost home, princess.'

'Inferno-X, this is Flight Com, stand by...'

'Just a few more minutes, Kul-X,' he said over the one-to-one.

'This is *Heart of Granite* Flight Command, good work, Inferno-X. Even you, Hal-X, I'm looking forward to our chat. So is the marshal general, I understand.'

Moeller waited for the hoots and catcalls to die down.

'Skies are clear, the *HoG* has the watch. You will come in in pairs, flying honour above the cortege. The cap's still with Hal-X... You're coming in first, boy, don't let me down.'

'Copy that, Flight Command. Inferno-X, this is Hal-X; form up on me.'

The solar arrays slid back, the glare shutting off sharply like dark clouds across the sun. The forty-millimetre batteries wound into place, twenty-five of them along the spine of the behemoth, ready to fill the sky with fire. Along her flanks were more than a hundred machine guns and, set down in the section cartilage, the frag bomb and fuel air explosive missile launchers would be active as well... just in case. It was showing off for Solomon, really, but you could never trust a Maf commander and daft suicide attacks weren't as rare as they ought to be.

'All right, Inferno-X,' rumbled Moeller. 'Come on in.'

'Inferno-X, Hal-X. Two-by-two. Let's form on the loop... always leave them gasping for more. Hal-X out.'

Max dipped his right arm and Martha peeled away, Kullani in impeccable formation. He levelled out Martha's flight before arching his back to send them sweeping up into the sky. Martha screeched delight, beating her wings hard and powering into the loop.

'On your three,' said Kullani. Max glanced across, but not for confirmation. More like he wanted a memory.

The pouch's fluid was working overtime in the steepening climb, the g-forces breathtaking. At the apex of their climb was an ephemeral moment of weightlessness. Max laughed, staring up at the sky. He twitched his body to make Martha perform a perfect barrel roll and he could see Inferno-X following his move, their synchronised rolls beautiful as they formed the loop in his wake, their positioning spot-on.

'Inferno-X, Hal-X, you look stunning. We are *so* far and away the best squad and even Solomon has seen it now.'

Martha screamed into the down arc, her wings trimmed for speed and balance, her body ramrod straight, in textbook position, with Kullani just a metre away. It was an incredible rush, the noise a glorious howl and whistle, the ground closing fast but they were always in absolute, millimetre-precision control. That was skill and Max just hoped Solomon was watching.

Max bent his head back a fraction and Martha began to level out. Ahead of them the *Heart of Granite*'s flight deck entrance was picked out in running lights beneath her slightly trembling curved-up tail.

'Now *that* is timing.'

The cortege was approaching the ramp as Max and Kullani scorched over their heads and into the harsh light of the flight deck. Halfway in, they flared their drakes' wings in a brutal braking manoeuvre.

Max stretched his legs and they landed, claws on the bone floor, surging forwards into a dead run, the wind whipping dust and scraps up in a whirl around them. Martha's feet pounded on the deck, wings beating back to slow her to a steady walk. At a nudge from Max she moved upright and walked serenely to the bay outside her pen. Max checked for Kullani, also walking steadily, unhurried and calm.

Gusts of wind and the reverberations through his feet told Max that Inferno-X was landing in his wake. He walked Martha into her humid, red-lit pen and triggered the pouch, spilling viscous fluid onto the deck.

'Catch you later, princess.'

Martha's body thrummed as if she understood. Max pulled himself out of the pouch and jumped down to the ground. Grimaldi was already there, hosing him down. She was ready for some banter but Max looked across the deck to Kullani, who was out of her pouch and standing by her drake. Her face was white and her expression lost while she was cleaned off.

'Speed it up, Grim.'

'I thought you won. Did I miss something?'

Max turned back to her, trying to speak but not finding the words. In the end, all he could do was shake his head, knowing the news would break her. She followed his jerk of the head towards Kullani.

'Shit,' muttered Grimaldi, staring up at him.

'Sorry, Grim,' said Max. Grimaldi stiffened. 'Don't let on, okay? Gotta keep this from the brass.'

Grimaldi's eyes were full of tears but she nodded. 'Shit, shit, shit. Yeah. You're good to go. Good enough, anyway. Don't let them take her.'

'Trust me. No one gets her but you.'

Max spun about and forced himself not to sprint over to Kullani. Halfway there, Valera fell into step with him. She was as half-clean as he was, the stink of lubricant sharp and powerful.

'You're going the wrong way.'

'They can wait,' said Max.

'They can't.'

'I—'

Valera caught his arm and glanced up at Flight Command, whose windowed control room spanned the entire deck fifteen metres up.

'You're not helping. Don't draw attention to the situation. We'll handle it.'

'I have to check on Kullani.'

'I'll handle it,' said Valera. Max started to turn away anyway.

'Don't even think it, Hal-X. The second you got out of that pouch, you stopped thinking.'

'I—'

'I get how you feel. But Moeller is watching your every move right now. What conclusion do you think he'll draw if you go straight to Kullani? You might as well march her into Landfill yourself.'

Max stared down at the floor, fists clenching.

'Go up there and take your medicine like a good boy. And while you're distracting Moeller, I get the time to look after Kullani, get it? And if he asks, tell him I was chewing you out, 'cos he's watching all of this and he ain't stupid. Now get going.'

Max closed his eyes briefly, cursing himself an idiot. He nodded mutely and headed for the stairs up to Flight Command, feeling everyone's eyes on his back.

The metal steps rang beneath his feet, two flights up to the gallery that ran along in front of the long windows. Max tried to appear unflustered while he walked to Moeller's office through the world of screens and the myriad lines of data, graphs, blinking lights and schematics they displayed.

He hated it in here but never more than today; Flight Command drones looked at him in disdain before returning to their oh-so-important tasks. It made him glad he still stank from the pouch; it'd give the desk monkeys a whiff of real life. Max flicked a bead of lubricant from his sleeve, satisfied to see it strike a screen, before marching up to Moeller's open door, knocking on it and drawing himself to attention.

'Max Halloran reporting as ordered, sir.'

Moeller waved him in from behind his desk.

'Close it behind you,' he said. Max did so, muting the hum of the command centre, the echoing cries of drakes, the clanging of metal and the shouts of ground crew.

Max took a glance round Moeller's office. It was massive, relatively speaking, sort of a conference room and executive study in one. Moeller's desk was a basic wooden affair boasting a pile of regulation textbooks, a beautifully sculpted model of a drake, three data screens and a half-empty mug of something. There were glass-fronted wooden bookcases behind the desk, both of them full, both neat and ordered. Moeller was a collector and this looked like the best of his collection. Max had thought about reading a book on the odd occasion but it had always seemed a bit of a waste of time.

Moeller got up from his plain metal chair, pushed it back under his desk and gestured Max follow him. He walked round a gleaming oval wooden table set with twelve chairs that dominated the room. Voice and video conferencing equipment sat dead centre and each chair was tidily tucked in.

Moeller opened the sliding doors overlooking the flight deck, where another squadron was on the runway. Two rows of five leather-upholstered seats were bolted to the balcony floor, relics from the days when VIPs and journalists had watched the drakes take off and land. Max had barely seen anyone up here in the nine months he'd been aboard.

Moeller took in the scene before facing Max, who snapped to attention once more. Moeller almost smiled and waved him at ease. There was never any malice in his weary face. He was in his fifties, grey-haired and fit with a gentle but precise manner. No one ever repeated the mistake of believing his gentle tone meant weakness.

'Holy Mother, you stink, boy.'

'Sorry, sir, but I was in a rush to—'

'Stop.'

'Sorry, sir.'

'Where to begin with you, Halloran,' he said, frowning until his bushy eyebrows almost met.

'Sir—?' Max said, before clamping his mouth shut on the career-limiting question he'd been about to ask.

'I'll do the talking, Halloran,' Moeller said, mildly.

'Yes, sir,' said Max.

'Tell me: how many squadrons of drakes do I command on this behemoth?'

'Six, sir.'

'That's eighteen chevrons. One hundred and forty-four active drake-pilot pairs. With their ground crews and Tweaker teams, that's four hundred and seventy-seven people on the flight deck alone before I even start on the ground forces.

'Order and discipline are essential, and every single person out there had them today, except you.'

'Sir, that's—'

'It's true.' Moeller looked directly at Max. 'You're a fantastic pilot, Halloran, but you're reckless and undisciplined. This was the fifth time you've been late to my flight deck and every time, you've risked your squad going out short and left your wingmate looking an idiot because it's implicit in your behaviour that you don't respect her. This is your last warning. Once more and you'll never fly for me again. Do I make myself clear?'

'Sir. You'll ground me, sir?'

'I'll transfer you to a training duty... one that reminds you every day how badly you screwed up.'

Max wondered if Moeller ever raised his voice.

'You're late for your appointment with the marshal general, and she's not as understanding as I am, you'll find. Later, you can thank me for resisting her calls to have you grounded.'

'Thank you, sir.'

'The rest of your performance with the cap was outstanding, though. Very much worthy of Inferno-X. Well done.'

'Thank you, sir.'

'Shame about Kullani.'

Max froze with his fingers cramping around the door handle. 'Sir?'

'It comes to you all. Remember those signs, because there's never any more warning it's started.'

Max turned, his mind churning. 'I'm not with you, sir.'

'Loyalty is a wonderful thing. But,' Moeller pointed to his eyes, 'these work and I have a decade's experience with drake pilots. You can't bullshit me.'

Max shrugged. 'Kullani had a near miss with an Águila in the dust cloud. Shook her up a bit. But she flew exceptionally today.'

'Uh-huh. You know, I have your best interests at heart so I'll give you a little advice: there are more sides to this war than you can count and not all of your enemies are in the sky. If you're going to extend your life to its maximum everyone has to be peak every time. One passenger and you could all go down. Where's your loyalty then?'

'I'll bear it in mind, sir,' said Max.

Moeller shook his head slowly. 'It'll sink through that thick skull of yours eventually, Halloran. I hope it's sooner rather than later. Dismissed.'

Max saluted and walked to the door, pulling it open and all but walking into Marshal General Solomon. He backed up hurriedly and stood to attention.

Solomon looked exactly like her press shots. Dark eyes that missed nothing, greying hair braided tight to her head, and beautiful mid-brown skin. She wasn't one for a lot of make-up and her uniform was creased from a long journey in the questionable comfort of a ground lizard, but her sheer presence made the details irrelevant.

'You stink.' She walked in, those eyes analysing him, daring him to make even more of a prat of himself. 'Good of you to let me freshen up before reporting to me, Halloran.'

'I didn't—'

'I know you didn't. I've been waiting like a good girl for you to come a-knocking, only I'm not a good girl and I hate being made to wait. Careers have folded for less. Don't look to your Flight Commander, he can't help you, especially as it seems you can't work out the chain of command. Guess that leaves you in pretty deep, doesn't it?'

Max couldn't speak, although he did manage to swallow on a dry throat.

'You were an unprofessional arse out there, Halloran. Pick up a shovel. Let's see if you can dig yourself out.'

CHAPTER 5

When alien technology and biological matter was discovered on the Ark asteroid, you could sense the world holding its breath. The day the commencement of experimentation on the fusion of alien and Terran DNA was announced, global politics changed forever.

MARIE RODRIGUEZ – NEW AGE POLITICS: THE RISE OF THE MULTI FAITH ALLIANCE

Max let the tepid water soak over him for a good long time before getting on with cleaning his flight suit and wishing he'd let Grim do a proper job. Lubricant and shock-absorbent fluid had dried in streaks on it while the marshal gen had given him a piece of her mind. He'd have gone to Gargan's Bar on tenways junction straight afterwards but for the fact that Kullani was in the Inferno-X rack. He wanted to check on her more than anything.

Valera had ordered him into the wash block, where he'd stalked around the eight shower heads on his own in an ever-worsening mood. He'd given his suit a particularly close scrub, then walked naked and dripping out of the showers to dump it at Valera's feet. She was sitting on a recliner, half-watching the news.

'There you go. It's clean, I'm wet, I was in there long enough to calm down. Now let me see Kullani.'

'Don't be a child, Max. And get dressed. Kullani doesn't need a naked dick-brained hothead right now.'

'Where is she?'

'I left her in her pod, trying to sort her head out. She wants to see you. Sort yourself and your suit out first.'

'Moeller knows,' said Max.

Valera looked up at him. 'Moeller suspects. Don't worry about it right now. Go on.'

Max nodded, scooped up his suit and hung it at the end of the rack. The duty flight crew would wheel it down to the flight deck later on. He grabbed a towel from the pile by the washroom door and wrapped it round his midriff before walking to his pod under the sympathetic gaze of the squad. He pushed open his door and found Risa Kullani sitting on his bed, looking at a picture of them taken just after he'd joined the squad.

'You're supposed to be in your pod. My lucky day, is it?' said Max.

'Well, it certainly isn't mine,' said Kullani.

'Don't talk like that. It's not what I meant.' Max gathered up some clothes, just jockeys, black tee-shirt and dark grey fatigues, and began pulling them on. 'Anyway, my door's always been open to you.'

'Yeah, but y'know, you were never quite my style, were you? And now everything is different.'

Max didn't know what to say so he just nodded, sat down next to her, and dragged his tee-shirt over his still-damp body. They both stared at the picture.

'So I'm going to ask the stupid and obvious question,' said Max. 'How are you feeling?'

'I thought you'd never ask.'

Max bumped her with his shoulder. 'Just answer the question.'

'I feel fine.' She shrugged. 'Now I do. It's hard to explain how I felt before. But I couldn't keep my drake out... She was right in my head with me, not beside me, *inside* me, suffocating me. It was frightening, Max.'

Max worried at his lip. He knew what it added up to and so, of course, did Risa.

'I bet. And you were saying some weird shit up there.'

'That makes me feel so much better.' But she smiled and punched him on the arm. Max made a play of being hurled aside by the blow and she laughed a little. 'It might have been weird but it was real. I could feel the cold. I saw the blood. It was *in my head*.'

'What's her name?'

Risa shook her head. 'Only freaks like you give their drakes names. It's an Extra Reptilian Construct, Max.'

'They aren't robots, though. Martha has personality and intelligence – though it's mostly locked away. And we can all feel them.'

Kullani shook her head.

'Not like this. It was speaking to me.' Risa's eyes closed briefly. 'I think it was, anyway... so many images. Shit. I don't know what to think. I didn't want this to happen.'

'You'll be fine. You—'

'I touched the Fall, Max. It's started.'

Then her arms were around his neck and she had buried her face in his shoulder. He clutched her hard, feeling her shiver as she tried to regain control.

'Too soon,' she said, her voice muffled. 'Don't let them put me in Landfill.'

'Not on my watch,' said Max, stroking her short fine hair. 'No one is taking you from my wing.'

Risa choked on laughter and tears and pulled away. Her eyes were bright and scared.

'We all know where it ends. Fuck it, Max. I should have had more time. Years.'

'Trust Valera. Trust the squad. We'll think of something. First we have to convince everyone nothing's wrong.'

'I'll try.'

'Great... so we do what we always do after a win? Gargan's for the toast.'

'I don't know. I'm not feeling much like celebrating.'

'I get it, but if we don't show there'll be questions. I'll look after you.'

Risa's smile was fragile but at least it was there. She shrugged. 'Just don't leave me?'

'I'll get Stepanek to buy all my rounds. How long do you need to get your head together?'

'Are you taking the piss?'

'Actually no, I was being unusually sensitive,' said Max.

'Uniquely,' said Kullani. 'Just a few minutes to hide the blotches.'

Max pulled deck shoes onto his bare feet and the two of them walked out.

'I think she knows her way home,' said Valera from their left. 'I need a word, Max. Several words, in fact.'

Max followed Valera through the squad, sprawled on their sofas and recliners. There were none of the usual comments or thrown missiles, which he supposed was a mark of the day's events, but he didn't like it – or their eyes following him. The computer games were suddenly profoundly irritating and the drone of reporters overlaid on images of the marshal gen's cortege boarding the *Granite* was loudly tedious. Mind you, the I-X drakes flashing into the flight deck looked bloody impressive.

'She's fine, all right?' he said very loudly. 'Get your arses ready for a toast at Gargan's.'

Valera took his arm and steered him to an empty seat where a mug of coffee and his named pill pack were waiting for him on a low table.

'That strikes me as a potentially disastrous plan. Take your settlers, coffee's yours too.'

'Thanks, boss.' Max picked up the mug and took a sip; it was strong and bitter, just as he liked it. He sloshed the liquid around in his mouth, fed in the pills and swallowed the lot. They equalised his mind after prolonged drake contact, helped him relax like they did for every pilot. 'I'll look after her.'

'Keep her off the spirits, all right? You too. Sit down.' Max complied. 'How are you doing? It's your first time facing the Fall and it's poor luck it's your wing.'

'I don't know... angry? This can't be it... We can't let her go, Skipper.'

'No, we can't,' said Valera. 'And we won't.'

'But she can't fly thinking like she is,' said Max.

'No, she can't.'

'What about Moeller? He saw it straight away. I denied it, but he knows.'

'But he can't get her tested until her settlers have taken effect or he'll get a false positive, so we have an opportunity to hide her condition from the brain-scrapers. You know how, right?'

Max thought for a moment. 'You're talking about heaters? But they're...'

Valera laughed. 'Wow, something went in that big head of yours and stayed there. Yes, they are, but if you're facing Landfill how much would you care about the legality of the drug that kept you out? She's your wing so it's your responsibility. I'll get the squad to chip in, and get you an introduction to the Blammers. After that, you're on your own. You're up for this?'

'Yes. Right now?'

'Patience! Remember, you're crossing a line from the moment you agree.'

'Yeah, but it's a line Moeller knows we'll cross. Why doesn't he do something about it?'

Valera grimaced. 'Well, it's complicated. Commander Avery practically sleeps with the regs manuals; she'd haul Kullani out of service now if she suspected anything. Our ExO wants to keep us in the pouch to the last second to save money. And Moeller's...

well, he's stuck in the middle. He does what he can... Look, never mind. Assume no one but the squad will support you.'

Max scrubbed at his head. 'I really need a drink.'

'I'll find you at Gargan's later. Tonight, just look after Kullani or I'll rip your balls off and wear them as earrings.'

CHAPTER 6

Chronic cognitive disassociation, the Fall, is an incurable complex condition with only symptomatic relief currently available. The earliest symptoms, hallucinations, nervous complaints and temporary paralysis, can appear up to eighteen months before the condition's trigger point. We have been unable to detect which factors combine to produce the trigger point, hence the potentially devastating effects of the Fall occurring while in flight.

PROFESSOR CARL ALDUS, NEUROLOGICAL SCIENCE
RESEARCH LEAD, ERC PROGRAMME

Gargan's was the place for loud music, cheap drink and the maximum amount of attention. Maybe even for taking a dig at the sand-eating infantry still shaking the desert out of their clothes. Max didn't want any of it tonight and, had it not been for toast tradition, he would have taken the squad to Rio's or, if he could blag it, the Bridge Bar, instead. Although given his run-ins with Moeller and Solomon, he might not have had a warm welcome.

So Gargan's it was, with its buzz, stale smell, sticky floor and the pheromone-fuelled dance of people seeking someone for fun, for a little comfort, even for love. Max felt disconnected when he and Kullani walked in. The music was a horrible distraction rather than a prelude to a long and glorious night flirting, laughing and celebrating their victory with his squad.

Max steered a subdued Kullani to the tables reserved for Inferno-X after their victory. Everyone was there; even Valera had arrived before him. The moment they came into view, the squad stood. Trays were passed around and each took a shot of spirit, either vodka or a single malt. His and Kullani's held shots of water.

With Max and Kullani among them, Inferno-X moved onto the floor and formed a shoulder-to-shoulder circle around Valera. The music was cut and the hoot of voices fell to a respectful quiet as everyone in Gargan's paused, some more grudgingly than others, to honour their comrades.

Valera raised her shot glass above her head and Inferno-X held theirs out to her. She turned slowly as she spoke.

'We are one. Today we flew, we fought, and we were victorious. We are Inferno-X! We are *Heart of Granite*!'

To a roar that shook the room, the squad downed their shots. Music kicked in again, voices rose to match it and Valera called Chevron Two into a huddle.

'You know one of your own needs your protection tonight. Watch out for each other. Enjoy your night and trust your squad. Get drunk, get laid... get a few hours' sleep.'

Valera broke up the huddle and leaned into Max before she left. 'I'll be back as soon as I can. Stay out of trouble, keep Risa reasonably sober, and if Moeller or Avery walk in, it's time to leave gracefully. Can you do all that?'

'Aye aye, Skipper.'

Valera patted his cheek and walked away.

Max watched her head towards the main corridor, people moving out of her way. He smiled and turned back to the squad, seeing the empty state of the glasses and bottles across their tables.

'But first, someone needs to go to the bar,' he muttered.

*

Alexandra Solomon smiled when the vidcom began to bleep for her attention. Few knew her direct code and she had been looking forward to this call. She finished towelling herself dry and got dressed, careful not to rush. The beeping had started to sound more insistent and it entertained her to keep her caller waiting.

It timed out after a while, and started again almost immediately. It had to be him and he'd know she was in her quarters. The question was, had he read the research she'd arranged for him to see or was this a social call? Solomon pulled her jacket over her shirt, adjusted her appearance in a mirror, and, checking that she was recording all that was to come, she enabled the link.

'Did you miss me?' she asked.

'Did you have any particular reason to keep me waiting?' President Corsini's voice was just slightly out of sync with his lips, making him look even more stupid than normal, which was quite a feat.

'You're fortunate I was just getting out of the shower and not just getting in,' said Solomon, 'or you'd have been waiting a sight longer, listening to my singing – and I only know songs about what a prick you are.'

'Dear me, Alex, you are frosty today. The water a bit cold, was it?' Corsini was middle-aged, and his olive skin was thick enough to take all her barbs. Still, it was fun hurling them.

'It's always cold. Something you'd know if you'd the guts to visit a behemoth. What do you want? I'm busy.'

Corsini's expression was stone but she was starting to get to him. 'I can't imagine anyone having more pressing concerns than speaking to their commanding officer.'

'You don't have to imagine it, you're looking at me. What do you want? Oh, wait... what day is it? You must have just seen the latest opinion polls.'

'You know my ratings are a burning behemoth carcass.'

Solomon's heart sang. 'So you must be calling to hear how I

can win the war for you by Election Day... Wow, that's going to be expensive.'

'And despite your recent, comprehensive report on targeted spending to achieve victory in Mid-Af, I can't increase your budget. It's time you earned your pay.'

Solomon stiffened fractionally. 'Is there a Maf behemoth outside your window?'

Corsini sighed. 'No—'

'That's because I'm already earning it.'

'That's a tired line, Alex. Try again.'

Solomon turned her back on the screen and walked to her dresser where her brushes and beads were laid out.

'Rainbow colours or something a little more serious and formal, do you think?'

'What?'

'If I'm to tell your flag carrier they have eighteen months to win this war of attrition without additional resources, I think I should adopt an appropriate look, don't you?'

'You have to be bolder,' he said. 'You used to be a risk-taker. What happened?'

Solomon barked a derisory laugh and turned back to the screen.

'That's all your years of battlefield experience speaking, is it? Or is it the advice of that fuckwit octogenarian in whom you apparently place so much faith?'

'General Baldwin has more tactical knowledge than you'll ever forget.'

'He's so old he still remembers petrol-driven cars. Last time he fought they were advancing behind fixed bayonets.'

'The general is merely suggesting a concentration of forces to break the Mid-African stalemate.'

'I see. And he expects us to do this by harnessing the power of nature and battling our enemies with insects and elephants or something, does he?'

'Your sarcasm does you no credit. You need to direct forces from the Balkan front. Even a fuckwit octogenarian can see that.'

Solomon smiled at him, plainly a reaction he wasn't expecting.

'A brilliant idea,' she said. 'Assuming you want to invite the Redheads into central Europe, force an alliance against us between the Sambas and Mid-Africa and push the Indian Subs into conflict to protect their border. But at least we'll have extra behemoths wholly unsuited to desert combat.'

'We have to end this war now.'

'Then by all means, make that your order. You won't have to worry about re-election, just what to wear for the show trial and firing squad. Tactics, my toned arse. Baldwin doesn't have a clue and neither do you.'

'Fuck you,' said Corsini.

'Once was a thousand times too many,' snapped Solomon.

Just for a moment, Corsini's jaw tensed and his eyes narrowed.

'If not Baldwin, then listen to Markov. At least she's still working for the common good. An interesting piece of research popped into my inbox. You're aware of it, I presume.'

Solomon shrugged, affecting disdain, though she felt a little excitement blossom; he had seen it.

'It's dangerous and untested,' she said. 'The data hasn't been properly analysed; I question the to-Fall time reduction versus the combat benefit assessment; and the cost implication matrix is, to say the least, creative. It *is* exciting, but given the early stage of the research we cannot expect to field-test for at least a year. We need a realistic solution, not this sort of promissory fancy.'

'This is realistic.'

Solomon shook her head, working out how best to lead him to the orders she wanted. 'It's not on the agenda. Not before the next election.'

Corsini leaned back in his chair. 'The options are few, Alex: the current war of attrition, this calculated risk, or the diplomacy table.'

'There will be no negotiated settlement. That's a betrayal of every life that's already been lost.'

Corsini slow-clapped her. 'Said with such passion I almost believe you. But I know how much uncaptured land you've been promised when we win. How many billions would it cost you if the war ended with the borders as they are right now?'

'About half as many as it would cost you,' Solomon snapped.

Corsini rapped the research report with his knuckles. 'Then we agree: be bold. Fast track this research. You're in the field now; get testing.'

Solomon rubbed her hands over her face. 'All right. Let me make this simple. That research reduces the average lifespan of a drake pilot from three years to ten months before the Fall takes them. The worst-case scenario leaves us with only fifteen per cent of test subjects still operational after nine months. Even you will realise I can't test this on any more than one squadron, if you order me to test at all.'

'Inferno-X can handle it.'

Solomon shrugged. 'If anyone can, they can. But it's a huge gamble. You're pinning all your hopes on one squad from one behemoth turning the tide in less than a year. If it fails, we've got nothing. You saw there's no mind-shielding? You'll be sacrificing our very best for this experiment.'

'Finances only stretch so far; mind-shielding is expensive.'

'I just want to be clear that you're comfortable with testing on our finest squadron.'

'We're all aware of their individual talents. They have the best chance of making it work for the longest time. I don't see any other choice.'

'You understand we won't even have enough space in Landfill to handle the burn-outs,' said Solomon.

'Burn-outs... You're as sentimental about your troops as ever.'

'That's what they'll be! This upgrade will create them by the sack-load, and if you can't increase our budget then I can't replace them in a hurry. You know how expensive training drake pilots is. And how long it takes.'

Corsini smiled; it was a most unsettling expression. 'So you missed the most interesting part of the research, then.'

'Go on.'

'The Specific Sentience Release programme means we can recruit pilots with lower aptitude, and they'll require a shorter, less intensive training period. This gives us more pilots for less money. It would also release all those currently in the programme for immediate active duty. Good, wouldn't you say?'

'That's not a training programme, it's a licence to slaughter our own.'

'But it could win us the war. If it does, the sacrifice is worth it.'

'You'll never persuade Markov to sign it off for live combat test.'

Corsini flapped his hands. 'I already have her signature. It'll be on the file when you receive it.'

'So let's be clear. You're ordering me to combat-test this upgrade on Inferno-X despite the objections I have raised. Any adverse consequences are on you.'

'Fine. Just win the fucking war with it. And be prepared for a wider roll-out if first reports are promising.'

Solomon fought to contain the smug feeling. 'Even so, if I'm to sell this in, it'll cost you, personally. I want the Virunga Mountains and the Bwindi rainforest.'

'Those are mine.'

'Not any more. Not if you want this test to happen.'

'You are a filthy, grasping bitch.'

'That is quite the nicest thing anyone's said to me all day.'

Solomon cut the vid-link and ended the recording of Corsini implicating himself in a deception. Now Solomon had exactly what she wanted and she didn't even have to fear the consequences. Sometimes it was almost too easy.

CHAPTER 7

I thought the war started because the oil ran out, only my dad said you had to go back further than that to when we were all mostly at peace and everyone shared their technology.

MAX HALLORAN, AGED 14 – SUPPORTED ESSAY 5: WHY ARE WE AT WAR?

'I need to get out of here,' said Kullani. 'There's too much noise. It's hurting my head.'

Max shuffled a little closer in the corner booth where they had retreated. Initially they'd been surrounded by the squad, but the natural ebb and flow of the human tide in Gargan's had dispersed them. Every now and again, Fellows, Roberts or Colette dropped by to leave more drinks but now he looked at their table, Max could see that his were largely untouched, but all of Kullani's were drained dry. Damn.

'Hang on a little longer. Skipper'll be back soon.'

Kullani shook her head. 'Max, I'm cold and I need to be alone and in peace so I can reach out to my drake in private. You're my wing. Get me to the squad rack.'

Max raised an eyebrow and stared at her for a moment. 'All right, Kul-X. We can go ... take it easy.'

She slapped away the hand he'd offered. 'Stop telling me what to do! You don't know. None of you get it; and it'll be too late when you do.'

'I hear you, Kullani. We've probably had enough to drink. So the squad rack – let's go, okay?'

'Oh, now you get it. Now I'm a little pissed and loud. Poor mad little me, eh? Best hurry me off to bed before I say something stupid, right?'

Max refrained from actually shushing her but did hold up his hands in surrender, hoping she'd calm down. He could sense that they were starting to draw attention.

'Whatever you want. I thought—'

'No, you didn't think. That's your problem. It's *all about you*, isn't it? Never mind what's happening to *me*!'

Max found himself lost for words. Instead, he hugged her, feeling the rattling pace of her heart and her quick, shallow breathing. While Kullani didn't hug him back, at least she didn't bite his head off. She began to relax.

'We're here to make everything seem normal, even though it isn't. Please try and hang on. Skipper'll be back soon and then I can get something to help you. Grim'll be here by then and you can leave together as usual. I know you're cold and scared but we'll fix this. Okay?'

Kullani heaved in a breath and nodded against his chest, head bowed to hide her tears, although her shoulders were visibly shaking.

'Damn,' she said. 'I'm sorry. I don't want it to be over.'

'It's not,' said Max. 'Not by a long way.'

'Max?' He looked up to see Anna-Beth and reached out a hand, which she took and held briefly. 'Can I help?'

'Have you seen Grim? She should be here.'

Anna-Beth jerked her thumb over her shoulder. 'I was prepping my drake for tomorrow when the whole duty flight crew got called for a flight deck emergency exercise at shift end. They'll be done soon. What is it?'

Max just shook his head, having to fight back sudden tears. 'Can you get her some water?'

Anna-Beth's eyes betrayed her understanding. 'Tell you what, you get the water and I'll do the hugging. Reckon it's my turn.'

Max stroked Kullani's hair. 'I've got someone far better than me to take over, okay?' He stood up and brushed lips with Anna-Beth. 'Thank you.'

'Bring me back a beer, eh?'

'You got it.'

Max hadn't moved two paces before he felt a heavy hand on his shoulder and a voice in his ear.

'Oh, Halloran—' His name sounded ugly, said with such a sneer. '—learned the truth, has she?'

'Fuck off, Meyer. She's just had some bad news from home.'

'That sort of grief only comes from seeing how tiny your prick really is.'

'You're hilarious. Now back off, this doesn't concern you.'

'Don't worry, there's a support group we can send Kullani to. Dick Dissatisfaction Anonymous, I think it's called.'

Max turned and faced Meyer, nose-to-nose. The powerful marine captain was a few centimetres taller than him, his short hair bleached by the sun and his young face creased and tanned dark.

'Sand in your ears again? I said, back off.'

'Whoa!' said Meyer, his smile broad and cruel. 'Didn't realise you were so sensitive about your... shortcoming. Fuckin' drake pilots never can take a joke.'

Max shoved Meyer hard and crowded him back further.

'Fucking sand-heads never know when to quit. Get out of my face.'

Meyer squared up, fists ready, and as fast as a hundred drinkers scattered away from them, another hundred filled the void.

'What did you call me?'

'You're the only one that didn't hear me. Need me to repeat it to get it through your thick, grunt skull?'

'Fuck you. Least my brains won't leak out through my ears—'

Max roared and swung a fist right for Meyer's fat nose. Meyer swayed away from it and thumped Max in the stomach. Max absorbed most of it but blew hard as he charged in, meaning to get inside the arc of Meyer's fists. He grabbed Meyer about the midriff and drove him back, scattering onlookers. Meyer was whacking him on the back. Max hooked a leg behind Meyer's and shoved, tripping him. They went down in a heap. Max raised a fist only to have his forearm grabbed hard.

'Let me—'

'Stow it, Halloran,' snapped Valera. 'Get up, the pair of you.' Marines and pilots were crowding in now, pulling their man away from the other. 'Get lost, Meyer.'

Valera's words carried through the noise of Gargan's with all the weight of her seniority and reputation. Max still burned with anger and struggled against the combined weight of Abraham and Kane to no effect. He swore as Meyer stepped away and the next thing he saw was Valera's furious expression.

'Time to turn in,' she said.

'I need to—' Valera's eyebrows rose slightly.

'Luckily, Inferno-X has your back,' said Kane, letting him go.

Max glanced back and saw Grim and Anna-Beth were sitting either side of Kullani, who looked calmer now. He nodded.

'Yeah, yeah... Time to go.'

Max stalked out of Gargan's, noticing Kirby, who was the *HoG*'s ExO, and Moeller staring at him as he left. The moment they were out of sight of the bar, Max felt a sharp clip around the back of his head.

'What the fuck are you playing at?'

'I— What?'

Valera set a stiff pace towards the aft section of the *HoG*, the set of her body tight and angry.

'They were simple instructions! Keep Risa sober, stay out of trouble, leave if Kirby, Moeller or Solomon appear. If you wanted to demonstrate something was wrong with the squad, you should have just told Moeller straight out.'

'I didn't ask for Meyer to mouth off.'

'You didn't have to rise to it.'

'I'm not going to bed,' said Max.

A second clip around the head followed, though this one was a little more playful.

'Of course you bloody aren't, you idiot. Now follow me, keep up and don't ask stupid questions.'

'You've set everything up, then?' asked Max, his irritation ebbing.

'Yeah. At least one of us can do what they're supposed to.'

Valera led him into the spine corridor of deck one. It varied between eight and ten metres wide and allowed the swift transit of personnel, machinery or supplies. This time of an evening, it was fairly quiet, mostly used by maintenance carts and teams or off-duty groups of personnel enjoying some down time. They threaded through the human traffic.

Out here the faint 'off' smell of the behemoth was wafting on the airflow and the lights were distinctly dimmer than normal. The gentle but distinct sway in the spine as the *Heart of Granite* travelled across the land was jerkier too.

'Getting worse, isn't it?' said Max.

'We're well overdue a regen cycle. That'll be something new for you, Max.'

'Fun. Is it?'

'Nope.'

'Are you worried we might be followed?'

'What did I just say about asking stupid questions?'

Max followed Valera down a left-hand passageway studded with glass-doored offices. At the end, she pushed open a heavy hydraulic door letting out on to one of the basic metal stairways that linked the three spine decks. Out here, outside the bone and beyond the sound-absorbent cladding of the living areas where the walls were just reinforced flesh, Max could hear the *HoG*'s lungs working; expanding with the sound of a spring tide over shingle, exhaling like the roar of a thousand drakes. All to the ponderous beat of its massive heart.

'Makes you shudder, doesn't it?' said Valera, heading down the stairs to spine deck three. 'Keeps you real, too.'

'Let's get back inside,' said Max. 'It bloody stinks as well.'

Valera patted a wall. 'Plenty of guts out there,' she said.

'You're disgusting, Skipper.'

Valera pulled open the door and ushered Max in. The passageway back to the main corridor was a mirror of those in the deck above and they were soon in among the mass of marine barracking.

'Welcome to grunt central,' said Max.

'Need I remind you that we're rather on our own down here?'

'It smells revolting,' said Max. 'As bad as outside.'

For explanation, Valera pointed to a junction of bone plates in the ceiling as a drip of brownish fluid fell to the large stain on the wall below it.

'Ever wondered why they call this deck "Seepage"? There you go. Imperfect bone alignment means the synovial fluid leaks through. Gets worse when we travel for lengthy periods and, like now, just before a big swim. There, I've taught you something.'

'And there I was thinking seepage was the drivel that oozes out of their mouths when they speak.'

'Say it louder, Max, and enjoy your beating.'

Eight thousand marines, artillery support and field medics were packed into Seepage, making the accommodations on deck one positively palatial by comparison. Deck two predominantly housed the endless administration division. The smell of food and laundry mixed with sour behemoth sweat to turn Max's stomach.

'Isn't there a better way to go wherever we're going?'

'Nope, and you'd better get used to it. Next time you'll be on your own.'

Valera led them past dorm after dorm, across open rec spaces, security stations and through training facilities, the occasional glance over her shoulder satisfying her that they weren't being followed. A hundred metres ahead, Max could see the guarded bulkhead doors to the tail storage areas sat closed.

'How long have you been on this behemoth?' he asked.

'Almost six years, now. Long time in our line of work.'

'Don't you ever think about—?'

'The Fall? Nope, and neither should you. Ever. Come on, in here.'

They were passing a window wall looking into a largely empty marine mess hall and heading in. The smell of food mingled with the clank of cutlery, the clang of pots and pans in the galley, and the low hum of scattered conversation from the few marines sitting to eat.

Valera moved quickly between the tables and into a small office that sat next to the serving area. The walls were adorned with schedules, rosters and stock charts, some on paper, some on screens. The duty sergeant, a black-haired, wiry and pock-marked soldier, was behind his desk. He stood to attention in a hurry.

'Squadron Leader Orin. Welcome. What can I do for you... both?'

His gaze travelled to Max and he frowned, already knowing the answer.

'Good to see you, Cooper. Got one for the heater girls,' said Valera.

The sergeant nodded and looked at Max. 'For you, is it?'

'No. A friend of his,' said Valera.

'Okay. And he's safe, is he?'

'I'll vouch,' said Valera. 'This is Max Halloran.'

Cooper raised his eyebrows. 'Oh right, heard of you. Got a big mouth, right? Probably best to shut it if you want access.'

Max bridled. 'What's that supposed to mean?'

'Listen carefully. I am Sergeant Jack Cooper and I'm your portal to everything you will ever want. One day you'll even beg and I have a heart so long as you have the money. The only reason you dragon-shaggers go for as long as you do is down to us. The only reason the slime-suckers don't puke their breakfast into their geckos is down to us. Today it's heaters, and if you want them for your friend you pay up and keep quiet. Discretion, Halloran. Or no deals. Ever. Are we clear?'

'I get it. No need to be so dramatic.'

Cooper looked at Valera. 'Make sure he's no trouble. I don't need jokers and arseholes.'

Valera punched Max. 'He understands perfectly, he'll be no trouble.' She stared at Cooper and the man flinched. 'I vouch for him. That's enough.'

Cooper waited for a long moment before he reached into a desk drawer and pulled out a data card. 'Okay, let's get this done. Open your p-palm.'

Max offered his left hand and Cooper gave him a sharp glance. 'Not you.'

Valera opened her left hand and the palm-screen glowed on her hand. Cooper pressed the data card to it.

'There's your code, on auto-delete as always... We're cycle seven – you know location seven?'

'D-one-four-four,' said Valera.

'Pay the girls directly. Cash only.'

'Halloran,' said Cooper.

'Yep?'

'You're doing the right thing. They'll help your friend stay in the pouch. Stop the visions and nightmares, keep them seeing straight, y'know? I hope your friend fights it.'

'Thank you,' he said. 'Yeah... thank you.'

He followed Valera out of the mess, heading towards the tail and the labyrinthine storage compartments. She kept her head down and Max fell into step beside her. He had a million questions but, even to him, it was obvious this was not the time to ask any of them.

About thirty metres from the bulkhead doors to the tail section, Valera took a left, and held her p-palm to the keypad screen beside an unmarked door. She waved Max into a large storage area, maybe sixty metres on a side. Row after row of racking fled away from them, leaving walkways wide enough for trolleys to pass between them. Each rack had five shelves and each shelf was stacked with wooden crates, metal drums, cans and bottles, everything barcoded and labelled. Each rack was assigned to a company galley.

'Where's this?'

Valera shut the door firmly. 'D-one-four-four. First time's always difficult... Just try not to throw up in there, okay?'

'What are you talking about?'

'It'll become really obvious, trust me.'

CHAPTER 8

> You'd think you'd be terrified of the Fall but my dad says it's not the length of life you lead that matters, it's the quality. And nothing beats being a drake pilot. MAX HALLORAN

The store room was a dead end unless you knew what you were doing and, naturally, Valera did. Cooper's company insignia was on a rack in the centre of the store. Valera traced her fingers along the ranks of three-metre crates standing on the floor before alighting on one.

'What about the security cameras?' asked Max.

'They only show what Cooper wants them to.'

The crates were all keypad-locked to stop casual pilfering. And this one, like every keypad lock, had a tamper alarm. Valera held her p-palm to the pad and the lock disengaged. She opened the crate and walked inside. Max followed her.

'Close the door,' she said, unhooking one of five head-torches and putting it on. 'You'll need one of these, too.'

Max took a torch and closed the door, hearing the lock re-engage. Valera's head-torch illuminated the insides of the crate, about two metres on a side and empty but for a very solid-looking rubber-edged metal plate in the floor. For a third time, Valera showed her p-palm to an input pad and the plate hissed and swung upwards, revealing a bone-edged cylindrical passage with a ladder leading down to a second plate.

'I hope you're ready for this.' Valera went first, indicating Max close the first plate after him. 'Remember what I said.'

'Yeah, don't puke,' said Max, a little anxious about what he was about to encounter.

The plate settled above Max's head and the lock clunked solidly into place. Simultaneously, a pale green light below pulsed and the second plate hinged down, releasing an unholy stench. It was all Max could do to cling on to the ladder let alone his guts. His eyes stung, his stomach lurched over and over, and he had to focus on not vomiting all over his skipper.

'Holy fuck, what died down here?' said Max once the gag reflex had eased.

It stank of effluent, blood and exposed flesh, and of rot and piss too. All wrapped up in a hot, sour breeze.

'Welcome to your first flesh tunnel. It is particularly horrible right now, but then the *HoG* needs a bath.'

'People work down here?'

'People *live* down here, Max. Come on, and try not to brush against the walls.'

Valera descended a short ladder and disappeared from view. Max followed her, triggering the plate to close on his way down. At the bottom of the ladder, he was presented with a narrow corridor made of a white flexible rubberised covering. Underfoot, it gave a little with every step and the whole tunnel swayed in response to the behemoth's movements and bodily functions. Fluid oozed from every seam in the rubber, and dripped through cracks in just discernible cauterised flesh.

'Where are we going exactly?' he asked, focusing hard on Valera's back and the beam of her head-torch as it moved over walls and floor.

'Into the tail. This is the tradesman's entrance, so to speak. It's not far. Not too far.'

It was like walking into hell, as far as Max was concerned. He began to sweat as the temperature and humidity rose, and the leaks became more pronounced as the tunnel sloped down. It worsened at the junctions they passed. The fluid pooled and ran underfoot, making the going horribly slippery, every step accompanied by an unpleasant squelch.

'And all at no extra cost...' he muttered.

Further on the movement left and right became more pronounced and he could feel a grating vibration through the floor, indicating they were in the tail proper. He saw light ahead and presently they crossed gratings in the floor, through which the slurry of fluid drained, and on to rough bone.

Max switched off his torch and stopped next to Valera in a crudely made hollow bone junction from which three passages sprouted. Max could hear chatter and also the rhythmic thump of some rock music. This junction wasn't oozing reeking, sticky fluids, which was the thinnest of silver linings as it still stank of an animal's insides.

'No welcoming committee?' asked Max.

'They know we're coming. Come on, this way.'

Valera took the right-hand passageway, which quickly became another poorly sealed flesh tunnel, but at least it had lights stuck to the ceiling. The light breeze that blew across his face carried something new, though.

'That is a uniquely disgusting smell,' said Max.

'And the answer to your prayers, you'll be delighted to know.'

The passageway was short and opened out into a combination lab, storeroom and kitchen. The music was coming from a line of micro-speakers stuck to a ridge around a central lantern that cast the surrounding grey bone in a harsh, bright light. There was a pan of something bubbling away on an effluent gas ring. There was also a wooden table and three chairs near the stove, but the space was dominated by a long bone-architectured bench on which sat reduction and refining stills – and a high-pressure, high-temperature oven. The heat in the chamber was stultifying and the acrid stench of chemicals laced with sweet rot was revolting.

Two people were standing over the stills, dressed in blue boiler suits, fabric gloves and heavy leather aprons that had seen better days. Both had long hair tied back from their faces and wore wraparound glass goggles. From the off-key singing he could hear, there was a third person beyond the lab.

'Hey, Sharmi,' said Valera.

One of the figures raised a hand without turning.

'One moment,' she said.

Max tried to see what they were doing. One of them was decanting a pale yellow liquid into a flask.

'... Twenty-five ... thirty. Okay, enough.'

Sharmi clamped the flask above a Bunsen burner and triggered the flame that burned blue and hot beneath it. Both of them turned and pushed their goggles up onto their heads. Through the grime on their faces, Max could see they were no more than thirty, but their eyes projected a sense of worldly weariness.

'Hey, Val, brought us a new bug, I see,' said Sharmi, giving Max the once-over while scratching behind one ear.

'Yep. Sharmi, Jola, meet Max.'

Max raised a hand. 'Hey.'

The pair of them grunted at him.

'So you're Max?' The third was now leaning against the opening opposite. She was older, fifty or so with greying brown hair cropped tight to her head and crow's feet around her eyes. She was no cleaner than the other two but at least wore a smile.

'My fame precedes me, I see.'

'Best not to get cocky, kiddo,' she said.

She walked over, stripping off a leather gauntlet. She enveloped Valera in a powerful embrace then thrust a hand at Max, which he shook.

'Max, this is Krystyna. Play nice or she'll break your arms.'

Krystyna laughed. 'Maybe not your arms, but I'll sure break your bank.'

Max nodded vaguely. 'I'm feeling a little lost. I mean, you're the heater girls, right?'

'S'right,' said Sharmi. 'It's one of our things.'

'Yeah, but… I mean, you *make* this stuff?'

Sharmi shrugged. 'You thought we cast a spell or something?'

Max glanced at Valera who offered no help, her serene expression suggesting she was enjoying his floundering.

'No, I… But I thought, you know, you'd get pills from somewhere, add your mark-up and sell them on. That's what Blammers do, right?'

'*What* did you just call us?' Jola's eyes were wide and then they were all advancing on him and Valera had taken a neat step to the left. 'P'raps you *should* be crackin' his limbs for him, Krys.'

Max held up his hands. Close to, they all smelled pretty rank. 'I meant no offence.'

'*No offence*? Then that's okay, girls.' Jola clapped her hands together. 'You think I'm a fuckin' sales rep, boy?'

'Of course I didn't think that. I just thought—'

Max looked to Valera for help again. She shrugged. The two heater girls closed in and Max backed away as far as he could before fetching up against a shelf and the uneven bone wall.

'What exactly did you just think?' asked Sharmi, her slimy leather apron pushed against his formerly mostly clean fatigues.

'P'raps old leaky-brain here can't quite recall,' said Jola. She shook her head. '*Blammer*. Are you for real?'

'He looks but he don't see,' said Sharmi, one hand in its filthy gauntlet stroking his cheek. He tried to pull back but only succeeded in cracking his head against the wall.

Krystyna clapped her hands.

'All right, back to work. We got orders to make up. Best not scare him away before he pays. They come in as buyers and end up as users, right?'

Sharmi gave his cheek a final, echoingly solid, pat before turning her back on him for her still. Jola's look of disdain was long and meaningful. Max was sweating a lot and not just because of the heat. He blew out his cheeks and Krystyna regarded him for a moment.

'How long you been on this lizard, kiddo?'

'Coming up nine months now.'

Krystyna raised her eyebrows. 'Barely out of the womb, then. Better get your ears and eyes open more and learn how things work.'

'I'm a flyer. I'm amazing at my job. Nothing else matters.'

'And because you're going to Fall it ain't worth investing in anything but flying and fucking, right, kiddo?'

'Frankly, yes,' said Max, belatedly discovering a little anger. 'I'm chucking away most of my life for the greater good. I deserve respect because in a few years I'll be dribbling in Landfill. You're just fucking pushers feeding off my sacrifice.'

Max heard Valera's sharp intake of breath and saw Jola and Sharmi spin back round. Krystyna raised a hand to keep them back.

'Well, you win the prize for being *the* most self-centred tool I have ever had the misfortune to meet, and given I meet mainly drake pilots, you're up against some pretty stiff competition.'

She turned to go and the others went back to their work. Max stared at Valera who shrugged in exasperation.

'What is wrong with you?' she hissed. 'Just remember who you're condemning right now, eh?'

Krystyna had disappeared back into the other room and had turned the music up. Max rubbed a hand over his face and followed her as far as the opening.

'Sorry... I'm sorry,' he said. Krystyna turned round and cupped a hand to her ear. Max raised his voice. 'I'm sorry!'

She flipped the music off bang on time and his apology bounced around the tiny space.

'You do deserve respect,' she said. 'And so do we. Apology accepted, this time. Now what do you want?'

'I need heaters for my wing. I've got money for thirty days' worth. Can we deal?'

Krystyna nodded and sparked up another cigarette. 'We can. Got the sample?'

Max's heart missed a beat and the look on his face gave him away. Krystyna smiled.

'Gotcha, kiddo.' She pushed past him. 'Okay, Val, hand it over.'

Valera pulled a small phial from her fatigues pocket, shook the red liquid within and handed it over. Krystyna took it and Max saw sadness in her eyes, just momentarily.

'Your wing... Kullani, right? I'm sorry, kiddo, tough on her. Good pilot. Make yourself comfortable, well, as comfortable as you can.' She gestured at the meagre seating.

'Um, what is that?' asked Max.

'Blood,' said Krystyna, flipping the phial to Jola who caught it deftly. 'Let's get this batch made up.'

'Blood.'

'Can't make a heater without it,' said Krystyna.

'I thought... Actually, I don't know what I thought. What else do you make them from, then? Stuff that smells bad for sure.'

'Spot on,' said Krystyna. 'We're not at the root of the tail by chance. Heaters are synthesised from digestive secretions harvested from a gland that runs by the large intestine... To put it bluntly, we stick needles in its arse to get what we need. All very glam.'

'Lovely,' said Max. 'How did you come by it? Just stuck needles in all sorts of places till something worked?'

Krystyna's easy smile disappeared. 'No, kiddo, I used to work for the ERC programme. We all did. Long story and none of your business but we need to stay close to the action, so to speak. We need data to improve our product. Just understand that I wouldn't be living in this craphole unless I felt I had no other choice, all right?'

Max shrugged. 'What does the blood do, then?'

Krystyna pursed her lips. Valera stepped in.

'You get on, Krys, I'll explain. He's like a curious child, isn't he?'

'*Like*?' said Jola.

Valera pointed at seats around the small table and they both sat. Max watched Krystyna and Jola pipetting Kullani's blood onto a petri dish and setting it inside a small machine that hissed when they turned it on. Further down the bench, Sharmi had set a flask of clear liquid on an effluent burner. A sour stench rose from it. He felt uncomfortably small and ignorant.

'It's simple enough,' said Valera. 'Heaters have to be DNA-typed to the individual. They use the blood to synthesise a horribly complex chemical linkage that allows them to blend the base structure with the human DNA.'

'So, not simple at all then,' said Max. 'Expensive business.'

Valera hunkered down in her seat and folded her arms. 'Very. Now if you don't mind, I could do with some rest.'

'Sure.'

Max watched her close her eyes and then open one and pierce him with her stare.

'Tell me you brought the EM stick.'

'I brought the EM stick,' said Max, patting his pocket. 'The squad were very generous.'

'Good.' She closed her eye. 'And good night.'

Max tried to doze too, and he probably did nod off from time to time, but mostly, he was plagued by an image of a clock ticking round with excruciating sloth. He tried to watch the heater girls work but that was dull too. At one stage, Sharmi pointed out the kettle and coffee grounds and he made them all a drink heavily tainted with the all-pervasive smell in the lab and he was glad of the distraction.

He had so many questions, now he had the time to think about where he was and what it meant, but the only time he opened his mouth to ask one of them, a sharp kick on his ankle betrayed the fact that Valera wasn't quite as asleep as she made out.

It was three hours before Sharmi set a small cardboard box on the table in front of him.

'It's all in basic doses,' she said, handing it over. 'Hypo in there too. One shot into the top of the thigh every day, works in a couple of minutes. That's fifteen hundred Euro Marks up front.'

Max pulled the EM stick from his pocket and handed it to Sharmi who flicked out her p-palm and made the off-grid transfer.

'Don't spend it all at once,' he said, taking the stick back and noting the small untraceable balance still on board.

'Remember, heaters are only one product we offer that stops this behemoth's crew going collectively insane. We've got uppers, downers, sleepers, stimmers, gutfulls, shitters, skyhighs, doubleOs, grainers, flip outs and halos. And that's just the common stuff.'

'Good to know. Thanks.'

'You'll do all right, kiddo,' said Krystyna. 'Time to go.'

She gave Valera a hug, punched Max on the shoulder and turned away. Sharmi blew him a kiss. Jola didn't even acknowledge their leaving.

Back in D-one-four-four, Max found himself trembling. Valera closed the crate.

'You all right?' she asked. 'Good to go?'

'I think so. I just... Someone'll be doing that for me, one day. Makes you think...'

'You were due some perspective, I guess. Shame it had to be this way.'

'Why don't the brass just shut it down?'

Valera blew out her cheeks and walked towards the warehouse door. 'That's a big question. Later, all right? We need to get back. Kullani can't wait.'

CHAPTER 9

> The sheer excitement of being one of those chosen to study sentient alien biology was only topped by the honour of that calling. I remain blessed by my fortune, but saddened by the direction the research has taken.
>
> DOCTOR HELENA MARKOV, HEAD OF RESEARCH,
> EXTRA REPTILIAN CONSTRUCT ORGANISATION

'Where the hell have you been?' Jessy shot up from her chair the moment Valera and Max entered the otherwise deserted common room. 'Moeller's about to page the whole behemoth for you. You were wanted an hour ago and it was urgent then.'

'Well, I guess he knows where I've been… Where's everyone else?' asked Valera.

Jessy shrugged. 'They were all sleeping when the call came. Funny how everyone had seen you at Gargan's and then gone straight to bed, isn't it?'

'What did you say?'

'Not a lot. I mean… Everyone's free to sleep wherever with whoever after a mission, right? And it is the middle of the night.' She noticed the box in Max's hands. 'It really took you this long to get that?'

'They had to complete some other orders first. You know how

it is,' said Valera. 'I'd better head to Flight Com. Put the call through and stop the all-hail.'

'Aye, Skipper.'

'You know what to do, Max. And when you're done, get some sleep.'

'Good luck, Skipper,' he said vaguely, eyes already on Kullani's pod.

'Your support is overwhelming.'

'My what?'

'Never mind. Go away.'

Max hurried along the corridor and rapped on Kullani's door.

'Go away,' came a groggy voice. 'She's not in here, I've told you already.'

'Can't do that,' said Max. 'I've got something you need.'

'Oh, it's you. Thought it was that fucking lackey from Flight Com again. Door's unlocked.'

Max walked in, the light from outside framing his shadow and casting it long over the bed. The room smelled of sex and alcohol and he grinned.

'Hey, Grim.'

'Morning, boss.' She was the second hump on the far side of the bed.

'Glad you two are having fun. I've been shouted at by smelly scientists in an even smellier flesh tunnel all night. Just the evening I had planned.'

Max closed the door and Risa Kullani flicked the low light on. She squinted at him and cast about for her tee-shirt as Max perched on the bed. Next to her, Grim was on the move too. She hopped out of bed and pulled on her sweats.

'No need for you to go,' said Kullani.

'Well, I thought...'

'Not on my account,' said Max. 'Besides, you might need to do this sometime.'

Grim nodded. 'Okay.' She scrambled back on to the bed and

sat behind Risa, legs straddling her and arms locking around the ailing pilot's waist. She leaned her head on Risa's shoulder.

'I should take a picture,' said Max. 'But it would make everyone cute-puke.'

'Just open Pandora's box, will you?' Kullani was trying to smile but couldn't take her eyes from the plain package Max was holding.

'It's really simple,' said Max, unclipping the fastenings and lifting the box lid off. 'Thirty shots, one into the top of your thigh last thing every night. It'll make you really hot for an hour or two afterwards; that'll wear off before you have to report to the ERC for a briefing.'

Max had been staring into the box, pointing at the phials and hypo. He looked up and both Risa and Grim had tears in their eyes.

'It'll be okay,' said Max. 'This stuff'll keep you flying forever.'

As if by prearranged signal, they hugged him.

'You're an idiot, Max,' said Risa. 'But I'm glad you're our idiot.'

'Hey, any time,' said Max, enjoying the embrace, his imagination wandering a little. They seemed to sense that too and pushed him away. 'Want to give it a go? A jab, I mean. Of the hypodermic.'

Grim dissolved into laughter, falling backwards onto the bed, hooting as she tried to calm herself. Risa just shook her head.

'There really is no better sight than a man digging an ever deeper hole for himself. Come on, hand it over. Grim, get a grip, you're doing this for me. Can't stand injections.'

Grim snorted and gathered herself. Her nimble fingers quickly assembled hypo and phial. She spread her hands.

'Pick a thigh.'

'Left... no, right, no, left.'

'Holy arse,' said Grim. She shifted Risa's tee-shirt up a little, placed the hypo on her left thigh. 'Ready?'

Risa bit her lip and nodded. 'The fight starts here.'

Grim triggered the hypo. 'No turning back now.'

'It's *cold*,' said Risa.

'Not for long,' said Grim. 'Come on, best you lie down again.'

Grim plumped up a couple of pillows and Risa lay against them. Even in the dim light, Max could see her cheeks beginning to flush and sweat appear on her brow.

'Wow,' he said.

'You should try being on this side of it.' Kullani shifted in sudden discomfort. 'Fuck.'

'One day I will be.'

Max had to force himself to stay while Risa's body heated up and the pain intensified. She stripped off her sweat-soaked tee-shirt. Grim grabbed a towel, soaked it in cold water and mopped her down repeatedly, though it had precious little effect. Risa's eyes were wide and frightened, her body shook and she writhed, contorted and gasped but she never once called out.

Unsure what to do at first, Max soaked another towel and held it to her wrists and mopped her torso. He stared into her eyes, trying to give her something to focus on, and wished he hadn't. Kullani was terrified, desperate for it to stop. The unfairness, the random nature of when the Fall struck, lit a sharp anger within him. Their commanders never saw this. Perhaps they should.

'Keep looking at me, Risa. You'll get through it and then we'll fly again. Hold on to that. Hold on to me.'

She shook the towel off her wrists and grabbed his hands, a horrible spasm racking her body and drawing a moan from her slack mouth, from which hung lines of drool. Her nails dragged at his skin.

His anger intensified. That she should be so desperate to get back in her drake she'd put herself through this. He wondered if command ever considered the human suffering at the end of the glory times of drake piloting. Of course they didn't.

It was more than an hour before Risa cooled off enough to lie still. Her breathing calmed to a more moderate and regular pace and she shuffled back under the covers. Even the fear in her eyes subsided.

'That had better have been worth it,' she managed, her voice dry and croaky.

'It gets easier, doesn't it?' asked Grim, looking squarely at Max.

'I don't see why it should,' said Kullani. 'Thanks for sticking around, Max. Max?'

Max stared at Kullani and all he could see was himself dialled forward a couple of years, when the Fall began to sharpen its claws and rake at his mind.

'I always assumed I would be okay. That it wouldn't bother me. But now I've seen this shit first-hand, I'm not.'

'Not what?' asked Risa.

'Okay with it. Not at all.'

'What are you talking about?'

'This! Risa... it's not right. This thing will destroy you. The price for flying shouldn't be so high. There has to be another way.'

'We all go through it,' said Kullani quietly. 'Think I first saw it about three months out too. First time facing the Fall and it's no longer something you can dodge, is it? It stinks, but the only thing to do is get back in your drake and remind yourself what a fucking amazing gift it is.'

'And then remember nothing when my brains start rotting.' Max flushed and squeezed his eyes shut. 'Sorry, Risa, I didn't—'

'No sweat. They say you never forget the touch, though.'

'Who says?'

'The Fallen.'

Max studied his lap and the box of heaters that leered up at him, representing inescapable pain and a haunted, miserable fate.

'I should go,' said Max, voice catching in his throat. 'Try and get some sleep.'

Kullani nodded. 'Thank you, Max.'

Max shrugged. 'For what, putting you through all that? Hard to believe it's worth it, you know?'

'It's worth it,' said Kullani. 'You'll understand when your time comes.'

Max pushed himself to his feet, feeling drained and hollow. 'Try and get some sleep, eh?'

'Don't you dare fly without me, Halloran.'

'Never without my wing.'

When the door closed behind him, Max leaned against the wall for a moment, his sighing breath reminding him he was tainted by the stench of the heater girls' lab. He should shower but he honestly didn't think he could stand for that length of time. Even the few paces to his pod looked an impossible distance.

It was quiet. The squad rack was otherwise at peace and the movement of the *HoG* evidenced by the gentle vibrations through her body. Max forced himself along the corridor and into his pod. The light was on and Anna-Beth was waiting for him.

'Oh, thank God,' he said and fell into her embrace.

'Let it out if you need to,' she whispered.

'There'd be no way back from there,' he said, needing to distract himself and finding a way. 'Thought you were on an early.'

Anna-Beth gently loosened the embrace. 'Not now. All sorties are delayed. We've all been invited to an outpouring of nauseating bullshit from President Corsini via vid-link tomorrow at oh-nine-thirty.'

'That would normally be terrible news,' said Max.

'How did she do?'

'She was incredible. I was the wreck. Pathetic, really.'

Anna-Beth kissed him. 'You were there for her, that's what counts. Come on, come to bed.' She began pulling his shirt up over his head. 'Hmm, thought it was just your clothes that stank but it seems it's your skin as well.'

Max found himself laughing. 'Sorry. I'll go shower.'

'Don't be an idiot, I don't care. Not tonight, anyway.'

'She's so strong, you know? Risa, I mean.'

'Yeah, but you need to watch her.'

'She'll know when it's time to stop,' said Max.

Anna-Beth's face was sad. 'That's the trouble, she won't.'

CHAPTER 10

We could combine alien and Terran DNA in every other Extra Reptilian Construct but with the firedrake, every attempt failed, hence their keen minds. We have to balance the need for drake intelligence against that to protect the human mind in order to deliver an effective weapon. Every further move we make tips that balance in the drake's favour.

PROFESSOR CARL ALDUS, NEUROLOGICAL SCIENCE RESEARCH LEAD, ERC PROGRAMME

The theatre had originally been designed for live performances but its primary use was as a briefing hall for ground and air missions. Every one of the two thousand seats was taken. The *Heart of Granite*'s command team, along with Alexandra Solomon, were seated among the drake pilots, ground lizard jockeys, senior civil servant administrators and army officers. The remaining seats had been allocated to carefully selected marines.

It made for a bright and noisy atmosphere which, along with the glaring ceiling lights, was most unwelcome for Max, who needed another three or four hours in the sack. He kept Kullani in front of him and they were directed to the fifth row, centre block, right behind Flight Commander Moeller.

Max swore under his breath. 'Morning, sir.'

Moeller turned his head fractionally and raised an eyebrow. 'You'll recall how I mentioned that nothing on this behemoth ever happens by accident?'

'Everything you say is a learning experience, sir,' said Max.

'I don't even want to feel your breath on my collar.'

'It would be an honour to hold my breath for the duration of our glorious leader's inspirational speech, sir.'

'And how are you, Kullani?' asked Moeller, his gaze fixing her abruptly.

'Fine, sir,' said Kullani brightly, perhaps too brightly.

'Really? Halloran told me you had some nasty bruises from yesterday's skirmish. Your squadron leader said you were extremely tired. A remarkable recovery, then.'

'A cold compress and a good night's sleep work wonders, sir,' said Kullani, her voice even and confident. 'Bruises come with the job.'

'Mind how you go. Remember to get checked out if you feel there's anything amiss.'

'Of course, sir.'

Anything else Moeller might have said was cut off as the main lights began to dim and Commander Avery walked on stage. The audience stood to attention.

'At ease. The president has recorded a video address. Please refrain from spontaneous applause until it is complete.' Laughter rang around the theatre. 'For context, I should remind you all that the presidential elections are in eighteen months' time. When the address is over, the following will remain for mission briefings. Inferno-X, Lavaflow-A, Hammerclaws-G and second battalion, first regiment . . . the Annihilators.'

Avery made a hand signal and walked quickly from the stage. The remaining lights dimmed and the huge screen displayed the flag of United Europa, a graphical representation of all the territories within its compass set on a background of three vertical blue, black and yellow stripes. Easily the dullest flag of all the warring factions.

The flag faded to a shot of Corsini behind his desk, all oily smile and bespoke suit. Exactly how he thought a statesman should look. The ornate wood adorning the walls; the paintings of ancient battlefield victories; the leather inlaid mahogany desk; the banks of information screens set on the left and right of the desk; and his hands resting on the desktop, fingers linked.

'My friends! I wish I possessed your courage. For almost seven years, you have kept our borders secure and our children safe, and we are in awe of your valour.'

Max prayed this was going to be a short version of one of Corsini's trademark inspirational speeches, rather than a long address, but it hadn't started in promising fashion.

'Today I want to send you one clear message: I've got your backs,' said Corsini. 'There are minorities, vocal minorities, who would have you pulled from the battlefield; returned home without the victories you fight for every single day. Without recognition of the sacrifices you make, and those who lay down their lives each and every day. So I am fighting, every day, to support you. To ensure your return will be with victory in your hearts, to give meaning to sacrifice.'

There was some applause then, desultory and brief.

'But be aware! I stand against the appeasers, hiding their cowardice behind sympathy for your families – ignoring your choice to fight for our cause. They are blind to the dangers of withdrawing from the battlefield. If I am not here to stand with you following the election, I fear what the future holds. Not for me, for you.'

This speech wasn't going quite the way Max had expected and, uniquely, he found himself listening; and the quiet in the theatre meant everyone else was too. Despite Corsini's unusual honesty, however, there remained an inevitability to his direction.

'These appeasers need to be stopped and you, the true backbone of United Europa, can deliver that blow.'

Here it comes, Max thought.

'It is in your hands to win this war and return as heroes. I know you are tired. I also know you are on the brink of a breakthrough in Mid-Africa. Meanwhile our armies in the Balkans gain momentum and we have successfully halted enemy advances in South America.

'In the terms of historic wars fought across our lands, it is time for the final push. One extra effort from each of you serving in United Europa's extraordinary armed forces in Mid-Africa. We are on the brink. With one mighty heave, we will break them.

'You can do this. You will do this. For your country, for your comrades and for those you love. Honour the memory of those who cannot return. United Europa needs you now. Thank you.'

'Corker,' said Max. 'There's no way we can fail now.'

There was a murmur of conversation, growing in volume, as people begin to file out.

Moeller stood and turned a bleak look on Max. 'Keep it to yourself, Halloran. Still, you'll soon have your first chance to prove your point. You're off on an Obs and Recon Circuit this afternoon.'

'An ORC? Why, with respect, are you sending Inferno-X?' asked Valera.

Moeller smiled. 'It's an ORC with attitude.'

'Sort of an Uruk-Hai then, you mean?' said Max.

'Holy Mother, you've read a book?' said Moeller. 'I'm almost impressed, Halloran.'

'Well, I saw a vid...'

'Oh? The ancient Jackson classic or the truly awful Katasami remake?'

'Who's Jackson, sir?'

'Never mind. Hope kindled by you is only ever a brief spark in a deluge, isn't it?' Moeller sighed and moved towards the stage.

The theatre was cleared except for those required to stay and hear the briefing and they bunched up in the front ten rows. Solomon and Avery had left with Kirby, leaving Flight Commander Moeller the last of the executive team in the room.

'Right, I'll make this brief,' said Moeller. 'We've been conducting long-range recon, and we've identified a Mid-Af behemoth in the central Vermelho Sea zone, alone and seriously overdue a regeneration cycle. Clearly, we need more intel so we have increased our pace and are now running ahead of the *Steelback*.

'Naturally, that means we have increased our risk as there are three Mid-Af behemoths in the zone. So, Annihilators, you are on point for the next four-day cycle and will pay close attention to southern vectors. Lavaflow and Hammerclaws, you are on combat air patrol. Full details to follow in the briefing ping. Inferno, you'll be flying obs and recon.'

Pilots from the other squads jeered and Inferno-X gave them the mandatory finger.

'Enough,' said Moeller. 'I need observation on speed, leg sync, how quickly they launch their drakes, what they have on the ground. Potential vulnerabilities; get me shots of dry armour if you can – and on no account engage. Fly smart, C-One in, C-Two on point and C-Three on high obs. If your intel confirms it's vulnerable, you'll be heading back in for a strike in a couple of days.

'Any questions, Val-X?'

'Has the lizard got a name, sir?'

Moeller smiled. 'Sadly it isn't the *Virunga*, so don't get too excited. It's an older one, the *Maputo*. This is the break Corsini was talking about, so bring me back something, eh?'

'Are we testing enemy drake fitness on the chase?' asked Valera.

'Negative. Don't risk yourselves. We assume the drakes will be on peak or close to. But the *Maputo* might be sluggish, making tail-up a trial. That's the sort of intel I need. If we're a go for assault, it'll be our last before the *Granite* takes her own big swim so let's go out on a high, okay?'

'Roger that.'

'You're all away at fourteen hundred. Fly well and don't Fall.' Moeller stared squarely at Kullani, who smiled back. 'And before you fly, report to the ERC for brain pattern scans. Dismissed.'

*

It was another day of blazing sun and scorching heat along the northern borders of the Nubische Desert. The battle for the Vermelho Sea coast was into its second year and the prize for United Europa, should they prevail, was dominance of the entire North-Af and Cen-Af region on a line that could be drawn almost exactly along latitude five degrees north. A distance of almost four thousand kilometres coast to coast. This was Corsini's goal and it was no coincidence that Solomon had arrived just before yet another final push.

Max had no idea if it would win them the war, but even he could see the huge geographical superiority the territory would give them. And the land they'd captured, once reformed, irrigated and planted... It would make United Europa the most powerful bloc in the world. Trouble was, the Mafs and the Sambas wanted it for exactly the same reason. The Mafs were regrouping, having lost the fight on the shores of the Mediterranean, and still controlled the south central region; and the Sambas, a long way from their South American homeland, waited to frustrate any army that looked like it might be getting the upper hand. Right now, that was UE, of course.

All any side needed was someone else to make an error. And it looked like the Mafs had made one: leaving a behemoth too far from water when it had to replenish. Slow. Weak. Vulnerable.

The squadron was flying high in the glorious blue sky on a south-south-easterly heading. Vision was excellent, the thermals were riding easy and the prevailing wind blew across them, east to west. Beneath them, ground forces advanced across uncontested land with Geckos, Iguanas and Basilisk outriders making up the bulk of the movement.

Somewhere down there, the Annihilators would be pressing out even further, trying to establish line-of-sight with the potential battleground. And just beyond it, was the *Maputo*.

It was best not to look too hard at the ground itself. Years of war, the advance and retreat of five different regional blocs trying to take control, had left much of it ruined beyond recognition. Max wasn't one to worry about what had been destroyed by war, but every now and again the scale of the devastation, the destruction of land in order to own land, got to him. And holy shit alone knew how many species had been eradicated in the process.

It was a fucked up world and he was doing his bit. Whether he was making it more or less fucked up, though, he'd leave to the armchair philosophers.

'Chevron orders,' said Valera. 'Step-X and C-Three: High altitude observation. Hal-X and C-Two: you have my back. C-One, you're coming with me to stir the nest. Under no circumstances wander into the *Maputo*'s firing arcs. Stick to your patterns, keep the chatter to a minimum and break on my order. No one gets a toasting, everyone comes home.'

'Roger that, Skipper,' said Lankowski of C-One, echoing the squad.

'Inferno-X, Flight Com. Contact imminent. We have a small group of enemy drakes at your ten o'clock, ten blips in all. Not a threat but be aware. Flight Com out.'

'Inferno-X, Val-X. Form chevrons, mission is green.'

Max opened his chevron com. 'C-Two, listen up. We'll be taking in the sights of the stunning Nubische Desert from a height of four hundred today, with views of the beautiful *Maputo* with its peeling scale, comedy multiple leg limp and, we hope, arthritic tail lift to your right during the flight. We will also observe the piloting skills of C-One, and while we are unable to toast any fucker who comes too close, we can shout and make funny arm gestures to scare them off.

'I trust you'll all have a lovely afternoon.'

There was silence for a moment.

'You really are a prat, Max,' said Monteith.

CHAPTER 11

> It was apparent early on that the aliens used organic matter in all their machines, and all their vehicles. It took the world's best a decade to work out how, and the revolution in battle hardware came hard on the heels of that discovery. Such strength of structure combined with such a lack of relative mass was extraordinary and game-changing.
>
> PROFESSOR HELENA MARKOV, DIRECTOR,
> EXTRA REPTILIAN CONSTRUCT ORGANISATION

Behemoths could be spotted by the dust they threw up, which drifted on the prevailing winds, causing clouds to form at low level, slowly rising on thermals to be dispersed by stronger winds.

Far to the east, a dull smudge indicated the *Virunga* and a similar distance to the west, the third Maf behemoth trudged along, playing its part in the endless game of behemoth chess. And there, clearer as they closed in, was the *Maputo*, moving steadily northwards and not looking to be in any particular distress.

'Hey, Risa, you passed the brain pattern scan then,' said Max.

'Never doubted it. I'd have paid to see Moeller's face when he got the results though.'

'How're you holding up?'

'Honestly? Better than ever,' said Kullani. 'Weird, but it's almost like nothing happened yesterday.'

'That's got to be good, right?' said Max, Anna-Beth's warning sounding in his head.

'I'll let you know.'

Max focused on the *Maputo*. There was some degradation on the spine and flank armour, visible as pale smears even from C-Two's distance, but nothing that might signify cracking. He opened the chevron com.

'Can anybody see a limp?'

'She looks pretty smooth from up here,' said Losano. 'Though she's slowing.'

'Copy that, Los-X. Eyes open, C-Two. Let's see if there's any crackle in her tail raise. Keep your distance. Skipper, we are on point.'

'Copy, Hal-X,' said Valera. 'C-One going for the close-up.'

Below them, the *Maputo*'s spine ordnance bristled. Forty millimetre auto-cannon sat in their retractable housings on each vertebra. Anti-aircraft launchers swivelled and tracked. The *Maputo* came to a halt, dust surging from her thirty pairs of legs. Immediately the tail began to rise and the flight deck would be deploying from her belly. Max could see no evidence of any struggle as the mighty muscles engaged and the tail tip began to curl up from the ground.

'Anything anyone wants to say?' he asked.

'What time are we meeting in Gargan's?' asked Calder.

'Usual time and it's your round, Hal-X,' said Borini.

'Musing over alcohol would be a better use of our time,' said Schmidt.

'Keep it tight, folks,' said Max. 'Here we go, she has got problems. Circle on station.'

Max watched the *Maputo* make a slight lean forwards. Her head dipped and the front eight pairs of legs bent to varying degrees at the knee. She was struggling to lift her tail, no doubt about it.

Max thumbed his open com. 'Flight Com, Val-X, Step-X. C-Two has intel. Distinct muscle and spinal degradation indicated by extreme effort required to raise the tail.'

'Confirmed,' said Valera. 'We're seeing significant muscle vibration in all legs along the right flank. Flank armour appears dry. Evidence of minor cracking.'

'Flight Com copies. Inferno-X, prepare to disengage. Step-X, I am tracking the ten blips inbound on your altitude. Confirm spots on a heading of one-six-five.'

'Step-X copies.' There was a pause while Stepanek and C-Three searched the sky. 'Spots confirmed. Observation suggests extreme pace. Flight Com, please confirm M-and-M.'

'Step-X, Flight Com, blips indicate make and model are dragon-class hunter-killers. They're drakes, Step-X.'

'Copy, Flight Com,' said Stepanek. 'Turbo-charged too. Jes-X, Rob-X, eyes on the incoming.'

'Recommend you complete obs and head home, Val-X.'

'I hear you, Flight Com. Complying.'

'Flight Com out.'

'Inferno-X, Val-X. Let's form up. C-Two, C-Three, merge at one thousand. C-One will complete inspection. Single circuit of target then ascend to one thousand. Keep an eye on those drakes. Val-X out.'

'Distinct grind in the aft launchers,' said Abraham. 'They're taking on too much sand from fifteenth vertebra backwards.'

'Copy, Abe-X,' said Valera. 'No closer. Jak-X, you too, move out fifty.'

'I hear you, Skipper,' said Jaks. 'Forty-mils tracking, can't see any degradation from here.'

'Time to go, Martha,' whispered Max. He twitched his right arm up and back and Martha swept into an easy climb, her rotation allowing her to take in the approaching enemy, presumably dispatched by the *Virunga* to chase Inferno-X away. Max noted a very slight tremor through Martha's flanks. 'What's up?'

With C-Two climbing in his wake, he continued his rotation. Using Martha's eyes, he could see Stepanek and C-Three heading towards them.

'Holy Mother, but those boys are coming in quick,' said Roberts, Stepanek's second in the chevron. 'Descending and tracking, still incoming. Are you getting this, Step-X?'

'Copy, Rob-X,' said Stepanek, his voice measured and calm as always. 'I reckon we're about to be buzzed. Heads-up, C-Three, let's not get complacent.'

'Good call, boss,' said Fellows. 'I'll try not to poke the nest.'

'You too, C-Two,' said Max. 'Dudes don't look friendly.'

'Well, we are assessing one of their behemoths for an assault,' said Schmidt.

'Hardly an excuse,' said Borini.

'Bloody Mafs, just can't take a joke, can they?' said Losano.

The two chevrons merged at a thousand and formed a three-sixty degree defensive flight pattern. Drake necks craned, pilots' eyes squinted, all of them watching the incoming enemy. Their relative numbers didn't suggest an attack but Max could sense the disquiet among the squad and the com silence confirmed it. He knew how confident Inferno-X was, but he also knew Martha was uneasy and no doubt the other drakes were too.

'What is it?' he asked her. She couldn't reply but he felt her desire to accelerate. 'I feel you, princess. We'll be fine.'

The enemy were at about three klicks and closing hard when Martha barked a warning.

'Inferno-X, Hal-X, there's something astray here. Suggest C-Two and C-Three adopt assault formations and increase speed. Val-X, are you done?'

'Nearly, we just need—'

'They're breaking! Five of them coming down to the deck.' Jes-X's voice was loud and urgent.

'Inferno-X, assault formation,' ordered Valera. 'We're coming to you. C-One, break off and climb hard. Five incoming. Flight Com, we are under attack.'

'Flight Com copies. I see no more bogies, they are ten in all. Break and retreat. We do not need a fight today.'

But we've already got one, thought Max, still surprised the enemy would risk it with fewer numbers. Inferno-X drakes broke observation formation. Wings and bodies crowded close as the chevrons formed up in wing pairs. Max and Kullani rose through the middle of the throng, swinging about to face the incoming Maf drakes. They were quick, and Martha's vision swept ahead of his, sensing threat.

The Maf drakes were already on them. Borini was still climbing and turning and couldn't see the danger. Max turned to help.

'Bor-X, fold and fall. Fold and fall! Enemy inco— Shit!'

Fast, too fast, the Maf drake battered into Borini's back, thrusting its claws deep into the Inferno drake's scales. Borini was driven hard across the sky, his drake's wings washed back by the force of the impact.

'Kul-X, let's toast that fucker,' said Max and drove down to attack.

The enemy drake shuddered violently and Borini and his drake were encased in a powerful blue light that fizzed and crackled over, under and between the scales. Borini's howl of pain over the com was matched by his drake's agonised roar. The enemy let go, smoke pouring from cracks in the Inferno drake's armour, and she dropped dead from the sky, wings tattered and burning.

Max and Kullani shot through the smoke trail after the enemy drake, which had already dropped into a steep dive to gather speed.

'Bor-X is down! Break! Break!' yelled Max. 'Don't offer them targets. Combine for assault and stick to your wing. Val-X, we need you.'

But Max could see Valera had problems of her own. C-One

had been spaced around the *Maputo*, circling out of flank fire range, and was trying to reform on the climb up to the rest of the squad. The other five Maf drakes were on them, chasing and scattering them. Two swept across the *Maputo*'s spine and pounced on an Inferno drake in a steep climb, separated from her wing partner. The first snagged her tail with its jaws, as the second swept around her and played searing fire all the way up her belly and across the pilot pouch.

The pilot shrieked and fell silent and the ruined drake stalled before falling end over end towards the ground.

'Lankowski!' yelled Valera. 'Get your wings out. Lankowski!'

'He's gone, Skipper. Inferno-X is two down.'

'Copy, Hal-X. Inferno-X, Val-X, orders, orders.'

'Enemy on your six, Jes-X, roll and dive, I'm in your wake.' Roberts's voice cut across Valera. 'Still on you. Loop up. Shit! You're not steep enough.'

'Where is he?' said Jes-X.

'Tight ninety right and dive! Tight!' called Roberts.

Max searched the sky and saw the final moments. Roberts caught the attacking drake a fleeting blow on its right flank but it barely flinched from its trajectory. Jes-X was hard into a right-hand loop and the Maf drake surged inside her turn. The beast's jaws clamped the top of her drake's and fire engulfed its head. Those jaws bit down harder and the Inferno drake was beheaded. Jes-X screamed as she plummeted to the desert.

'Jessy!' roared Roberts. 'You fuck. You filthy Maf fuck!'

'Inferno-X, form on me in fours and threes at eight hundred. Keep it calm, keep it steady,' ordered Valera. 'Flight Com, Val-X. Inferno-X is three down.'

But Max could hear the shock edging her voice and in the com chatter, their indomitable confidence was shaken.

'Copy, Val-X.' Moeller couldn't hide his shock either.

Max searched the sky, using Martha's eyes to help him try and identify the paths their enemy would take. In among the sweeps, dives and rolls of the Inferno drakes he saw the smears of slate-grey enemy drakes weaving serenely through the chaos his squad was creating to deny them clear targets.

Kullani moved up to his right just a few wingbeats away. The airwaves were full of location calls and warnings. Fire strafed the air below him as Monteith and Nugent whipped by in pursuit of an enemy.

'Kul-X, let's—'

A flash of grey and Kullani was suddenly shunted through the air towards him, her loss of forward momentum taking her behind him. Max arched his back and neck, simultaneously dragging his arms into his sides and Martha snapped her wings closed and set her body into a tight backwards loop.

'Fight it, Kul-X.'

'He's not quite got me,' replied Kullani. 'Rolling here, Max, I need you.'

'Coming round hard.' Max used Martha's eyes to fix on Kullani and, when he saw her, he unwound the loop and powered Martha forwards. Kullani was barrel-rolling, keeping the enemy from taking a hold. 'Steady on my mark.'

'Copy, Hal-X.'

'Now.'

Kullani's roll ceased and her drake spat fire into her attacker's scales. The Maf drake grabbed at her drake's spine with its talons and in the same moment, Martha thumped hard into it, her own talons raking along its flank and sending it spinning away. Max suggested tight fire and twin beams of flame spat out into the empty space where the drake had been.

'Thanks, Max.'

'Any time. Clear air low.'

Max and Kullani dived into the narrowing airspace between C-One and the melee. Messages on the open com were urgent but remained calm despite the stunning start to the attack and the losses they had suffered. The Maf drakes were reforming in a

‘V’ formation about half a klick to the north of Inferno-X. They stayed on station, and began flying a helix pattern in formation.

‘Very pretty,’ muttered Monteith.

‘They were good enough to give us a bloody nose,’ said Valera.

‘Got some weight and ordnance too,’ said Redfearn.

‘All right, people. We’ve lost some and now it’s our turn. You have your threes and fours. Go tight com in your fire teams. I will retain open status.’

‘Inferno-X, Flight Com. Break and return to the *HoG*. Do not engage.’

‘Negative, Flight Com. They aren’t going to let us through.’

‘Roger that.’ Moeller sounded irritable. ‘Minimise contact. Flight Com out.’

‘Copy, Flight Com. Inferno-X, you heard the boss. We’re going straight on till morning,’ said Valera.

‘We’re running away,’ said Stepanek.

‘We’re living to fight another day. Something about these drakes stinks and we need a weak spot,’ said Valera. ‘We have our orders, doesn’t mean we can’t give them a scratch or two on our way past.’

‘Sounds good, Skipper,’ said Max.

‘Your support warms my tired old bones,’ said Valera. ‘Break and strike. Reform two klicks south at fifteen hundred. Sun’s out, let’s use it. Val-X out.’

The fluid formation of Inferno-X gave the enemy no hint of their intent. Valera led them on, the trios and quartets of drakes flying over and around each other as they came. Max felt the thrill through Martha’s body and wondered for a moment why the Mafs wanted to take them on, never mind their marginal technical superiority.

‘Kul-X, Mont-X, Nuge-X, you hearing me okay?’

‘Sadly,’ said Kullani.

‘For my sins,’ said Monteith.

‘Like a waking nightmare,’ said Nugent.

'May you all suffer maddening crotch itches every time you fly. So, bottom of the V is ours. We're going to count them off as they burn in the sand. Mont-X, Nuge-X, fly the flanks for follow-up to complete the kill. Kul-X, we're going straight in, rip the fucker up a little.'

'Go, Inferno-X,' said Val.

The squad surged forwards, Max suggesting maximum speed to Martha. He was pressed back in his pouch, Martha's roar joining the chorus. Max led his quartet out to the right; Valera's dived under him, Redfearn's over him and Stepanek's chasing across behind. He tipped his left arm and Martha swooped across the line and squared up with the target, now just a few beats away and heading for them.

'In we go,' said Max.

Monteith and Nugent pressed ahead on the flanks. Kullani came to his right-hand side. Nothing else needed saying. It was payback time, whatever Flight Com had ordered.

'Hope your teeth are sharp, Martha,' he said. 'They've got some armour by the look of them.'

Slate-grey and sleek, his target loomed ever larger. Max imagined a grappling attack and Martha tensed her neck and claws. The enemy came on, determined not to flinch first in the deadly game of chicken. Max accelerated further, Kullani at his side, both drakes homing in. Still the Maf came on. Kullani edged left and up a fraction and Max smiled; the bastard was caught.

Max imagined the strike and Martha cocked, swivelled and struck, jaws snapping on empty air, claws grasping at nothing. Max flew on a heartbeat into clear air before he understood what had happened. It just wasn't possible to change direction and move away that quickly.

'On me, Kul-X,' said Max.

He dropped his right arm hard to his side and stretched out his left arm, sure that the Maf drake had gone past him high and to his right. Martha turned hard, her head craning to see.

'He's on me,' called Nugent. 'Holy shit he's fast. I'm— Shit!'

Max raced for Nugent, seeing the grey shape batter into the Inferno-X drake and pour fire over her back and onto her left wing. Monteith hurtled in, his drake's claws thumping into the enemy's flank, sharp teeth sinking into its neck. He tore the beast from Nugent just in time for Max to line up.

'Max, on you!' shouted Nugent.

Max sensed the threat in the next moment and threw his arms up, slapping Martha's wings together above her head. They dropped out of the sky, the Maf drake breathing fire through the space where they'd been.

'Thanks, Nuge-X, I owe you. Where are you?'

'On your three and going down. Think I can control it. Dammit.'

Max pushed Martha up again and she began to rise back into the combat zone. Right in front of him, two enemies engulfed an Inferno-X drake. One tore through a wing and the other grabbed its tail in its rear talons, shaking its victim like a puppet on a string before severing it with a single bite.

The drake shrieked in agony and the two drakes let the stricken reptile go. She tumbled away, rudderless, her tail spouting blood, her one wing flapping in futility.

'Who went down!?'

'Fellows,' said Kullani. 'Get back up here, Max, I need your eyes.'

'Copy that, Kul-X. Monts, the Nuge is down. Shield him; we've got your back.'

'Copy, Hal-X,' said Monteith.

Max took in the scene while Martha closed in on Kullani. The enemy squadron was everywhere, reacting faster, turning harder and flying more powerfully. It wasn't much of an edge, but it didn't have to be. Max flew hard through the centre of the combat. A Maf drake shot in front of him, chased by three drakes including Valera, whose mark he could clearly see on the shiny underbelly of her drake.

The Maf drake dumped electronic counter measures from the base of its tail. All drakes had that capacity, creating sparking, crackling globes, fifty centimetres in diameter, to deflect incoming missiles. But these ones didn't float; they flew like they had a purpose.

Max turned Martha on to a curve trajectory over the chase, using her eyes to sweep for threats and his own to watch the battle unfold. Valera had seen the ECMs and her trio rolled and bucked to dodge the balls of lightning.

'On your six, Hal-X,' said Kullani. 'Monts and Nuge are out of it, no pursuit.'

'Good. Follow me and watch this bastard fly. We need to get an angle on what they're about.'

A huge burst of flame to his right distracted him for a moment. A quick glance showed him another crippled Inferno-X drake plummeting from the sky and two Maf drakes soaring through the smoke trail, four Infernos on their tails.

'Holy Mother, Inferno-X five down,' he muttered. 'I'm so sorry I couldn't protect you, Los-X.'

Valera was flying with Abe-X and Xav-X on her flanks. She rolled hard right, a globe brushing her drake's belly, leaving a dark smear and causing it to jerk sharply. Abe-X climbed steeply away, a trio of ECMs scorching a path below him, but he fell behind as a result. The Maf drake dived and released more globes ahead of Valera and Xavier.

The pair followed their target, swooping through the cloud of reptilian bodies, great wings, flame and smoke. Beyond the centre of the combat, Max caught sight of a pair of Maf drakes searching for their next target. No, they weren't searching, they were waiting.

'Val-X, Hal-X. Break right, break right.'

'Negative, Hal-X, we're closing. He's tiring.'

The enemy drake threaded through another skirmish. Calder and Redfearn had flanked an enemy and were spearing flame into its neck, driving it away from its support, weaving around it in a tunnel of drake flesh. It was awesome flying and Schmidt was trailing them, ready to pounce.

'Negative, Skipper, he's leading you onto another two. Check your nine. Break right, break right.'

The Maf drake drove into a climb, allowing Abraham to close the gap. He was greedy, he wanted all three of them.

'I don't see them, Hal-X, and we have him.'

'Pull out!' yelled Max. 'It's a trap. Trust the squad!'

A moment's silence. 'Copy that, Hal-X. Abe-X, Xav-X, hard right on my mark.'

Max watched them close on the waiting enemies who were flying in at frightening speed.

'Now, Skipper,' he whispered. 'Come on...'

'Mark! Break right, break right...' Valera and Xav-X dipped their right wings and sheared away, turning slow rolls, losing height fast and taking themselves from the jaws of the trap. 'Abe-X, break right! That's an order.'

Max watched Abraham's drake. He was right on top of his quarry, on the tip of his tail. The Inferno drake's mouth opened to breathe but the Maf drake dropped away in a stunning dive turn, ducking away from the oncoming pair who were poised, flaring their wings back, claws outstretched.

Max winced at the violence of the impact. Abraham was driven backwards, his drake venting flame into clear sky, mouth open to roar her frustration. The forces in the pouch must have been horrendous, too much for the muscle and lubricant to absorb. The enemy drakes poured fire over Abraham and one of them bled electricity into its body until the drake jerked spasmodically, and fell limp, dead before it began to fall.

'Bastards! Abe-X is down,' shouted Max. 'Kul-X, with me, let's have one of those fuckers.'

Max angled Martha into intercept.

'Negative, Hal-X. Break off, head home.'

'Skipper, it's—'

'Break off, Hal-X,' said Valera and then, much more quietly. 'We're running.'

'Copy, Val-X,' said Max.

'Inferno-X, Val-X. Break, break, break. Best speed to the mother ship. Watch your injured, shadow the slow. Hal-X, take the rear.'

'Count on it,' said Max. 'Kul-X, you with me?'

'Always, buddy.'

Inferno-X's escape procedure was second nature, though Max had never thought he would hear the order. The squadron broke off across the conflict and dived for the desert floor to reassemble in broken chevrons at seven-, eight-, and nine-hundred. It was an hour's flight to the *HoG*, an hour to safety within the behemoth's devastating firing arcs.

Max and Kullani flew across the back of the squad, watching the enemy for evidence they were done. The Mafs gathered at higher altitude and used the sun to obscure their positions and direction.

'What have you got, Kul-X?'

'Not a lot but glare, Max. They're tracking us I think.'

'Copy, Kul-X, stand by,' said Max. 'Mont-X, do you copy? Where are you?'

'On our way home,' said Monteith after a pause. He sounded tired. 'We had to pull some stunts on the way down, though.'

'What do you mean "we"?'

'I couldn't leave him there for ground evac,' said Monteith. 'He's hurt, Max. It's pretty bad. I've got him in the claws, gentle though.'

'Your call, Monts. Don't Fall.'

'Hear you, Max. Mont-X out.'

'There's nothing more you can do for him, Hal-X,' said Valera, her open com relaying everything to her. Mostly, it would be silence. 'Keep your eyes up, keep them off us, we've got some sick birds up here. This isn't going to be quick.'

'Copy, Val-X.'

Max turned a circle, squinting into the sun through Martha's eyes. All ten of them were still up there, still tracking.

'What are they doing?' asked Kullani. 'Seeing us off?'

'I wish,' said Max. 'They're waiting for our formation to show them who the weakest are. We'll have our work cut out getting home.'

'Flight Com, are you reading all this?' asked Valera.

'Copy, Val-X. We'll advise as we see it. Good luck.' Moeller sounded tired.

Max left Martha tracking the Maf drakes and looked down at Inferno-X, making best speed back to the *Heart of Granite*. He could see two with minor wing tears, one with a trailing hind leg and another with a tail burned black but mercifully still intact. Nothing the Tweakers couldn't fix when they got home. He could only guess at the condition of his squad mates. Everything he could see, they could see too.

'Val-X, Hal-X, do you copy?'

'Go ahead.'

'We have to use the injured as bait, Skipper.'

'Don't joke with me, Hal-X.'

'He's right,' said Kullani. 'They're so obvious from up here. If the Mafs attack, they'll target the weak. They want dead drakes on the ground, not a squad we can patch up and send back out.'

'Suggestions?'

'We can't defend them at close quarters. At least if we stand off we can call in threats as they go. Put a spotter on each injured flyer, a wing defence on each spotter and everyone else flies diversion and break-up. What do you say, Skipper?'

'I say it's our best option. Brief it out.'

'Okay, patch me across the squad. Who's the one with the grade three tear in the left wing? Our real sloth?'

‘That’s Roberts,’ said Valera. ‘You’re patched. Do it, I doubt the Mafs are going to wait much longer.’

‘Inferno-X, Hal-X, orders orders. All injured drakes to fly line astern of Rob-X. Roberts, you have to keep pushing.’

‘There’s a lot of whistle through the wing, Hal-X, and I’m a little bruised but okay to lead,’ said Roberts.

‘Copy, Rob-X. Right, here’s what we’re going to do…’

CHAPTER 12

> I saw a behemoth in the growing tank once. Well, it was more of a growing warehouse, a really big one. It was fully submerged and fed by a single tube into its stomach. It was weird because it was only about twenty metres long and the tank was over a kilometre long so it would fit when it was fully grown. That was going to take a year, apparently. How boring is that?
>
> MAXIMUS HALLORAN, AGE 15

The bridge of the *Heart of Granite* (Avery preferred 'Command and Control Centre') was as tense as she'd known it in months. The term Bridge just didn't do it justice at all. It was two hundred metres long, a hundred and eighty metres wide at its base and narrowing to sixty metres wide at the head, just behind the snout. It was full of sound and colour, busy with chatter and the energy of its staff and right now, alongside the tension was the ill-odour a behemoth exuded when it needed a regeneration cycle.

Avery had walked from the neck walkway through the main bulkhead and it seemed everyone from every department wanted her. Doors had opened from Weapons Control, Radar, Life Systems and even the ERC Systems Integration Unit, and people filled the space around her. She'd brushed them all aside and walked around the top of the brain, which was some sixty metres in diameter, and gave her usual shudder at the memories it evoked.

To aspire to the position of behemoth commander, one of the pre-requisite jobs was that of a movement and functions manipulator. That meant shift after endless shift wired into the sluggish reptile's synapses with your hands in thin superconducting gloves as you and your five co-manipulators relayed orders through the kneading and probing of the revolting sludgy tissue in the 'pockets' architectured into the brain. It felt almost nothing like dough, yet *bread-heads* was the popular slang; had been for years.

Avery had been told she'd grow to love the touch of the great beast. She had always utterly hated it.

The world beyond the brain was her domain now. The tactical tables, the ornate meeting table, the operations portals and the wall-to-wall video relays giving a three hundred and sixty degree view of the outside. And if that wasn't enough, they had a direct feed from the *Heart of Granite*'s eyes, which gave them light in a slightly different spectrum. It was particularly useful for spotting incoming spyflys and a critical aid at night.

One of the things she loved best was bringing important dignitaries up here, the ones who assumed commanding a behemoth was a simple task, and watch them gape and shrivel as the confusion of information, of sound and vision, battered them. The mighty were rendered insignificant and all their condescension washed away to be replaced by proper respect.

The politicians always thought they were in command. They didn't have a fucking clue. It was a shame that Solomon did, of course she did; she'd been commander of the *HoG*'s sister behemoth, the *Steelback*, before her astonishing, incomprehensible, appointment to the top of the pyramid.

'Commander?'

Avery turned from the vast main screen and rubbed a hand down her face.

'Flight Commander Moeller. Good. Come with me.'

She led Moeller to an unoccupied tactical table for a little relative privacy. The two of them stood side by side, Avery punching up data, radar and predicted flight paths.

'What the fuck is going on?' she asked. 'God's teeth, Gerhard, can you feel it in here? Our elite squad is being ripped up.'

'It's a mess,' said Moeller. 'And Valera has rejected help from other squads.'

'Overrule her.'

Moeller sucked his top lip. 'Come on, Nicola, not Valera. She says it isn't about numbers, that more drakes won't help and that we may lose more getting Inferno-X home. I trust her judgement.'

Avery stared at Moeller, searching for doubt. 'All right, what am I looking at here? This is one screwed-up formation.'

Avery tapped the tactical radar on which the Inferno drakes were represented by bright green blips and the enemy in red... well, you had to be traditional sometimes.

'They're running a distraction and obstruction defence. Those four in a line are the wounded. It seems to be working... so far.'

Avery shook her head. 'What do you really think?'

'I think I trust Inferno-X.'

'Right... And what have we got on these Maf drakes?'

'We'll have to wait until they're back and we can upload all the tactical data from the drakes, but we know they are slightly bigger, stronger and faster.'

'Is it an unlocking or a fleshware upgrade?'

Moeller blew out his cheeks. 'Mostly fleshware, I'd say. But it's hard to be certain.'

'All right, what do you need from me?'

'A firing solution, forty-mil-based, something I-X can get below. Flight path and entry grid too.'

'No problem. Where's my chief gunner? She was dogging my footsteps like, well, a dog just now... Lieutenant Edney, where are you when I need you?'

'Right here, ma'am,' said Edney.

Avery spun round. Lisa Edney was just a few feet away, hands behind her back. She was mid-height, with bobbed black hair and wore glasses in defiance of everything technology had to offer. She said her face was too soft and it needed hardening up. Avery understood her point.

'Right. Good. Thought I'd need you, I suppose.'

'It seemed probable,' she said.

'We have work to do.' Avery indicated the tactical radar tracking the approach of Inferno-X. 'Inferno-X is being pursued. They have injured. I need a firing solution for a south-easterly approach, rolling round to a north-westerly entry. No missiles. Stick to forty-mil and flank guns. I need it in about ten minutes.'

'I'll have it in five, Commander.'

'Smart arse. In that case I want it in three.' Edney turned and strode away towards the weapons control room at the back of the command centre. 'Right, Gerhard, anything else?'

'The ExO and I have medical and ERC emergency teams already on station. But we'll need to think how to handle the PR.'

Avery shrugged. 'PR can wait. Get as many of them home as you can first. I'll find you in Flight Command if I need you.'

Avery watched Moeller go before turning back to the tactical screen.

'What the hell are we walking into?'

'Two on approach from the west, approximately two-eight-zero degrees,' said Calder.

'Copy, Cal-X,' said Max. 'Intercept with Red-X.'

Max watched them move in. Down to his right, Valera and Stepanek were chasing off another. Three more were circling very high above them which left four...

'Compass point attacks incoming!' Nev-X's voice cut across the com. 'Steep angle approach.'

'Sal-X here, I have north,' said Salewski.

'Gur-X here, I have south,' said Gurney.

'Kul-X, with me, we'll sweep east to west,' said Max. 'Rob-X, you have six incoming, four on compass point approaches.'

'Top three diving,' said Pal-X.

'This is the big one,' said Max. 'Top cover move to intercept.'

Max dived, seeing the Maf drakes approach in the clear air. Below, their quartet of wounded made steady progress across the desert floor and at least had sight of the *Heart of Granite*. The *Granite* would have them on screen by now, via the hi-res long-lens cameras mounted on her snout. This was probably the enemy's last chance to make a statement, and in front of the flagship behemoth of the UE fleet would be the best place to make it.

'Kul-X, where are you?'

'Tracking the easterly approach. Sweep west. I'm going low to high to play a game of chicken.'

'Copy that,' said Max.

Max trimmed Martha's wings to still some vibration and heard the whistle and whine across her scales as she gathered yet more speed. He was approaching from the south-east and the thrill took him.

'I'll be coming across your left flank, Schmiddy,' he said. 'Be ready.'

'Copy, Hal-X,' said Schmidt. His drake, with a burned tail, was in the centre of the quartet and struggling to maintain his line. 'Don't blow me off course.'

'I think I can fly high enough to avoid that. Stand by.'

Max was certain his target had seen him coming. In fact, he was counting on it. Martha's body rippled with a passing anxiety, something she sensed and couldn't communicate.

'What is it, princess?' asked Max.

He was at close to top speed and his mind was focused. He'd be on the Maf drake in half a minute; he had his trajectory right and assuming the Maf drake intended to take out Schmidt, he was going to get in the way at the perfect moment.

'Show me, Martha. What's the problem?' He sent the impulse with his mind, too.

Martha looked pointedly at the drake coming in from the south, then the one from the north. Max projected their impact points using pure instinct to make the complex calculation.

'Gur-X, Sal-X, this is Hal-X. Which of you is on target first?'

'Gur-X,' said Gurney.

'Agreed,' said Salewski.

'Pull away a hundred metres from your target point. Turn hard, don't look back. They're setting you a trap.'

'Copy, Hal-X. Thank you.'

'I live to save others,' said Max.

Max scorched in, bringing his arms to level. Martha flashed across the desert floor, no more than fifty above the undulating sand and less than ten above the stricken drakes when she reached them. It was all laid out before him. He was behind the enemy drake heading in from the west; it was Kullani's target. He could see Kullani hammering in from the bright eastern sky, descending hard, ready to test the enemy's courage. They'd flinch or they'd both die; after all, she was Falling. She didn't care any more.

The first Maf drake flew in from the south. Gurney was closing at extreme speed and Max prayed he'd time it right. In the split second before the potential impact point, both drakes pulled away; the enemy went left and whipped past Max. Gurney went with it. Max's target had been tasked to take Gurney out but now, without a target, it came straight on.

'Hello, hello,' said Max.

He washed over Schmidt, rolled ninety degrees and suggested lances of fire. Martha obliged and her flame raked along the enemy's left flank and wing. It was there and gone in a blink, but was a strike nonetheless. A beat later, Kullani flew straight into her target, her drake's claws dragging across its back as it tried to dive aside. He saw a wing tear appear before they separated.

The final attacker flew in on a collision course with Roberts.

Salewski roared by overhead, her drake's mouth already open, ready to bite and breathe. The Maf drake jerked up, whipped over her head and down again. Max blinked, not sure he believed what he was seeing.

'Schmiddy, roll left!'

'I— Holy shit,' said Schmidt as he saw the Maf drake rushing for him.

Max kept Martha's eyes on him and executed a sharp left turn. The Maf drake drove in. Schmidt, his drake wobbling, attempted to turn aside but he was too slow. The Maf ran fire across his wings and stamped down with its claws, fatally unbalancing him. The burned tail sought vainly for purchase and balance. Schmidt's left wing tip dipped violently, making a ninety degree turn and slowing far too fast. With no time to react, Jak-X and her drake ploughed straight into Schmidt and the pair of drakes tumbled hard into sand.

'Fuck!' shouted Max. 'Jak-X and Schmidt-X down, I repeat both down. Inferno-X is eight down.'

'Inferno-X, Flight Com. Firing solution acquired. Immediate drop to fifty on my mark. Forty-mil fire imminent. Skirt the *HoG* along her eastern flank, emergency entry authorised. We're ready for you. Come on in.'

'Copy, Flight Com,' said Valera.

'Inferno-X, Flight Com. On our mark. Three, two, one, mark.'

The remainder of the squadron dropped steeply towards fifty metres. The *HoG* was close now. Max could see her eyes and the slight rolling movement of her legs at rest was a thing of pure beauty right now.

Across her spine, scale plates rolled back and the forty-millimetre cannons spiralled up, swivelled to the south and filled the sky above Inferno-X with a deluge of armour-piercing slugs. Max shuddered to think of those things ripping into Martha's body. He flew down alongside Roberts.

'You made it, Rob-X,' he said.

'Only just, buddy.' Roberts's voice came in gasps. 'Gonna need some help getting out of my pouch, I think.'

'Do you need brakes on landing?' asked Max.

'Could do.'

'Tuck in behind me,' said Max. 'I'll see you in.'

Max put Martha ahead of Roberts's drake and turned past the *HoG*'s snout, dropping immediately down into the lee of her eastern flank. Machine guns bristled from their turrets all the way along while down on the sand, marines were ready to provide further cover fire.

'Some days, you even have to respect the grunts,' said Max.

He moved Martha out from the *HoG*'s shadow, turned a gentle left and lined up on the flight deck. The landing lights were flashing and further in, he could see red pools of light indicating medic teams. It was going to be busy in there.

'On my tail, Rob-X.'

'Copy, Hal-X.' Roberts sounded vague. 'I'm with you.'

'Stay that way,' said Max. He brought Martha over the ramp, seeing the lights flaring and the white lines of the runway hurrying beneath him. He flared Martha's wings and came to a quick stop about three quarters of the way into the hangar.

'Brace yourself, Martha. Take a look, would you?'

Martha turned her head. Inferno-X drakes were crowding outside where the sound of gunfire had ceased. But seventy metres away and slithering desperately along the bone floor came Roberts, plainly unconscious inside his pouch.

'This is going to hurt,' said Max.

Max hunched his shoulders and relaxed his back. Martha hunkered down in response, drawing her wings forwards and out of harm's way. Roberts's drake careered into her, shunting them along the runway and rattling Max about painfully despite the best efforts of muscle and fluid. Martha jammed her claws against the bone floor, the resultant shrieking sound forcing ground crew to turn away, hands over their ears.

Max gasped at the impact, keeping his feet pointed down and Martha groaned at the effort, backing her wings on Max's signal and bringing them to a complete stop. The shrieking ceased and Max slumped forwards momentarily, taking in a huge gulp of air and sending Martha a wave of love before triggering the release on his pouch.

'Grim'll have you now. Be good and get some rest.'

Martha rumbled something in her throat in response. Max scrambled out of the pouch, the lubricant cascading off his suit. He slid quickly down her chest and onto the floor and raced back to help Roberts. The air was full of the sound of orders, the whirring of machinery and the cries of drakes. Dull thumps beneath his feet signalled other drakes landing.

MedCarts and stretchers hummed in towards every drake. Tweakers with the big 'ERC' logo on the backs of their overalls hurried in to assess reptilian damage. Max moved quickly under the neck of Roberts's drake and patted her at the top of her chest to make her stand up. He scooted back a couple of paces as she complied.

'Where's Risa? Is she safe?'

Max flashed Grim a smile while climbing the drake's chest.

'She's peak. Flew the best I've ever seen her today. Bringing up the rear with the Skipper. Get Martha into her pen and go find her. But first get one of those MedCarts over here. Roberts is hurt.'

Max climbed up to Roberts's pod. His eyes were closed and he was slumped forwards.

'Roberts? ... Johannes, it's Max. Come on, buddy, time to get out.'

Max found the manual release and the top of the pouch rolled back and away. He fumbled briefly inside the pouch until he found the manual trigger stud. The pouch eased forwards, lubricant cascading out, and Max scrambled around to the side.

'Holy Mother, how hard did they hit you?'

Robert's left arm was broken at the shoulder. His collarbone had snapped and protruded from his skin. Blood had soaked down his suit. The shoulder was clearly dislocated and yet he had still flown all the way home.

'Shit, but you're a hard bastard,' said Max. 'Come on, we need you out.'

The stricken pilot moved his head and moaned as his collarbone shifted. He mumbled something but Max couldn't pick it up.

'Easy now, buddy. Help's here.'

'Hal-X . . . Max?'

Max looked down. 'Hey, Gordy, got a sick one for you here.'

The great bald and barrel-chested medic with 'Gordievski' on his overalls nodded solemnly. 'He's not the only one. Get down, we'll take it from here.'

Max dropped to the ground and almost fell onto his hands and knees. Gordievski put a hand under his shoulder and helped him back up.

'You need a massage, some anti-inflammatories and a whole lot of rest,' he said in his gloriously thick eastern European accent. 'But you'll ignore me, I know.'

'Until the moment I've counted the squad in.'

'Do what you have to do.'

Max gasped in a breath. 'Hey, did you see Monts? He would have come in with the Nuge in his claws. They're both all right?'

Gordievski nodded. 'Monteith practically laid Nugent on a stretcher before he landed. Top flying. They're both up in medical. Nugent's been smacked about pretty hard but nothing that won't heal.'

'Good.' Max managed a frail smile. 'That's good.'

Max looked down the length of the flight deck. He could see the Inferno-X drakes cluttering the runway. He could see pilots being helped onto stretchers while others were still in their pouches, being stabilised before they were moved. He walked down the line, seeing the expressions on the faces of ground crew and medics alike. A glance back and he could see the Flight Command balcony was packed with a disbelieving audience.

Max wanted to walk tall, to show them it wasn't so bad. Only it was and he couldn't. But he kept on walking and at last found something to smile about. There were Valera, Kullani and Stepanek, walking towards him and checking the squad one by one. He jogged down to meet them.

'Hey,' he said. 'Glad you could all get out on your own.'

Valera turned to him, the shock of all she was seeing on her face.

'Just look at this mess,' she said.

CHAPTER 13

The problem with the glorious design of the firedrake is that it was undiluted by any strands of Terran DNA. We couldn't engineer indigenous DNA into it and make it work. So the dragon of myth is an alien lifeform and people immediately speculated whether aliens ever flew them in our skies in centuries gone by. Our issue was more pressing. What would happen to the humans asked to fly them?

PROFESSOR HELENA MARKOV, MANAGING DIRECTOR, EXTRA REPTILIAN CONSTRUCT ORGANISATION

Gargan's was quiet that night. Plenty of people were out, and dancing, but there was none of the normal frenetic energy about it. Mostly they stood in groups and talked. And stared.

Max nursed a glass of whisky into which the ice had long since melted. Those few with him had only left the rack out of a sense of duty and in the wake of further bad news. None of the downed drakes or their pilots had survived. That made it official: Inferno-X was eight down.

'We have to have a naming,' said Max.

Valera nodded. 'I know, but we aren't all here.'

'Barring those in medical, only Risa's missing,' said Max. Risa, who had shut her door on it all and was alone with Grim. 'Come on, Skipper. Get it done and we can move on. I think the whole bar is waiting.'

Valera sighed and pushed herself to her feet. The squad, just eleven of them left, assembled in a circle. The music fell silent and everyone in Gargan's with it. Valera raised her glass.

'And you're all going to drain yours when I'm done, right?' she muttered to them before raising her voice. 'To our lost, we name you. We remember you as heroes of Inferno-X. Abraham. Lankowski. Jaks. Losano. Schmidt. Jes. Borini. Fellows. You made the sacrifice. You are gone but will ever remain Inferno-X. Salute!'

Glasses were raised and drained. The silence in Gargan's was brief and then applause began to grow. It boomed around the tenways space, louder than he had ever heard it, and Max closed his eyes and let it roll over him, soaking in the emotion until it faded and all that was left was an echo in his memory.

'Thank you,' said Valera to all who could hear. 'Now let's celebrate their talent and their lives.'

Gargan's closed early that night and Inferno-X had returned to their racks long before the last dance.

Max woke well before the bells and let Anna-Beth sleep on, letting the sounds of the *HoG* settle into his body just like he had the first night he'd been on board. First there was the hum, a bass tone with a slight rhythmic throb. It was always there in the background; blood pumping through arteries as thick as tree trunks. It was a sound of comfort and security. Next, there was the distant vibrating rumble and thud, one every fifteen seconds or so; the heart beating, powering the blood. The sound of life.

Third, there was the titanic dull roar that surrounded everything, the wind you would never feel; breath entering and leaving the cavernous lungs. It was the sound of health, if you felt you needed to hear it. And lastly, there was the repeated heavy *crump* that reverberated gently through everything; thirty pairs of giant clawed feet impacting the ground in a rhythm more akin to a centipede's than a giant iguana's.

'You okay?' Anna-Beth was staring at him.

'Yeah, not so bad,' said Max. 'Sorry I wasn't great company last night.'

'Or the night before... but I think I can find it in my heart to forgive you.' Anna-Beth sat up. 'I need to go. Got a brain pattern scan this morning and the Hammerclaws are out on earlies.'

Max sat up and drew her to him, kissing her and burying his face into her neck, breathing her in. 'It would be so much worse without you.'

'Are you going soft on me, Halloran?'

'Maybe.'

'Good.' Anna-Beth got out of bed, pulled her clothes on and gave him a peck on the cheek before going to the door. 'My place next time. Your pod smells too much of sweaty man.'

When the bells sounded a few minutes later, summoning them all from their pods, Max pulled on his sweats and walked out to the squad room, the gentler sounds of the *HoG* having reminded him that life went on. One look at his friends, silent and drawn when he strode in, reminded him that, for some of them, it didn't. Not straight away.

What struck Max most as he walked to the coffee machine to pour himself the obligatory half litre mug, was how sparsely populated the squad room was, how few of them remained fit to fly. Eight of them were dead, another four were hospitalised with broken bones, severe concussion or internal injuries from the sheer force of impact.

Everyone was sitting in their usual places, which only emphasised the great gaps that had been torn in the squad. Max sat between Redfearn and Kullani, who bumped their shoulders with his in a half-hearted version of their normal boisterous greeting.

'All right, Reds?'

'So-so,' said Redfearn.

'Risa?'

'The nightmare is running through my head on endless loop. There is so much more I should have done,' said Kullani.

'You can't afford to think like that,' said Gurney, who was seated opposite them, by Jes's empty place. 'Check the data. It's incredible so many of us survived.'

Max nodded. The room fell silent again. Max tried to catch the eyes of as many as he could, asking them with a raise of his eyebrows if they were all right. The response was patchy at best, though Stepanek at least seemed pumped for some reason. Eventually, all of them switched their attention to Valera, who was studying her p-palm. She was waiting for something, if her constant refreshing of the screen was anything to go by.

'Skipper?' asked Palant. 'What's happening?'

Valera looked up. 'Sorry, Pal, sorry, everyone, it's—'

The door to their rack squeaked open and in came Grim, pushing a trolley. Scents of hot food and fresh baked bread heralded its cargo and Max realised that he was hungry, so not absolutely everything had gone to shit.

Grim wheeled the trolley over to the drinks point, looking intensely uncomfortable under the gaze of every pilot but trying to smile. She shrugged.

'I thought... You know, you might not want to sit and eat and have everyone staring at you, so, you know...'

Valera took her hands.

'Grim, you are an absolute angel. Thank you.'

Grim relaxed and her smile broadened. 'Oh, great, well it was nothing, you know... Right, well I'll be going.'

'Like hell you will,' said Valera. 'Eat with us.'

Grim scrubbed her hands down her fatigues, blushing. 'No, it's not my place. This is a drake squad room.'

'Grim, you're practically family,' said Monteith. 'Sit down. Max'll make a space for you.'

‘Yeah, of course,’ said Max, springing up. ‘Sit down, let me get you something.’

Grim made a half move and then stopped. Valera caught her eye.

‘I’d have all of you up here if I could. Every medic, every flight crew… Picking us up yesterday when we got home, you have no idea how much it means. So do as you’re told and sit down and we’ll serve you for a change, all right?’

Kullani held out her hands and Grim shrugged and went over to a cheer from the squad.

‘Eggs is it, Grim?’

‘Yep. Scrambled. On toast and with a few beans. And a coffee if that’s okay?’

Max grinned. ‘Your wish is my command.’

He walked to the trolley, leading a surge of hungry pilots grabbing plates and descending on the food. Max delivered Grim’s breakfast and took his own over to sit by Monteith, who put an arm around his shoulders and pulled him in hard, almost dumping his food on the floor.

‘I love you too, Monts, even with your scratchy hair.’

‘Hey, you should have seen me when I had dreads.’ Monteith rapped a knuckle on his skull for good measure and headed off to the trolley.

‘All right, people,’ said Valera, sitting down and talking while she ate. ‘It’s oh-seven-fifteen now and we have our debrief at oh-eight-hundred in the flight deck briefing room. It’s going to be a hard day, let’s not pretend otherwise. But we’re Inferno-X. Yesterday was tough, but today we’re the flagship squadron and I need you all to act like it though you might not feel like it, okay?’

Valera looked around the squad and nodded at what she saw.

‘Good. So shower. Shave if you’re hairy, make sure you smell nice and put on clean fatigues if you’ve got any,’ she said, giving Max a stare and drawing a chuckle from the rest of them. ‘Get down to alpha deck and spend a moment with your drake before the debrief. It'll be a fact-finding exercise so keep your emotions out of it. If you can't, don't say anything at all.'

'Any news on our medical cases?' asked Redfearn.

'I was coming to that. One by one: Roberts has a broken collarbone, dislocated shoulder and some whacked out tendons and ligaments in his arm and across his shoulder and chest. He's out of it for six weeks. The Nuge has electrical burns to his face and neck, muscle tears in his biceps and quads from his crash landing and also sustained a concussion. But he's not as bad as we feared. Monteith saved his life: the Mafs circled back to make sure his drake was dead.'

Monteith inclined his head modestly. The squad applauded him and Max gave him a big kiss on the cheek.

'That is disgusting,' said Monteith. 'I won't be saving you if that's what I can look forward to.'

'That was for saving the Nuge. Just imagine how grateful I'd be if you saved me.' Max winked and pouted.

'Should that horror arise, I will don my armoured underpants immediately.'

'All right, you two, enough of the love,' said Valera. 'Kane is in a bad way but it's not life threatening. He has a severe concussion, whiplash injuries and a broken leg. We won't be seeing him for some time, I'm afraid. And finally, Colette... Well, she's pretty much one giant bruise. She's suffered some internals and had abdominal bleeding. She's stable but like all of them, some rehab time will be necessary before she's fit to fly. Go see them all regularly. Out of sight is not out of mind. Not in my squad.'

Valera blew out her cheeks. 'Lastly, I can confirm that all the bodies have been recovered along with our drakes, so we have our people back for remembrance. Nothing has fallen into enemy hands. The memorial will be in the reflection room at fourteen hundred tomorrow with cremations immediately afterwards.'

'Got a suggestion,' said Gurney.

'Fire away.'

'Since we're debriefing on the flight deck, how about doing a run?' He shrugged. 'I mean, we could all do with the cardio and a little energy burn and it'll send the right message. What do you think?'

'I think last one to their drake pen does the squad laundry for a week. Be back here at quarter-to for the starting gun,' said Valera.

For those few minutes they forgot everything but the race. Every dirty trick in the book was played. The pushing, jabbing and tripping were all way over the top, as if the attempt to exorcise yesterday demanded they risk further serious injury.

Going across the flesh bridge towards the inner scale, Max was just behind Calder at the head of the pack and that was only because she'd shouldered him into the wall just before the left turn on to the bridge. Valera had chosen a quiet route, conscious of appearing disrespectful to their dead, knowing there would be some who would misinterpret their high intensity determination for plain high spirits.

But there were always some people about and when Calder was slowed by a group of flight crew heading towards their mess hall, Max took his chance. He got right in her boot prints, stooped and tapped her ankle with an outstretched hand. She careered to the right, colliding with a railing. Max left her to dust herself down and continued the chase.

He was in the clear and heading for the stairs. The next moment, he felt a blow to the back of his leg and he was tumbling into the dust, dirt and marbles of desiccated behemoth flesh.

'Fuck it,' he growled, hearing a triumphant shout as Gurney vaulted his prone body and hared off.

The bastard was fast, Max would give him that. Max drove to his feet and accelerated along the bridge. Redfearn, Nevant, Xavier and Valera were all past him by now. He hit the stairs, used the rails for balance and vaulted down flight by flight, as they wound down towards the flight decks.

He burst into the echoing space, feeling the exhilaration of the run, pissed that he wasn't first but buzzed he wasn't last either. Valera was at the door, counting them all in, logging who was last. Max's money was on Salewski. She was a great flyer but a total slug on the sprint.

But the moment his feet rang on the bone deck, he slowed and stopped. The deck was clear but the place stank of blood, ERC shit and cleansing agents. Everything came flooding back and the muscles in his arms began to ache at the memory of Roberts's drake crashing into his on landing, and the mess he'd been inside his pouch.

Max sucked his lip, put it behind him, and jogged towards Martha's pen, already feeling the warmth of her in his mind. Grim was at the door to the pen, her fresh overalls already sporting smears of dirt and drake oil.

'She okay?' asked Max.

'Subdued,' said Grim and she shuddered. 'Can't you feel it? Not just her but every drake, every ERC for that matter, whether ground or air lizard. They know. I think they grieve.'

Max saw the conviction in her face. He paused to take in the atmosphere and the noise and had to agree. There was a dampening of energy in here, a pall of shock – or that's how it felt. And it didn't just come from the crew.

'Weird.'

'Not really,' said Grim. 'You think about them like I do.'

'You've got me there.' Max unlatched the pen and walked in, blowing out his cheeks at the wash of heat. Martha was lying down, her tail along the length of her body and her neck curled back along her spine. She was plugged into the central ERC system that fed her the exact quantity of nutrient she needed and constantly monitored her condition. She raised her head in greeting and brought it towards him. 'You look tired, princess.'

Martha stared at him and opened her jaws wide as if yawning to confirm his words. It was hard to define the feelings he got from her. There was warmth, but there was something else too and perhaps it *was* loss.

'Reckon we might not be flying for a while. Not until we can make ourselves whole again, you know? Become the Inferno-X we should be. Hard to do with only half your people. I can't stay but I'll be back soon. Rest up, okay?'

He turned to go only to find her head coming to rest on his shoulder, weighing him down. It was a brief moment and he turned his head just in time to catch her eye and see the depths of her emotions before she pulled back.

'Did you see that?' he asked. Grim nodded. 'Bloody hell.'

'Sometimes I envy you,' she said. 'You can feel her and I can only look.'

'Aye but one day, I'll fall into those feelings and never come back. You can look forever.'

Valera walked by, leading the squad. 'Come on, Max. We're all going in together.'

'See you later,' he said.

'Good luck,' said Grim.

The flight deck briefing room was large enough to accommodate all six drake squadrons but today only a handful of chairs and tables were set out facing the wall screen. There was water and biscuits on every table and Max dumped himself down between Valera and Nevant, who had the tidiest beard on the *HoG*, at the front. He poured them all water and helped himself to a biscuit. It was a little stale.

'I wonder who's coming to tell us everything's all right,' said Nevant and, not for the first time, Max wished he had a French accent too.

'The ExO is my guess,' said Max and he was proved right moments later when Kirby walked in, flanked by two of his senior staff; Moeller entered alone, looking like he'd been handed his cards; and lastly came Doctor Eleanor Rosenbach, a very senior

Tweaker for a mission debrief, even one as difficult as this. Max felt a sweep of unease.

The atmosphere in the room switched from apprehension to tension in a blink. Everyone straightened in their chairs to watch the execs as they gathered under the screen. One of Kirby's people, a thin-faced ping-pusher called Hewitt who seemed glued to his ExO's side most of the time, tapped up a few inset screens of data and video using his p-palm. Up popped a stream of stuff Max couldn't care less about, some transcripts of com chatter and an HD vid of Inferno-X's final approach.

Kirby faced them and waved a hand at the screen. He was a tall man with a powerful frame and had served in the army on combat duty before moving to his executive position. The endless hard decisions his job demanded were reflected in the lines on his face and in the grey marking his neat beard and moustache.

'Don't worry about all that, it's just background to the real issues in play here,' he said. 'The first of which is: how are you feeling? How's your morale? Where are your heads right now and how are your bodies faring? Squadron Leader Orin, I'm sure you speak for the squad.'

'Thank you, sir, and on behalf of the squad, thank you for your concern. I won't gloss over this: while those of us here are fine physically, we're in an average state at best. We aren't used to losing our people, let alone eight in the same mission. So we've had a sleepless night, a whole lot of guilt-ridden nightmares, and now we're about to relive the whole thing. Not a whole lot of positives to be had, sir.'

'Understood, Valcra. Thank you for your honesty. I can ease your minds on one score: we're not going to hold a blow-by-blow analysis of the mission. We have drake cam footage, voice records and all your flight data. All we're lacking is your take on the enemy drakes. We saw almost nothing of them on the mission downloads. I'll open the floor for this one… Yes, Gurney.'

'It's easy to sum up: they were bigger, stronger and faster than us. Their weapons suite was more powerful – flame hotter and ECMs that could discharge massive amounts of electricity. They could also fire their ECMs like seeker missiles. The fact we're better pilots means we got home at all but even so, ten of them took out eight of us and whacked four others into hospital, sir.'

'Great start, thank you. So was this upgraded fleshware, or are we facing a sentience unlock?'

'I'd say there's been a sentience tweak,' said Salewski. 'Some of their turns defy belief unless the drakes have more autonomy.'

'I disagree,' said Xavier. 'If a fleshware upgrade sped up transmission of human impulse to drake, I think you can explain their reaction speeds.'

'But we can only think so fast,' replied Salewski. 'If you factor in their raw speed, which diminishes reaction time still further, I can't see any other way to do it. They must have allowed the drake some freedom in evasion moves at the very least.'

'There must have been musculature enhancements, though,' said Gurney. 'How else do you explain some of their wing positioning and switching moves?'

'Does it really matter?' asked Max, bitterness surfacing momentarily. 'They were better than us, end of story.'

'Yes, it does matter,' said Rosenbach. She had an earnest expression on her soft round face, endless eyes and delicate long fingers that danced over her p-palm. 'If we're to match them quickly, we need to know if we're looking at physical systems, impulse transmission, drake thought processes or human improvement. Otherwise, how do we direct our work?'

'Then I'll throw this in,' said Valera. 'Their co-ordination impressed me. At times, it was as if they were responding to a single set of commands rather than individual impulse and physical movement instructions. Do they also have a more advanced com, something that can disperse umbrella commands to a whole squad of drakes?'

Rosenbach stared at her for a moment before nodding and making more notes. 'Very interesting, thank you.'

Kirby held up his hands. 'This is an excellent start but you can already see we're not going to find all the answers from this one encounter. We need more data, and we must press on with our pursuit of the *Maputo* now you've confirmed she's struggling. I feel sure the launch of the new drakes and her current situation are not coincidental.'

Every pilot in the room wanted to ask the same question but none of them wanted to hear the answer. Kirby gave it to them anyway. Just before he opened his mouth, Max saw Moeller take half a pace away. And with every word towards his inevitable senseless conclusion, Max's gorge rose a little further.

'We have to test them. Explore and expose their weaknesses. We can't implement upgrades to fleshware at the drop of a hat. We have to combat them with what we have. It doesn't matter if they're more advanced, there are still humans in control, and humans make mistakes – which we can observe and use against them. So you want revenge for the bloody nose they gave you? You can have it. Get out there with Lavaflow-A and show them what Inferno-X can do. You fly tomorrow at eleven hundred hours. Any questions?'

The silence was ephemeral.

'*Bloody nose*?' shouted Stepanek. 'Perhaps you weren't watching when the Mafs handed us our fried balls on a bed of toasted scales?'

'We're still mopping the blood from the flight deck and you want us to go out again?' said Xavier.

'Did you visit medical?' asked Salewski. 'Perhaps you can teach Roberts to fly with one fucking arm.'

'Why?' demanded Max. 'Didn't enough of us die yesterday to satisfy Solomon?'

'Silence!' roared Kirby, all softness gone and replaced by

something altogether more familiar. 'Squadron Leader Orin, you will control your squad.'

Valera stood up and held her hands up for quiet. 'Make your points without shouting, eh?'

She was turned far enough from Kirby that he couldn't see her wink and when she turned back to face him, she held his gaze for longer than she should before sitting down. Max glanced at Moeller, who was impassive.

'Such outbursts will not be tolerated,' said Kirby as Max raised his hand. 'Go ahead, Halloran. Carefully.'

'I apologise for raising my voice, sir,' said Max. Kirby inclined his head. 'With the greatest respect, sir: why? Didn't enough of us die yesterday to satisfy you and the marshal general?'

Next to him, Valera's breath hissed through her teeth. Any remaining colour drained from Kirby's face. He walked forwards to stand right in front of Max, glaring down at him.

'You will do as you are ordered and you will not question my integrity or that of the marshal general. Am I clear?'

'I was just—'

'Am I clear, Halloran?'

Max gritted his teeth and forced himself to stay in his seat.

'Absolutely, sir. I meant no offence. But we lost eight, we've got four in medical and we barely laid a claw on them. Even though we outnumbered them more than two to one—'

'Halloran...' warned Kirby.

'—so what is the point of going out there and having it done to us again?'

'Are you questioning my orders, boy?'

Max bit back on his first thought. 'Yes, sir, and I am looking for clarification as to how this decision was reached.'

The ExO leaned in and laid a finger on Max's chest. 'You are treading a very fine line, Halloran. Be careful you don't slip off.'

'It'd be a problem though, wouldn't it, sir?' said Stepanek. 'If we lose one more pilot we will be below the minimum required to form a combat squadron.'

Kirby straightened to direct his ire at Stepanek, while behind him, Hewitt took a pace forward, his presence drawing the eye.

Hewitt paused a moment before speaking. 'Calculated insubordination because you're too cowardly to face the enemy, is that it?'

'Fuck did you just say?' Max pushed away from the table and stood, his self-control fracturing. 'Perhaps I didn't hear you right.'

Hewitt shrugged. 'You don't have the courage to face them again? I get it. But don't hide behind regulations.'

The whole squad was on its feet now and Max led the shouts.

'Calm down!' ordered Valera, but her tone held no conviction. She wanted this confrontation as much as they did and she wasn't sitting down either. No one was.

'You'd better listen,' said Kirby. 'Final warning.'

'Hewitt has called our courage into question. He has disrespected our dead. He apologises now.'

'Sit. Down.' Kirby's voice was stone and the pace he took towards Max carried undisguised threat.

Buoyed by the support of his commanding officer, Hewitt oozed a smile.

'Halloran isn't terribly good with orders, sir.'

Max shot him a glance. 'No, dickhead, what I'm not good at is offering my squad up for slaughter. The odds were against us yesterday. Today they're impossible.'

Hewitt shrugged. 'Typical. You're happy to enjoy the fame, unhappy to face the enemy. It's pure cowardice.'

The final piece of Max's self-control broke. He pushed past Kirby, all but picked Hewitt off his feet and slammed him against the big screen.

'Halloran!' shouted Kirby.

'I am this close,' hissed Max, hearing the rising volume behind him, the shrieking of chairs and the pushing away of tables. He pinched the thumb and forefinger of his right hand together. 'No one, certainly not a whining office fuck like you, calls Inferno-X cowards.'

'Let him go, right now,' said Kirby, laying a heavy hand on Max's shoulder.

'I don't have to call you a coward,' sneered Hewitt. 'You do it to yourself.'

Max punched him in the mouth. His fist split Hewitt's lips and he felt teeth give under the force of the blow. Hewitt's head whacked against the screen and his hands flew up as the blood started to flow.

It was pandemonium. Kirby heaved Max aside violently enough that he almost collided with Moeller and Rosenbach, who had been backing towards the door as soon as it looked like trouble. Moeller, a veteran of briefing room slanging matches, had a defensive arm across the Tweaker, who was gazing at the unfolding chaos in disbelief.

Hewitt was staring at the blood and teeth in his hands; Moeller was roaring at Valera to get control. Max had lost his footing and as he scrambled to his feet, Andersen, Hewitt's aide, rushed him, his fists bunched. Max was in no stance to defend himself and raised his arms to try and deflect the coming blows as Stepanek stepped in front of him and decked Andersen with a straight punch to the chin that knocked him square on his arse.

'Enough!' roared Valera, just too late to stop Stepanek's glorious punch. 'Inferno-X, stand down!'

Max stood and straightened his fatigues. He looked at his fist, happy with the red marks on his knuckles, then at Hewitt, whose face was white and whose uniform was streaked with blood from his mouth. Max was breathing hard, but his anger had barely diminished and when he faced Kirby he was ready for more. Standing behind the ExO, Valera saw Max's expression and gave him a palms-down gesture.

'Halloran, Stepanek, you will place yourselves in my custody immediately. Orin, get your squadron out of my sight. Your orders stand. Consider yourself reprimanded ahead of a formal hearing.'

Max sighed. 'This sucks. I acted without orders, sir.'

Kirby jabbed a finger at him. 'I advise you to say nothing unless you are addressed directly.'

'Enough, Max,' said Valera. Then she mouthed, 'Thank you.'

Max winked and turned his mouth up in a smile. Inferno-X began to file out and every one of them clapped either him or Stepanek on the shoulder or patted him on the head. Max saluted Kirby, as did Stepanek.

'Executive Officer Kirby, Stepanek and Halloran placing ourselves in your custody.'

'You are both charged with causing an affray and with the assault of a crew member. You will remain here until representatives of the military police arrive to accompany you to the brig. You will not speak to anyone nor seek to make contact with anyone. Your charges will be heard at a time of my choosing of which you will be advised in due course.'

Kirby shook his head. 'I cannot express how disappointed I am in your actions, pointless and damaging as they are.'

Both Hewitt and Andersen were on their feet and Kirby waved them out and followed them, pausing to hiss something at Moeller, whose reply was pitched just loud enough.

'You made it perfectly clear I was attending as an observer. So I have . . . observed.'

Kirby cleared his throat and stalked out. Moeller stared at Max and Stepanek and there was a glint in his eye though he was trying to be disapproving.

'That Hewitt is an utter prick, isn't he?' he said.

CHAPTER 14

> The Tweakers, I mean the lovely scientists in the ERC programme, reckon drakes have no emotional responses on any measurable scale. They couldn't be more wrong but they won't listen to us. Scientists... if you can't put a number on it, it doesn't exist. Twats.
>
> MAXIMUS HALLORAN

The *HoG*'s brig was a sterile affair of fifty bone-architectured cells, each one sporting a metal bed, basin and toilet. It was located at the base of deck two, where the lack of any air-circulation and artery-rich area made the cell block chilly and stuffy at the same time. Doherty, the single guard on duty beyond their locked metal-mesh doors, had a fan on her desk to blow the stale air around.

Still, it wasn't all bad. The block was very sparsely populated and she'd put him and Stepanek in cells opposite each other so they could at least sit on the end of their beds and talk across the couple of metres of brightly lit grey corridor. Well, they could if Stepanek ever sat up.

Max was silent for a while and fixed his eyes on Stepanek's shoes, hoping to make them smoulder and burst into flame by the power of his mind alone. They remained stubbornly undamaged.

'Pretty good straight right, by the way.'

Stepanek sat bolt upright and Max smiled. '*Pretty good*? That punch was world class and don't you fucking forget it. Pretty good, my holy arse...'

'All right, all right, it was a beauty, no argument there. But why did you of all people wade in for me?'

Stepanek chuckled and massaged his right fist. 'I've been lying here, rather than in my altogether more comfortable pod, wondering the same thing.'

'So: why?'

'You're Inferno-X. What else could I do? If you stand up against fuckheads like Kirby and Hewitt, I'm going to be at your shoulder no matter how much of a dick you are.'

'You're not going to start giving me all that team shit like Valera, are you?'

'No,' said Stepanek. 'And you know why? Because it's stronger than that. You're family. Maybe the moron bastard son of my psychotic fifth cousin, but family just the same.'

Max laughed, the sound echoing against the bone and metal. 'That's supposed to make me feel loved, is it? Sound of that family, I could easily be your son or your uncle. Or both.'

'Fuck me, if I was your father I'd have the snip to kill the threat of any more.'

'And if I was your son, I'd chop mine off to end the line of bloody Stepaneks.'

They sat in companionable silence for a while.

'Fact is you did okay, Max. I was almost proud of you.'

'And I've still got my awesome looks because of you, so thanks.'

'You owe me for the rest of your short, shallow life, you bastard.'

'Well, at least you don't hate me any more.'

'I've never hated you, you idiot. You were an utter dick for three months after you joined, mind you, and I might have said some things I shouldn't. But back there you said what we were all thinking and you had a big enough pair to take the rap for the squad. And while you still own the definition of "selfish twat" there seems to be a little more to you than I thought.'

'I'll take that as a compliment.'

'Yeah, well, don't get all wet-knickered about it, you've got a long way to go yet.'

'Right. Best not to extend too much hope,' said Max. Stepanek grinned. 'What's going to happen to us?'

'What should happen is, we get hauled in front of the commander, she gives us a verbal kicking and confines us to the squad dorm between missions for as long as she sees fit. But who knows? Kirby and Moeller seem to have fallen out.'

'Think we'll get away with it?'

'I'll be surprised if we get much worse than a booze ban.'

The door to the block squeaked open. Max pressed his left cheek to the mesh so he could see who had come in.

'It's Kirby,' he said, feeling a brief rush of anxiety. 'Think he's come to apologise?'

There was a short buzz and the two cell doors swung open. Kirby marched along the corridor. Both pilots stood to attention.

'Stepanek, get out of here. You'll find your charge notes in your p-palm and nailed to the door of your pod. Halloran, you and I will talk.' Kirby's expression was bleak.

'Will you make Hewitt apologise for accusing us of cowardice?'

'That will never happen.'

'Agree with him, do you?' Max sat on the end of his bed.

'You refused to go into action,' said Kirby. He remained standing.

'Then you go right ahead and have your chat and I'll exercise my right to say absolutely dick all, sir.'

The ExO blew out his cheeks. 'You really will have to learn to curb that tongue of yours.'

'And disappoint a behemoth full of women?'

'Fucking hell,' said Kirby through a sigh. 'You have to respect the chain of command. There is no other way.'

'Poor old ExO, eh?' said Max. 'Avery or Solomon twisted your arm into sending us to our deaths? So what? A shit order is a shit order.'

'I understand your anger. But we have to get more data about those drakes.'

'Then send a cloud of spyflys.'

'We need tactical information not still photography.'

'You aren't going to get that by sending us out to get our arses fried again, are you? Why don't you get that?' Max threw up his hands. 'Why are you talking to me anyway? Just punish me, sir.'

'Don't play the martyr, Halloran. I'm talking to you because I have a solution, but I need your help to see it through.'

'Why would I do the first thing to help you?'

'Because it'll give you the upgrade you need to go out and rip those Maf drakes' heads off their scrawny necks.'

Max frowned. 'Are you talking about a sentience upgrade? Skipper'll fight that all the way.'

'And so here I am talking to you. You can persuade her.'

Max felt himself flush. 'I'm insulted you think I'm so easily bought, sir.'

'I don't think that. Bloody hell, Halloran, you're a top pilot and no one wants to see you grounded. Help me out and I can reduce your and Stepanek's charges to minor misdemeanours. Everyone benefits, not least Inferno-X.'

'Is that what I'm looking at? Time out of the pouch?'

'Why so surprised?' asked Kirby. 'Both of my aides are in medical, both keen to see you hung out to dry.'

'All right.' Max held up his hands. 'What do you want me to do?'

'We've just got a new sentience upgrade on the slate. It's good and it's been dry tested. It's safe. Valera will object, because she always does – and more Inferno-X will die without it.'

'Why?'

'Because I can't change the order.' Kirby cleared his throat. 'And because you were right, it is a shit order, so you need something to help you fight. I'm offering it to you.'

Max needed a moment. It was a stitch-up but it made perfect sense.

'The skipper will hate my guts for it.'

'Only until she sees what we're offering you. I'm not asking you to sell it, just persuade her to listen rather than quote the testing standards at me.'

'Oh, right. No field testing's been done, has it?' said Max.

Kirby shook his head. 'That would be part of Inferno's brief.'

'Wow. So why didn't you mention this at the debrief? Could have saved a lot of trouble, sir.'

'I had no knowledge of the research until two hours ago. It was completed at a level above my security grade.'

'Bloody hell.'

'Quite.'

'And say I try to convince Valera, Steps and I walk free?'

'As I said, a reduction to a minor misdemeanour only. No stain on your record. After all, Hewitt does have a big mouth.'

'Even bigger after my fist got stuck in it.'

'Enough, Halloran.'

'And he'll apologise to the squad. We aren't cowards.'

'Don't push your luck. Will you do it?'

'Sure. Didn't like the décor in here anyway,' said Max. 'So, what does this upgrade do, then?'

'Max!' He turned from his pod door to see Valera tucked away in her favourite corner of an otherwise empty squad room. 'I heard you were out.'

'Bad news travels fast, huh? No interviews, not until I see my lawyer.'

'Very funny. Get your arse over here.'

'Where's the squad?'

'Anywhere but here,' said Valera. 'I wanted to speak to you alone and my pod's a mess.'

Max walked over, trying to assess Valera's mood as she poured coffee into two mugs and shoved one across the table at him, indicating where he should sit.

'This is a bit formal, isn't it?'

'What did Kirby have to say?'

'It was a bit weird, really,' said Max, sitting opposite her. 'He was trying to bribe me... But he did have a few interesting things to say.'

Valera scowled. 'Anything he said was at best a half-truth. Spill it.'

'He said there's a sentience upgrade available, something to help against the new Maf drakes because we still have to go out. He wanted me to help convince you to accept it. Something like that anyway.'

'And I suppose he told you it was all tested and a hundred per cent safe, right?' said Valera, her scowl deepening.

'I— Yes, how did you know?' said Max, starting to feel like he was passing on second-hand news.

'Lucky guess. So what does it give us, this uniquely safe upgrade?'

Max smiled apologetically. 'It speeds up drake reaction to stimulus and would give us back our competitive edge. It sounds like what we need to kick those bastards in the teeth. But I know how you feel about these upgrades so I'm not going to do the hard sell he wanted me to. I answer to you, not him.'

Valera smiled. 'Kirby always sounds convincing but he's a sly bastard. He wouldn't be pushing this unless it helped him. Yes, we need to get an edge over the Mafs but not at any cost. Sentience upgrades might be very effective but they push us into the Fall quicker. Fleshware is almost as good but far more expensive. Don't be naïve about this. Our well-being will be bottom of the list.'

'I get it, but—'

'But nothing, Max. There are plenty of ongoing projects that promise genuine results, but none have even reached field testing. Whatever this is, I guarantee it's poorly tested and unsafe.'

'Are you sure? Kirby said it was completed above his security level. It'll be shielded, right?'

Valera sighed. 'If that's true then it's definitely dangerous. Kirby's on the upgrade oversight committee and if he really hasn't seen data, it means it's being pushed from way, way up high. That cannot be good for us. Moeller warned me something was coming. Now I get why he looked so unhappy.

'This is like a magic trick, Max... Hey, you got beaten up in the sky yesterday and so... ta dah! Here's an upgrade to help you kick their arses.'

Max took a moment to let it all sink in. He couldn't escape the disappointment.

'So Moeller spoke to you. About this?'

'Yeah, he said an upgrade approval meeting was coming and to ensure we were all fit.'

'Why?' asked Max.

'Because, contractually, we have to be retested before a sentience upgrade is initiated and it's a lot more than a brain pattern scan. He knows I'll invoke that clause to force a delay and he said he'd sign any of us off sick I wanted.'

'Bloody hell.' Max's mind was whirling. Valera was almost certainly right but he couldn't see what it really changed. 'What can we do? We have to fly and without help, we'll get slaughtered.'

'Quite.'

'So you're going to the meeting?'

'You bet your arse, I am. But I'm supposed to go with your ringing endorsement, aren't I?'

'Do you think he'll notice I didn't give it?'

'I think I'll tell him we had a frank discussion about it.'

'Can you refuse the upgrade?' asked Max. 'Can you afford to?'

Valera sighed. 'I don't know… on both counts. Shit but Kirby's done a job, hasn't he? Pretty obvious what he'll throw at me if I object and a fleshware alternative seems unlikely, and probably couldn't be designed and installed in any sensible timeframe anyway? The more I think about it, the more we're screwed whichever way we jump.'

'But…' Max grasped for a way to say what he really wanted. 'Surely it's better to, y'know, live to fight another day.'

Valera smiled but it was forced. 'I can't argue with that logic but without any field testing – and I've seen no data on it *at all* – it could even be riskier than fighting the new Mafs just as we are. Just because it's possible doesn't mean it works.'

'I'm not with you… I mean, if we go out as we are, we'll just get burned again.'

'But with an untested sentience upgrade, we really could all Fall first time out and remember, once it's done, the upgrade can't be undone and if it *is* unsafe… Well, you work it out.'

'Sorry, Skipper.'

'For what?'

'Well, y'know, if I hadn't lost my rag.'

'Don't beat yourself up, Max. You twatting that prick was the best thing I've seen in ages.' Valera drained her coffee. 'Someone knew about the upgrade before the briefing, they must have. Why didn't they make it known as an option sooner? The fact they were prepared to order us out with nothing else is what really pisses me off.'

'So what're you going to do?'

Valera shrugged. 'I have no idea.'

Alexandra Solomon loved seeing people's faces when she unexpectedly attended their meetings. And this time she had two to enjoy. Moeller came in first and his face fell heavily, even as he greeted her with priceless forced warmth.

Valera Orin, she of the iron mind and unnatural longevity for a pilot, walked in next, saw her and almost tripped. She regained a measure of composure and mumbled a greeting but her body language telegraphed her anxiety with every movement. Perfect, and the best bit was still to come: as soon as Kirby, Avery, Moeller and Orin were seated around the small circular table, she played her joker.

'Literally,' she muttered, then louder. 'Thank you all for coming. Since this is such a key matter, I would like to welcome our sixth attendee.'

Solomon tapped her p-palm and the screens at either end of the meeting room displayed President Corsini's beaming countenance. Orin's face went sheet-white. Moeller's gaze went blank.

'Good afternoon, *Heart of Granite*,' said Corsini. 'Sorry I couldn't be with you in person. I trust you can all hear me.'

'Loud and clear, Mister President,' said Solomon. 'I think you're familiar with everyone here but Squadron Leader Valera Orin, one of our finest pilots.'

'One of?' said Corsini. 'Surely the famed leader of Inferno-X is our very best pilot!' Orin blushed and shifted in her seat.

'Before we start, Valera,' continued Corsini. 'May I say how personally sorry I was to hear of your losses in the service of United Europa. Irreplaceable people but I know you'll rise above it and strike back as you always have done.'

'Thank you, sir,' said Valera, her voice a little dry.

Solomon reminded herself to congratulate Corsini on delivering his lines with such aplomb... so far. There was still plenty of time for the idiot to screw up.

'Mister Kirby, the meeting is yours,' she said.

'Actually, if I may?' asked Orin. Kirby, halfway out of his chair, sat down with a heavy sigh and waved impatiently for her to go ahead. 'This is a meeting to discuss an internal matter concerning the welfare of Inferno-X drakes and pilots, and a potential sentience upgrade implementation process. With respect, might I know your interest, Mister President, and yours, Marshal General Solomon?'

Solomon ticked her head and forced a smile on to her face. Disappointing that Orin had been off-balance for so brief a time.

'A sound question. Good to know our staff are fully versed in the minutiae of regulations. As a senior ranking officer I may attend any meeting as part of my over-watch duties. Mister President?'

'My concern is to understand the problems facing my forces on the front line so I can better direct our scarce funds to the correct cost centres,' said Corsini. 'Do you wish me to withdraw, Squadron Leader Orin?'

'Of course not, sir. Forgive me.'

'Not at all,' said Corsini, oozing good grace. 'If we are not all properly informed, how can we make properly informed decisions?'

Solomon let the silence settle before nodding for Kirby to continue.

'We've had very exciting news,' he said. 'A genuine game-changing breakthrough. Just a few hours ago I was handed the results of some understandably confidential research conducted by Professor Helena Markov. The Extra Reptilian Construct design and research team have isolated the key synapse trails and a single DNA strand shared by human and firedrake. Together they allow significantly quicker drake reaction times to both neural and physical stimuli.'

Solomon glanced around the room. Corsini was reacting as if he'd heard the word of God; Orin looked as if someone had puked in her dinner; while Avery was failing to contain her excitement and Moeller was failing to appear neutral.

Kirby tapped his p-palm and the research data popped up on everyone's screens.

'Let me take you through the detail on this fully dry-tested and safety-one rated sentience upgrade.'

Kirby was a pro, Solomon would give him that; an excellent ally despite his own ambition. They all knew Orin would be reluctant so he was focusing on Avery and Moeller. With them onside, this was a done deal. They all listened intently, Orin studying the data on her p-palm while Kirby ran through the brief and drew his conclusions.

'The key advance is the neural adjustment. Slight but powerful, it offers exceptional pilot security and longevity as well as value for money. The dry testing showed no adverse results for human or drake and gave pilots in combat situations faster reaction times, faster targeting and quicker, keener delivery of flame, melee and ECM weaponry.

'It is the ultimate zero-risk upgrade and I recommend it for live combat field testing without reservation. Are there any questions?'

'How can you call it risk-free?' asked Orin, and Solomon saw Kirby tense. 'There has been no field testing, hence no data for potential feedback or bleed-through analysis. Every other DNA-synapse linkage has been proven to be a two-way system, yet there is no recommendation for mind-shielding. This upgrade is not ready.'

'You're questioning Professor Markov's conclusions?' asked Kirby, a frown on his face.

'I can't even find her conclusions, just the results of early-stage dry testing. Hard to believe her name is there on the sign-off.'

'Yet it is there,' said Corsini.

'We have a situation here,' said Solomon, already bored by Orin's line. 'We must attack the *Maputo* but these new Maf drakes are a problem. This upgrade will help you remove that problem. You need to accept it.'

'So you admit it's being rushed through?'

'It's being prioritised,' said Kirby. 'And it's your weapon to strike back.'

'Only if it works under combat conditions,' said Valera. 'The field-testing records are littered with the problems associated with heightened drake brain activity under stress. You're risking pushing us all into the Fall in one hit. How can that be worth it?'

'Is it worth the risk flying without the upgrade? Because fly you must. What if there are more than ten enhanced Maf drakes?'

'This attack will go ahead,' said Corsini. 'The joint chiefs are in agreement. Take the upgrade. Fight the enemy.'

'I urge you to reconsider,' said Valera. 'I cannot approve this upgrade and I can't understand why Markov has – she's never signed off anything this incomplete before. It concerns me that the two things not currently on the table, fleshware and mind-shielding, are coincidentally the most expensive to implement yet would both better protect your most prized assets from the Fall.'

'Our window for the attack is too brief to allow a fleshware upgrade.' Solomon spoke firmly. 'Mind-shielding will be considered following the attack on the *Maputo*, you have my word on that. Meanwhile, without trusting this upgrade, and Professor Markov, further Inferno-X losses are guaranteed. But thank you for your input, Orin, we all understand and respect your position.'

'I hope so, ma'am,' said Orin. 'I'd hate to think what would happen if pilots got to thinking that drakes were a more valuable commodity than their pilots.'

'I can assure you that will never happen,' said Solomon, her smile forced.

'Do you have any further comments before you go?' asked Kirby pleasantly.

'Go?'

'Of course. We needed to hear your concerns first-hand. Unless you have more to say, now we need to discuss financial implications.'

Orin shrugged and pushed back her chair. She looked squarely at Moeller.

'Our contracts and your responsibilities are quite clear. I don't understand why this upgrade has been brought forward and the fleshware tweaking we had begun to discuss with Rosenbach has been abandoned. It smacks of expediency and we've seen throughout this war that expediency trumping sense costs pilots' lives. There *is* time to implement minor fleshware improvements but it requires you to approve the spend.'

Orin turned and strode from the room, the door closing softly on its hydraulic hinge.

Solomon stared after her for a moment. 'She was supposed to come here with an open mind, Robert. What the fuck just happened?'

'She is a woman of singular determination,' said Kirby.

'She's loyal to her squad, that's what she is,' said Moeller.

'This upgrade is going ahead, I presume?' interrupted Corsini, irritation plain in his tone. 'We've heard her bleating and now we need to push ahead.'

'Unfortunately, given Orin's objections, the current contractual structure makes swift implementation difficult,' said Kirby.

Corsini nodded but Solomon could see he was about to explode.

'So which fucking moron drew up a contract giving power to the bloody *pilots*? This is a fucking war! Who gives a shit about the rules when *you* need to win a war and *I* need to win an election to keep you bastards in your jobs. She was supposed to roll over. What a fucking backfire. Who wants to go first?'

Solomon raised an eyebrow at the trio of senior military executives squirming under the president's cold anger.

'It's very simple,' she said. 'We have an enemy behemoth to attack, we know it is weak and we are closing on it. This upgrade must and will go ahead. I simply do not understand why she would refuse something that will save the lives of her and her squad.'

'She's looking beyond the current fight,' said Moeller.

'Without the upgrade there won't *be* any "beyond",' snapped Solomon. 'Find out what she's angling for and give it to her.'

'Within budget,' added Corsini.

Solomon's smile was thin to vanishing point. 'Mister President,

I'll report back to you with a solution and timescale later this afternoon. I'm sure you have better things to do.'

Solomon stared at him until he nodded fractionally and cut his connection. She rounded on the three of them.

'You're all a fucking embarrassment. I will not play upgrade poker with an upstart drake pilot. I want her minimum requirements delivered to me in two hours from now and if I don't like what I read, I'll send her and her squad out to die and upgrade the Hammerclaws. Am I clear?'

She stood and strode from the meeting room.

CHAPTER 15

When the risks to drake pilots became clear, there was a hurricane of controversy. While young men and women lined up to join the programme, lawyers were tying the military in knots and the final contracts placed real influence in the hands of ranking military personnel. For the military, it enabled their most powerful weapon. For me, it approved some incredible new research.

PROFESSOR HELENA MARKOV, MANAGING DIRECTOR,
EXTRA REPTILIAN CONSTRUCT ORGANISATION

Avery leaned back in her chair. 'You know, I think that went rather well.'

'Were you in a different meeting?' asked Kirby. 'And you didn't say a word.'

'Speaking out didn't play well, did it?' Avery replied. 'Think it through. We tried a quick argument, it hasn't worked and now we have to go a little more carefully.'

'She won't go for the upgrade,' said Moeller. 'Our own contracts have tied us up in knots. Who did write them, anyway?'

'Solomon did, of course, and Corsini signed them off back when the risks seemed so extreme that getting anyone to sign up without a lawyer next to them was like pushing behemoth shit uphill with a hay fork. Offering them a veto on upgrades seemed a smart move. Doesn't seem so smart, now, eh?'

Avery felt warm inside. 'Best bit is that Solomon knows the moment that screen went blank, Corsini ordered some minion to find out who drew up the contracts. Wish I could overhear their next conversation.'

Kirby huffed. 'Oh good. Solomon's in the shit with the rest of us. What exactly are we going to do? Moeller?'

'Approve the mind-shielding add-on,' said Moeller, shrugging. 'It's the only way.'

Kirby shrugged. 'We can't fund it, or afford the inevitable integration delay.'

'Surely the cost is justified? We can't bring down the *Maputo* without Inferno-X. We need them at the top of their game – *with* this upgrade. And the shielding secures our best pilots in our best drakes. Plus we have to offer Valera something. She won't change her mind on a whim and she knows we're aware sending them out without an edge in combat is suicidal.'

'So tell her there will be mind-shielding,' said Kirby.

'You're backing my recommendation?' asked Moeller.

'I want her to approve the upgrade. I think we have to tell her what she wants to hear.'

'You want me to lie to her?'

'I know we don't always get on but I do have the best interests of all personnel on this ship at heart... I'm the ExO, for God's sake, it's my duty. I genuinely believe we have no choice but to implement the upgrade. So how about this for a compromise? You persuade Valera to take the upgrade out on combat test and I'll persuade Solomon to approve the shielding afterwards.'

'Fine. But what if she doesn't approve it and I've already pushed the upgrade through?'

'If this upgrade *does* mean pilots Fall faster, then the cost of training new pilots to I-X standard will be higher than adding the mind-shielding because we'll need more bodies. I can work up the figures to prove it.'

Moeller shrugged. 'Show me the figures and I'll talk to Valera.'

'Good,' said Avery. 'One last thing: you both know the *HoG* is running on empty. We have seventy-eight serious systems issues, she stinks and Seepage is beyond filthy. We should be heading for our regeneration cycle already and we'll be seriously vulnerable if we don't go in the next five days. We can and we must take the *Maputo* down in that timescale or we'll be easy pickings on the way to the Vermelho Sea. I will not have that as my epitaph.'

Moeller knew Valera would have been waiting for a summons from him or Kirby so he decided to drop into the Inferno-X squad rooms instead. It seemed to do the trick. Her smile was warm once the surprise had faded. Valera poured them both coffees before showing him into her pod, which had a couple of armchairs and a small table in the extra space afforded her as squadron leader.

'What's the verdict, sir?' asked Valera, frostiness replacing the warmth now the door was shut on the concerted gaze of the squad.

'I think we can drop the formality. There's been no "verdict",' said Moeller gently. 'I'm here to find out what will persuade you to take the upgrade.'

'I don't like being backed into a corner, sir,' she said. 'Feels like we were ordered out to face the Mafs just so the upgrade could be forced on us.'

'Even for you, that's cynical.'

'Is it? We get a pep talk from Corsini, an attack goes wrong and shortly after the Tweakers presumably reported how expensive a fleshware upgrade would be, a mysterious and very cheap sentience upgrade pops up. Cheap because it isn't complete. I'm a drake pilot, I don't do coincidences.'

Moeller took a sip of his coffee while he framed his reply.

'How about it's a genuine offer to give you the control you need to take them down?'

'Had it come from you, I might have believed it. From Solomon via the ExO... Look, sir, the problem I have, the problem my squad and all the pilots have is the lack of shielding. And for me, personally, Markov's absence was very telling. I've been coming to upgrade meetings for six years and this is the first without her. I don't trust it.'

'But without it, you stand to suffer more losses. Is mind-shielding the red line for you?'

'You know it is. And even then I'm suspicious of the data and testing. Barely past modelling stage, is it?'

There was such disappointment in Valera's eyes it drew Moeller up short.

'You're feeling betrayed?'

'Ha, it's worse than that. You can fight against betrayal. I feel like we're being sacrificed.'

Moeller nodded. 'The pressure from the top is severe. Time is running out.'

'So it's okay to throw pilots on the fire and hope the gods smile on us, is it?'

'Come on, Val...'

'They just don't get it,' she said. 'Doesn't matter how much we love it, every time we fly, it's there... the shadow of the Fall... and in the dead of night it's what brings on the terrors. So we have to be sure we're being protected from it; that we *matter*. Doesn't much feel like that right now and trust me, you don't want to be sending pilots out like that.'

'Of course you matter.'

'To you, maybe.'

'Don't go all petulant teenager on me,' said Moeller. 'You're better than that.'

'Sorry... Sometimes it seems that stamping and throwing toys is all that's left.' She shrugged. 'I was talking to the squad...

We're all excited at the potential of the upgrade, but the thing that should scare you is that we'd rather go back out and face the Mafs with nothing rather than risk it without shielding. *That's* what avoiding the Fall means to a drake pilot.'

Moeller stared at her. 'You're serious, aren't you?'

Valera nodded and jerked a thumb at the door. 'Ask 'em.'

'All right,' said Moeller. 'Look, we can meet you partway. Kirby has said that if you agree to the upgrade, he'll produce the figures making agreement to mind-shielding a formality.'

'What do you mean, "partway"?'

Moeller sucked his lip, feeling guilty even as he spoke. 'You'll have to do that sortie without the shielding.'

Valera gasped. 'Holy shit, sir, you can't expect me to agree to that.'

'We can't delay. We have to put the Maf drakes to bed so we can attack the *Maputo*.'

'With respect, you're missing the point. You can't undo an upgrade. If I agree, I lose my bargaining power. Solomon can just shrug her shoulders at the ExO's figures, however compelling.'

'But she won't because he's going to compare cost of shielding with potential cost of training new pilots if the upgrade provokes a faster Fall.'

'Why haven't they done that already?'

Moeller had opened his mouth to reply before he realised he had no idea. 'That's a very good question.'

'And I've got the simple answer but let's not go there. Will they do it? Will they retrofit the shielding if we take on the upgrade for tomorrow, risks and all?'

'You have to trust your commanding officers.'

'I trust you,' said Valera.

'And despite everything, I trust Kirby when it comes to staff. He'll work the figures, he'll persuade Solomon.'

'This is a massive call.'

'Discuss it with the squad, then. Privately if you want to.'

'You may as well hear what they have to say… but it's squad room rules, okay?'

Moeller held up his hands. 'Nothing you don't want reported gets reported. Now that I can promise.'

Valera led the way back to the squad, who were scattered around the sofas and chairs doing a poor job of appearing disinterested. At sight of Moeller, Stepanek shouted them to attention only for him to wave them back to their seats.

'Right, listen up,' said Valera, standing where they could all see her. 'I need to put something to you. Speak freely but you will not resort to personal abuse. I trust I'm clear.'

'Is it me or is this a lead-up to a big "but"?' said Palant.

'And there's no butt bigger than yours,' said Max to a concerted groan.

'Just couldn't resist, could you?' said Kullani.

'Nope,' said Max. 'Ow!'

'That's for being a twat,' said Kullani.

'Just listen!' snapped Valera. 'And think before you speak.'

She stared at Max before continuing.

'So, we have to go fight the Mafs tomorrow. The upgrade is cool and it would give us an edge but it has no shielding. There's been movement but we have to blink first. If we agree the upgrade, fly the sortie, we get shielding on our return. It's as close to a promise as I can get – that Mister Moeller can get. Think it over. Take your time but hurry up all the same.'

Moeller was fascinated by the breadth of their reactions. Gurney was smiling; Redfearn looked pensive and Stepanek was unreadable while both Calder and Nevant were nodding their heads where Palant and Salewski were shaking theirs. Halloran had opened his mouth to speak but Kullani dug him in the ribs.

'Ow, bloody hell,' he hissed into the contemplative quiet.

'Something to say, Max?' asked Valera.

'Quite a lot springs to mind,' he replied.

'Which is why I jabbed you,' said Kullani. 'To filter the stupid stuff out.'

'There's no going back once we're upgraded,' said Max. 'You said so yourself.'

'That's why it's a call I won't make without you,' said Valera.

'S'about trust, isn't it?' said Calder.

'When have the exec screwed us over before?' asked Gurney.

'Last briefing,' said Max.

'You know what I mean.'

'Yeah, I do, and it feels to me we're being screwed. If we can get shielding the day after tomorrow, why couldn't we have had it the day before yesterday?'

Valera turned briefly to look at Moeller and he hoped his eyes conveyed how careful she had to be.

'The official line,' she said, 'is that the upgrade is believed to be safe, hence no need for shielding.'

'And Markov's signed it off?' asked Redfearn.

'Her signature is on the file,' said Valera.

'But what did she say?' asked Redfearn.

'I haven't spoken to her yet.'

'Then how…' Redfearn trailed off as Valera held up her hands.

'Look, I-X, we are where we are. We can go over how we came to this point at our leisure another time. Right now, I need to know whether you want to risk a sortie with an untested upgrade or go out without anything new.'

'Do you think they'll approve the shielding retrofit?' asked Calder.

'That's a matter for you, it's why I'm talking to you. For what it's worth, I'm with Mister Moeller – I think we have to take the ExO at his word.'

Max snorted but Monteith stood up.

'Can I say something?'

'Me saying "no" has never stopped you before,' said Valera.

'We're thinking about this all wrong. Bloody hell, the negativity in this room is depressing. We're Inferno-X, for fuck's sake, and we're scared of nothing. So we don't back off the upgrade, we take it, we love it, we get out there and toast the Mafs with it. We show them, and we show the ExO and Avery and Solomon and whoever the hell else is watching, that they cannot win without Inferno-X. *That's* how you really get the shielding. Right?'

Moeller felt the mood in the room transform and saw smiles replace frowns. All except Halloran who was still closed and angry. But he was on his own now; Moeller could see that clearly enough and so could Valera. She waited to see if anyone else had anything to say before turning to him.

'All right, we'll take it,' she said.

Max had known it the moment he entered the flight deck. They all had. The mind-touch was cleaner, clearer, like pure song and crystal glass. Settling into the pouch was like ducking his body into a freezing cold plunge pool, leaving his mind sharp. Despite his misgivings, he couldn't deny it was incredible, like the potential of him and his drake was finally unveiled.

'Oh, Martha, we are going to rip them claw from scale,' he said.

'Inferno-X, Flight Com, the *Maputo* is two hours south of your position. Plenty of time to familiarise yourselves with your upgrade but let's not give too much away when you hit tactical radar range.'

'Copy that,' said Valera.

'Feeling good, Val-X?' asked Moeller.

'Feeling even better about the mind-shielding to come. But this is a thoroughly awesome sensation.'

'I hear you, Val-X,' said Moeller. 'I'll have confirmation on your return.'

They'd chosen to fly as they were, twelve strong. Valera had refused to share the upgrade risk with another squadron and their injured quartet didn't have to make their decisions until they were fit to fly

'Inferno-X, you heard the boss, let's air test.'

'Good luck, Inferno-X, Flight Com out.'

'Hey, Skipper!'

'Hal-X, does the upgrade confer the right to ignore com protocol?'

'Sorry, Skipper. Val-X, Hal-X, just wondering if anyone else feels like they should be scared by how open their mind is but feels fucking amazing anyway... Y'know, natural like daylight, like someone's opened a channel, taken away all the blockages.'

'Copy, Hal-X. I'm sure we all feel the same.'

'It's just a question who's really in control, right?' said Max.

'I hear you, Hal-X, but right now, we're out here to honour our dead and see those Maf fuckers plough the sand. Got it?'

'Aye, Skipper!'

They flew in almost total silence to begin with, each of them recalling those they had so recently lost. The Inferno-X family, flyers they should be sharing the sky with right now. Well, Max assumed everyone was. He brought Schmiddy's laughing face to mind and used it to focus his mind on the task. Revenge with control.

They were about half an hour out when they began to adopt a few formations – as if they'd all come to the same idea simultaneously. Red-X had led a subtle change to their standard close-form chevron and then they were all into their inter-squad display tournament routine... But this time they could use the sentience upgrade.

Max pushed with his mind and Martha was right there, hanging on his every thought and urging him to slip deeper into her consciousness. The danger was so close but he could feel, almost *see* the line beyond which he must not go. He imagined a descent of fifty metres and she acted upon it, rendering his arm movements irrelevant beyond minute adjustments to her trim. He moved her eyes to scan the squad and she acted on the thought so fast he had to fight to keep up. This was freedom in flight; combat would be a dream but the cost was still to be quantified.

The Inferno-X drakes slipped, slid, darted and swooped with effortless precision. Gently they tested and each time they were rewarded. It was so tempting to push further and Valera knew it.

'Inferno-X, Val-X, enough for now, folks. Let's remember we have no shielding so don't risk getting lost in it, only use what you must. All right, we're four a chevron. You know your places. Standard attack tactics on the way in, then feel your way. Flight Com, Val-X. Talk us in.'

'Flight Com copies. Stand by. Screen is clear, *Maputo* is on bearing one-seven-nine. Continue at present height, stand by for further orders.'

Max opened his wing com. 'How's it feeling, buddy?'

'Like a new crisp and chill dawn,' said Kullani.

'Nothing scary?'

'Given that I'm leaking my brains out of my ears? No. In fact I feel freer than I have in months. It's a breath of new life.'

'Don't go crazy,' said Max.

'Crazier,' said Kullani.

'Very funny.' Max looked down and ahead and spotted the scattered dust and sand clouds indicating the three Maf behemoths. They had closed formation a little to protect the *Maputo* and there was no doubt they were heading directly towards the Vermelho Sea. 'You're not getting there, you big, sick, old lizard.'

'Really think we can bring her down?' asked Kullani.

'Right now I think we can do anything. But the realist in me says it's a huge job. Depends on how many new drakes they've got. And how many of ours take the upgrade.'

'Inferno-X, Flight Com, I have blips on screen from the *Virunga* on an intercept course with you. Ten blips... Guess who?'

Max felt a thrill and Martha shivered. 'Yeah, baby, this time you get to do the chewing.'

Martha roared, the other drakes taking up the call, and Max imagined a roll and turned his body minutely to the right. Martha's reacted at the speed of thought.

'C-Two, Hal-X. Form up on me. On contact, maintain height, split to wings and cycle back in. Call your targets and feel it, people, but let's not get cocky. These boys are good.'

Inferno-X were close-formed, the three chevrons no more than fifty metres apart in a vertical stack. C-Two was Max, Kullani, Monteith and Redfearn. Below him, and just ahead, he could see Valera's drake, the sun glinting off her pearl-white scales and her neck ramrod straight and beautiful.

'Here they come, Inferno-X,' said Valera. 'Give nothing away. We know what they're capable of, let your instincts lead you. Watch out for each other. Good luck.'

'Kul-X, you hearing me?' asked Max.

'Need you ask?'

'Straight through, no deviation, then break hard right and come back onto my wing.'

'Copy that, Hal-X.'

'All right, Martha, let's play chicken.'

Max straightened his body and Martha trimmed her wings and stretched her neck and tail out. The slate-grey Maf drakes were closing hard, moving directly into their path, confident in their ability and superiority. The only question was who would blink first. Two klicks out became one in a few wingbeats. And then the sky was full of scale and wing and fire and the roars of drakes, sparkling white and slate grey. Max felt Maf and Inferno drakes peel off in all directions. Monteith and Redfearn went low and right, leaving him and Kullani driving straight on.

Ahead, their target drake opened her mouth and spat flame into the air to have it wash away in the wind of her passage. Two beats to collision. Max forced himself to stare. For the briefest of moments, he saw the Maf drake's fangs, the pulsing flame fuel arteries and the slits of her eyes.

Her pilot blinked first, taking her up and over. Max caught a glimpse of the pilot, eyes wide. Max imagined a flick and Martha's tail whipped up, her spike connecting with the drake's rear quarters as she passed.

'One-nil,' he said, ripping Martha into a left turn. He scanned with her eyes, seeing his target climbing high, its lower abdomen cut.

'On your three, Max,' said Kullani. 'What a rush.'

'On me, I've nicked one.'

Max drove up after the injured Maf drake. Ahead to his left, the sky was crowded with combat. He saw Valera all but stand her drake on its tail to bring her round onto the back of an enemy and disgorge tight beams of fire over its wings and spine. It fell into a steep spin, smoke trailing from multiple wounds. Beyond her, two Mafs were harrying an Inferno wing pair. Max watched breathlessly as the quartet danced, twisted and rolled through other skirmishes, into empty air and back again, the Maf drakes unable to get close enough to strike, the Infernos unable to shake them off.

Martha's eyes were fixed on her quarry. The slash of her tail hadn't disabled the enemy but there had to be discomfort and that might make all the difference. Max saw the white streak on the Maf drake's belly that indicated blood.

'Get on her tail, Kul-X, I'll be right above you. Keep at her; let's see what she's got.'

'Copy, Max.'

Kullani moved in front of Max, who ghosted a few metres higher. Ahead, their target turned and saw them before shooting down and left some two hundred metres ahead of them. Kullani adjusted instantly, taking the intercept line and closing fast. The Maf switched into a sharp right as Kullani dropped into her slipstream. Kullani followed without hesitation, her drake closing her left wing momentarily and stretching her right, pivoting about it.

'Wooo!' shouted Risa.

'Oh yeah!' yelled Max, following her move and feeling g-forces press him back in Martha's pouch.

'He's bloody good,' she said.

'We're better!'

The Maf dived, dropping like a stone and sweeping its wings back along its body. Again Kullani followed but this time Max changed his angle, making his dive less acute. A Maf drake shot past him not thirty metres distant, chased by a pair of Infernos.

'Go, go,' he muttered.

He knew what his enemy was going to do. There was pattern to her flight and it was revealing itself in her turn selection. It was so familiar Max was convinced he'd faced this one before. There was no doubting that the enemy would have to pull out and would do so as low as possible and as sharply as possible, hoping to leave Kullani no time to react. But something inside Max told him it wouldn't be a vertical climb. The Maf would angle left or right to drive back into the main conflict at a more advantageous angle to strike.

Max smiled. He knew which direction he'd take. He watched the Maf and Kullani screaming down towards the desert sands.

'What's your altitude, Kul-X?'

'Two-fifty.'

'Don't leave it too late.'

'I've got this.'

Diving past the four hundred mark, Max twitched his drake left. The Maf drove out of his dive with speed and beautiful timing, Kullani ripping at his tail. He had speed into the climb, his back to Max, and his drake was looking up and not behind.

'Lovely,' said Max and stretched out his toes and jerked his legs straight.

Martha stamped down with her claws open. She slammed into the enemy, driving her claws straight through its scales and into the flesh sheath around its spine. The Maf was shunted forwards violently enough to stun the pilot, if the sudden slump of the drake's neck and wings were any indication.

But he gathered himself fast and the drake's head swivelled, its jaws agape and coming at Max, flame ready. He curled his toes, simultaneously imagining a back beat. Martha complied, flaring her wings to apply the brakes and beating them hard to drag the enemy backwards.

The enemy drake squawked in pain as Martha's claws tightened. And in the moment's delay, he brought Martha's head around and asked for tight fire, all ducts. The octet of beams speared out, burning into the enemy drake's face, blinding it and roasting its brain inside its skull. The head and neck dropped, Martha released her claws and the carcass hit the sand with a resounding crump.

'Great work!' yelled Kullani. 'One for the lost.'

'Teamwork, Kul-X,' said Max. Martha exulted. 'Let's get back up there, see who else we can catch.'

Max drove Martha quickly back into the sky, heading to the conflict which had scattered across a wide area. Two drakes, one grey, one white, dropped past him locked in a claw fight, twisting in each other's grip, tumbling and rolling, their wings fouling. Jaws sought purchase, tails were entwined and talons jabbed and raked, looking for the vital opening. He followed the fight, seeing the Inferno drake get the upper hand, still the rotation and bite down on the top of the Maf's neck. The enemy juddered and its wings flailed, desperate to push away. The Inferno drake dragged its tail free and slashed it up the other's belly. Blood surged into the sky. It was as good as over.

'Skipper, Hal-X, how are we doing?'

'A whole lot better than last time, Hal-X. Stand by ... Have some of that, you fucker. Run and hide, drake shit tic turd!'

Max searched the sky and found what he was looking for. Valera and Nevant whipped across from behind him, chasing a drake with great slashes in its back, a hole in its left wing and smoke trailing from burn marks at the base of its neck. It was heading away from the fight, back towards the *Virunga*.

'Sorry, Hal-X, Head up on over-watch. I think we've got this in the bag. Gurney has a burn but otherwise we're all fine.'

'Good. We've ploughed one in so that makes them five down, by my count.'

'Hal-X, Mont-X, coming by you in three,' said Monteith. His drake swooped across Max's bow, his drake's claws battering into the belly of his target and her tail slicing deeply into flesh. She opened her mouth and scorched the pouch black.

'Correction, Val-X. Six down,' said Max.

And with that it was done. On a signal the surviving Maf drakes broke and headed home, chased by Palant and Stepanek.

'Pal-X, Step-X, let 'em go,' said Valera.

'Copy, Skipper' said Stepanek. 'Looks like we shaded this one.'

'Looks like we ripped them up!' said Palant.

'Inferno-X, Val-X, great work, everyone. I think we can call that a win. Gur-X, your condition, please.'

'Still here, Skipper,' said Gurney. 'But I should be heading home. No need for a nanny, I'm okay.'

'Free to go,' said Valera. 'Did you copy all that, Flight Com?'

'Confirmed, Val-X. Congratulations, Inferno-X, looks like we're back on track. Be aware: skytime has been granted so all drakes are coming out to play. Go ahead and test the upgrade a little more but don't push yourselves. You'll all be needed for ERC tactical and neural debrief on landing. Have fun, Inferno-X, you've earned it.'

'Copy, Flight Com, and thank you,' said Valera. 'Inferno-X signing off feeling a whole lot better about life than we did yesterday.'

'You know it,' said Moeller. 'Flight Com out.'

'All right, folks, looks like we're done for the day,' said Valera. 'You know the skytime zones, make your own way there and enjoy the free time.'

Skytime. The often dreamed about and seldom granted free

flight benefit. Apparently there were cost implications to do with the extra nutrients required because of the extra flight time, blah blah. Max couldn't care less. He was going to soar, he was going to dive, and he was going to irritate the shit out of anyone else he could find. For as long as it lasted, he was going to enjoy it.

'Correction,' he said. 'Martha... *we* are going to enjoy it. It's gonna be better than sex. Well, almost.'

CHAPTER 16

> My dad said that some of the old nuclear submarines lasted ages but eventually the behemoths got them. They could read the radiation signatures and chased them down and crushed them then took them to dry land so they wouldn't contaminate the oceans. My dad said if you listen hard enough in the water, you can still hear the metal screaming and the submariners begging for mercy.
>
> MAXIMUS HALLORAN, AGE 15

With the *HoG* large on the landscape ahead, Max could make out the dots representing the other five squads, a hundred and twenty in all. He could see a few games going on. There was some netting, some stall chasing and the obligatory chicken and sprint contests. Today, though, he fancied relaxing into the upgrade and seeing a little more of what it could do, how much he had to push to get where he wanted. Martha's mind-touch warmed him to his soul. She wanted it too.

'Hal-X, Val-X, sorry to intrude.'

'Not a problem, Skipper, what can I do for you? I'm not signing up for a stall dare, okay? Scared myself shitless last time.'

Valera laughed. 'Oh yes, brown pouch time indeed. No, it's not that. Got a call for you.'

'Who is it?'

'Trust me. Go ahead, com is closed, Val-X out.'

'I'm about to demonstrate skills beyond your wildest dreams, whoever you are. Are you ready to be proved inferior?'

'Max, it's me.'

'Anna-Beth?' he croaked.

Max's heart leapt into his throat and hammered away up there. Martha's whole body shook in disapproval. She could be a jealous beast.

'Oh, I have the unflappable Max Halloran off balance, do I?' she said.

'I might be coerced into admitting that even your voice does things to me,' said Max.

'Fancy some up-close-and-personal? I need to talk to you.'

Max felt a thrill rush through him that brought a growl from Martha. 'You never know when we'll get another chance.'

'Quite.' But something in Anna-Beth's tone wasn't right.

'Where are you?'

'See the line of dunes a klick west of the *HoG*? There's an old camel herd's hut still standing there. Unbelievably. I'm at a thousand above it.'

'I'm on my way,' said Max. 'Are you okay?'

'Tell you in a moment.'

He knew he shouldn't but during the short flight to Anna-Beth, whose dappled red and white drake he could see circling, he wondered if he was about to be dumped. Stupid but he felt the anxiety nonetheless.

Max flew low over the hut, seeing corrugated iron bolted to steel piles sunk into concrete. One or two panels hung loose, the roof was half gone, the remains of a camel pen remained in evidence, along with a washing line, while old litter still blew about inside, surviving against all the odds; splashes of bright colour against the background of sand.

'Nice place you've got there,' he said, flying up towards her.

'I wrote down all the obvious clichés and that was number one.'

'The decoration needs attention.'

'Wow, Max, two for two. Get up here. Skytime won't last for ever.'

'Can't it wait until we're in bed later?'

'It's hard to get into bed with a Landfill inmate.'

'You mean the upgrade? It'll be okay.' Max turned tight and came alongside Anna-Beth. 'What do you want to do?'

'Twine,' she said, looking across at him. 'What else?'

'Want to go on top first or shall I?'

'Do you ever think about anything other than sex?'

'I'm sure I've no idea what you're talking about,' said Max.

'Whatever. You take position one. I'm ready when you are.'

Max side-slipped away about twenty metres and matched Anna-Beth's drake beat for beat.

'Check this out,' he said. He rose a few metres, turned a single roll and finished directly above her. Martha roared her pleasure. 'Cool, eh?'

'Actually, yes. But how about this?'

Anna-Beth switched onto her back, had her drake twine Martha's tail in hers and moved her head up so the two drakes touched muzzles. She furled her drake's wings, Martha's snapping out in response. The pair began to descend, Max putting Martha on the glide, the extra weight making manoeuvring difficult.

'All right, that's even cooler.'

'Good, aren't I?'

Anna-Beth's voice came to him like he was sitting next to her. It was a wonderful anomaly of twine flying, still the best method for a fit drake to land a wounded one, that they could speak directly through their rides. He switched off his com and looked down at her, seeing only her eyes and nose.

'You're amazing,' he said.

'How long can you keep us up?'

'Reckon we can take the strain for a good ten minutes at this height. I'll let you know if we need a switch.' Anna-Beth was regarding him with a seriousness that concerned him. 'What's up?'

'You can't take the upgrade,' she said.

'We—'

'*Listen to me*, I've got to get this out. It's because I trust your instincts when you smell a rat that I did this.'

'Did what?'

'Got some information out of the ERC about your upgrade.'

'How the hell did you manage that?' Martha was buffeted by a whack of clear air turbulence. Max beat her wings and put her in a shallower glide. 'Okay, steady.'

'I wouldn't sleep with anyone else but you aren't the only man who finds me attractive, all right? Do I need to draw you a picture?'

'No,' said Max, a little more petulant in tone than he'd intended.

'Deal with it. Just listen. That upgrade is less than half-cooked. The data doesn't support deployment, only second stage modelling and partial field testing. It is unsafe. There isn't even a neural map yet.'

'But the skipper saw the report.'

'She saw *a* report and Markov wasn't there to endorse it, was she? She saw what they wanted her to see.'

'But with shielding we're protected anyway, right? It's going to be retrofitted.'

'You can't retrofit mind-shielding.' Anna-Beth's eyes betrayed her anxiety. 'It's never been done because it's impossible.'

Max felt empty, like someone had stolen his guts. There was a rushing noise in his ears and even his embryonic satisfaction at being proved right was scant comfort. Martha wobbled in flight. He felt horribly exposed and vulnerable. His first instinct was to shrink from her mind. They dropped a hundred metres.

'Max!'

'Fuck!' He stabilised Martha. 'Sorry.'

'What the fuck?'

'Moeller promised...' said Max, aware he was sounding a little vague. His heart was pounding away and all he wanted to do was land and get away from Martha and that reaction made him feel terrible. Angry too, very angry.

'Then Moeller has swallowed the same shit as Valera. Just don't let them fool you.'

'They already have.'

'What?'

'I'm flying with the upgrade now. All of Inferno-X are.'

The widening of Anna-Beth's eyes almost broke him.

'How do you think we toasted the Mafs just now?' he managed.

Anna-Beth loosened the twine and spun her drake a hundred and eighty degrees before tightening again and beating her wings. Max reacted, Martha's wings beating in sync to avoid fouling. It was inefficient but it gave them some lift.

'I'm driving,' she said, her tone cold and determined. 'Don't you do a fucking thing.'

Max felt sick. Vindication of his suspicions was a hollow triumph. The rest of I-X were still at play, diving, sparring and cavorting, their moves so accurate, so much cleaner than the others in the sky with them.

'We have to tell them,' said Max.

'You can't go open com with this,' said Anna-Beth.

'Who else knows?'

'No one.'

'I'll tell them when they're home,' said Max, his anger burning his cheeks. 'I'll fix this.'

'Just don't try fixing it with your fists, okay?'

'What can we do?' asked Max, suddenly lost. 'We're screwed, aren't we?'

'You've got to try and keep calm. Talk to Valera. I'll stand with you if you want me, tell her what I've just told you. She'll know what to do.'

'What difference will it make? It's too late.'

'Don't go there, Max. In a few days we'll be off to the Vermelho Sea. There'll be time then.'

'That's five days!' snapped Max, unable to quite contain his rage. 'That's five more sorties away at least. Twenty-plus hours unshielded in an untested upgrade. They've taken a gamble with my life and the lives of all of Inferno-X, haven't they? That we'll take down the *Maputo*. How fucking dare they! I'm not ending up in Landfill to get some other fucker a medal.'

'No,' said Anna-Beth. 'You're not. I'm not losing you, Max.'

'I love you,' said Max before he could stop himself.

Anna-Beth was quiet long enough Max thought he'd made a huge error.

'I love you too.'

Anxiety washed through Martha and juddered through Max's mind. He shook himself.

'Did you feel that?'

'Yep.' The calls of drakes at play had changed to mournful calls and Martha took up the chorus too. 'Oh no.'

'What is it?'

Anna-Beth didn't need to answer him. Martha's head swivelled right and up to track a drake plummeting towards the ground. Max's breath caught in his throat. Its great body led the Fall, its tail and neck reaching upwards, its head wobbling in the dirty air. From everywhere, other drakes charged in to try and get beneath it, alongside it, anything to help. Max was transfixed. He knew there was nothing they could do, nothing anyone could do.

The open com surged with orders and counter orders, the shouts of pilots trying desperately to get through to the victim. Max stared, keeping Martha on the glide. The drake pushed out a wing and brief hope kindled but it was a twitching beat, an innate reaction, nothing more. It turned lazily as it fell.

'Pull out pull out pull out,' whispered Max.

Down they fell, pilot and drake. Everyone knew why, everyone watched on, seeing themselves in the tragic dive. They watched all the way down until the sand billowed, the drakes roared fury and the command com sounded.

'Skytime is aborted,' came a gruff voice. 'Landing protocols to follow.'

The flight deck was sombre where it should have been buzzing and that suited Max just fine. The Fall was part of life on a behemoth but seeing it played out so publicly had taken the wind from the sails of victory. But Max felt hollow for other reasons too. Once he'd watched the rest of Inferno-X land, he'd given Anna-Beth a desperate hug before walking off the deck arm-in-arm with Kullani, needing to know she was okay.

At the squad victory dinner in the executive restaurant up in skull deck three, alcohol lightened their mood and talk soon turned to the mission, the upgrade and their stunning victory. Max forced himself to join in, acting as the life and soul of it all, and led the toast to the ERC team.

He soaked up the banter around the table and saw the light in his friends' eyes when Moeller, Avery, Kirby and even Solomon dropped by to offer their congratulations. Solomon told them they'd struck the first decisive blow that would bring the war to a swift conclusion.

When she left them, genuine hope had swept round the table. They could be the squad who finished it, who got out of the pouch before the Fall took them. A chance to go home to families they thought they'd never see again and enjoy their pay. And with mind-shielding how could they fail . . . ?

What a job she'd done on them all. Max had to fight back the rage and keep the smile on his face.

'You all been to tech debrief?' he asked.

Kullani and Gurney were either side of him and Stepanek was across from him. All three nodded.

'Haven't you?' asked Gurney.

'Not got round to it.'

'Oh right, I think Skipper thought she was the last,' said Gurney, and then called along the table to her. 'Hey, Skipper, is the ERC still open? Max hasn't quite got in the chair yet.'

'Bloody hell, Max. Get your sorry bollocks up there, will you?' said Valera. 'They were winding down when I left. Only the duty tech in there by now, I should think. Off you go.'

Max pushed back his chair and gave an extravagant bow.

'My friends, duty calls. Think of me while you drink and make merry.'

The response was loud and predictable. Lucky the marshal gen wasn't within earshot.

It wasn't far to the ERC complex. Every behemoth had a significant facility as part of the medical services on skull deck two so Max walked past a couple of the wards and the passageway that led to Landfill ward. It always made him shudder. One day he'd make that walk and once the door closed behind him, he'd never walk back out.

The ERC development was a series of offices and laboratories split over a section of the deck that surrounded the brain sheath. The sheath itself was transparent, reminding anyone passing by they were inside a living organism. The tech debrief lab was just off the main research laboratory, which itself was a place of tables covered in screens and confusing equipment and whose walls displayed the physiology of man and drake.

DNA maps and models sat as ornaments, half-empty mugs stood forgotten on desks and cables spread like voracious plant life, threatening to obliterate floor, walls and ceiling if left unchecked. Despite the cable weights, taping and covers all over the floor, Max had learned to tread carefully whenever he came here.

'Hello?' he called. 'Anyone at home?'

'Yup!' came a voice from his left. Max looked round and a

tall young man appeared. He was probably no older than Max. 'Can I help you?'

'I'm Max Halloran. Are you the duty tech?'

His freckled face lit up with a smile. 'Ah, excellent, Hal-X, very good to meet you. Fantastic result today.' He came forward and stuck out a long-fingered hand, which Max shook. 'I'm Carlos Ashanti.'

'Unbelievable day,' said Max. 'I need to debrief.'

'Of course, of course, this way.'

Max had been here a few times but he followed along dutifully, working out how best to get the information he wanted to back up what Anna-Beth had told him. It would be easier if Ashanti was a twat but he appeared irritatingly pleasant. The tech debrief room was dominated by a sensor chair and a single workbench set with multiple screens. Max settled into the chair, slipped his hands into the gloves and let Ashanti pull the sensor-encrusted skullcap down on to his head.

Now every neural pathway would be mapped, every emotion and muscle movement recorded and every word he said during the debrief would be overlaid on a map of the mission. All he had to do was answer some questions and give a few opinions. Science would do the rest.

'Are you comfortable?'

'Have you ever sat in this chair?' asked Max.

A series of green lights and a single red one blinked and steadied on a panel above Max's head.

'Nope,' said Ashanti. 'But we're good to go, we're recording. This is Carlos Ashanti, Extra Reptilian Construct research and development team, technician first class—'

'First class, eh? Good work.'

'Thanks, yes, well... We all try to do our best.'

'Most of us.'

'Ha! So... This is the tech debrief of Pilot Hal-X of Inferno-X following upgrade thirty-seven, H-I-O, enhanced sentience activation and adjustment of neural interface. Right, Hal-X—'

'Call me Max.'

'Max. We'll begin with some simple questions to normalise the reading input. Did I give your correct call sign and squadron?'

'You did.'

'What did you have for breakfast this morning?'

'Scrambled egg, toast, appalling tinned bacon and strong coffee.'

Ashanti smiled. 'And do you feel hot, cold or normal temperature at the moment?'

'Entirely normal, thank you, no need to adjust the aircon.'

'That's not a question about the air—'

'I know what it's about.'

'Right, great. We're normalised within standard parameters, so... How did you feel approaching your drake this afternoon?'

'Can we pause the recording? I need to piss, sorry.'

'Ah, sure.' Ashanti tapped the screen behind him and the big red light dimmed away. 'I'll get you a sample phial for analysis later.'

Max took his hands out of the gloves and pushed the skullcap back.

'Can I ask you something?'

'Sure,' said Ashanti.

'How old are you?'

Ashanti frowned and shrugged. 'Twenty-three, why?'

'Same as me. Looking forward to a long, happy life beyond the war?'

'I'm... Well, sure, aren't we all?'

'I'm a drake pilot, Carlos, I get to look forward to a slow, irreversible decline into the most depressing of deaths unless I manage to Fall on the wing.'

'Sorry. Sorry.' Ashanti held up his hands in a placatory gesture. 'Sorry.'

Max pushed himself half out of the chair and gave Ashanti a

playful punch on the shoulder. 'Don't beat yourself up; I knew what I was signing up for.'

'Toilet's just down the corridor, third on the left.'

Max stood up and made to go before pausing and turning for effect. 'I watched one of our pilots Fall today. Even so, it's a great life but it's short and I'd hate to think anyone would deliberately make it shorter.'

'Heaven forbid,' said Ashanti – and there was a shine to his brow.

Max leaned into his discomfort. 'Why do we need mind-shielding, Carlos?'

'Well, a drake's mind is inherently stronger than a human's so it delays decline into the Fall,' said Ashanti.

'But it's seriously expensive.'

'Yeah, I mean, ridiculously. You wouldn't believe it.'

Max joined the laughter, then sobered in an instant. 'And without it?'

Ashanti's eyes wouldn't light on Max suddenly. They searched for a way out but Max had closed in to deny him escape.

'You know,' he said.

'Remind me.'

'Um – well, depending on the scale of open neural interaction, decline of an unshielded pilot can be very swift.'

'Hmm, fascinating. Define "very swift".'

Ashanti held up his hands. He was breathing hard. 'I know what you're driving at.'

'And I don't blame you. You're just a monkey like me when all's said and done. But answer my question.'

Ashanti relaxed a little. 'Anything from first sortie onwards. Risk of the Fall increases with hours in the pouch anyway but it's exponential without shielding.'

'Thank you,' Max turned to go then paused. 'I need to confirm one thing. Can you retrofit shielding?'

'It's never been done,' said Ashanti.

'That's a bullshit weasel response, Carlos. I thought we were going to be friends... Take your hand away from that screen. If that red light comes on, I'll break your arm.'

Ashanti started and hesitated. 'No, I mean because it's not possible.'

'For sure?'

Ashanti nodded. 'I'm sorry.'

'It's okay, shooting messengers isn't my style. But you know what they've done to us, right? Think about it and about what you might do to help.'

'Perhaps... perhaps it's time you went for your piss,' said Ashanti, hands trembling.

'Is that supposed to be a joke?'

'N-no, no, not at all. It's just that you said you needed one, and we need to finish the debrief.'

Max stared at him. 'You can stick your tech debrief up Markov's arse. I'm giving you nothing. Inferno-X might be screwed but no other squadron needs to be. And you're in charge of the data, Carlos. Do you get me?'

CHAPTER 17

> The voracity with which the alien technologies were gobbled up by the world's superpowers had an unpleasant, almost bestial quality. It left comparatively few of us asking really important questions like 'Where did they come from?' The problem is, the answer to that sort of question doesn't confer any battlefield advantage. PROFESSOR MEHMET GOVANI, DIARIES

'Max, you need to calm right down.'

'Why? You've been lied to, so has Moeller. So have all of us.'

She'd pulled him into her pod pretty much as soon as she'd seen his face. Apparently, he looked like he was about to detonate. He felt he was masking his anger rather well. They had agreed to differ.

'Where did Anna-Beth get her information?' Valera was still in denial.

'Some Tweaker ex of hers, but it isn't just her, is it? The tech I went to see, Ashanti, he's confirmed it. It's impossible, so no one's ever tried it and they aren't going to start now. Mind you...'

'What?'

Max shook his head. 'Nothing, it's nothing. I-X has been sacrificed on the altar of Corsini's lust for power. Pure and simple.'

Valera took a breath, walking round in a small circle. 'These are serious allegations. But we're in a fix. Never mind who's implicated, we've got this upgrade and I need to work out what, if anything, we can do. Markov signed it off, after all.'

'And is nowhere to be seen at the moment. You've seen the signature that Kirby showed you, but he's a lying bag of shit so it's probably forged. Why are you defending an upgrade you didn't want?'

'What I want is information I can use, not hearsay and the word of a tech you threatened.'

'You don't believe me?'

'Of course I believe you but it isn't as simple as marching into the ExO and issuing accusations. I have to be sure of my ground and "Max's-girlfriend's-ex-fuck-buddy-says" isn't going to cut it.'

Max sighed. 'We don't have time to screw around, Skipper. One after the other, we've been up to the Tweakers and told them how brilliant it is. That's going to green-light pushing the upgrade to every squad. We cannot allow that to happen. Bloody hell, Landfill's going to burst with new inmates, all in the name of money and power. There's no honour here, no respect.'

'Quiet down!' snapped Valera. 'I know you're angry—'

'That doesn't even *begin* to explain how I feel.'

'I get it! But we have to have some evidence. So here's what I'll do. I'll ping the other skippers, make them aware of the potential problems with the upgrade. Next I'll go and speak to Markov, if I can find her, and Rosenbach if I can't, and confirm what Ashanti told you.

'Then I will approach Moeller and Commander Avery. Am I clear?'

Max nodded reluctantly. Protocol was bullshit. 'Kirby needs pinning against a wall until he coughs up the truth.'

'See why I'm skipper and you're not?' Valera opened her pod door. 'Come on, go to bed and neither you nor Anna-Beth says *anything* to anyone until I say so.'

'Why? People have to know.'

Valera nodded. 'And so they will. But in the right way. That's my way in case you weren't clear.'

'Why aren't you raging?'

'Who says I'm not?'

Max sat up in bed and looked at the time. It was five thirty a.m. His heart was thumping away with the broken memories of half-dreams from fitful sleep. His anger was keeping his mind whirring and his body tense. Try as he might, he couldn't shake it off. He wasn't sure he wanted to.

He looked down at Anna-Beth, who had the sheet pulled up over her shoulders and was facing the other way. He'd fought it all night but he couldn't just lie here and hope. No way, *no way*, was that upgrade happening to her. No way was some dragon going to steal her mind from him. Kirby could stop it happening but if Max was to see him, it had to be now, before it was too late. He got out of bed and started to slip on some clothes as quietly as he could.

Valera's plan was all very well but it was too slow; it was pretty obvious they'd upgrade every drake at the earliest opportunity, whether they got squadron agreement or not. That probably meant along with their first feed of the day in about an hour and a half. Then it would be job done as far as Kirby and Solomon were concerned and they could go and tell Corsini what good little subjects they'd been. Shortly after that, drake pilots would start dropping out of the sky. Anna-Beth might drop out of the sky.

Max slipped on his shoes and headed for the door.

'Where do you think you're going?'

Max started and looked around. Anna-Beth was staring at him.

'I thought you were asleep.'

'Oh, yeah. Nothing easier than sleeping with a huffing, cursing, twitching goon next to you, I can tell you.'

'I couldn't sleep.'

'I'd never have guessed.'

'I thought it might help if I sat in the squad room, had some coffee or something.'

'It's still last night and if you're heading out for a quiet cup of coffee, then I'm a slime-sucking gecko rat.'

Max managed a smile and sat on the edge of the bed. 'Busted,' he said. He put a hand on her shoulder and she turned over onto her back. 'You were pissed off with me last night, weren't you?'

'No, it's just a little hard to be sympathetic in the face of a prolonged rant.'

'I'm sorry,' said Max, attempting sheepishness. 'I was very angry, wasn't I?'

'With good reason. You've just been handed what amounts to a death sentence—'

'I'm more concerned they'll hand it to you next.'

Anna-Beth's eyes sparkled. 'And I love you for that but you needed to listen to me and trust your skipper and you weren't about to do either. I had to close you down.'

'Sorry.'

'So, what particularly stupid thing are you thinking of doing?'

Max shrugged and tried to appear relaxed while he lied to her. 'I was hoping it would come to me. I just can't sit here and do nothing and then find out it's too late to do anything. I won't let them kill you like they're killing me.'

Anna-Beth smiled and stroked his arm. 'Tough, isn't it, finding out you care about someone other than yourself?'

'It's a nightmare without end,' said Max.

'Well, at least you haven't lost your sense of humour... You were joking, right?'

'I'm not sure, actually.'

'You can't do it all by yourself, love. So go and have that cup of coffee, realise anything you do will cause more trouble and then come back to bed. Like I said, it's still last night...'

Max kissed her then levered himself off the bed. 'I get you. Should I bring you anything?'

'Just yourself, in about half an hour.'

'Done.'

Anna-Beth turned over and Max walked to the deserted squad room where he'd only have the whirring of fans for a distraction. For a moment he actually contemplated sitting down in the minimally lit gloom and thinking things through but the clock was ticking and those things needed to be said.

Max headed towards the main door. Even though the air-circulation system was beginning to wind down as they approached the time for a regeneration cycle in the Vermelho Sea, the early air was fresh and cool. The central spine corridor was almost deserted, allowing Max some peace and quiet with just the regular thump of the *HoG*'s feet and the working of its cavernous lungs for company.

Sure, there were a few crew about heading for whatever task they had to perform but up here, where the dormitories were thick on the ground and no one had been called for a dawn sortie, it was beautifully... *empty.* So much so that he stopped for a moment, turned a slow circle and took in the corridor, its doors and side passages and the melodic, echoing sounds the *HoG* made, sounds usually covered up by the cumulative din of ten thousand humans.

He took a short walk towards the neck, whose walkways became stairs should it steepen its normal gentle angle to give the head more elevation. It had no rooms but plenty of conduit space plus engineering and Tweaker access. Max hurried along it and headed up to skull deck three, where the execs all had their sizeable suites of rooms.

Max's pass granted him access to all three skull decks and he exchanged pleasantries with the couple of sets of security personnel he passed on the way. If anyone asked, he was heading for the exec gymnasiums ... but he wasn't stopped. After all, he was Inferno-X.

To be fair to the Exec, although their rooms were larger, there were no particular additional touches of luxury ... same old bone and metal floor with its rubberised coating, same old wall panels and even a tiny bit of seepage – though nothing like the grunts had to endure.

Max arrived at Kirby's door, raised his fist to knock and then paused, the first motes of doubt creeping into his head. Valera might be right about following procedure but they had to let Kirby know they were on to him, didn't they? He had to know that upgrading more widely couldn't be sanctioned.

Max rapped on the metal door, the sound ringing dully in the corridor and presumably within. He stepped back and waited. He was wondering how long to wait until he knocked again when the lock clunked back and the door opened. Kirby was wearing sweats but didn't look like he'd just been dragged out of bed.

'What the hell do you want?' he asked.

'I need to talk to you, sir.'

'The desire's been burning you all night by the looks.'

Kirby raised his eyebrows and shook his head before pushing the door wide and wandering off inside. Max followed and closed the door. He was in a small, sparsely decorated living area with a desk, a round table and four chairs, a two-seater sofa and a high-backed armchair. There was a single door leading off to the bedroom and washroom and faint music was coming from within.

Kirby went to his desk, which had a drinks unit next to it. He put a mug under the spout and thumbed a selection.

'Want a coffee or something?'

'No thanks, sir,' said Max, fighting to stay calm despite the nonchalance of the lying shit in front of him. 'You don't seem surprised to see me.'

'I'm not really, though I hadn't expected you to come knocking till a little later. Ashanti mentioned your refusal to test in his report and I guessed you'd want to see me. I expect you're angry.'

Max felt completely wrong-footed. Kirby smiled, picked up his mug and gestured to the sofa.

'Go on, sit down. I suspect you've rarely seen this time of day.'

'Only when I'm angry, apparently.'

Kirby sat in the high-backed chair and waved Max down. He sat on the sofa, his visions of how this would go disintegrating.

'You'll find nothing is quite as clear-cut as it seems.'

'It seems pretty clear-cut to me,' said Max.

'To you, yes. That's why you're in here while Orin, who I'm sure you've told all about this, is tucked up in bed. You know why?'

'Yeah: because she wants to collect hard evidence that you're lying,' said Max.

'You know, Halloran, you've walked the wrong side of the line pretty much ever since you joined the *Granite*. And you screwed up after our chat in the brig. But I'm still going to offer you one last free piece of advice.'

'What is it, "don't trust your ExO"?'

'Don't fuck with your ExO.'

Max took a breath. 'It's too late for me, I get that—'

'Actually, we think I-X will be just fine.'

'Really? Reckon my source who says we're all utterly screwed is more reliable, don't you?'

'That data I've seen supports my view.'

Max gathered himself. 'You promised us mind-shielding that we will not get. You lied to us.'

Kirby didn't even flinch. 'I gave you the means to strike back. Maybe make the decisive break. Have you really no idea what bringing down the *Maputo* will do? Win the war, walk away a hero, alive and with your mind still your own. Without the upgrade, the stalemate continues and every pilot on this behemoth goes through the Fall before the war ends. My way, we have a chance so you have a chance too. Can you understand that?'

'I'm not here for me, sir. I want you to promise me you won't roll out this upgrade to the other squads. We had no choice. They deserve one.'

Kirby sighed. 'Your desire to save your girlfriend is very noble. I presume that's what this is really about?'

'So I care. So what?'

'Your request is noted. And now I have to go back to making the hard unpalatable choices that keep me awake all night.'

Max blinked. 'That's it?'

'What else were you expecting?' said Kirby shortly.

'I dunno… Some acknowledgement that you won't make the same mistake with the other squads.'

'What mistake?' snapped Kirby, then tensed, his face set.

'That…' The ExO's eyes betrayed him. 'You knew, didn't you? You knew all along.'

'Like I said: unpalatable choices. Drop it, Halloran. You're dismissed.'

'Probably not even impossible to retrofit, is it?' said Max, his face hot. Kirby stared at him, his expression cold. 'Fucking hell, I'm right, aren't I?'

'You really should have let Valera handle this. Goodbye, Max.'

CHAPTER 18

My mum kept on saying I never thought of anyone but myself.
Good career move as it turns out. MAXIMUS HALLORAN

Max started running the moment he reached the neck. There were more people about now as the *Heart of Granite* began to prepare for the new day, but the corridors were still quiet. With every step he tried to go faster, stretch his legs that little further and pump his arms a little harder.

The run was short and energising and he fetched up at the squad rack panting hard and feeling a little light-headed. His anger had been swallowed up by a kind of revolutionary excitement that quickened his pulse still further. He needed everyone out of their pods to hear how they'd been betrayed. He started by hammering on Valera's door.

'Skipper, get up, you've got to get up!'

He stepped away and hollered down the corridor. 'Inferno-X, get your arses out of bed! Up, up!'

Max snapped his fingers together and headed for the com panel near the dorm door. His finger was on the red alarm stud when Valera's voice stopped him.

'What the hell do you think you're doing?'

'He's throwing us away,' he said, spinning round and walking towards her, his mind so full of words he didn't know which to say first. 'He always knew there wouldn't be shielding.'

Valera stilled his words with a curt hand gesture.

'What did you do, Max?'

'I went to see him. I confronted the bastard.'

The blood ran from Valera's face. 'Oh, holy fuck. Who?'

'Kirby! That lying, seething bag of turd.'

'You fucking IDIOT!' Valera bellowed the word right into his face so loud he staggered back a pace.

'I... What? You wanted proof and I got it.'

Doors were starting to open along the corridor and bleary-eyed pilots were emerging, heading towards the shouting.

'No you didn't.' Valera pushed her hands through her hair then grabbed his shoulders. 'Why can't you ever listen?'

'I don't understand. We've got him, Skipper.'

'Got what, exactly?'

'Proof that he lied to us. Only there's more. He—'

'What does it matter?' spat Valera. 'You had to trust me to do what had to be done.'

'I couldn't sit around and wait for him to kill Anna-Beth,' he said.

'But instead you've confronted a senior officer and accused him of lying.' Valera's expression was draining the energy from him. 'I should have shackled you to your bed. Fucking hell.'

The dorm door smashed open and cracked against the wall and both Max and Valera backed away towards the squad room.

'What the fuck?' Stepanek demanded from behind them.

Hewitt, his face bruised and swollen but with an ugly smile on his face, walked in with six military police. Four of the Mips formed a barrier between Valera and Max and the rest of the squad. Two of them came past Hewitt and straight for Max.

'Get your fucking hands off me!'

'Shut up and walk out or we'll carry your thick arse out unconscious,' said Hewitt. 'It's up to you.'

'You're not silencing me. Your boss is a lying, treacherous scumbag and every pilot needs to know what he's doing!'

'Hold him,' ordered Hewitt.

The Mips, big men, grabbed an arm each and it was like being held by a pair of vices. Beyond them, Monteith, Kullani and Stepanek led a surge forwards. Zapons were enabled, their hiss malevolent.

'Let him go!' shouted Kullani. 'Skipper, they can't do this?'

Her call was taken up by the rest of the squad but Valera could only wearily order calm. Max stared at Hewitt as he tried in vain to break the grip of his captors.

'All I had to do was wait. I knew you'd louse up soon enough. Revenge is the sweetest thing.'

'I-X, listen to me,' said Max. 'Kirby's lying. It's not i—'

One of the Mips punched him in the stomach, winding him. Zapons whirred as I-X threatened the line. Hewitt moved in surprisingly quickly, a hypo stick in his right hand. Max aimed a kick at his groin but the desk polisher dodged it easily enough.

'Bye-bye, Halloran.' He jabbed the hypo into Max's shoulder and stepped back.

'Fuck you, Hewitt.' Max stared at I-X, straight into Anna-Beth's sheet-white face and wide, dark-rimmed eyes. He felt his strength flooding away and his mind begin to fade. 'You were right! Don't let them... Don't let them do it...'

As Max's eyelids drooped he saw Hewitt's fist fly towards his face. He didn't feel the impact.

The silence in the squad room was as complete as the din had been moments before. Confusion and anger warred as Max was dragged away, Hewitt hissing a threat into Valera's ear as he went. Valera waved the squad to follow her and she went and slumped in her chair, her head in her hands, hearing the others join her. There was a restless silence, broken by Monteith.

'Skipper?'

Valera raised her head and they were all staring at her, of course they were.

'Where's Anna-Beth?'

'I'm here,' she said.

Valera looked to her right and saw the distraught Hammerclaw pilot sitting on a chair with her knees pulled up to her chest. She was wearing some of Max's sweats.

'What happened last night?' asked Valera.

'He couldn't sleep. He got up at about half five for a coffee and never came back. I'm sorry, Skipper Orin.'

Valera held up her hands. 'Not your fault. "Headstrong" does not adequately describe our Max. Are you all right to stay? You're part of this now.'

Anna-Beth nodded.

'Try not to worry,' said Valera. 'He's in a shitload of trouble but none of it's terminal. I'll check in on the brig later.'

'Thank you.'

'No problem. All right, you lot, I'll tell you everything I'm allowed to and a couple of things that will not leave this squad room.'

Max had the most spectacular headache when he woke up. The rhythmic pain was intense enough to force him to keep his eyes closed, fearing what the light would do. It felt like his brain was trying to escape through the base of his skull.

He was lying on a pallet, which was something, and chose to stay still – might be best if everyone thought he was out cold. There was no rush, given the shit he was in, and anyway, he reckoned that if he moved his head at all, he'd probably puke.

The first thing that impressed itself upon him was the smell, or the combination of smells. For starters, it was fragrant though he couldn't identify it... sort of grassy or maybe it was the seaside. Whatever. But there was more to it; the faint scent of excrement underlying disinfectant; lingering old food and stale coffee as well. It told him that he wasn't in the brig... Maybe in medical?

It was quiet... There was music – violins and a piano – from somewhere, all very gentle and calming and with no chance of making any playlist of his until he was dead. And there were a few voices. Max listened harder, but it wasn't conversation.

Someone was mumbling incoherently – and sadly, from where Max was. Someone else was crying quietly. To his right there was rhythmic rustling and then a woman cleared her throat and turned the page of a book.

So, medical then. There was certainly plenty of light through his eyelids to support that view. And yet he still didn't open his eyes... It couldn't be medical, it didn't feel right. There was misery here. The crying briefly rose in volume and there was a moan of pain – of loss – within it.

Max's next breath caught in his throat and his eyes flew open to be greeted by a wash of bright and friendly colours. There was a mural on the ceiling, a pure blue sky across which beautiful white drakes flew. The walls to his left and right were bright yellow and painted with flowers and birds and grass, and the whole thing felt more like a child's nursery than the hideous dead end he knew it was.

Landfill.

'What the fuck am I doing in here?' he whispered, barely moving his lips.

Landfill, the end-of-life ward for drake pilots who had lost the fight against the Fall; it was the place to decline when heaters couldn't hide the signs any more and the pilot fell prey to the full and awful range of symptoms, both mental and physical. The Fall, which every drake pilot feared more than anything, but which they risked because flying a drake was a high like no other. Max, like every other pilot, had secretly believed he would be the one to beat the Fall or that he'd die a glorious death in the pouch long before it claimed him.

The pain in Max's skull was diminishing slowly but his anxiety was rising in its wake. He'd never been here before. No one ever came here unless they were dragged. This was where Kullani would end up, unless she managed to die on the wing and Max prayed that she would.

With a deep breath, Max hauled himself slowly up onto his elbows and then shuffled backwards against his headboard. He took in the cameras placed around the walls and in a central ceiling rose, and then edged his eyes around his surroundings as if moving them slowly would make his head hurt less.

The ward held twenty beds and, including his, nine were occupied. There were doors in three of the brightly coloured walls. Almost directly opposite him, an open door allowed a view of plants, warm lights and what looked like the edge of a fountain. To his left was a closed door with a single window letting him see enough to know it was the washroom. To his right was the big, solid door to the rest of the *HoG*. The floor was covered in rugs.

Max's pulse was uncomfortably high and he felt his horror rise as he gazed at his fellow inmates. There was no one in the beds adjacent to him and it looked as though all the current inmates had been placed to maximise individual space. Max was at one end of the rectangular ward.

Opposite him were two recumbent forms and he could see little of them. They were barely moving, suggesting they were catatonic, since sleeping only led to nightmares of blood and fire... or so they said. Down the left and right, where fourteen beds were split into two sets of seven, three were occupied on either side.

Closest to him, a woman was propped up reading a book, and to all intents and purposes looked entirely normal. She had a drink on her table, a pair of headphones over her ears and colour in her cheeks. Normal... only her legs twitched and quivered violently beneath the sheets and she cleared her throat every few seconds with an agonising rasp.

Beyond her, another woman lay looking away from him. She

muttered and moaned and waved imaginary things from before her eyes. And at the end of the left-hand beds, a man was sitting on the edge of his, staring down at his legs as if willing them to move while his hands and head shook.

Max had to drag his gaze to the other side. A woman lay on her side, face a rictus of terror while drool slipped from her mouth and her eyes searched everywhere and lit on nothing. Another lay flat on her back while her whole body shook. She cried out intermittently, demanding to see the sky and yelling warnings of the fire she imagined consumed her before lapsing into muttering. And there was a man staring straight at him, or straight through him, with eyes that were bottomless so lost was he.

Not one of them would be over twenty-seven, though they all looked so much older, with grey skin, hair loss and mouths filled with rotting teeth. It was impossible to imagine them as the fit, strong drake pilots they had been. That's what the Fall did.

Max's lower lip was trembling and he tried to still it, not wanting to break a sob. Here was his fate; the one he'd signed up for willingly because he, like all of them, didn't believe it would ever come to this. It was the one coming for Kullani right now and it would come for Anna-Beth too because he had failed her, failed them all. Stuck in here, Max could bellow about lies and deceit all he wanted. No one would listen, or care, because it was already too late.

So much wreckage, so much waste. So much unshakeable destiny.

Max drew his knees up to his chest and sobbed.

CHAPTER 19

How majestic the behemoths looked, gazing down on us tiny humans with their benevolent eyes. How graceful their movement and how welcoming their bones to the humans who rode within them. It should have been the beginning of an age of wonder. History will give it a far more damning title.

PROFESSOR HELENA MARKOV, CEO, ERCP

Flight deck alpha was busy with preparations for the day's sorties. All the drake squads were going out to scout, the basilisks were on a forward recon, and there were infantry ground exercises on the slate too. Orders were echoing out of loudspeakers and the activity in Flight Command was brisk and busy.

Grim walked over to Martha, pushing her arms into her bright yellow overalls, hearing the drake kicking at her pen and the metal reverberating to the blows

'What are you so ticked off about?' Grim zipped up her overalls and looked through the wide window. 'Restless for some action?'

It wasn't that, though. Drakes didn't exactly have a wide range of facial expressions but her body was tense and her eyes were wide and unhappy. Grim unlatched the pen door and closed it behind her before she turned to stroke Martha's cheeks. The drake raised her head and shook it gently.

'Missing your man, are you? Well, don't worry, he'll be down here any time. He'll be late of course but he wouldn't be Max otherwise, would he? Let me disconnect your tubes and we'll give you a good brush down, okay?'

Grim turned and pulled up abruptly. Flight Commander Moeller was at the side door to the tech area.

'Grimaldi.'

'Sir?'

'Can I come in?'

'Of course, sir. I'm just getting her ready, sir.'

'Yes, about that,' said Moeller, entering the pen.

Grim watched him, a frown on her face and knowing that no good was going to come of this encounter. She tried to think of any transgressions she'd made but there was nothing; certainly nothing that would require Moeller's personal attention.

'Can I help you, sir?' she asked.

He smiled rather sadly. 'No, I'm just here to pass on the news that Max won't be flying today and you should stand this drake down. You know the procedure.'

Martha's rear claw whacked against the back of the pen and she rattled fluid deep down in her throat. Moeller started and backed towards the door.

'She don't like bad news all that much.'

'Very funny, Grimaldi,' said Moeller, his face a little pale. 'If only they could talk, eh?'

'Why isn't Max flying, sir?'

'He's injured, in a non-flying incident,' said Moeller, too quickly.

'Which ward is he in, sir? I'll get off and see him.'

'He's not... Look, Grimaldi, I need to take the comparison readings from your data point.'

Grim felt as if she'd been slapped across the face. 'Why?'

Moeller tried a mollifying smile but it was weak. 'It's nothing to worry about. File work... you know.'

Grim shook her head, there were no good reasons he'd need

that data. She reached into her pocket, though, and proffered her access card.

'Here,' she said, her tone deliberately sullen. 'Sir.'

Moeller might have reacted badly but he merely nodded. 'Thanks, but I've brought the master key.'

'Then, with respect, why even ask me, sir?'

'Because I respect those who work for me and, more importantly, Grim, because you *need* to know. I hope you understand.'

Grim nodded and led the way to the data point, hooked to the pen by her small workstation and screen. She stood and watched while Moeller scanned his access card then downloaded the data set onto his p-palm. When he was done, he managed a curt nod before striding off.

Grim turned to watch him go and caught Valera's eye, leading a solemn Inferno-X along the flight deck. Valera's anger was apparent with every pace she took.

'What's going on, Skipper?' asked Grim.

'Kirby's goons took Max this morning.'

'Not injured then, like Moeller said.'

Valera shook her head. 'Well, Hewitt punched him but I doubt he felt it.'

'Why?'

'I don't want you to get involved in all this.'

Grim bridled and gestured behind her at Martha's pen. 'I'm already involved.'

'True. Risa can fill you in when we get back.'

Grim nodded. 'All right... Where is he?'

'I don't know. He's not in the brig... Wherever he is, we'll get him back. But he's in a shitload of trouble with command.'

'Be quick. You saw what Moeller did?' Grim jerked a thumb at Martha's data point.

'Took the latest readings?'

'Yes. Don't let them take Martha.'

Valera's expression hardened yet further. 'They'd be doing it over the cooling corpses of every member of Inferno-X.'

Grim smiled. 'Thanks, Skipper.'

Valera dragged her into an embrace. 'We'll work it out, but right now we've got to go. Look after Martha, okay?'

Valera led Inferno-X away towards the rest of the pens, each one of them patting Grim on the back, kissing her on the cheek or in Risa's case, enveloping her in a desperate hug. She watched them enter their individual pens before going back to try to placate an increasingly unhappy firedrake.

Max hadn't moved. He just stared at the ceiling. If he'd believed in any god he would have prayed for a swift end for the tortured souls in Landfill. Come to think of it, why had any of these pilots allowed themselves to be admitted and endure this agonising insanity? Anyone could opt to be euthanised.

To date, Max's short life had been crammed full of direction and focus. He'd never doubted his destination, whether it was to get a coffee, pursue a woman or become a drake pilot. But here, there was nothing for him to do, no way to move forward. The thought scared him more than he expected. He may not have been mad when he was dumped in here but it wouldn't take too long for him to become so.

Abruptly, renewed pain ricocheted around Max's skull. Different to that caused by the drug Hewitt had injected and far more acute. He cried out involuntarily and clutched the sides of his head, falling forwards onto his bed and gasping for breath. In his mind, he could hear screaming, wait... It wasn't screaming, it wasn't human at all. It was roaring and bellowing – the sound of anger and frustration and the hurt of being alone and left behind.

'Martha?' he managed.

The howling pain ceased as abruptly as it had begun, leaving him with hollow echoes of sadness and confusion. He lay stunned for a while.

'Don't be frightened by it.'

The even-toned woman's voice startled Max and he shot upright, almost falling off the bed. The woman with the twitching legs was looking at him.

'By what?'

She had a long, tired-looking face, deeply lined and framed by brown hair shot through with premature grey. She looked far older than she could possibly be.

'By hearing your drake in your head. It isn't what you think.'

'What makes you think that's what it was?'

She stared at him pointedly. 'I'm in Landfill? I know all the signs.'

'But I'm not going through the Fall.'

She smiled. 'I know. It was clear from the moment you woke up and kept your eyes closed while you tried to work out where you were. That's way too normal.'

Max nodded. 'Fair enough. Though you sound way too normal yourself.'

'Ah, well... Tell you what, come and sit with me and I'll tell you all about it. I'd come to you but my legs have minds of their own. Think I might have the op to still them, the drugs aren't working any more.'

Max walked over and sat on her bed. 'I'm Max Halloran,' he said. 'Inferno-X.'

She raised her eyebrows. 'Inferno-X, eh? You must have done something remarkably dim to get yourself chucked in here early. I'm Diana Kovlakis, formerly of Hammerclaw-K, now an incumbent of the home-from-home that is the Chronic Neural Trauma ward, aka Landfill.'

'Why aren't you shouting and beating the wall down? There's no way you need to be in here.'

'That is a lovely sentiment, Max Halloran... Hal-X, right? Yeah, heard of you vaguely. Big mouth, I heard.'

'Among other things,' said Max, cracking a smile at last.

'How old are you, Max?'

'Twenty-three.'

'Same as me, only I look fifty-three, don't I? S'all right, I'm past being upset by my wrinkles and grey hair. Let me tell you a little secret. You're feeling okay because you believe you'll get out of here. When you realise you won't, that's when the shouting starts.'

'But that doesn't explain why you're in here now. I get some of the others... but look at you...'

'Good days, bad days and mood stabilisers,' said Diana. 'They give us heaters too, but you have to be in here to get the treatment and believe me, I needed it. My mistake was thinking they'd let me go when I was stable again. Probably tells you how deluded I'd become.'

'No. Never going to happen, was it?'

Diana smiled. 'Well, I'm hardly an advert for Hunter Killer pilot recruitment, am I? I don't think I could cope on the outside now. Anyway I'm a research case, more useful to them here than out there. A lab rat, one in luxurious surroundings for a behemoth.'

'They can't do that.'

'Who's stopping them? We're where we are, no one can visit us, and we're so drugged half the time we can barely recall our names, let alone the affront to human rights that we represent.'

Max couldn't take it in. Everything he'd heard suggested no one went into Landfill until they were well into the decline... although Moeller was already interested in Kullani, so perhaps all he'd heard was wrong.

'But you're, you know... sane. Why can't you protest? Surely someone will listen.'

'I'm having a good day today and the balance seems to be right but it might not be like that tomorrow. Tomorrow I could be like Sarkovic or poor little Franny over there.' She pointed at two of the occupied beds. 'And even if I did protest, who's listening? Who cares? I'm here for the greater good. There's no danger of our protests being heard or leaked out, even if we voiced them. Can't have anyone learn the truth. Can't put off the recruits.'

'But they are trying to cure you, right?'

Another voice cut across the conversation, male this time, gruff and full of phlegm.

'Of course they bloody aren't. Why spend time tryin' to reverse somethin' that don't need reversin' and killin' us all in the process? Can't change evolution, brother.'

'What's he talking about?'

'The truth,' said Diana. 'But no one listens to us. We're insane. Apparently.' She rolled her eyes and flapped her hands.

Max smiled. 'I'm listening.'

'Hey, Leitch?' called Diana to the man. 'You solid?'

'Fuckin' legs stopped workin' and I'm freezin'. Hot head, but not hot enough to move the old pins. Yeah, I'm solid, my Grecian goddess of love.'

'He's a real charmer,' said Diana quietly. 'Luckily his paralysis stops him acting out the cruder of his fantasies. Mind you, I've paid him a visit every now and again. The treatments do amazing things for your libido.'

'That's the awful truth? Fall drugs make you desperate for sex?'

Diana barked a laugh. 'It's the best and worst side effect.'

'So what is the truth? You want me to guess?'

'No. She wants me to tell you. Sayin' the words gives her the shakes,' said Leitch.

Apparently even thinking about it was enough to make Diana's hands shake. Her smile was suddenly thin and fragile.

'Good days and bad days,' she said. 'Sometimes on the same day.'

She turned back to her book without another word, though her hands were shaking enough that reading must surely be difficult. Max looked over at Leitch, who still sat in the same place. He looked awful. Pasty skin, a bad case of the shakes and straggly blond hair, most of which had fallen out. He could pass for fifty but he was probably no more than mid-twenties. He saw Max staring.

'Treatment does it,' he said. 'Ages you faster n' a drake can fly. I could do with some help gettin' into bed. I'm cold, brother.'

'Sure.' Max patted Diana's twitching legs and walked round to Leitch's bed. He was already shuffling himself towards his pillows and Max moved his legs up onto the mattress and helped him under the sheets. 'All right?'

'Thanks, brother.' He held out a shaking hand which Max grasped in both of his. It was warm to the point of sweaty. 'Dylan Leitch, Flamehawk-G. I know who you are, I was listenin'.'

'Good to meet you. That's two of you in here who are pretty, you know...'

'Sane... lucid?' Leitch nodded. 'Bit of a coincidence, eh? Not.'

Leitch had wide, wild eyes and his smile was unsettling. Perhaps 'sane' was an exaggeration. He stared at Max for a long blink. Eventually, Max shrugged.

'Go on, then, spill it.'

'Where to start?' He eyed Max suspiciously. 'Can I trust you?'

'Well, I've been dumped in here because I called Kirby a lying sack of shit, does that help?'

'Whoa... You know you're never gettin' out of here, right?'

'Why not?'

'They mus' already think you've sussed too much. I'm about to tell you the rest. If they were goin' to let you go, they wouldn't let us talk to you, brother.'

Max had to fight to ignore that logic and to remain believing Valera and Inferno-X would see him safely back to the squad rooms.

'Then there's no harm in telling me everything, is there?' he said.

'Guess not.' He reached out and gripped Max's shoulders. 'The Fall don't kill you.'

'Bullshit. I saw it happen yesterday. Drake fell right out of the sky. Bang!'

'That's only 'cos the poor unfortunate was in the air when they fell. Listen, you don't have to believe me. I'm in the Fall now, right? Talkin' rubbish and descendin' to gibber and drool. S'okay, I get it. But you're goin' to find out I'm right. When you've begun the Fall proper, it's takin' you from your drake makes you sick, and the drugs they give you in here speed you along graveyard road.'

Max shook his head. 'No... it's not like that. They take over your mind until you're not you any more. We all know that and we still fly. We all want to believe anything that would let us fly for longer but the facts are the facts.'

'No. That's what they want you to believe. When you get in here you know it's a lie 'cos of all the things you heard and felt before they put you in here. And you should worry, 'cos they will treat you even though you ain't sick yet, 'cos they need you to get sick to prove their lie.'

Max swallowed hard. 'They can't do that to me.'

'You heard Diana, they can do whatever the fuck they want. You do believe me, don't you?'

'About what?'

'About the Fall.'

'I don't know what to believe any more.'

'Well, you have to believe *me*,' said Leitch. 'Look at me. Look at Diana. Not quite as mad as you assumed we'd be, eh? That's proof, that is. The Fall's not a disease, brother, it's... progress.'

'*What?*'

'They link our minds and our bodies,' said Leitch. 'The drakes know it, they soothe our minds when the change starts and the heaters keep our bodies on the level. They talk to us, tell us it's goin' to be all right.'

'So why did I see a pilot Fall yesterday? Explain that.'

Leitch shrugged. 'You can't refuse to fly. Jus' bad timin', I guess.'

Max wanted to laugh right in Leitch's face. Tell him he sounded exactly as insane as everyone assumed those in Landfill were. But there was such belief in him. His eyes shone with it. The poor man was completely lost. Wasn't he?

'Drakes can't talk.' It was all Max could find to say.

'Yes they can,' whispered Diana, making Max start. 'It starts with empathy. Sharing their emotions. But to begin with you don't believe it. You think it's you going insane but really it's the beginning. You and your drake becoming like one.'

'That's just a myth,' said Max quietly. 'You know that deep down, right?'

'I know that's what I used to think,' said Diana.

'But you don't know and we do,' said Leitch, his tone impatient. 'Why is it so hard to believe? You feel your drake all the time and we saw what happened to you just now. It's no stretch for the emotions to become words and images you can understand.'

'What do they tell you?' asked Max, hating himself for starting to believe them.

Leitch glanced at Diana, who had retreated back into herself, her shaking hands and her book. 'That the only way you'll both survive is to go through the Fall.'

'No way. They tested it in the early days. Every jockey died with the drakes. Every time. No one's mind or body is strong enough.'

'Then they researched it wrong. You'll know it for sure when they re-engineer your drake. The pain, brother… What you felt just now was like a splinter in your hand. S'like someone rippin' out a part of you because that's jus' what they're doin'. And you know your link with your drake? That's what they steal from you when you get in here. S'what does your mind and body in and sends you into a tailspin to the grave.'

Leitch whistled and whirled his fingers, crashing them into his sheets to illustrate his words.

Max was battling hard to maintain a sense of balance. Everything Leitch said would mark him as losing his mind but he said it with *such* clarity, *such* passion it was hard not to believe him.

'Why don't you tell them? Make them do the research?'

'You think we haven't?' said Diana. 'We know what's going on here, the other agenda. Having lab rats.'

'Yeah, but Leitch said they were trying to reverse the effects in you. Surely that's an attempt to cure you?'

'No,' said Diana and there were tears on her cheeks. 'Just to find ways to keep you flying for longer when the first symptoms of the Fall start.'

Max shook his head. 'You're wrong on this one, really. I mean, the only drug that works is heaters, right? And it's illegal. That's going to apply to anything that blocks the Fall. They're too scared of the consequences of apparent sudden onset.'

The thought brought Kullani to mind and he feared for her if he didn't get out. Feared that she'd be in here with him all too soon.

'Tell yourself what you like,' said Diana. 'We were like you, don't forget that. We believed the medics in here were soothing ruined minds. But we know what the drugs do. Trouble is, if we complain that we're lab rats all that happens is the medics say we're paranoid.'

'I believe you.' Max found himself saying.

'Yeah, it's a great side effect of our agonisin' deaths, ain't it? So much experimentation and all measured through here.' Leitch turned his head and pushed some of his remaining hair aside to reveal a chip embedded in the base of his skull behind his right ear.

Max frowned. 'And they've been doing this the whole war?'

'Suppose,' said Leitch, his shrug more of a shudder.

'So what are they doing with all the data? I mean, unless I'm missing something, any research has led to absolutely fuck all legal treatment so far.' As soon as he said it, Max sucked in a quick breath. 'Bloody hell.'

Leitch was staring at him, his eyes dancing in their sockets as he tried to maintain concentration. 'You got clarity, brother?'

'Yeah... Just something someone said to me.' Max tried to recall everything Krystyna and the heater girls had told him. It all fitted together. 'The black market drug makers and the ERC are colluding.'

'Wow,' said Leitch, his eyes steadying. 'There's more to all this than they'll ever let on, I reckon. Makes me wonder what really landed you in here. Got too close to somethin', didn't you?'

'They lied about our latest sentience upgrade, risking every pilot on my squad. I found out the truth. If that upgrade goes to every squad it'll be three to a bed in here.'

'Holy fuck.'

'Yeah.' Max got up.

'Where are you going?'

'I need to think. Decide if I believe everything you've told me.'

'I feel sorry for you, Max. You'll never experience the real joy... You'll never really become a pilot.'

'What are you on about?'

Leitch's expression was almost happiness.

'There's this moment, the breakthrough... when the voice in your head makes sense. It's the day the fear lifts and you realise the heaters might have checked your symptoms but didn' slow the change and actually, that's jus' fine. That whoever invented heaters knew exactly what they were doin' and that if you and your drake could only escape, you could become somethin' greater than you ever imagined.'

'I have to get out of here,' said Max.

Max lay in his bed and stared at the images of drakes on the ceiling. He had no idea what time of day it was and that was unsettling for a military man for whom time and routine were everything. Well, routine, anyway; he'd never been that great with time.

A little while later, a medic came through the ward, dishing out food and drugs which those who were conscious had taken dutifully.

'No point in not,' Leitch said, grimly. 'Or they knock you out and give you 'em anyways.'

'Do the pills help?'

'Sometimes,' Leitch said and then turned his attention to the medic. 'You know there's nothin' wrong with him, right?'

The medic said nothing but paused fractionally as he administered an injection to one of the more advanced cases.

'Come on, Barney, you're a proper human. Not like some of the twats you work with. Can you really let a fit man get ruined? I'm tellin' you, you'll never sleep properly again.'

Barney's big frame stiffened and his friendly brown eyes flicked to Max. He gave Max a long look before moving on, his movements less assured. It wasn't much, but it was something.

Max refused food and drink, mistrustful of what they might be concealing, and when Barney left, he wandered around his new home instead. It was impressive, he gave it that. There were places to sit in peace among plants and water features; a small library; a vid screen and film library; hydrotherapy pool; a music room and three well-appointed single rooms. They were all occupied and Max realised they were also fully soundproofed. The glimpse he got of the inmates was profoundly depressing.

Max's bed seemed the safest place to stay, though he guarded himself against sleep. He monitored the quiet whirring of cameras moving and zooming in and out, trying to gauge if there was a pattern. He noted the passage of medics in and out, sometimes with guards, more often without. He was hungry and thirsty and he used the discomfort to keep him sharp as he did on a long return leg from a sortie.

The moment he thought about the joy of flying, and that it would be denied him forever, despair hit him like falling rock. It crushed him and his calm and focus. His future was gone – he'd be forced to endure being killed slowly and painfully in the name of research.

'Get it now, don't you, Max?' said Diana from the gloom.

'Yeah,' said Max. 'I get it. I have got to get out of here. Put all this straight for all of us.'

'That's just a dream,' said Diana.

'I don't dream, I do. I'm Max fucking Halloran.'

It was probably the first time real laughter had been heard in Landfill.

Valera had forbidden all talk of Max during the sortie. Closed squad com or not, if the brass really wanted to listen in, they could. She'd issued a no-deviation standard landing procedure order but had felt the weight of discontent. God knew she wanted to make a statement too but now was not the time.

Once they were all showered, their suits washed and hung and their energy drinks and pills downed, they gathered in the squad room with the *HoG*'s com disabled and the whole dorm swept for bugs. It was useful to have an electro-head like Calder on the squad sometimes.

'You're wasted as a pilot,' said Gurney.

'You're so right,' said Calder. 'I often dream of building my own super-robot so I can crush your puny lizards and mince your skulls inside the scaly remains.'

'You're a freak,' said Redfearn.

'And you are right to fear me, mortal.'

'Let's get to it,' said Valera. 'Moan away and then I'll tell you why everything I did was right and everything you wanted to do was wrong.'

'We should have made a statement on the flight deck,' said Kullani. 'Lined up in front of Martha's pen and stared until the gallery fell down. Something to let them know we won't accept this.'

'We should have refused to fly without him,' said Stepanek. 'He stood up for us and we have to support him.'

'Stepanek's right,' said Gurney. 'Flying without Max is wrong.'

'We don't even know where he is,' said Redfearn.

'It stinks, Skipper, and we're doing nothing,' said Monteith.

Valera heard them all out before she spoke.

'I'm as angry as you are but we have to be careful. I love your idea, Risa, but all it does is draw unwanted attention. Stepanek, if we strike they can hit us with insubordination, and then we can't help Max. Reds, I agree: we have to know what we're up against. We know Moeller took a data dump from the pen today; that's the first step to grounding him and re-engineering Martha. I hope it's just a threat.'

She paused to consider her next words. 'Look, I'm in a horrible place here and if I haven't misjudged him, Moeller's in a worse one. However fucked up it seems to be, we have to respect the chain of command. Max is wherever the hell he is because he didn't. While we should never over-estimate our importance, we are Inferno-X. If the Exec won't give us Max back, we'll leak everything we know and let the backlash do the job for us.'

Valera stopped talking at a sharp hand gesture from Salewski, who was positioned closest to the dorm door.

'Got a visitor,' he said.

There was a decisive rap on the door, and Valera nodded to Salewski to let whoever it was in. It was relief that quickly became concern when they saw Grim's face.

'It's Max,' she said. 'They've put him in Landfill.'

The silence was complete enough that they could hear the *Heart of Granite* breathe.

'They've fucking what?' growled Stepanek.

'Are you sure?' asked Valera, feeling cold all over.

Grim nodded. 'A mate up in medical saw them taking him in. There's nothing to stop them now, is there? They could take Martha and leave Max to rot. What's going on, Skipper?'

'Right.' Valera stood up. 'This is a clear breach of crew rights, detention regulations, and charge protocol – and I can take it to the ExO. I'm sure he'll be expecting me.'

'Want some backup?' asked Stepanek. 'I mean, he's dumped one of us in there...'

Valera nodded into the calls of support for Stepanek's idea. 'Witnesses are a good idea. Monts, Palant, Calder, Gurney, you're with me. Stepanek, you're in charge in my absence. Sit tight and don't say a word about Max until I find out why the hell he's in there in the first place and I shudder to think of the lie I'm about to be told. Grim, give Martha the most detailed brushing and cleaning she's ever had. Keep her fed too, know what I mean?'

'Sure thing, Skipper,' said Grim.

'Reds, Xavier... probably time you had one-to-ones with your flight crew, make sure they keep eyes on Martha too, okay?'

'Any of you wondering if there's more to the marshal gen's visit than meets the eye?' asked Nevant.

'Could be a coincidence,' said Palant.

'I'm a drake pilot,' said Valera. 'I don't do coincidences.'

CHAPTER 20

When criticised about the way countries were invited to join United Europa, the first president elect, Maria Deschamps, was reported as saying: 'We were fair, and we offered them a choice: join on our terms or be invaded.' I'd love that to be true.

ALEXANDRA SOLOMON, MARSHAL GENERAL,
UNITED EUROPA JOINT FORCES

The door to Kirby's quarters was open and he was behind his desk when Valera walked in. He nodded as if he'd been expecting her and gestured her to the seat in front of his desk. She shook her head curtly.

'Close the door behind you, at least,' he said.

'I've got some of my squad out there. I want them to hear us.'

Kirby shrugged. 'Bring them in.'

Valera waved her people in and they arranged themselves around the wall, Calder closing the door behind her.

'I won't tolerate interruptions,' said Kirby. 'Only Orin speaks. Squadron Leader, when you're ready.'

'First of all, I accept that Max was out of line to come to you.'

'Out of line does not scratch the surface of his insubordination or his unfounded accusations. It did illustrate his state of mind, though.'

Valera paused, wondering what Kirby meant by that last statement. 'Nonetheless, Max Halloran is being held in La— the Chronic Neural Trauma ward, which is not a designated detention area for non-medical cases. It breaches seven articles of Halloran's rights to counsel, pre-hearing visits and living conditions. He must be released from the ward immediately.'

For a moment, Valera thought Kirby was going to applaud her. 'Your grasp of regulations is second to none.'

'It's always an advantage to be well-informed. Release my pilot, sir.'

'And that's why I always am.' He tapped his screen twice and Valera's p-palm beeped an incoming message. 'Max Halloran is in Landfill because he's going through the Fall.'

'Bullshit.'

The quartet behind her gasped and Kirby fired a warning glance in their direction.

'Read the tech debrief. It includes vids of Halloran. Perhaps you'd like to see them now?'

Kirby turned his screen and tapped an icon to show two short clips. One was of Max in tears, staring into space, another was of him clutching his head and shouting, though there was no audio.

'These are out of context, sir. I'd shout and scream too, if I were in there for no reason. If you maintain he's going through the Fall then I demand a retest, which I will attend.'

'Don't make me laugh, Orin. We both know what any retest will reveal.'

Valera dug her nails into her palms. 'Are you implying, in front of these witnesses, that the result is predetermined?'

Kirby leaned back in his chair. 'I'm implying nothing of the kind. But tread carefully. Your new upgrade has thrown up some very interesting data. Makes a few of you borderline cases already.'

Valera waved a hand at her pilots for quiet while fighting for control herself.

'Please don't threaten us, sir. You may not place a pilot in

Landfill without following the proper legal procedures; hence I will be bringing charges against you for these breaches. I will be taking this matter to higher authorities as a matter of extreme urgency.'

Kirby shrugged. 'Go ahead, Orin. You have the file. I'll even set up appointments for you. Who would you like to see? Avery? Solomon? It won't help – whatever you think you know about the upgrade and its mind-shielding issues, it *will not* become ship-wide knowledge. It *will* roll out to other squads. Don't risk ending up like Halloran.'

Valera shook her head and hoped Calder's device was recording the whole conversation. 'This is only the start. I'm getting Max back, and I'm coming for you unless you come clean about the mind-shielding you promised us.'

'There are some things you should understand,' said Kirby, unfazed by Valera's charges. 'Drake pilots are the most talented of the lower ranks and you have tough contracts, but ultimately you have no real power or influence. You are military personnel and you will follow orders or be suspended for insubordination. Get back to your pit, Orin. You can file your charges from there. They will be given full consideration in due course. Inferno-X is confined to quarters and on coms lockdown until the attack on the *Maputo*. Dismissed.'

The lights were up, the fountains were on and the piped music was playing. The *Heart of Granite* was moving so the day's sorties hadn't begun yet. It was most likely still early because the *Granite* didn't travel too much in the heat of the day, preferring night-travel despite the chill making the beast a little sluggish of mind. *Heart of Granite* command could then let her bask, with her solar panels glittering and outer armour retracted, when the sun was high.

Max yearned to be with his squad, it was another punch to his bruised spirit. He still hadn't eaten but he'd drunk from the fountain. It was stale and recycled but probably free of drugs, and he was in a recliner in the garden sifting through potential escape plans when Leitch's coughing alerted him to a visitor.

Max had been wrestling with the problem of the only door out. Whenever it was open, it was guarded by at least two orderlies, often three. Three was too many for Max to both surprise and take down; two was marginal at best. He'd dismissed taking a medic hostage. His only realistic chance was to rush the guards and get clear, which was insanely risky, or plead with Barney who was the most likely candidate to give him some help. The trouble was, Landfill was for sick and desperate pilots. No doubt there had been escape attempts before.

Max was expecting the visitor to be a medic but the harsh voice demanding his whereabouts told him it was Hewitt, no doubt come to crow. Kirby's toerag sauntered in flanked by Mips. He fingered plant leaves and dipped his fingers in the fountain pool, shaking them extravagantly when he removed them and scattering drips everywhere. He smelled his fingers.

'I wouldn't drink that. It stinks,' he said, walking over towards Max. 'Still, desperate times and all that.'

'Anything you wouldn't do is automatically a good thing,' said Max, putting his hands behind his head. 'Make yourself comfortable, Hewitt, take the weight off all that bruising.'

'You're not looking so pretty yourself,' said Hewitt, remaining standing.

'You punch like a child,' said Max. 'What do you want?'

'Just checking you're enjoying your new home and making friends, not that they'll remember your name for too long. Mind you, neither will you.'

'Fuck off, Hewitt, I'm busy.' Max's brain was wired with Hewitt's words and his pulse raced. *Bloody hell.*

'So I can see. I also have some news.'

Max shrugged.

'Time's almost up, Halloran. We're just a couple of signatures away from re-engineering your drake. "Martha", isn't it? How sweet that you named her. Soon she'll be a blank brain and so much malleable muscle for a new pilot.'

Max clung to his calm. 'And you think that will anger me? You need Martha for a new pilot. Make sure it's someone worthy of her scales.'

'It's tough, you know? Without the proper medical withdrawal process, when we wipe your scaly girlfriend, your brain will suffer enough trauma to kick you into terminal decay. Hard way to go.'

Max smiled and met Hewitt's eyes for the first time.

'I'm going to get out of here, and I'm going to come and find you.'

Hewitt curled his lip. 'You still haven't grasped it, have you, Max? You're in here. You're already dead. Maybe this will help you understand – it'll be in everyone's inbox in a couple of days. It's rather good, I think.'

Hewitt took a square of paper from his thigh pocket, unfolded it and laid it on Max's chest.

'Perhaps someone can help you with the big words.'

'You get funnier every day.' Max picked up the paper and his sneer fell from his face. Hewitt was already halfway towards the door as Max let the paper drop. He didn't need to read past the headline.

Top pilot in Fall shock – Tragically early exit for call sign Hal-X, the finest ever Inferno jock – An obituary by Squadron Leader Valera Orin

Standard procedure, he knew, but it struck him hard.

'I will not die in here,' he whispered. 'Don't forget me, Skipper.'

Valera led the team back towards the squad dorm. The pace of events was cranking up and one slip now could mean Max and Martha were lost for ever.

'Reds, get everyone back to the squad rack. Calder, clean up that recording and hide copies absolutely bloody everywhere. I'll join you shortly – I need to see Moeller. And none of you say a word to anyone about anything, got it?'

At the base of the neck, Valera headed towards Flight Command, dropping down through the decks to enter the flight deck area as publicly as possible. Kirby would assume she'd try and see Moeller and she'd hate to disappoint the ExO. She walked across the centre of flight deck alpha, climbing the stairs to Flight Command. Even from a distance, she could see Moeller's office was empty.

'Hey, Yarif, where is he?' she demanded of his assistant, a perpetually harassed-looking young man who was unbelievably efficient and destined for great things in military administration.

'Got a call then headed out looking angry,' said Yarif, barely looking up from his screen. 'Dammit, why do people think his every free moment needs to be filled with a meeting? See this? "Monthly debrief on moral and ethical standards adherence". For fuck's—'

'My heart bleeds. When will he be back? I need to see him urgently.'

'It was the ExO who called him, they had a fraught conversation, then he hurried off. Apparently, that shouldn't surprise you.'

Valera sighed. 'No, it doesn't. But when will he be back?'

'Soon, I hope.'

'I'm back,' said Moeller from behind Valera. 'Come into my office.'

Valera followed him in and closed the door behind her. Through the glass wall panels she could see the eyes of at least half the Flight Command staff on the office. She wondered how much they knew and how much was still just rumour.

'I need your support,' said Valera before Moeller had reached his desk. 'Kirby is holding Max in Landfill in breach of five separate regulations. You cannot let that stand.'

Moeller held up his hands. 'Let's take this one step at a time, all right? It's a complex situation.'

'It's a simple issue of false imprisonment, sir.'

Moeller pointed at various icons on his screen while he spoke. 'There's the tech debrief report and brain pattern assessment saying he's begun the Fall. There's confronting a senior offer within his own quarters and making wild accusations. There's vid. It's compelling stuff.'

'It's complete fiction. Just like your promise to include shielding on the latest upgrade. Kirby has confirmed we aren't getting it because it's actually impossible to retrofit. Presumably he expects us to die in the pouch before any charges against him are considered. Again and again he's lied to us. And to you, sir.'

Moeller punched up the tech debrief and scanned it. 'Kirby told me you dropped by. You're not doing yourself any favours by bringing charges against him. But of course you know that.'

'What should I do, sit back while Kirby destroys the *HoG*'s best pilot and drake? Not to mention Max is a personal friend of mine, not to mention he's my fucking pilot, not to mention he's *your* fucking pilot. Why won't you look at me? He's sentenced me and my squad to death into the bargain. Has he got to you as well?'

'I resent that remark, squadron leader.' Moeller looked up from the screen. 'Max is a valuable member of the flight team and I have not turned my back on him.'

'So what *are* you doing? *You* took the data point reading from Martha's pen, sir. It certainly looks like you've turned your back on us.'

'It's protocol to take a data point comparison when pilots behave erratically, whether they return to duty or not. You know that.'

'With respect, sir, you're hiding behind regulations. It's time to decide what you really care about: your crew or your bosses.'

'It's not that simple.'

'Yes it is. Pick Solomon and the ExO and Max will die in Landfill. Then, inevitably, so does the rest of I-X. Pick Max and no one knows you gave me anything. You *know* Max isn't Falling.'

Moeller held her gaze. He said nothing and she understood that he couldn't. But he closed the data file and rubbed his hands together.

'I understand you're being confined to your squad rooms. You'd better go.'

'Tough course you're navigating, sir,' said Valera. 'Don't let the tide push you on to the rocks. Max needs you. I-X needs you.'

Moeller rubbed a hand across his clean-shaven chin. 'I will do everything in my power to secure Max's release. But it doesn't look good. The evidence against him appears solid, the signatories are in place and the wheels of drake decommissioning are ready to roll. If you or your squad take pre-emptive action you're liable to end up in there with him.'

'Kirby is lying, sir. And he laid that threat at my door too and I simply don't believe it. At least force a retest. Max is entitled to it – and protocol requires one now I've requested it.'

Moeller nodded and the ghost of a smile crossed his lips. 'Leave that with me. I'll see it happens.'

'Don't leave us wondering in the squad room,' said Valera.

'If you're right and the evidence against Max is fabricated then his allegations still have to be contained and dealt with by the executive. I will not have my pilots inciting a riot on this behemoth. Do you understand?'

'How long I keep my counsel depends on Max's chances.'

Moeller nodded. 'Fair enough. Dismissed.'

'Sir.'

Valera walked through the bustle and noise on the *Heart of Granite*. There were more Mips on duty than normal, or maybe Valera was just more sensitive to them. Every man and woman on duty seemed to be watching her.

Gargan's was already busy. She lost herself in the crowd for a moment, seeing life on the behemoth going on as normal. And it made her angry. It was weird to experience clarity in a stew of alcohol, thumping music and a press of bodies. Just a couple of days ago, they'd celebrated victory over the Sambas and seeing the marshal gen safely aboard.

Now their world had gone to shit. She had no choice but to trust Moeller for now. But would he do anything when push came to shove? Valera was sceptical.

While there were no Mips actually guarding the squad rack, there might as well have been. Valera smiled sweetly at the pair leaning against the corner of a corridor a few metres up. It was a pathetic attempt at nonchalance.

'If you're being all undercover and stuff, at least wear casual clothes,' she called.

The moment she opened the door, she was greeted by angry voices from the rec. She blew out her cheeks and listened for a few moments.

'Half of them would join us in a strike,' said Redfearn.

'Wouldn't matter if they did,' said Nevant. 'A strike? You're dreaming. They'd shoot the lot of us rather than tolerate a walk-out.'

'They wouldn't dare,' said Monteith. 'Take out half the drake squads? I don't think so.'

'Monts is right,' said Redfearn. 'They won't line us up, but one by one we'd all end up like Max. There has to be another way.'

'Storm the med centre, like I said,' said Stepanek. 'Get a guard on Martha too. Get Max back.'

'You're all missing the point,' said Gurney. 'The Exec is set against Max. We're watched, so is Martha. Some big gesture might make us feel better, but if we want to help Max, we have to be a whole lot smarter and more subtle.'

A chorus of shouts poured scorn on Gurney's words. Enough. Valera walked into view, her presence inspiring instant quiet.

'So this is revolution central, is it?' she asked. There was a smattering of awkward laughter. 'I wish I had good news to report but I don't. First, secure all thoughts of an uprising. Moeller has agreed to try and force Max's release. He's going down the retest route. Meanwhile, hard though it is, we have to sit tight and wait. But that doesn't mean we can't plot our endgame.'

There were various grudging grunts of agreement.

'Then gather round and let's see…'

'So she came to you, too?' Kirby marched into Moeller's office despite the closed door, and the meeting he was holding with his senior staff. 'Your meeting's over. Get out.'

Moeller was sitting at the head of his table and had his back to Kirby. He made sure his people saw his expression before nodding. He stayed seated. 'Last one out, close the door.'

When he heard the click, he pushed back his chair and stood. Kirby was by his desk, drumming his fingers on the edge, impatient and irritable. A normal day for him, then.

'You will never speak to me in front of my staff in that manner again. I do not report to you, I do not tug my forelock to you and I do not appreciate being dragged into the great pit of dung you're digging.'

Kirby cleared his throat and strode towards the gallery windows overlooking the quiet flight deck.

'Did she come to you?' he asked again.

'Take a wild guess,' said Moeller, not joining him. 'How do you plan to deal with it?'

'It's done. Halloran is finished.'

Moeller adopted a neutral expression.

'So, Solomon, Markov and Avery have all signed off on effective murder of our finest ever drake pilot?'

'The marshal general and the president agree that the issues at stake outweigh the loss of one pilot.'

Moeller raised his eyebrows. 'And in doing so you will earn the mistrust of Inferno-X, the undying hatred of Valera Orin and every squadron leader fearing being undermined. I could go on, but that little list describes a behemoth's Exec failing in its core duty and all because you lied without thought to the likely result of its inevitable exposure. Why didn't you come to me?'

'I don't need your agreement,' said Kirby, a sneer on his face.

'Not for my agreement, you idiot, for advice from the only man on the Exec who knows how to handle pilots. You sat in the meeting and you lied to me, to Avery and to Valera. You made me repeat a lie to Inferno-X and, as a result, a dangerous and untested upgrade is in place. And instead of admitting your error, you've made Max a scapegoat to keep everyone else in line. Didn't work, did it? You should have come to me.'

Kirby's face was all belligerent outrage. 'All right. And what do you suggest, in your wisdom?'

'I'm ordering a retest on Max and it will prove he isn't Falling.' Moeller held up his hand to still Kirby's protestation. 'You cannot prevent me from doing so. Sell it to Max as a change of heart. Get him onside. Try a little honesty, you'll be amazed how often that works. Don't toss him on the scrapheap because he knows a truth.'

'Are you kidding?' Kirby's face was incredulous. 'The boy's a flying genius with a big mouth and a little knowledge; and that's a poisonous combination – especially when he's just discovered a few principles. He can't keep his mouth shut, and I do not want a hundred angry drake pilots lining up outside my door demanding answers I cannot give them. You're being naïve, Moeller, and even if you weren't, it's out of our hands.'

'No it isn't. He's our pilot on our behemoth. I don't care who's exerting pressure, this isn't happening. You need to stop it.'

Kirby shook his head. 'There's a world outside the *Granite* and Max made too much noise. Solomon and Corsini want him silenced. So go get your retest, it won't change a thing. We're fighting a war and sometimes it requires unpalatable decisions and dangerous conditions. We have to win and win fast. No one can get in the way of that.'

'I used to think there was more to you than this,' said Moeller, and he felt genuinely sad at the death of their friendship. 'You've become exactly what you used to decry.'

'We all have our masters. Yours is Avery, mine is further up the chain. I can live with that.'

Moeller felt a chill run down his spine. 'Avery doesn't know about Halloran's situation, does she? The truth, I mean. How did you pull that off?'

Kirby's face was stone. 'Commander Avery is aware that Halloran is going through the Fall, so has reluctantly signed the necessary releases. It would be a grave mistake for anybody to give her any contrary information now or in the future.'

'Wow,' said Moeller. 'Drawing up battle lines, aren't we?'

'Move on,' said Kirby. 'This is finished. We're re-engineering Halloran's drake tomorrow, as soon as her digestive tract is empty. Max has his first treatment at pretty much the same moment.'

'You'll burn for this,' said Moeller.

'I doubt that. You've picked the wrong side. I'm sure the undying respect of your pilots helps you sleep but you should be looking ahead. When the war is done, who's going to reward you for your loyalty to them?'

CHAPTER 21

The need for alternative energy changed the global landscape. Wind harvesters ploughed the heavens, their kilometres-long cables tethering them to earthbound batteries; every roof glittered with solar panels; coasts were awash with tidal generators. But biofuels could not hold sway in the fields when so many billions needed food. The war began for land. Land to feed your own and damn the rest.

PROFESSOR JULIA NICHOLLS –
WHEN THE EARTH STOPPED GIVING

It was plain none of the squad trusted him and Moeller was comfortable with that, or so it looked to Valera. The Mips would report it, but there were a hundred reasons for him to visit a squad in isolation. It meant Inferno-X could see his eyes. Valera was quietly impressed but she regarded him with a healthy suspicion nonetheless.

'Get Flight Commander Moeller a coffee, Stepanek.'

'How do you take it, sir?' asked Stepanek.

'White, no sugar,' said Moeller.

Valera indicated a chair. 'Take a seat, sir.'

Moeller sat and was followed by the rest of the squad, crowding close and staring at him like he was a zoo exhibit. Stepanek handed him his coffee and Valera could see that Moeller was not about to deliver positive news, it was just a question of how bad.

'So, we're honoured,' said Valera. 'You know that fraternising with Inferno-X currently carries a health warning?'

'I think I'm already infected by implication.' He sipped his coffee, nodding appreciatively though it was sure to be as crap as everyone else's. Then he set it down. 'Listen closely. I trust you all and I want your confidence in return. Your friend and my pilot, Max Halloran, is in deep, deep trouble and all official channels to help him are closed, all file work is complete. There is nothing I can do. At dawn tomorrow, assuming the data point calculations are correct, his drake will be re-engineered. That is all the time we have to save both drake and pilot.'

'So we break him out,' said Stepanek into the shocked silence. 'Storm the fucking place.'

'And what then?' said Moeller quietly. 'He'll be a fugitive and you'll all be criminals. Think what would happen to all of you.'

'Then we strike. Other squads will support. Show Kirby we won't fight until Max is freed,' said Redfearn.

'And what then?' repeated Moeller. 'Kirby's orders are still carried out, and one by one, you're all disciplined for insubordination. Only the strike against the *Maputo* is keeping us from beelining to the Vermelho Sea right now, for a regeneration cycle. If you strike, we'll pass the *Maputo* baton to the *Steelback*, the *Flinthorn* and the *Ironclaw*. Then what leverage do you have? You'll destroy yourselves and Inferno-X. This is still a war.'

Valera found herself fighting a rising despair and Moeller's deconstruction of their options merely deepened it.

'We have to do something,' she whispered. 'What can we do?'

'Tread carefully. I am neither deaf nor blind on this behemoth, much as our ExO loves to think I am. Max has the very slightest opportunity and he'll have to see it and act on it. If he does, he'll need help. Any contacts you have need to be ready to make him disappear in about three hours.'

'We can do that,' said Valera. 'What is it that you know, sir?'

'Best not to ask that question.' Moeller smiled. 'We're relying on Max a whole lot here. None of us can be seen helping him. He has to seize the moment and take the risk for himself. Think he'll deliver?'

'Now, let's see,' said Monteith. 'Max doing something for himself and himself alone… will he deliver? That's a tough one.'

Laughter ran around the squad room and the tension eased. Redfearn high-fived Monteith.

'All right. I've said all I can. Spread the word, and sit tight, Inferno-X. None of you is to leave this squad room.' Moeller stood up and drained his coffee. 'I should have seen it coming.'

'What's that, sir?' asked Valera, sensing something of weight was about to come their way.

Moeller thought for a moment before deciding to continue. 'The politics of war. Election day is a year and a half away. If the war's still on, then Corsini loses. Never mind this incident, watch for whatever's coming down the line in the next few months. I told Max that not every battle would be fought in the sky. I should have listened to myself.'

'What about the retest, sir?' asked Valera. 'Won't that help?'

Moeller cleared his throat. 'How do I put this delicately? No one who… *matters* cares a damn about its results.'

Valera felt sick to her stomach. 'How can that be?'

'It's for another day. Get Max out first, then we can turn to I-X's situation. Right now, no other squad has been upgraded but I'm not sure how long I can hold back the tide.'

'What's happening, sir?' asked Kullani.

'People *really* want you to take down the *Maputo*, that's what's happening. Making that happen might be the only way to save all of your lives.'

He nodded to them, turned and strode to the dorm door, which slammed behind him with an impressive echo.

Valera scanned the squad. 'Before everything else, and boy

is there a lot of that, let's set this up. Anyone with any useful Blammer contacts, come to me. I've got the odd favour to call in myself. And use squad encryption for anything you send by p-palm. You never know who's watching.'

Leitch lay in his bed and wished it wasn't so cold. He was uncomfortable. There were echoes in his head, voices he chased but could never quite catch up. He thought it was his drake; still out there somewhere but muzzled. It was the most painful thing: knowing it was alive but knowing he would never know the mind-touch again. It made his head hurt and his legs cold and dead.

He remembered feeling quite excited when Max arrived. Max listened and Max believed. That made Leitch feel good, something that had been in short supply. Trouble was now he had nothing new to tell Max. And that made him uncomfortable because Max was still here.

So he focused on the big empty black space in his mind where his drake had been, though he knew he shouldn't, and he felt a rush of blood across his vision and it was chill and choking. The flames were inside him and he craved the voice telling him it would all be all right. There was no one to tell him, only the echoes. There would never be someone and the flames melted his eyes and boiled his cold blood and he turned to dust in the fire and he was falling so fast the flesh was torn from his body and there was screaming in his ears and it might have been his own and there was nothing to calm him and he would open his mouth and consume himself and his death would be in never-ending agony and—

'Dylan.'

—so he cried because it wasn't the right voice and his eyes opened all by themselves and he shivered so hard he thought his eyes might fall out and his neck break and in front of him wasn't his drake like he craved but it was Barney—

'Dylan.'

—and Barney was standing over him, one gentle hand rocking his shoulder.

'I'm sorry, Dylan,' said Barney softly.

'No,' said Leitch, desperately trying to surface.

'You're right, I am a human being and I don't want to live with guilt.'

Leitch had to search hard through his scattered mind to link up Barney's words with the memory. 'That's great, he needs to go.'

'Talk into your hands. Some of them lip-read, remember?' Barney crouched down and held Leitch's wrist as if taking his pulse. He put his mouth in close so he could whisper. 'You need to remember this. I know you can because you're not gone, not yet, but sometimes the deep dark won't let you go, will it?'

Leitch was aware tears were rolling down his face and on to his pillow and he wasn't really sure why. 'Am I awake?'

'Yes. You're going to do something very important. More important than your last drake mission, okay?'

Leitch blew out a laugh on the back of a sob. 'Liar. What's happening?'

'You don't like Max being here, do you?'

'And you feel guilty,' said Leitch, finally making the connection and feeling some of the cloying cold blood drain from his mind, leaving him a little freer to think. 'Is he going, then?'

'Only with your help.' Barney shook a little pot he had in his free hand. 'I'm going to give you your pills. Pretend to take them now, actually take them later.'

'How much later?'

'When Max has gone.'

Leitch smiled. 'I can do that.'

'I know it's hard when you wake up from the dark place and I know it's harder to think when you don't have your pills,' said Barney. 'But it's important you understand. Tell me: what happens if someone is cross with you?'

'It's okay because I always have my pills.'

'But what if you haven't had your pills?'

'I get very upset.'

Leitch's heart was suddenly beating very fast and very hard and he needed the chill of the blood to calm it down but it wasn't there.

'Today, that's a good thing.'

CHAPTER 22

> Ten thousand people live on this behemoth. We carry enough ordnance to flatten a small country. I can send out a hundred drakes to burn the sky and eight thousand marines to turn the sand to glass. Sometimes, that weighs heavy. Should one person be in command of so much capacity for destruction?
>
> NICOLA AVERY, COMMANDER, HEART OF GRANITE

Max was going to have to eat soon. Well, he didn't *have* to but he was starting to question why he was enduring hunger pains and food fantasies, particularly when he had no reason to doubt Hewitt. His was a well-directed cruelty and Max fully expected him to reappear carrying the force-feeding tube or massive hypo or whatever else they'd use to force Max to take his life-limiting drugs.

He'd tried most of the plants in the garden and merely reminded himself how marvellous meat tasted, even when it had been freeze dried and reconstituted. He was still drinking from the fountain and the garden's irrigation system and was suffering no ill-effects.

He had to get out...

Max hadn't quite given up, but he knew the routine, he'd heard all the stories and time was running out, first for Martha and then for him. He hadn't heard her in his head since that one violent outburst of loneliness.

He lay on his bed in the half-light and heard the music come on, which meant the medics would be coming round with pills and jabs and then some food. He wondered if he'd give in and eat this time. When the door opened, Barney walked in with the tray of medications and intravenous bags. A trolley of food, smelling unbelievable, was pushed in by another medic who retreated immediately and closed the door.

Max watched in silence as Barney visited every bed. He was different from the other medics and their cursory, dehumanising attitude. Obviously that was why Leitch had targeted him for the guilt trip. Max had thought him sullen before but now he looked more carefully, it was more like he was trying to keep his emotions in check. Who'd have thought it, a nut nurse who cared?

Barney paused to speak with Leitch at some length and then did the same with Diana. He sat them both up, moved their tables across their beds and gave them their plates of food and cups of water. Satisfied with his patients he brought the trolley past Max.

'You should eat,' he said.

Max almost jumped out of his skin. 'I thought I was the invisible man in here.'

Barney shrugged. 'We know why you're not eating. Most pilots do it but we've never laced the food with meds. Don't have to. When we want you to take them, you take them, remember what Leitch said? So eat. You need your strength.'

'Yeah, you're right,' said Max. 'All this lying down is really exhausting.'

'You're going to need your sense of humour too,' said Barney. He moved Max's table across his bed and put a covered plate of food on it. It allowed him to move closer to Max. 'Eat. It's safe. Be ready.'

Max tried hard not to react, though his pulse had skyrocketed. Barney straightened and poured Max a cup of water.

'Stay quiet, the others don't like being disturbed when they're eating.'

'I'm brilliant at chewing silently,' said Max, trying to calm himself down a little.

'You're a real comedian.'

Max waited until Barney had moved off before he took the cover off his food, staring at it as his pulse returned to something approaching normal. Chicken, vegetables and gravy, plus a fresh baked roll. Max's stomach attempted to leap from his mouth and grab it all in one go but he forced himself to take a sip of water first and then cut an altogether smaller amount than he really wanted.

'Might as well savour it,' he said.

It was the best food he'd ever tasted. He tried to eat it slowly, he really did, but in a tragically short space of time, his plate was gleaming clean, any remaining specks of gravy wiped away with the roll. Max drained his water and sighed in satisfaction.

'Hey, Max, I'm talking into my hands. Do the same so the spies can't see your mouth.'

Max smiled and turned to plump up his pillow with great focus and concentration.

'Hey, Dylan, you all right?'

'I will be when you're gone. No offence.'

'None taken.'

'You'll hear all sorts of shit. Ignore it and do what you got to do, okay?'

'Okay.'

'Goodbye, Max,' said Diana, her voice a little muffled too.

'Bye, Diana. And thank you. I'm going to blow this right open, you know that.'

'I know it, Max-fucking-Halloran,' said Diana. Max only just managed to suppress a belly laugh.

'Make it right,' said Leitch.

'For all of us,' said Max.

'Too late for us. For the rest of you.'

'I promise.'

The two stricken pilots fell silent and all Max could do was watch them and wait. He'd learned quickly how fast their moods could change, whether they'd had stabilisers or not, and pushing either of them could lead to a confused and uncomfortable silence. So he focused on his toes while he listened to the clanking of cutlery on plates and the sound of pilots in various states of mental and physical incapacity and prayed for the door to open and for whatever it was to begin.

The wait was interminable. Just to be a little cruel, the door opened once to admit an orderly and a medic to clear the plates, and then once more to resettle one of the sicker inmates who had begun to twitch, whimper and shout.

Max's anxiety grew. He'd imagined his triumphant return to the squad rack and a night of celebration in Gargan's but it wasn't going to be like that. He'd have to hide, effectively exchanging one prison for another. Until he could be cleared or Kirby was stopped from carrying out his plan, he'd be reliant on others for absolutely everything.

And then there was Martha. Someone would have to protect her too. But how could you protect a drake on a behemoth flight deck? Max felt heat in his face as he realised there was only one option that would save them both, and even then probably only in the short term.

The door opened again and in walked Barney wearing a serious expression and carrying a covered hypo. The door remained open and a pair of orderlies watched as he strode over to Leitch.

'Leitch, your readouts show you didn't take your pills. If you don't then I have to inject you and you don't like that, do you?' Barney's tone was nauseatingly patronising.

'Am I coming out today?' asked Leitch.

'Well, let's see, shall we?' said Barney. 'Perhaps if you take your pills.'

'You bloody liar!' said Leitch. 'No one gets out.'

'All right, Dylan,' said Diana in an overloud voice. 'Remember the drugs give you hope.'

'Hope,' snarled Leitch and the tension in the ward went vertical. 'Stupid, stupid when my blood is so cold and my head is burning and my legs are rotting and my mouth spews shit.'

'Please don't talk like that,' said Diana. 'I don't like it when you talk like that.'

'Come on, let's just take a breath,' said Barney gently.

'You just don't want to hear the truth so you can go back and pretend it isn't so bad and there is no pain, don't you, Barney? Well there is and I hate it I hate it I hate it!'

The orderlies made a move in but Barney held up his hands to keep them back.

'It's okay,' he said, but there was sweat on his brow and Max wondered how much of this was play-acting and how much was real.

'Where's Hayley?' demanded Leitch.

'Hayley can't come,' said Barney and he glanced over at Max. 'We explained why, didn't we? No one can have visitors here.'

'And why would she want to? Poor mad Dylan, no more than a dribbling animal now.'

'Stop it! Stop it! Stop it!' cried Diana and Max could hear her breaking down into tears. 'Why are you talking like that? I'm sure she still cares.'

'Noonefuckingcares!' snapped Dylan.

'No noise, no noise!' sobbed Diana. 'Please, I hate it.'

'I need you both to quiet down,' said Barney, his voice carrying no urgency whatever. Other inmates were starting to react. The orderlies edged in and this time, Barney didn't stop them. 'Especially you, Dylan. Now, are you going to take your pills?'

'Oh, am I being a bad boy, Barney? Please put me on a charge. That's so much worse than having your brain slowly dissolve into a puddle of sludge.'

'He just wants to help!' wailed Diana. 'Why do you have to be like this?'

'Because I'm fucking dying in fucking agony!' roared Leitch.

'I hate the noise,' whimpered Diana into the short silence.

From Max's right came a whirring noise. He turned to see the camera swinging round to focus on the left side of the ward, which was descending into impressive chaos. Barney took a pace towards the head of Leitch's bed, brandishing the hypo. Despite his lower body paralysis, Leitch hinged at the waist and landed a remarkable punch on Barney's left cheek.

Diana screamed and began to cry, her voice falling and rising like an alarm. Barney fell back, swearing equally impressively. One of the orderlies pressed the panic button by the door and they both ran to help. A klaxon went off in the corridor.

'Forget me, calm Diana,' snapped Barney, stretching his jaw and rubbing his cheek. 'Dylan's not going anywhere, after all.'

But he was trying to. The former pilot thrashed in his bed, jerking his hips from side to side in an effort to move his useless legs and succeeding only in dislodging his bedding and juddering himself closer to the raised bars that kept him from falling out.

In response to the alarm, two security guards ran in, banging the door back against the wall and giving Max a glimpse of freedom. A third guard was hurrying along the corridor.

'I need him in the garden. Get him away from the others so I can jab him,' said Barney, who had a bruise swelling on his cheek.

'No problem, Barn,' said one. The pair marched up either side of Leitch and grabbed a shoulder each, their combined strength only just able to counter his frenzy. 'Come on, Dylan, let's go see the flowers.'

'Fuck you. I don't need flowers, I need Max to go. Go away, Max, go away!'

Max froze where he was sitting up in his bed. The two guards glanced at him and then at the door where the third guard was now stationed. Max just shrugged.

'That's not going to happen,' said Barney. 'Come on, Dylan, enough.'

Leitch continued to heave and thrash as he was helped out of bed, trying to butt the guards. Spittle was flying everywhere, Leitch was frothing at the mouth and Max felt a deep sense of responsibility. However much this had been controlled at the outset, it certainly wasn't now.

Max dared a glance at the third guard who was no more than three metres away and staring at the hysterical pilot. The struggle was moving steadily towards the garden, with Barney walking along behind, his large frame obscuring much of what was happening behind him. The two orderlies were both faced away from Max, one calming Diana's hair, another helping her swallow mood stabilisers. It was now or never.

Max leaned to his right to get his water and instead up-ended his whole table. There was nothing on it barring the plastic cup and it made precious little sound but it caught the eye of the guard, as did Max hopping out of bed to set things right, jamming his feet into his softies as he went.

'Shit, shit, shit,' he said. 'Sorry.'

The guard took a half pace towards him, and the door began to close on its hydraulic hinges.

'Back in bed,' she said.

'Sure,' said Max. 'Let me just...'

He leaned forwards to pick up his empty cup, came up fast and cracked a fist into the guard's chin. Her eyes rolled back and she crumpled. The door was almost closed and Max dived headlong for it, snared it a few centimetres from the point of no return and dragged it back open.

He looked around. Leitch, still shouting at the top of his voice, and his helpers were in the garden. Behind him, Diana had started screaming again and the two orderlies hadn't looked round. The alarm klaxon was still sounding, covering all but the loudest of sounds. Max breathed deep and walked out of Landfill, letting the door click shut behind him.

With the klaxon still going, there would be more attention on the ward soon enough but Max reasoned that few enough people knew he was an inmate. He was wearing standard patient fatigues anyway, so he wouldn't stand out.

He forced himself to walk calmly up the corridor, past the medic station and guard post doors, turning a sharp left into the central walkway, through the medical centre where no one paid him the slightest attention. Max hurried round the brain sheath and finally found what he was looking for. The digital clock told him it was seventeen thirty-five.

He caught his reflection in a ward window too and rather wished he hadn't. There were stale sweat patches on his tee-shirt, he was unshaven and looked sunken-eyed, though that might have been the light and glass playing tricks on him. He consciously kept his head up and a bright expression on his face.

Max kept moving at his unhurried pace, however much he wanted to sprint. He strode purposefully to the metal and bone bulkhead doors that stood open onto the neck walkway. The neck was at an angle of about thirty degrees meaning the *Heart of Granite* was still tracking drakes and ground forces. It gave Max a good view down the busy moving walkways. The doors at the base of the neck stood open, guard posts were empty. So far so good.

Max moved onto the walkway, walking quickly down the left-hand side, excusing himself past people and scanning everyone he could in case he was about to pass one of Kirby's inner circle. He was halfway down when the ship-wide com sounded and announced a security level three lockdown rehearsal and everyone was to have their passes ready for inspection. So his escape had been discovered, then.

CHAPTER 23

> Surely the greatest sacrifice is mine? If we lose this war, I lose everything. So if we win, should I not benefit?
>
> GILLES CORSINI, DIARIES

Max moved more quickly but he still wasn't fast enough. Below him, at the bulkhead doors to the torso, military police were gathering. They stood in four pairs, two either side of each entrance, and began checking everyone in and out. The movement on the walkway slowed dramatically as the bottleneck built up and the walkway gently came to a stop, sensing the building problem.

A quick glance back showed him another ten Mips heading down the walkway at some speed and barking commands to clear the way. There was no other way out but to carry on down and nowhere else he could think of to run but back to the heater girls and the dubious sanctuary of the flesh tunnels.

Max was less than ten metres from the bulkhead doors into the main spine now. He could see the Mips notice that someone was causing ripples. One of them moved his way, calling for people to stop pushing. Max pushed harder, trying to shove people to either side.

His pushing was creating a minor panic. People shoved back. A fist jarred against his shoulder and the anger spiked up a level.

The Mips were closer now, he could hear them ordering people to stop, demanding calm. Max made sure they didn't get it. He pushed again, and gave it everything.

At the head of the queue, some of the crew had stopped but there was no such compliance with the police orders further back. A woman in front of Max, with one of his hands on her back, stumbled forwards and fell heavily into the marine ahead of her. He moved diagonally, colliding with another who turned to complain but was pushed backwards and toppled over.

Like chaotic human dominoes, the wave of people trying to keep their feet moved outwards. It broke against the Mips at the head of the queue and people spilled out into the spine corridor. Max saw his chance, leapt over two people scrabbling to rise, pushed off the flank of a third person and shouldered his way through the bulkhead opening.

'Sorry!' he shouted, bolting into the spine corridor and sprinting away.

Over the sound of the Mips ordering him to stop, he heard a call of support. Max put his head down and ran. Deck two was a mixture of bars, fitness areas, and a couple of restaurants along with a recreation area. Elsewhere, marine dorms were mixed with army administration offices, civilian, ground lizard and crew quarters and, towards the tail, storage and the upper section of the plastics recycling, remoulding and printing facility. Max thought as he ran, shouts behind him confirming the pursuit was well and truly on. He ducked down the next left into a short corridor accessing crew quarters and a laundry room.

He ran down it, hauling open the door at the end and thumping down the metal stairs to deck three. Hitting the deck, he ran back up to the central corridor, reaching it just as a Mip rounded the corner at a run, his hand to his ear, receiving orders. He reacted fast, raising his zapon.

Max feinted left and threw himself right, rolling over his shoulders and using the corridor wall to push himself back to his feet.

The zapon hummed over his head, dragging his hair upright in its static trail. Max shoved the Mip hard into the opposite wall and ran into the spine, seeing it busy with marines heading off to their assignments, many in full kit running towards the flight deck access passageways. There would be police flooding down here too and he still had to make it most of the way to the tail. Cooper was the only man who could help him now.

'Which way, which way...'

The *Heart of Granite* was enormous, almost a kilometre long, not including the tail, but there were so few places to get out of sight and move quickly. He couldn't risk being trapped, and finally a solution presented itself. With at least one Mip behind him, he ducked into the rack of the nearest marine company, seeing the 'Exterminators' insignia on the doors.

Max slapped the double doors open onto a dorm crowded with marines suiting up for a mission. He dashed through the throng, ignored by almost all of them, but as he sprinted the hundred or so metres to the exit, one stepped into his path.

'Unbelievable,' muttered Max.

'What the fuck are you doing in my rack, sludge-brain?' demanded Meyer.

Max slithered to a halt. 'Holy fuck, Meyer, help me out? Mips on my six.'

'You must be in some trouble.'

'The worst. End-of-life stuff.'

'You are one walking charge sheet, man.'

'Come on, give me some space, will you? Sorry about Gargan's the other night, okay?'

Meyer looked over Max's shoulder in response to growls of displeasure from his crew.

'Mips in my rack,' he said. 'Get lost, Halloran, and remember, you owe me.'

'I owe everyone.'

Max ran on as Meyer roared orders.

'Rank up, Exterminators. Central spread. Fill the floor.' And a moment later. 'You have permission to come in here, Corporal?'

'We are in pursuit of an escaped prisoner. No permission is required. Get your people out of my way.'

Max pushed through the doors, ran into and through the galley and laundry and back out into the spine, dropping into an easy walk. He was right behind two Mips, both walking fast towards the tail and he fell into their footsteps, walking silently in his softies.

He glanced back and saw others behind him. Ahead, more were stationed at the entrance to the sports courts which had multiple exits... and there were bound to be Mips in the tail too, in case he tried to hide in the maze of storage areas and shelving.

Max followed the Mips as closely as he dared, seeing his goal come closer, metre by agonisingly slow metre. But then the Mips Meyer had delayed burst back into the corridor and everything went to shit again. They ran along the corridor, Max just about holding his nerve until one of those in front got the message. He tagged his partner, turned round and saw Max.

'Max Halloran, you're—'

Max punched him hard in the gut, sending him sprawling into his colleague and pushed past them both, running as hard as he ever had. There were people everywhere, every one of them a potential collision. Boy, he could do with Martha's eyes right now, an extra pair would go a long way.

He ran like he was flying into combat anyway, flitting around crew, ducking gesticulating arms, anticipating changes of direction and pace, and scouting ahead for the inevitability of more Mips. It was an exhilarating run and he was leaving his pursuers behind in a race where a couple of metres might make all the difference.

Max was closing on the fourth and fifth company mess when the six-strong patrol appeared from the right not thirty metres ahead of him. He wasn't hard to spot, being the only idiot running at full tilt while almost everyone else stood and stared. The patrol spread across the corridor and moved through the few crew in between them, zapons ready to smack him down and beat him. Oh, the joy of pain.

'Fuck that,' muttered Max and bolted down a left-hand turn, then hard right through the first door he came to, praying it would lead somewhere.

He found himself in a services block and hared through it, fearing a dead end. Beyond the laundry were the toilet stalls and the showers. Hope bloomed bright: he knew exactly where he was. Max ran on through the locker room and straight into the dorm. It was all but deserted, just a couple of cleaner crew with brooms.

Max sprinted towards the doors opposite and flung them back, darting across the narrow corridor to get into the four and five mess. He heard the swish of a thrown zapon and felt it brush his trousers. A thunk of electricity fled through him, throwing spasms across his body. He half fell against the mess door, just managing to twitch the bar down so his momentum carried him inside.

He rolled and staggered to his feet, his body juddering with pain. A few dozen faces lifted from their food. He stumbled heavily into a table, scattering cutlery, drinks and plates. Three marines shoved their chairs back, dodging sauce and water as it poured off the table.

Max met the angry stare of one, jerked his head behind him by way of an apology and shakily ran on. He heard the Mips piling into the mess to give chase, yelling at him to stop. Max barrelled into the galley, ran down the lines of stoves and sinks and cabinets. Ahead, the swing doors out into the non-perishable food storage zone were tempting. They'd give him a way into the next galley but it wasn't where he had to be. Time to take a chance. Knowing the Mips would be on his heels in seconds, he ducked right around the end of the work surfaces and pushed through the door into the serving area, keeping low.

He crept to the end of the counter, the kitchen staff ignoring him with commendable aplomb, and glanced into the mess. The Mips were in the galley after him. He ran in a crouch to Cooper's office, headed in and closed the door behind him.

'Morning, Halloran, Valera said you'd drop in.'

Max was gasping. 'L... love my skipper... Give me a pass... Flesh tunnels. Please, Cooper.'

Cooper smiled. It was a wholly unpleasant expression. 'Two things: this is going to cost you so much you'll be eating sand the rest of your life. And if you're caught and give up my people, I will personally poison your drake and watch your brain explode.'

Max almost snapped something back but in his head he heard the disapproving sound of Valera clearing her throat. Or maybe it was Martha.

'Just hide me, man.'

'You got it.'

Inferno-X had all been monitoring messages on their p-palms and the news of a sudden lockdown rehearsal had been greeted with cheers and tension. Valera had insisted there be no communication once the plan was set in motion, and that had led to a growing frustration when they knew a pursuit was underway but could do nothing to help.

Valera's faith in Max's ability to escape was unshakeable. And despite the lack of information, she was certain they would hear from the top soon enough. Anxiety was quickly replaced with satisfaction when Kirby marched in, all jabbing fingers and red face to confront the whole squad who were delighted to hear Max had evaded capture so far.

'Where is he?' demanded Kirby.

'Who?' asked Valera.

'Don't fuck with me, Orin. You're deep in this.'

'I'm not with you, sir. We're confined to quarters.'

Kirby sighed. 'I suppose I should expect this moronic denial. You know all p-palm communication is tracked.'

'I hope you haven't been reading our personal mails, sir.'

'I'm petitioning Commander Avery to allow decryption of the most recent spate of communications from this squadron. We'll link you to Halloran's escape, I can promise you that.'

'Max has escaped?' Valera tried hard not to punch the air but there was no keeping her heart from singing, nor was there any stopping the cheers that echoed around the squad room.

'And I *know* you know where he is. When I find a shred of proof you were involved, like organising the theft of one of his flight suits, you'll be taking his place in Landfill. All of you.'

'We've had no communication with Max, sir. He's Falling too, according to your fascinating report. Better find him. You don't want Falling pilots getting all flappy-mouthed in public, do you, sir?'

Kirby walked close to Valera and stared down at her. 'He won't be so hard to find. Just think, when I push the button to wipe him from his lizard's memory I'll be able to hear his screams from whatever filthy hole he's stowed in. Can't wait; think I might do it now. The beast is ready, I wonder if Halloran is.'

He stalked towards the door. 'You think you're so clever but you've only worsened his suffering. He'll be wishing he was back in his nut-bed when the pain strikes. The second we reach our regeneration cycle, Inferno-X is history, dishonourably decommissioned. I'll scatter you across the fleets to fly your last missions, disgraced and humiliated.'

Valera let the echo of the rack door slamming die away.

'Well done, everyone. Keep it down, though.'

'He'll go for Martha now, won't he?' said Redfearn.

'Yep. Now everything hangs on Grim. Hold tight a little longer, everyone, we're not quite there yet.'

When Grim received the message she was ready. It meant brig time but she didn't care. She would not let Inferno-X or Max down. It didn't stop her hands trembling though and she dug them deep into the pockets of her filthy overalls. As she entered the flight deck it suddenly seemed a huge, unfriendly space filled with the cries of geckos, basilisks, komodos and drakes.

She felt like a pariah, shunned by her crew mates as she strode to Martha's pen. They looked at her with pity; everyone knew what was going to happen to Martha and they didn't want to be associated with her in case it meant they were next. Stupid, really.

There were two guards on Martha's pen and they watched her approach just as Kirby's agents did, up on the gallery.

'What do you want?' asked one as Grim approached. She was a thin-lipped woman whose badge named her as 'Lewis'. She was tall and her helmet gave her face a robotic quality. Apt.

'I came to say goodbye, give her a last rub down.'

'Pity you can't bring it a last meal, eh?' Lewis laughed at her own joke and her partner nodded his head in approval.

'Been working on that one a while, have you?' snapped Grim.

'Never understood why you lot get so emotional about the ERCs. One dumb lizard is just like another, right?'

There was a solid kick to the inside of the pen. Both guards jumped and swung round to the door.

'Dumb lizard has good hearing,' said Grim. 'Let me in, and I'll try to persuade her not to have you as a light snack.'

'You think it understands us?' asked the second guard, Carter, whose face was altogether kinder and sat atop a body stacked with muscle.

'Not even the Tweakers know,' said Grim. 'But they hear and feel and deserve our respect. Now I want to say goodbye so maybe your mate could keep her sharp comments to herself.'

Carter nodded and unlatched the pen.

'Don't try anything,' said Lewis.

'Like what? I can't fly her, can I?' Lewis shrugged. 'If you're so bothered then leave the door open.'

Carter shuddered. 'We trust you.'

'Good call.'

Inside with Martha, Grim felt complete again. The drake was lying down, having made her point with her kick of the pen. Her head and neck were laid across her back in the resting swan position and she lifted her head to look at Grim, her eyes brimming with intelligence but her body weakening through lack of nutrition. Grim reckoned she'd missed four feeds, and with her energised metabolic system that was a major problem.

'Hey, you,' said Grim, moving forwards to stroke her flank scales, feeling them dry and rough. 'How are you doing?'

Martha opened her mouth wide and rocked her head in what Grim had come to know as an expression of displeasure. She snapped her jaws shut and moved her head closer to Grim, wanting her muzzle rubbed. Grim obliged and spoke into her ear slit.

'Ready for some fun?' she whispered. 'Going to try and get Max to you, princess.'

The mention of Max's name made Martha shiver and Grim chuckled. She checked the drake out, noting nothing amiss beyond the obvious effects of her enforced starvation. The data and flow pipes were still connected to her, providing the drugs which kept her relatively docile, and the endless flow of information so beloved by the Tweakers.

'Fancy some food?' she whispered. 'Course you do.'

Martha rattled the phlegm in her throat. Her fuel ducts were dry and the sound was raw. Grim glanced back at the pen door and Carter.

'How's it doing?' he asked, raising his voice to carry through the glass and ignoring the equally loud tut from Lewis.

'Her name's Martha. And she's okay, under the circumstances.'

'Holy bollocks,' muttered Lewis.

Grim glared at Lewis. 'I'd hate to live in your world. What a cold and miserable place it must be.'

'Are you finished?' asked Lewis.

'Almost. Just need to check her data stream.' Grim tugged at her forelock. 'If that's okay, ma'am.'

Lewis almost smiled. 'Knock yourself out.'

Grim gave Martha a pat on the top of her head and leaned as if to kiss her muzzle. 'Get ready to fly, princess,' she whispered.

Grim let herself out of the small side door and into the technical area that sat next to the pen. She made sure her arms were folded and looked at the data screen from a pace away, shaking her head sadly. Lewis and Carter couldn't see her from where they stood but the Mips stationed in the gallery were staring at her.

Grim smiled and backed off, looking at Martha while she gathered her nerve. Martha had relaxed back into her resting position. She ran through her steps, the number of touches she'd need.

'This is for you, Max,' she said.

Grim put her hands back in her pockets and moved casually back to the screen; her left fingers toyed with her access card. With a final breath, she fed it into the side slot. The screen came alive. Her fingers danced across it and she ignored the shouts from the gallery as she enabled the feeding system.

'Grimaldi!' snapped Lewis. 'Step away.'

Grim heard them coming round the pen towards the technical area. She selected the level and mix of nutrients Martha needed, and heard a zapon buzz as it was activated.

'Last warning,' said Lewis.

Grim tapped the activation pad and the feed started to flow. Then she turned, with a swell of pride at her own bravery.

'So cuff me. No one's wiping Martha now.'

CHAPTER 24

The beauty of the alien DNA was its capacity to produce creatures to almost any specification, and combine enormous strength with low mass. It allowed us to create behemoths to march the land and drakes to fill the sky. I still weep at the beauty of it all, but more so at the gift we humans inevitably bent to destruction.

DOCTOR DAVID WONG

'Smoke?' Krystyna proffered a tatty packet.

'Bad for my health,' said Max.

Krystyna laughed; a rough throaty sound. 'Now that's funny coming from a drake pilot. I think it's about time you started, kiddo, what with the shit storm you've kicked up.'

Max was sitting at the table in the heater girls' lab. Jola and Sharmi were in the back, sleeping. The whole place stank of chemicals and behemoth viscera, leaving Max feeling nauseous and already wanting to leave.

'They know I'm down here somewhere, right?'

'Despite recent evidence to the contrary, Kirby isn't entirely stupid. Right now, he has to be careful which tunnels he decides to expose – and he still needs us. He'll probably make a statement and raid someone way down in the tail where the low-level narcos and pros ply their trade. I'll eat my still if he comes down here...

Besides, he can wait you out. He knows your only option is to get to your drake before he re-engineers it. So you've done well to get this far, but there's worse to come.'

'Just tell me how to get to her, okay?'

'It's in hand, so be patient. Gather your strength and your luck; you're seriously going to need both and even then your chances are pretty slim.'

'Thanks for the pep talk.'

Krystyna chuckled. 'I almost like you, kiddo. What's up?'

Max realised his expression must have changed, because he'd paused to think ahead for the first time since he'd left Landfill.

'I'm just wondering if it was worth the bother of escaping.'

'Your options are becoming depressingly clear, are they?'

'I'm dead whichever way I turn, aren't I?'

Krystyna waved her hand to disperse some smoke. 'It's not quite as clear-cut as that.'

Max raised his eyebrows. 'Really? I'm surprised Kirby's so dead set on finding me. Might as well let me take Martha and go, then I'll die in the desert and he can blame the Fall.'

'Believe me, he's far more scared that you'll survive it.'

'What? No one survives the Fall.'

'Not yet.'

'You should probably explain that,' said Max sharply.

Krystyna took a long drag on her cigarette and chained another one before stubbing the end out.

'Look, back when the Fall was a new phenomenon it threatened the whole ERC programme. There were tests done that led directly to mind-shielding technology and prolonging the active service of drake pilots. But they also suggested that the Fall wasn't a death sentence, that it was the ongoing process of mixing alien and human DNA. It was never a surprise that transition affected the human brain.'

'So what's wrong with that?'

Krystyna gave a dry laugh and stubbed out her cigarette. 'It depends where you stand. If you're a scientist, it's fascinating and demanding of further research. If you're a pilot, it means longer in the pouch. But if you're a humanist, it's playing god to wage war. A pilot who went through the Fall wouldn't be completely human any more; none of us knows what that means. And all the test subjects died, so further direct research was suspended. We've continued researching the ideal conditions for the Fall, just using existing data to model Fall-survival.'

'"We"?' he said and noticed her hands were trembling.

'I was part of the team, Max. I truly don't know whether to be ashamed or proud. We lost lives but we discovered so much.'

Max felt a cool anger growing. 'Yeah, and you've ended up in this stinking bone lab and never see the sunlight. I'd say there was more shame than pride and there bloody should be. Lab rats, right?'

'How's that?'

'Everything I heard in Landfill. It's not the Fall that sends you mad, it's losing your drake that does it, made worse by the drugs they give you. Or perhaps they're wrong in there. Perhaps that's part of the madness.'

'Oh boy, you got stuck in with a real live one, didn't you?'

'Leitch. He knows the drugs are killing him but he takes them anyway. Diana called herself a "lab rat". And that's right, isn't it? Someone's passing data to you, aren't they?'

Krystyna paused and picked a shred of tobacco from her lip. 'Yeah, but it isn't how you think it is. All I've ever done is try and help drake pilots live.'

'Lucrative business too, eh?'

'Go fuck yourself, Halloran, you know nothing,' spat Krystyna. She pushed away from the table, snatched her pack of cigarettes and tapped another one out, which she jammed between her lips and lit from the lighter in her apron pocket. She tapped her chest. 'I'm the one true ally you've got, kiddo. Get back in your box and stop mouthing off about things you don't understand.'

'So make me understand. Why did you leave?'

'Landfill, Max, why else?' Krystyna sighed. 'Look. Public opinion went hard against the mixing of alien and human DNA so that coward Corsini made a big show of shutting down the Fall research programme and diverting all the funding – ha! – into finding a cure for what can't be cured. And that left all the Landfill victims being experimented on with incredibly dangerous shit to halt symptomatic advance of the Fall.'

'Great. So rather than stand and fight, you scuttled off to make a load of cash making drugs yourself.'

Krystyna snorted a laugh and Max looked past her to see Jola standing in the doorway to the living area. Sharmi levered her way past Jola, wandered over to the coffee machine and poured a couple of mugs.

'We left the ERC to come here and develop heaters. Still the only drug that actually helps pilots suffering early Fall symptoms,' said Sharmi. 'And keeps them flying.'

'Yeah, so you're part of the problem!' shouted Max, images of Diana, Leitch and all the Landfill inmates crowding his head. 'You're profiting from the misery of pilots... You're like fucking leeches on their brains, sucking out anything useful and casting the husks aside. They die in horrible pain, screaming at the walls in soundproof boxes for fuck's sake!'

'So what?' yelled Jola right into his face.

'I... it's... What do you mean *so what*? What the fuck kind of an answer is that?'

'You're all drake pilots! You knew the end when you signed up. And while you're dying you provide incredibly useful information for people like me who are *still doing the original research*. Fuckwit.'

Jola moved back a pace and glared at him. Max focused instead on Krystyna while he tried to unscramble his thoughts.

'What about the pilots in Landfill now?'

'There's nothing we can do for them,' said Krystyna. 'They're lost and all the medics can do is make them comfortable and gather data to make better treatments… some of which comes our way.'

'They should put them to sleep, it would be kinder.'

Krystyna blew more smoke. 'Yes, it would. But we can't be seen to be killing our heroes now, can we?'

Max shuddered. 'What about all the other drugs you push? Some sort of altruistic motive behind them too, is there?'

'Sure, we make money selling drugs for all sorts of needs but we have to in order to buy the materials to continue our research. I'm not trying to pretend we're angels, we want money like everyone else. But we also want to find the formula to keep a pilot in the pouch while he or she goes through the Fall in relative safety. That's what we came to the ERC to do. We're getting closer but we're still way off.'

'I've misjudged you a bit, haven't I?' said Max.

'Maybe a fraction,' said Sharmi.

'Believe me, none of us want this but without Landfill, we wouldn't get the raw data and without that, we can't devise the silver bullet that lets you all Fall and closes the wards across the fleet for good.' Krystyna smiled. 'And what a fucking shit storm that'll create. Can't wait.'

'Can't help me though, can you?' asked Max.

'We are helping,' said Sharmi.

'No, I mean, after I leave. I'm going to go through the Fall, aren't I?'

Jola shrugged. 'If you stay with your drake, it's inevitable. Or you can leave your drake to die in the desert. But when it does, you'll get your mind shredded while you're dying of thirst under the blazing sun. Or we can take you back to Kirby and you can have your space in Landfill back again.'

'No drugs you can give me for any of that, then?'

'Like I say, we're not there yet.' Krystyna touched him briefly on the shoulder. 'And I won't lie, alone-in-the-desert isn't ideal conditions for successfully negotiating the Fall.'

'Heaters?' suggested Max.

'You're going to Fall. All the way, probably quite quickly. Heaters can't help with that.'

Max stared into his coffee mug. He was fighting a sense of unfairness and part of him wished for blissful ignorance. He thought Valera would have handled all this much better… but she'd have done everything differently. He suddenly fervently wished he'd kept his stupid mouth shut. Too late now.

'Any advice, then?' he asked.

'Jeez, kiddo, who knows? Everyone else has died trying. Could be mental frailty, could be physical frailty. Post mortems showed all sorts. I dunno… Believe in yourself. Trust yourself.'

'You'll come to terms with it,' said Sharmi. 'Right now, you need food, fluid and sleep. Follow me.'

Max pushed himself to his feet, hungry, despite his Landfill feast, and exhausted now both had been mentioned. The living area was really tight. A tiny bathroom and another doorless room, just big enough for three single cots.

'Going to be tight fitting us all in there,' he said, nodding at the bedroom. 'I'm happy to share, mind you.'

Sharmi regarded him from really rather beautiful blue eyes. 'You have got to be fucking kidding.'

CHAPTER 25

My dad said that we always underestimate the length and consequences of war. He said we never learn and that the young always pay the price because we have to hold the guns and do the flying. I'd like to see my dad again but I never will, will I?

MAXIMUS HALLORAN

Max was partway through an early breakfast when Krystyna's p-palm beeped and she gave them all the thumbs-up. The *HoG* was still moving but with dawn only an hour away, she would stop soon, the tail would arc up and the flight deck lower from the cavernous belly. He had time still, but he had to leave his rather strange sanctuary with the heater girls.

Max was a bundle of nerves, a most uncomfortable and unusual experience.

'They'll be expecting me to make a break for it, won't they?' he said.

'Yes. Don't think about it,' said Sharmi. 'Right, here's your suit. We've taken the locator chip out but don't go putting it on until you're in the pen or they'll know something's up – the suit'll ping them an error message.'

'Thanks,' said Max, taking the suit. 'What's that for?'

Sharmi was holding out a sheathed scalpel. 'You'll need to

excise your drake's coms and locator chip or they'll be able to follow you wherever you go. Do it as soon as you can.'

'Right, yes, great idea, thanks.'

Sharmi smiled. 'Not just a brilliant scientist, eh?' She pointed the way to the exit. Max got up and they started walking. 'You know where the tunnels will take you, right? Any questions, now is the time. Beyond that, it's up to you.'

'They'll have drugged Martha, won't they? Sedated her or something.'

'I'd be surprised if they didn't,' said Krystyna.

'What?' Max stopped in his tracks. They were heading down towards the plastics Blammer, Stephane Marsan, who had his own access tunnels. 'How can I fly a sleeping drake?'

'As it happens, there are many things the ERC ignored when they stopped the Fall research and opened the Landfill programme instead. Trust me, when your minds come within range, it won't be the problem Kirby expects it to be.'

Max turned to face her full on. 'Thank you, Krystyna, and you, Sharmi. Maybe if I'm successful, you'll be able to get out of here and into a proper lab.'

'Don't go dissing our lab,' said Sharmi.

'You know what I mean.'

'Good luck out there, kiddo,' said Krystyna.

'Give my love to Jola.'

The two heater girls laughed.

'Only if you come back and clear up her puke,' said Sharmi.

'Get lost, Max,' said Krystyna. 'Marsan's expecting you.'

Max trotted into the Frenchman's lair and pulled up short. It was like falling into some demented dream of times gone by. Plastics of every hue and shape hung from the ceiling on wires or were stacked on shelves or piled on the floor. Much of it was in broken pieces, difficult to identify, but there were a few bits that were almost whole or obvious enough by shape or colour. Light and monitor casings, partial mouldings from tables and chairs, poles, a complete and surely ancient computer keyboard, clear covers...

'It's more a museum than a warehouse, no?' said Marsan, appearing from behind a particularly unruly stack of what might have been paper file folders.

'What the hell do you do with all this stuff?'

Marsan's smile was warm and knowing, revealing remarkably white teeth that were somehow at odds with his stubble and the untidy shoulder-length curly black hair that framed his grimy face.

'More valuable than diamonds.' He shrugged and pointed the way to go. 'To some people anyway. Everything in here is saved from the recyclers, the murderers of historical artefacts in the name of the military.'

'It's just bits of old plastic. Mostly broken old plastic.'

Marsan shook his head and kept Max moving quickly through the room. 'You're a philistine. This is a museum. You'd remould all these treasures to keep the C.A.C. looking pristine, would you?'

'I don't know, but I mean, what do your buyers *do* with this rubbish?'

Marsan shrugged. 'Mostly it goes off the behemoth with whoever bought it and sold on to collectors back home, wherever home is. I've seen mosaics, framed pieces, sculptures... all sorts. You think it's rubbish? You should see what I sell my rubbish for. Doesn't matter what it looks like, it matters that it's rare. You're in the wrong business.'

'I'd agree with you but I couldn't live in this hole.'

'A hole while the war lasts, a mansion when it is over.' Marsan shrugged again, an extravagantly Gallic gesture this time. 'Enough, though. We are both busy men. Come, I'll get you back to the real world.'

'Whatever.'

There was a poorly fitting door in the bone at the far end of Marsan's bizarre storeroom and the stench that funnelled out when the Frenchman opened it was extraordinary. It was hard to identify the odour but old meat, faeces and burnt oil were in there somewhere.

'I'll take you to the first junction,' said Marsan.

'It's not necessary,' said Max. 'You probably have some plastic to polish.'

Marsan looked at him, trying to gauge whether he was being insulted or not. 'No, I insist. You're paying for it, after all.'

'I am?'

'Oh yes,' said Marsan, his eyes sparkling. 'A lot.'

He led the way into the flesh tunnel and after a few metres, Jola's description was proved entirely accurate. The luxury of wall plating gave way to cauterised flesh. The matting beneath his feet was covered in a revolting slime that Marsan was happy to tell him was an antiseptic mixture produced by the behemoth's immune system. Max had no desire to see biology at work this close up. Even worse, it was soaking through his softies and starting to squelch between his toes.

'We don't all have the money for bone architecture,' said Marsan, his voice dulled by the gently undulating flesh surrounding them.

'Or you're too tight to spend it.'

'Comes to the same thing.'

The place was a maze and became increasingly more depressing as they headed deeper. The dripping fluid from roof and walls was a background to the desultory sound of voices emanating from side corridors. He heard a screech and some rhythmic moaning along with discordant music. The smell of the tunnels was overlaid by questionable cooking smells, and steam and smoke curled around the ceiling and crawled up the walls. Max recognised some harsh narcotic fumes within the complex stench.

The noise grew, as did the brightness of light, and the filthy passage let out into a bone space packed with people, goods and stalls.

'You have got to be kidding me . . .' breathed Max.

'Welcome to the *Heart of Granite*'s best marketplace,' said Marsan. 'Anything you want... Drugs, food, clothing, plastics, whores, weapons, your friendly agent can negotiate for it here. Notice anything?'

They'd paused at the entrance and while Marsan was getting nods, waves and calls of recognition and welcome, Max was attracting far more hostile attention.

'Beyond the fact they all seem to hate me on sight?' said Max.

'Why do you think that is?'

Max had a good look at the forty or fifty people in front of him. All shapes, sizes and ages, all civilians, in dirty, creased or old clothes. There certainly wasn't much money in evidence here. Or hygiene, for that matter.

'I dunno... There's no uniforms here?'

'So you and your fatigues stick out like the proverbial here. Please say nothing and stay with me, or you won't make it to the other side of the market.'

'Why do you think I'd say anything?' Max felt a little hurt.

Marsan favoured him with a tiny shake of the head. 'Your reputation precedes you.'

The distance to their destination flesh tunnel was no more than forty metres but it was like walking through an alien society. Max barely understood a word, such was the speed and accent of the barter patter all around him. Deals for drugs, fresh fruit and low grade plastics were being made with great energy, all on behalf of agents and clients within the *HoG*.

Everywhere he moved, and always in Marsan's shadow, the chatter quietened and people stared like he was some sort of freak exhibit. Max did his best not to catch anyone's eye or react to the remarkable number of elbows and shoulders placed in his path, or the heels that managed to find his toes through the thin fabric of his sodden, stinking softies.

Marsan, aware of his rising temper, kept a firm hand on his

forearm and made plain he was passing through, nothing more. It didn't seem to make any difference.

'Hey, soldier, remember me when you need a little company.'

The young man to Max's left, leaning on a narco's stall, had deep eye sockets, and a skin infection that was weeping pus from beneath his fingernails. Classic signs of a Regen addict close to the end.

Max smiled. 'You'll be the first to know. And I'm not a soldier, I'm a—'

'Hsssst,' said Marsan, a beat too late as it turned out.

'Drake pilot?' guessed the addict. 'I have special services for your kind.'

A hush fell momentarily as the whole marketplace took in the gift that had just walked into their midst. Marsan tugged him forward at a greater pace but the crowd began to press in and the volume grew.

'Heaters... Best price on the best heaters, flippers, doubleOs, and hardhats.'

'You jocks love a peach. I've got them, fresh from hydroponics. Originally destined for the Commander's table, now destined for yours.'

Hands were all over him, fleecing him, and he brushed them off as best he could, pulling his suit back from grasping hands eager for the payday it represented.

'Share the wealth.'

'Keep the market thriving, friend.'

'I'm just passing through,' said Max.

'Not without spending, boy.'

Max stopped to stare at the rat-faced man elbowing his way forwards to loom over them. He had a grey, unruly beard, long fingers and blank eyes. Marsan swore under his breath.

'He has spent. With me. He bought safe passage to C-Tunnel, past the gland locks and all the way to alpha. A deal is a deal, Feral, you respect that. We all do.'

Max could feel Marsan's anxiety despite the confidence in his tone. His body was tense, poised to move forwards, but Max was tired of the jostling and looking for a chance to get involved.

'Yeah, Mars, a deal's a deal and we want to make a few more. Share the wealth, right?'

'My client's funds are seriously diminished,' said Marsan.

'Enough to pay you, right? That's pretty rich,' said Feral, drawing approving noises from his audience.

'Even if I wanted to trade,' said Max, 'your friends with the clever fingers would have lifted any cash sticks I had. How about I drop back this way when I'm not so pushed for time?'

Feral laughed and a nervous titter followed from the otherwise quiet crowd.

'There's a rule in the marketplace, jockey. A promise ain't worth shit unless it's delivered with Euro Marks attached.'

'*Mes amis*,' said Marsan, edging forwards, intending to stand in front of Max. 'You have to respect me or where is our marketplace?'

'Ours?' barked Feral. 'When did you last trade here, Mars? Too elite for us now, eh? Collectors not mods-men now, so I heard.'

'Does that make me disloyal? Have I been disrespectful? Let us pass. My client has no funds.'

The *HoG* was slowing. Dawn would be in full cry outside and the time to tail-up was getting short.

'It's been lovely talking to you all,' said Max. 'But I really must dash.'

Feral's eyes lit up like someone had plugged him in. He grabbed Max's shoulder in a painfully strong grip.

'You're Halloran,' he said. 'Fugitive, that's why you're down here. Price on your head, right? Looks like a payday just walked in, my friends.'

This was going to go south, really, really fast, so Max did what he did best: he acted completely without thinking. He slapped Feral's hand away and smashed a fist into the Blammer's gut.

Feral staggered back and Max leapt at him, jabbing an elbow up into his face and bringing them both crashing to the ground. He cracked in another punch as they fell, and the back of Feral's head bounced from the bone floor, stunning him.

While the crowd in the marketplace assimilated the speed and ferocity of the attack, Max was back on his feet, one foot on Feral's throat with enough pressure to choke him. Max scanned the crowd, who were beginning to twitch.

'Any one of you moves on me or Marsan, Feral stops breathing. Feral? Move a muscle and I'll crush your throat. Now. Enough of this. I have somewhere to be.'

'You won't kill him,' said a voice from the crowd. 'You haven't got the guts.'

Max pushed a little harder and Feral, his eyes wide and desperate, squawked a protest. He grabbed at Max's leg. Max increased the pressure and the scrabbling became weaker and more desperate.

'Before Feral chokes to death, be aware I've just escaped from Landfill,' said Max, his body feeling like it was rippling with sudden energy. 'If I am caught, I will be killed. If I escape, I'll probably die anyway. I'm a dead man walking, and I'm really happy to take a few of you along for the ride.'

Seeing his cue, Marsan moved in front of Max and the prone Feral.

'How about you make us a path? I don't think my client's foot can stay so gently on Feral's throat for much longer.'

Reluctantly they began to move aside and Max could see the flesh tunnel just ten metres away. He kept the pressure on and made a point of staring all around him, noting those who had moved in.

Marsan was at the flesh tunnel entrance now and there was sadness in his face that made Max regret what he had done but for once, the disappointment wasn't aimed his way.

'All I wanted was the safe passage I negotiated,' said Marsan.

'You have all let yourselves down, disrespected the rules of the market. We should talk when I get back. Put ourselves right. Come on, Max.'

Max moved quickly, taking his foot from Feral's throat and striding to the tunnel, feeling their discontent like a weight across his shoulders. They were filling in the space in his wake and Max sensed Feral was back on his feet and risked a glance. He was grey-faced and massaging his throat.

'We'll talk more on my return,' said Marsan.

'I have nothing to say to you,' said Feral.

Max strode off up the flesh tunnel and back into the stinking, slushy gloom. Marsan hurried to catch up with him and diverted him down a right hand spoke that began to angle down gently.

'I'm sorry,' said Max. 'I think I've made enemies for you.'

'It'll blow over,' said Marsan. 'Anyway, Feral needs a lesson every now and again and I have other routes in and out of my place. He was right about one thing, I don't need the marketplace.'

Max smiled. 'How far is it?'

'Just a couple of turns to alpha junction.'

'Good. I'll be fine from there.' Max blew out his cheeks. 'It's a different world down here. Can't believe the military let any of it be built.'

'Ha! They didn't know it was happening to begin with. Those were fun days. It's a bit different now, and we're just about tolerated but there's still plenty of space they can't close down because they don't know it exists. Fortunately for you, that includes alpha tunnel. They told you where it comes out, right?'

'Yeah. I was thinking you might want to architect it right into Martha's pen.'

'I'll get right on it,' said Marsan. He paused mid-stride. 'Martha?'

'My drake.'

'*Merde*.'

They passed more unfortunates in drug dens, where Marsan

said poorly cut drugs were smoked or injected, further shortening already pitifully brief lives.

'So much for the thriving black economy,' said Max.

Marsan shrugged. 'The weak fail.'

'You're one big bowl of compassion, aren't you?'

'It does not pay to care. You of all people know that.'

'I'm paying right now.'

'My point exactly. Right, here we are.'

Max was somehow expecting alpha tunnel to be a grand entrance of some kind, but of course it was just like all the others. There was rough structure at the junction to stop a collapse or even a regrowth... a 'heal', as the illicit architects called it. But beyond that, the walls were cauterised like everywhere else and the floor matting just as full of ichor. It made Max crave fresh air.

'Where are we exactly... relative to the behemoth proper?'

'We are in the starboard flank beneath Seepage. Your path takes you round the belly, through the muscle and fat and down to your exit point. It's tight up there and you'll have to pick a careful path to your drake across the deck. If you're spotted, you're toast...' Marsan smiled and shook Max's hand. 'Good luck, *mon ami*.'

'I'll need it. Hey, be careful back there. It's an ugly crowd and I don't just mean the beards.'

Marsan chuckled. 'Look to yourself. And if you live, remember, you owe me.'

'Surely you won't allow me to forget.'

Max headed along alpha tunnel, seeing the downward slope in the gently moving flesh and the way it curved in an anti-clockwise direction, following the belly wall. He began to plan before realising the futility of it, since he knew bugger all about how the flight deck would be when he arrived. It was the key smuggling route for goods coming onto the flight deck, but that's all he knew. Its whereabouts was the most closely guarded secret on the *HoG*... Another reason that if he survived he'd be broke for the rest of his life.

CHAPTER 26

> I argued that thirty pairs of legs were too few but unfortunately more would mean losing architectable living space. So we went with the minimum. At least I convinced them to increase tib and fib bone density. Even so, the loss of just five pairs would leave a behemoth struggling to move unless it was entirely unloaded.
>
> PROFESSOR HELENA MARKOV,
> ERC COMMAND LOG ENTRIES

The quality of the tunnel improved as it spiralled gently down towards the flight deck. The base plating became a more solid rubber matting and the walls were coated in increasingly large sections by rubberised panelling. It didn't diminish the smell at all but at least Max could shake the notion that he was paddling in behemoth guts.

He made quick progress through the well-lit tunnel and knew he was closing on the flight deck when the sounds of reptiles of all shapes and sizes began to echo up to him. They were bookended by metallic clangs and, more dimly, by orders booming across the cavernous space of the flight deck. He paused for a moment, struck by the normality of all he could hear and feeling a pang of regret that he had to leave it all behind.

Max saw the end of the tunnel from a hundred metres or so

away. It was ringed with lights, the central one of which, above the round-cornered square doorplate, was a solid red.

'Wow,' said Max when he reached the door. 'High security or what?'

He studied the screen set on the wall to the left of the door plate. It was split into three sections. The upper panel showed the view directly outside, which was just a bunch of equipment crates, no signs of life. Bottom left were the readings from four movement sensors and even Max could see that there were people near two of them, wherever they were positioned. Bottom right was the input panel which displayed a single command tile marked 'Open'. It was currently crossed through and coloured red.

'No prizes for guessing what that means,' muttered Max.

He sat on the tunnel floor and waited for the light to go green. He stared at the levels on the two offending movement sensors, willing the people to start moving away. While he waited he plotted and listened, straining to hear Martha but getting nothing bar a muffled soundtrack of a flight deck bursting with activity. He didn't want to be waiting too long; he was desperate to see Martha again and he could afford to miss the wonderful chaos of the first missions of the day.

Max felt he should be able to feel her now, just on the outer edges of his consciousness, but there was nothing when he pushed his mind out towards her. He wondered if Inferno-X was out there, or Anna-Beth. He'd give anything to be looking into her eyes right now.

Max slumped where he sat, trying to control his anticipation and his fear. He brought his hands up in front of his face and turned them over and back to confirm they were actually trembling. So much had changed; so much more would if he escaped. Whatever came next, there was no coming back. The thought brought tears to his eyes and he shook his head and growled.

'Dammit.'

He knew that his anxiety should have peaked when the exit

light went green but instead he felt relief from the torture of waiting. He took a deep breath and pushed the screen tile. The door plate slid backwards with the merest hiss and he moved out into flight deck storage. He heard a minimal beep and the door slid shut behind him. He turned to see it close.

'Wow,' he breathed.

He was facing a bone wall, set with air duct grilles floor to ceiling and a large stencilled sign above them saying 'No stowage'. He'd just walked through the opening and he still couldn't see where the seams met the rest of the duct-heavy section of wall. He put his hand to a grille at chest height and found it had airflow.

'Wow.'

The beautiful violent sounds that characterised the flight deck registered the next instant and he was reminded of his precarious position. He was in the middle of a short corridor which, the grilles excepted, was walled by storage shelving and stacked metal crates. The flight deck storage facilities were open-fronted areas about a third of the way down the deck – there was one either side of the runway.

While much space was given over to equipment specific to the flight deck's smooth operation, the zones were also used for temporary storage of anything and everything that came onto the flight deck before onward transport to its final destination... or its smuggling into the flesh tunnels and the Blammers' hands.

The din of the flight deck was coming from Max's left, so the pens were all across the deck and up toward Flight Command. It meant a walk across open space. Tricky but at least it would be busy.

Max needed a hidden spot to assess his chances of making it there unseen. He looked down the aisle; he was at the right end of the storage zone but he couldn't see without poking his head out so he walked to the back of the zone and then along the ends of the twenty numbered aisles, glancing down each one before ambling across to the next, appearing very much the ordinary flight deck crewman.

With each glance, he gained a snapshot of the flight deck. Every time he did, he felt a pang that he wouldn't be able to stride across it ever again, head held high and proud as he prepared for a mission or returned triumphant from one. There were drakes on the runway and he yearned to be lining up with Inferno-X. This lot were the Firestorm.

'Don't Fall,' he whispered.

Looking at Firestorm waiting for the go, a thought struck him and he hurried to the end of the zone and walked down aisle two, staying in the shadows. He reached the end and let his gaze travel up the deck. It wasn't quite as bad as he feared.

Max was about three hundred metres from Flight Command and more concerned by the possibility of being recognised by a wandering security guard. He could see all the way up to the bulkheads on the right side of the deck, and sure enough, they were guarded. Same with the back stairs and stores lifts. It would be the same on his side.

With drakes on the runway, the geckos were watching on warily, stilled by the proximity of predators. For their part, the drakes ignored them completely, standing serene, gazing out at the sun-drenched desert and the heat washing in, warming the chilly interior.

The Flight Command alert tones sounded and the pre-recorded message began. 'Attention, flight deck. Launch imminent. Clear the runway. Lights up in thirty seconds.'

Across the flight deck, the orange lights flashed and rotated. Along the flight deck, green arrows lit. Drakes roared and their pilots moved them to the ready position. The lead Firestorm drake beat a talon against the bone floor then charged off. The noise and spectacle were all-consuming, even for those who had seen it a hundred times.

What Max needed was the cover of another squad. He peered

out again and could make out Hammerclaw pilots mustering outside the guarded locker room, watching Firestorm take off. His breath caught in his throat. Anna-Beth would be among them. He was desperate to let her know he was back and okay for now. For a moment he considered trying to reach her before she flew. He sighed . . . One way or another, she'd know soon enough.

Max dragged his gaze away from the Hammerclaws and watched a couple of Firestormers depart before hurrying back into the depths of the storage area to strip and drag on his suit, storing the scalpel against his thigh. He knew when he did it would go active, but at least without the chip they wouldn't know where he was, nor have his ID. With any luck, it'd be dismissed as a rogue signal.

Luck. Right.

Max dragged the hood over his head, zipped up the suit and was back at the entrance to the deck in time to see the Hammerclaws heading to their pens. Max watched until he'd counted the last of them leaving the locker room, mouthing a prayer for Anna-Beth to be safe.

He pulled his zip up all the way to his throat. 'I'm coming, Martha,' he whispered.

He hesitated a moment, then headed out onto flight deck alpha.

CHAPTER 27

Am I shallow? If you call the link between jockey and drake 'shallow', then yes. If you call the camaraderie of a drake squad 'shallow', then yes. If you call choosing to shorten my life to help guarantee my family lives in peace 'shallow', then yes.

VALERA ORIN, SQUADRON LEADER, INFERNO-X

Gerhard Moeller was normally a man of complete focus and direction. His entire life had been drawn around certainty. Today he had none. He was conflicted and it made him intensely uncomfortable. He'd barely slept, questioning everything he'd done and said since the Halloran incident had blown up and he still couldn't work out if he'd done all, or indeed any, of the right things.

Walking into Flight Command well before dawn he'd been more deliberate than ever: checking the schedule had no holes, no possibilities for confusion and that there was the maximum chance for Halloran to get to his drake and escape. Not that he thought for a moment Max would succeed, not least because Kirby had ordered a hefty dose of tranquilisers fed down his drake's feed tube. Martha couldn't be wiped yet, but she was deeply asleep.

He wasn't sure he wanted Max to succeed, even in getting as far as Martha's pen. But if he didn't, why had he gone to Inferno-X last night and risked his career? Actually, he knew the answer to that: it was so that whether Max made it or not, Valera and her squad wouldn't hate him. He shouldn't have cared about that but he did, and it made some of Kirby's words ring loud in his head.

This time, though, he reckoned he'd called it right. If Max didn't get away, he was Kirby's problem. If he did, well, escaping with Martha was its own death sentence. One way or another, Max was a problem that was going to solve itself.

Moeller stood at the open gallery windows in his office and scratched at some irritated skin on his arm. He'd just watched the Hammerclaws leave and there'd been no sign of Halloran. Whiteheat were due in-pouch imminently and they were the last squadron flying today. Ground forces were already deployed and Kirby had arranged for the flight deck to be retracted until the squads returned. Halloran didn't have much time.

'Probably overslept again,' muttered Moeller and chuckled at his own joke.

It was at the moment that Marie O'Regan led the Whiteheats out onto the flight deck that he decided he wanted Max to escape. If he found a way to expose the truth about Landfill, which he undoubtedly would if he could, it would be expensive for Moeller, but that would be outweighed by seeing Kirby falling flat on his smug, entitled face. It would probably be enough to take him from the race for the next behemoth command post.

'Ah yes, I knew there was another reason I went to see Inferno-X...'

The Whiteheat drakes were roaring and kicking their pens, the shuddering thumps against the metal echoing around the flight deck. They could feel their pilots when they were suited up, every filament live and broadcasting stimulus to the drake mind and nervous system. The pilots were hurrying to their respective pens, their flight crews waiting to open the doors, check their suits and lube levels and disconnect the data feeds.

Moeller's gaze wandered further up the flight deck to Martha's pen with its guard of twelve military police. There were others guarding every entrance to the flight deck, including Flight Command. It made for an impressive net but Max had very smart people helping him out, and there were other ways onto alpha deck if you had the right connections.

Still, getting into Martha's pen wouldn't be easy. Moeller let his gaze wander back down the flight deck. And there he was: trotting up the deck dead centre like he was just a little late to Whiteheat's party. Moeller wondered how long it would be before someone counted the crew and realised he was surplus to requirements.

Halloran put a hand to his ear as he ran then tapped the side of his head and spread his hands. Moeller opened his p-palm and tapped up the com feeds, selecting the open com. Whiteheat pilots were looking round to see who the focus of attention was.

'...you are still dark, call sign guest. Are you picking me up at all? More hand signals appreciated.'

Halloran wobbled a hand then put a finger to his lips.

'If I understand it, transmission is intermittent and quiet. We have no data feed, repeat, your suit is dark. You need to get your spare. Signal acknowledgement.'

Halloran wobbled his hands again and kept on coming. He was halfway up the Whiteheat pens now, and with all their doors open and the first drakes coming out onto the deck, it was a matter of time before the maths didn't add up.

'Come on, Max,' whispered Moeller. 'Make me proud.'

There was no open announcement but just as he'd begun to hope, Moeller saw Mips disengaging from entrance guard and begin to move on Max from three directions. Moeller wanted to shout a warning but all he could do was bite his lip and pray Max had some idea what to do. For a few horrible, yawning seconds, Max didn't notice them at all but then he hesitated, checked behind him and broke into a sprint.

Moeller stepped to the front of the gallery, gripped the rail hard and stared.

*

There were six of them in front of him and a few more were coming from behind, but he couldn't worry about them. He was in the midst of the Whiteheat drake pens and the edges of the runways were becoming ever more crowded with reptilian predators. Max knew he wouldn't be able to break the ring of Mips so he ran to his right across the one hundred and forty metre wide deck.

The shouts to stop were lost in the bellows of drakes and the stamping of taloned feet ringing loud on the bone floor. Over the PA, Kirby's voice – he thought it was Kirby's – ordered him to give himself up. The level of noise was rising sharply and Max had to concentrate on his pursuers, coming in fast, straight down the middle of the runway. They were coming way too quickly down the empty space and were just fifty metres away. Max needed help… and he never doubted he'd get it.

Dead ahead, a drake with signature aquamarine blue flares running down its neck stuck its head out of a pen.

'O'Regan…' He really should ask how she'd got those flares approved… 'Come on, show you can see me.'

Max waved his arms and ripped his hood back off his head, hoping they had some notion of what had happened to him. O'Regan saw him. Her drake ducked her head and moved swiftly towards him, head glancing back and forth, indicating she knew where the Mips were. Max took a deep breath and ran on, trusting their instincts wouldn't let them down.

O'Regan's drake opened her mouth and emitted a battering roar. Max caught the force of her foul breath full in the face and loved it. It was a warning: drakes on the runway, clear the deck. O'Regan brought her drake round. Her head reared up, giving clear passage for Max. Thirty metres the other way, her tail slewed around low and fast, making an onerous 'whoosh'.

All but one of the Mips saw it coming and scattered backwards or leapt the swinging, spiked tail. The other took a glancing blow in mid-calf and was thrown across the deck, tumbling over to lie screaming in pain, one leg at a horribly unnatural angle.

Max ran under the drake's neck and turned left to run up the deck towards the Inferno pens. Ahead of him was a mass of reptilian bodies, mostly broadside to him, all waiting the call to move onto the runway and providing an excellent barrier to his pursuers. He loved Whiteheat; they were a great squadron.

The Mips were regrouping and moving in from his left. Kirby was relaying his position but his people were more cautious now, the cries of their broken comrade still echoing from the bone arches above. Max slid under one gently lifted tail, hurdled another laid down for him and broke into the brief space between Whiteheat and Inferno-X pens. His pursuers were converging from ahead again now, as well as from the left. It was tight.

He made the Inferno pens and became aware of a growing roar from drakes up and down the flight deck, as if they knew he was running for his life, for all their pilots' lives, and were willing him to succeed. It was weird, like running through a freeze-frame. Every drake on the runway was looking at him. Every flight deck crew was transfixed. The gallery was packed, as if the best live event ever was going on below them.

'Enjoy the fucking show, Kirby,' muttered Max.

The pens were in back-to-back pairs with back-to-back tech areas in between. He only had two pairs to pass before reaching Martha but it looked a tall order. Mips were running down the rank towards him. Others were forming a ring around Martha's pen again, zapons buzzing greedily.

Max ran past the first pair of pens, belonging to Valera and Stepanek. Drakes battered their heads hard against the windows along the Inferno run, further disconcerting and distracting already nervous military police.

Max took his cue and leapt into the tech areas that came next. He dodged through monitoring equipment, feed control stations and over the feed and power lines that spread like exposed roots across the floor. He hitched over the rail dividing the two techs as Mips came in on his left, knocking the sophisticated kit aside, hollering for him to stop.

Using the side door of Roberts's pen, which partnered Martha's, he put a foot on the lock wheel and propelled himself upwards, just getting the tips of his fingers over the edge of the low roof that covered the door before sloping sharply up to accommodate a drake standing on hind legs in the pen. He was heading for the roof access ladders, which the maintenance teams apparently used only very rarely to fix fans and suchlike.

The Mips were on him now. They didn't bother with words, just cocked their zapons to strike. Max kicked one in the face and pulled himself up hard, getting an elbow onto the roof. Inside the pen, Roberts's drake was going crazy, talons hammering at the metal and bone walls, sending shivers through the structure.

A zapon whacked his trailing ankle and he jerked, his muscles contracting, body hinging violently at the waist as the pulse fled through him. He gripped the rough bone and metal mesh roof desperately, finding some unexpected upward momentum in the wake of the strike, and managed to pull himself up far enough to roll to temporary safety. He twitched on his back for a moment before hauling himself unsteadily to his feet.

'Shit.'

He steadied himself and climbed the ladder up to the pen roof proper, his body barely under his control. He could hear the Mips gathering themselves to climb up after him. The cacophony of drakes was undimmed, but Kirby's voice could still just about be heard over it.

Max reached the top and half trotted, half shambled across towards Martha's pen. She was silent; asleep, he assumed. His body still ricocheted with the electric pulse, his head hurt and his eyes swam. He forced in deep breaths, trying to relax tight muscles. It didn't entirely work.

Movement on his left. Mips were at the roof line. It was time to pray for maintenance sloth. He scrambled across to Martha's pen, Kirby's voice booming out again in a lull in the drake tumult. Below him, Whiteheat began to take off; the beat of wings and the stamping of feet accelerating along the runway were the soundtrack of his life. He craved the open skies, and he was so close.

Max reached his goal and stopped, looking down at the damaged ventilation fan. He could see Martha curled up, her form flickering between the slow sweeps of the fan blades. Mips were surrounding him now.

'Nowhere to go,' said one. 'Give it up.'

Max smiled, feeling his heart beat fast as the last of the zapon charge dissipated.

'Any of you boys and girls want to join me, you're more than welcome.'

Max raised his right foot and brought it down hard on the hood of the fan. Once, twice, three times. The fan brackets screeched and buckled. The weakest sheared and the whole unit fell into the pen, bouncing harmlessly from Martha's back.

Max didn't pause. He put his arms tight to his sides, feet together and jumped down after it. The moments before he landed on Martha's flank scales were full of the glorious scent of her; the heat of her pen; the warm red glow of the heater lights; and the strong smell of her waste in the slurry channel.

The fall was from no great height, six metres and change, and then down onto the slope of her flank. He relaxed as he struck and slid into a slightly untidy heap on the heated floor. Looking up as he rose and brushed himself down, he saw the Mips crowded round the opening.

'Come on down, join the party.'

'No need, you moron. You're caught. Thanks for the assist.'

Max smiled and trailed his hand lovingly along Martha's scales. He wiped at damp eyes and felt whole once again. The pain of his separation from her was gone and he breathed her in, letting himself dream of the open skies. He moved slowly, enjoying the touch and the edges of warmth in his mind. He paused at the feed lines, staring down at them, seeing them as parasites sucking Martha's life away to the beat of Kirby's warped heart. He bent down and uncoupled them.

'Not any more.'

He walked round to her head, that was partially tucked into a fold in her left wing. He could feel his suit energising with the closeness of her. All he needed was one thing. He knelt by her closed eyes.

'Come on, baby, wake up. Time to fly.'

The flight deck was quiet. Whiteheat was gone, the rest of them knew that Max and Martha were together. Kirby's voice on the PA and over his personal com was finally unimpeded by reptilian interference.

'Max,' he said, his voice soft and full of regret. 'That was one hell of a run. You're one of a kind, I'll give you that. I don't think anyone else could have got as far. But it's done now, okay? Fun's over. Whitehcat is sky-high and the tail closure cycle has begun. There's no way off, Hal-X. So come on. Walk out, come up to Flight Com and let's put this straight.'

'I haven't even started,' said Max over the com. He stroked the top of Martha's head and felt the merest shiver in response. 'That's it, baby.'

'The fact is,' continued Kirby, and Max wasn't at all sure the ExO was really speaking to him, 'there has been a series of unfortunate... misunderstandings, problems blown out of proportion... But it's nothing that can't be straightened out. We all want you back in the pouch, one of Inferno-X. But this isn't the way, Max. We've got to do things right. Step out and talk to us.'

Max bit his lip. The bastard was convincing and he couldn't deny he was tempted. He pulled in a deep cleansing breath and reached out with his mind, searching for Martha's. His whole body warmed, his suit channelled energy around his muscles.

Martha's eye flickered and opened and she regarded him with such *knowledge* that he gasped.

'There you are, princess.'

'What the fu—' Kirby's voice over the PA cut off abruptly.

It would be magnificent up in Flight Com. Lights and warnings would be triggered; neural activity readouts would be fizzing; physical status monitors would be moving from red to green. Max moved to stand in front of Martha.

'Don't even think about it,' Kirby hissed over the suit com.

'Too late,' said Max. 'It's all I've dreamed of since you shut me in Landfill. Now it's my turn to do whatever the hell I want. Best get your people away from the pen door.'

Max could almost see Kirby's writhing fury and he was certain Flight Com was alive with colourful language. Martha began to push herself up to a sitting position, leaning back on her hind legs and tail and raising her front claws off the ground. She lifted her head gingerly on her glorious long neck, the sedative still live in her system.

'What do you think you're doing, Max?' asked Kirby, the conciliatory tone back again. 'There's nothing out there. No food, no water, no drake feed. You're flying out to die.'

'Tell me how that's worse than what you planned for us.'

Martha's head swam on her neck. She was struggling to hold it up. Her neck shuddered under the strain but she managed to move it away from her chest pouch.

'Well done, princess.'

Max climbed her body and triggered the pouch release. It creaked open jerkily, the effort causing Martha to shift her talons, searching for balance. Max paused before climbing into the pouch, his dry suit buffing uncomfortably against the receptor space.

'Sorry, Martha. Almost there.'

Martha released more secretions, helping him slide into the sleeves and settle his back. She rattled phlegm in her throat and Max reached out with his mind, trying to encourage her, feed her energy. The pouch closed and he felt the familiar thrill of connection. Every part of her was open to him and he could sense the sluggishness of her muscles as she fought the sedative.

'Max,' said Kirby. 'The tail's closing. You can't get out.'

'Lucky I don't know how long it takes to complete the cycle. No, wait, I do, you idiot.'

'No one's unlocking the pen, Max,' said Kirby. 'You can't get out.'

Max laughed. 'I'm in a firedrake, dickhead. I don't need someone to let me out. Better get your people clear.'

'Stand down, Halloran. That's an order. Leave this behemoth and I'll have you shot down.'

'You lost the right to command me when you lied to me; you lost the right to command everyone in Inferno-X and every drake pilot on the *HoG*, sir. Five seconds.'

Max brought Martha's head round to the pen door. He could see Mips sprinting for cover. Martha's vision wasn't pin-sharp but she responded to his suggestions and opened her mouth. Her fuel lines swelled, though Max could tell her reserves were depleted.

Max imagined a full-spread flame delivered over maximum range. Heat bloomed briefly and Max's vision filled with fire. Martha's ducts spewed flame across the short gap with enough pressure to carry seventy metres across open sky.

Steel and bone mesh and glass were obliterated. The pen door exploded outwards in a hail of sparks and fire. Alarms rang, sprinkler systems kicked in and safety bulkheads slammed shut, sealing off the flight deck.

Max bent his toes and raised one leg minutely. Martha swayed, but then marched out of her pen through fire and melted bone and out onto the evacuated flight deck. They moved ponderously onto the runway; turning Martha was akin to directing a drunk round corners. He prayed she'd be able to take off.

'Last chance, Halloran,' said Kirby.

'Put Moeller on.'

'What?'

'Put him on.'

Max focused hard down the runway, seeing the tail making its gentle decline and knowing he still had a couple of minutes to get airborne. Martha was trembling and held her neck in an 's' shape for support.

'You can do it, baby. It's just you and me, same as always.'

Martha rumbled her pleasure and settled towards her ready stance.

'Hal-X, Flight Com.'

'Sorry it's come to this, sir.'

'Me too, son. You know we'll hunt you down. There's no escape… we'll track you.'

'Copy that, Flight Com.'

'You can still turn back.'

'No I can't, sir.'

'Copy, Hal-X.'

Max switched off his com and let his sense of Martha fill him. Her breathing was even but shallow, her pulse raised. He could feel the tremble in her body and sense the sluggish state of her mind. And everyone on the flight deck could see her neck swaying and dipping as she struggled to keep her head steady.

He wanted nothing more than to stand her down but instead, he moved his legs forwards, bent his body slightly and suggested speed. Martha barked a muted roar and set off down the runway. She leaned hard over with each pace, rolling uncomfortably from side to side, gathering speed slowly while she fought against falling.

Max gave her everything he had, trying to steady her, keep her running in a straight line. But she veered away continually one way or the other, staggering occasionally when she tried to compensate, and she must have looked for all the world like a sand-head after an all-nighter in Gargan's.

About halfway down, with the tail cycle cramping his take-off zone, Max began to entertain the possibility that she might not get airborne. The chevrons and coloured support pillars seemed to amble by. There was no blurring at the periphery of his vision and there was no energy in her legs.

'It wouldn't look good if we made our escape on foot,' said Max. 'Wake up, princess, this isn't one of those running-through-treacle dreams.'

He leaned in with his mind, knowing what he risked but fearing failure to escape more keenly. The potential of the upgrade was huge and he knew, without having to think or learn, what he could do. He sent her warmth and strength and sent her visions of the open sky, the sensation of heat on her back and memories of the joy of them flying free.

Martha steadied and drove forwards with renewed vigour. Max kept up the stream of sensory stimuli, mentally visualising the gauge of his own energy swinging steadily toward zero, like charge draining from a leaking battery.

Martha's neck stretched towards the free air, she moved fully into a take-off position and pounded down the runway. Max felt the press of acceleration. The painted white ground-speed zone was underfoot and beyond it, the take-off area. It was going to be touch-and-go.

Martha reached the take-off point and snapped her wings out angled for maximum lift as Max directed. She dipped sharply down, her claws rattled across the ramp before, with a single powerful beat, she achieved minimum air speed and flew north under the drooping tail.

Max kept Martha low, following the *HoG*'s footprints and deep tail. He didn't think Kirby would order a spine cannon or a missile launch, but the lower their profile the better. Max's heart was thundering away, every nervous, excited beat amplified within the pouch.

'Long way to go, princess,' he said breathlessly. 'And we need a place to hole up.'

CHAPTER 28

There was so much still unknown but the programme went ahead anyway, imminent invasion being the mother of all expediencies. When would we truly learn the effects of mixing alien and reptilian DNA? And, by extension, the mixing with human DNA? Well, when those effects made themselves known, of course. Hardly a basis for coherent science but there was no alternative.

PROFESSOR HELENA MARKOV, ERC COMMAND LOGS

Moeller took off his headset and walked back into his office. Beyond knowing things were about to get extremely difficult, he had little idea how to react. Fortunately, he had Kirby to crystallise his thoughts for him.

'What the fuck was that about?'

Moeller laid his headset down on his desk and poured himself a mug of coffee. Finally, he turned to see Kirby. The ExO had closed the gallery door and beyond him, the crowd was dispersing though few could resist staring into his office.

'Want one?'

'You tell him you're sorry it's come to this and let him go, and you want me to have a cup of coffee?'

Kirby's face was grey, his expression beyond anger and becoming fear as the consequences of Max's escape settled on him. There was a slight tremble in his hands as they gripped the back of a chair pushed under Moeller's meeting table.

'That's because I *am* sorry,' said Moeller, knowing his determined calm would enrage Kirby further. 'As should you be. This is the mother of all cock-ups and you're in the flame wash.'

'You're loving this, aren't you?'

'As your rival for the next command position, I am delighted to see you self-destruct. As a flight commander who's just lost his best pilot because you let your ambition cloud your judgement, I am disappointed, angry and profoundly worried about the consequences.'

Kirby stared at him and a faint hope glimmered in his eyes.

'It's convenient for you that Halloran escaped, isn't it? You even told him we'd track him, didn't you? I wonder why.'

'You're living in a dream. There is nothing convenient about all the crap that is going to descend in the aftermath of Halloran's escape. I wanted him to change his mind, to realise it was hopeless.'

'Bullshit. You warned him. You as good as wished him bon-fucking-voyage.'

Moeller took a sip of his coffee. It was fresh, hot and the perfect strength. Yarif was the best barista in the fleet. He smelled the aroma and let it calm him before he tried to slap the stupid off Kirby.

'Save your puerile attempts to blame me for Avery and Solomon,' he said. Kirby opened his mouth but Moeller cut him off. 'We're both in serious trouble. Your corner-cutting has led us directly here and I have the misfortune to be the flight commander who let an unauthorised drake off his flight deck. So thank you for that great scar on my record and how about we turn our attention to getting him back?'

'There's nothing to discuss. You're going to turn Whiteheat around and send them after him. You should have already.'

'Perhaps I'll put my coffee down and hit you after all.'

'What?'

'No one is changing Whiteheat's mission. It's the sort of mission that helps win wars. Finding Max will only save your arse. We'll adopt standard procedure for recapturing a rogue drake; there's no hurry. He won't escape tracker range in a day even if he flies non-stop.'

Kirby straightened. 'Only you *reminded* him to remove the drake's tracker. After all, he's already done it to his own suit. You have to react faster.'

'The drake trackers can only be removed by a local surgical procedure. Max doesn't have the tools to do it. And the delay is your fault: if you hadn't bulldozed through your request for a tail-down then Lavaflow, who are on standby, would be on the runway already.'

Kirby stared back down the flight deck, where the tail was almost down, when both their p-palms bleeped and vibrated simultaneously. Both men snapped out their screens and looked at each other.

'The blame game begins,' said Moeller. 'Remember, I know the truth.'

'You're about to learn how powerless you are. There'll be no life for you beyond this behemoth if you don't back me up.'

'Meaning?'

'Meaning my friends are way more powerful than yours. I told you to think ahead, about after the war, and going up against me is a dangerous error.'

Moeller drained his coffee and set the cup down. 'Don't threaten me, Robert, you really don't have the intellect. Meanwhile, I don't think Avery and Solomon want to be kept waiting. Shall we?'

Max's excitement quickly gave way to a more sober assessment of their situation. He was tired and had a headache building from the effort of keeping the stream of imagery going. Martha was beyond exhausted. Her fuel ducts were dry, she was hungry and she shuddered with every beat of her wings.

Max kept them flying due north for as long as he could, trying to work out how long it would be before he was pursued and so how long he could afford to be on the ground conducting minor surgery. No time at all, really.

Below them, the deep trough gouged out by the *HoG's* tail looked ideal. Max tipped his hands out slightly and straightened his legs. Martha landed in the trench, rear legs almost buckling. She slewed to a stop, kicking up clouds of sand and came to an upright rest, rocking on her haunches.

'Sorry, princess, but there's something we've got to do before we go and hide where we can get some rest.'

Martha almost purred. Max triggered the pouch release and clambered out. His limbs were shaking and his normally controlled slide down Martha's body became a fall. He crumpled onto the packed sand, heaving in each breath like it might be his last.

'Whoa.'

Max dragged himself to a hunched sitting position. His body dripped with secretions and his hands trembled. He shook with fatigue and even the thought of dragging his suit off to get at the scalpel was an effort too far. His head was pounding and he was still concentrating on sending a sense of freedom and open skies to Martha, the thoughts fading slowly and unwillingly.

He dropped his hands to find Martha's head very close and her eyes staring down the beautiful lines of her muzzle into his.

'Sorry, princess... Just need a moment here.' Martha fired a foul lungful of stale air into his face. In addition to the obvious irritation, he could sense hunger too. 'Point taken.'

Max leaned on the top of her muzzle and pushed himself to his feet as Martha shook her head, almost knocking him back on to the floor. The sun was only halfway into its climb but it was already a crushingly hot day and the cooling effects of Martha's secretions were short-lived.

The walls of the trough the *HoG*'s tail dug were taller than Max. He stared south as if straining to the limits of his vision would allow him to see her as a speck in the distance. There was no dust cloud on the horizon, indicating that she hadn't moved.

Max scrambled up the side of the trough to be greeted with a view of endless desert in every direction. There were no meaningful features, just rolling, wind-blown dunes, scraps of vegetation and an ocean of silent beauty. 'Well, that clears up where we are, exactly.'

Max slid back down and for the first time the disconnection between his life and the world through which he travelled was obvious. It was an uncomfortable sensation. The *Heart of Granite* was a windowless cocoon, a mobile hive with its grunts and pilots as its drones. They saw what they were told to see, flew where they were ordered to fly and were encouraged not to ask questions.

It presented Max with problems. He had to keep out of the way of the *HoG*, the *Ironclaw* and the *Steelback* and had only his own rough calculations to give him safe corridors for flying. Worse, the landscape offered precious few opportunities to hide and that made the inevitable search for him far simpler. He wondered what Valera would do, what she'd say to him.

The thought of his skipper triggered an uncomfortable slew of emotions. Max gazed up into the sky. He craved to be there but not alone, not without the radio chatter, the comfort of the squad around him and Kullani a wingspan away. With what he knew about the Fall he could really help her now... but not from out here. Max cleared his throat and switched his attention south along the trough. If he strained hard, he imagined he could hear laughter in the squad room and his arms around Anna-Beth.

Max shook his head. 'Perhaps I should just go back and throw myself on Commander Avery's mercy.'

He felt a rough-edged jab in his back and turned around. Martha's nostrils flared. She must have guessed what he was thinking.

They stared at each other for a moment, then she moved her head, turning it to the right and tipping it up to expose the soft skin at the base of her ear slit, beneath which sat the tracker.

'You're not supposed to know it's there, are you?'

In response, Martha spat a tiny ball of flame into the sand where it fused a few square centimetres to glass; well, when it cooled it would be, sort of. Max frowned and began shrugging off his suit so he could get at the scalpel tucked against his left thigh.

Pulling his weary arms from the suit and pushing it over his torso required a far greater effort than it should have and Max felt another twinge of anxiety. Kirby had done a number on them both and neither had the strength for much more.

Max pulled the scalpel from its resting place. It had cut his thigh, of course, but nothing serious. He gripped the blade the way he'd seen surgeons do on the medical shows, his hands trembling slightly, and placed the tip on Martha's body, stretching the scales away from the incision point with his other hand.

Her scales felt dry, having nothing of the slight oiliness of healthy lubrication. Across her body they ranged from dinner-plate-sized irregular pentagons to the thumb-sized, teardrop shapes beneath her ear slits. There was an artistry to how they meshed and moved, combining maximum protection with great flexibility. Max felt like he was about to commit a crime.

'This won't hurt a bit,' he said.

Max took a breath and pushed. The blade cut easily into the small section of scale-free flesh. Martha rattled phlegm in her throat but didn't react otherwise. However, Max was treated to a sharp pain below his left ear that made him wince.

'Very funny.'

Max cut a slit big enough to accommodate his thumb and forefinger then laid the scalpel on the sand. He pushed into the fat below the skin, feeling the edges of the diminutive bio-plastic chip almost immediately. Flesh had grown around it in places and an experimental tug proved fruitless.

'More slice and dice, Martha,' he said.

He picked up the scalpel again and widened the incision a little. Martha rumbled and Max made some ineffectual soothing noises. He found the chip with thumb and forefinger again then began to edge the flesh away from the chip, gritting his teeth at every scrape and jerky movement.

'Sorry,' he said. 'Nearly…'

He was treated to more prickly sensations under his ear and prayed he didn't do Martha any more serious damage. He gave the chip another tug, feeling it give but for the back right corner. He slipped the scalpel in once more, the chip came free, and he found himself sitting on his backside in the sand, Martha's baleful gaze upon him.

Max slapped her muzzle playfully. 'Here, take it out on this.'

He tossed the chip on the ground, where Martha stared at it for a second then dripped fire on it, melting it to a puddle. No more tracker data, no more drake cam feeds either. Max felt a momentary smugness.

'Bye-bye, Kirby,' said Max.

He rubbed the top of Martha's head and scratched her under the chin when she displayed it for him.

'What now, eh?' he said, though the answer was as glaring as the sun. 'Move on, stay under the radar and find a place to rest. What could be simpler?'

Solomon's quarters contained a small meeting room with a wooden table big enough for six, three walls hung with schematics of behemoths designed for desert, ice and rainforest, and a fourth dominated by a big screen. Moeller found himself staring at them a good deal in an effort not to enjoy Kirby's discomfort too much. After all, it would be his turn soon enough. What concerned him most was that Avery had so far said nothing at all. That was never, ever a good sign.

'Thank you for your version of events,' said Solomon in the wake of Kirby's report. 'You clearly have quite a talent for fiction.'

What little colour remaining in Kirby's face drained away. 'I assure you this is wholly accurate—'

'I asked you to perform two tasks,' snapped Solomon. 'They weren't hard. I didn't ask you to perform a solo take-down of the *Maputo* armed only with a box cutter, did I? No. I asked you to keep one pilot in the most secure medical unit on this behemoth and to ensure his drake's digestive tract was emptied and remained that way. So you'll understand I'm a little taken aback that you failed in both.'

'He had help,' said Kirby weakly.

Solomon stared at him. 'Deduced that all by yourself, did you? Most popular pilot, unjustly imprisoned, I mean, what were the chances, eh? Of course he had help! And why isn't every possible suspect already in the brig being questioned? Why is that sly bitch Orin still in her rack?'

'Because she had nothing to do with Halloran's escape,' said Moeller, immediately wishing he'd kept quiet.

'Oh, really? I'm in the company of not one but two master detectives, am I? Enlighten me, Sherlock… No, you're more Costa Khan. He can be Sherlock. How did you reach that astounding conclusion?'

'Orin and her squad were confined to quarters the entire time, as ordered by the ExO.'

'Like that makes one turd of difference.'

'Plus I know her, and you don't,' said Moeller evenly.

'Oh, really? And what do you think we'd find if we pulled their encrypted coms, eh?' said Solomon. 'Here's what will happen. Pull in anyone who had contact with Halloran, anyone with anything to gain from his escape. Get pressure on that upstart who fed the drake because I want to know who told her to do it. When we're done with staff, I'll be sending people into the flesh tunnels.'

Moeller hissed in a breath.

'Problem?' snapped Solomon.

'Ma'am, we need the Blammers, however fucked up that is.'

'But, and I get the irony, they're not above the law. A crime has been committed here and we will find and punish the perpetrators. Do I make myself clear? Good.

'Next, Nicola. Since I can't trust either of these two to tie their fucking shoelaces, you will lead the search and recapture of Hal-X. Presumably you already have resources committed. How long until you have him back here?'

Commander Avery finished tapping on her p-palm before leaning back in her chair. Moeller could feel Solomon's temperature rise.

'We will remain on station as per the current published schedule. A standard grid search has been authorised and given the drake tracker location, we anticipate a successful outcome today. If not, we will pass the search on to the support forces behind us and move on. Should Halloran or his drake remain missing for three days, they will be recorded as lost, presumed deceased. As you are aware, our attack on the *Maputo* must take place within the next two days or the window will close.'

'That is entirely unacceptable,' said Solomon. 'This behemoth goes nowhere until we have Halloran back on board.'

Moeller cleared his throat, half-expecting a frost to form on his breath so cold had the room become.

'This is my behemoth,' said Avery quietly. 'And I have orders to fulfil.'

'I am changing those orders.'

'With all due respect, ma'am, you may not do that without first consulting the joint chiefs of staff.'

'Three smart-arses in the room, just what I need. I will have their confirmation of those orders by dusk. This behemoth will not move.'

Avery shrugged. 'As you wish. Then for the record, and I will send all necessary supporting data to the joint chiefs, in my opinion the *Heart of Granite* will be unable to fulfil her primary mission parameters due to the imminent failure of critical systems and habitat priorities. She's already gasping, Alex, we're right on the edge. We have one chance to attack the *Maputo* and then we're hauling for the Vermelho Sea.'

Solomon mimicked her shrug. 'Then the *Steelback* will have to sub-in supported by the *Ironclaw*. I'll authorise the sentience upgrade across all squadrons in the Mid-Af theatre.'

'Forgive my ignorance,' said Avery, 'But this whole attack depends on the skills of Inferno-X in enhanced drakes, depleted though the squadron is, to create a gap that ground forces and supporting squadrons from all three behemoths can exploit. You are advocating removing a third of the firepower and the most influential drake squadron from the battle. We cannot bring down the *Maputo* that way.'

'Then get me Halloran. Quickly. Otherwise your fellow commanders will have to find a way to prove you wrong.'

'I don't get it,' said Avery. 'This is the break you and Corsini have been fighting for. If we take out the *Maputo* we will see victory in less than a year.'

'Believe me, if someone else picks up Halloran there will be no victory. None of us will see the end of the war.'

'He's one man,' said Moeller, aware that Kirby's silence meant he knew something Avery and Moeller didn't. 'Like as not he'll be dead in a day. Mar— His drake has minimal nutrients, Max is starving and there's nothing within exhaustion range. As Nic said, if we don't find him his chances of survival are minimal to vanishing.'

'Even if he dies, no one salvages his body or his drake but us,' said Solomon. 'No one examines them but Markov. News of their escape does not leave this behemoth. Otherwise we'll have a shit storm on the back of a fireball to deal with. Make your staff aware: whatever they think they know, they keep it to themselves.'

'He's a rogue pilot, it's hardly a PR disaster, is it? The public have seen it before and like all the others, he'll die in the pouch—' Moeller stopped when he felt Kirby's and Solomon's eyes on him. The pieces started dropping into place. 'You don't think he'll die, do you? You think he'll survive the Fall.'

'What?' said Avery.

Solomon and Kirby glanced at each other, and Solomon gave the slightest shrug and the curtest of nods. Kirby spoke.

'Yes, we do. He's a perfect, if difficult, test subject. Halloran has a uniquely strong physiology and brain chemistry combination. Why do you think Markov relocated here a few months ago? Why do you think Alex is here and the upgrade was pushed through?'

'Then why did you chuck him in Landfill?'

'Because he was about to expose everything. And if we couldn't monitor him in-pouch, we could still do critical research in Landfill. Simple, really,' said Kirby.

'You talk about him as if he's some kind of experiment!'

'Don't be so naïve, Gerhard,' said Solomon. 'They're all experiments. We know *everything* about every pilot.'

Moeller felt a chill across his back. 'Monitoring and measuring is one thing, experimenting on them to further your ambitions, that's something else entirely. This mess is a direct result of your misguided interventions.'

Solomon stared at him and the pity in her eyes made him want to punch her teeth in. Instead, he sat in silence while Kirby swelled with glee.

'And you want to be a behemoth commander? My advice: get your head out of the drake's arse it's been stuck in. God's holy prick, Nicola, where do you get your execs from, the idiot tree?'

Moeller felt his cheeks reddening.

'Fine,' he said calmly, using every mote of his experience to remain so. 'I'm not a political animal. But I am also the most effective flight commander in UE. Do you want to win this war, or just carry on playing your power games?'

'The fact that you think they're incompatible rather makes my point,' said Solomon.

'I'm not with you,' said Moeller.

Solomon rolled her eyes. 'We can agree on that, at least. Let me lay it out for you: I know the potential of every pilot in the service. Every. Single. One. So does Markov. And on the *HoG*, so do Avery and Kirby. Pilots with particular skills are gathered together for closer analysis across the fleet.'

Moeller winced. He'd known I-X were special but he'd never asked himself why.

'Every behemoth needs a gun squadron, the flag carrier more than any other. I didn't realise they were a mere experiment,' he said.

'Their skill is certainly a bonus when it comes to skinning enemy drakes but it doesn't end there.' Solomon sucked her top lip a moment then began to count off on her fingers. 'Orin – Iron Mind – her longevity is unparalleled. We've been experimenting with her endurance, trying to mimic her brain patterns for eleven months now. Stepanek's reactions are stunning; his synaptic velocity is off the scale. Something in Redfearn's mind mimics mind-shielding; we don't know how yet, but we think her mind might be even stronger than Orin's. Have you seen how smoothly Monteith flies? Something in his neural pathways and specific muscle chemistry gives him extraordinary control over his movements. Want me to go on? Everyone in that squad has a unique strength; we're working to develop it, clone it, and roll it out as an upgrade for every pilot.'

'And you think Max can survive the Fall?'

'He is the distillation of every other pilot in Inferno-X. If we can capture and share his strengths, we'll win this war.'

Moeller cursed himself for his naivety. 'This upgrade's all part of it, isn't it? Not just a financial win.'

'Now you're getting it,' said Kirby.

'But, unshielded it's not research and experimentation; it's gambling.'

'It's a calculated risk,' said Kirby.

Moeller laughed, he couldn't help himself. 'But if it fails you've tossed all of Inferno-X away.'

Kirby shrugged and Moeller almost punched him then and there. 'It's inevitable that the throughput of pilots will increase but remember, we save money on both time and training new jockeys.'

Moeller sat back in his chair. He felt like he was among strangers, listening to sedition, rather than meeting with people he'd worked with and mostly respected for years. But now he was on the outside, and it had only taken one word to convince him of that.

'*Throughput*,' he snarled. 'You're not fit to be the ExO. These are *human beings*, you soul-sucking, heartless reptile.'

'Yeah, that's right,' said Kirby, leaning in so Moeller had the full measure of his contempt. 'Human beings who watch vids of poster boys like Max and cannot sign on fast enough. They're ours, and even if the Inferno-X experiment plays out badly we'll have so many willing to take their re-engineered drakes that the Mafs and the Sambas will wilt under the barrage. But if this works and we have Max out there, a true drake pair, maybe others from Inferno will survive the Fall with him? We'll be unstoppable. We can't lose. So long as no one learns our pilots are surviving the Fall and that by default we had to be complicit in their survival. You do get that, don't you? That's why we have to get Max back here, alive or dead.'

Moeller's p-palm bleeped and he snapped it open rather than spend another second watching Kirby. Yarif had sent him a vid from all the newsnets in UE.

'Too late,' said Moeller, and swiped it up to the big screen.

It was a little shaky but there was no doubting the insignia in the background. There was an icy silence as they watched high definition sound and video of Martha demolishing her pen door and then taking off with that disconcerting drunken stagger.

'There goes your poster boy.'

Solomon turned from the screen and her face was a snarl.

'Fuck you, Moeller.'

CHAPTER 29

> Funny how times change. The sky used to be full of planes and helicopters. There are still a few left, powered by biofuel, but shit do they look weird chugging around up there. Clumsy, no grace, and seriously vulnerable too. The drake… that's the way to fly.
>
> MAX HALLORAN

Valera had taken one look at Kullani and knew why Grim had looked so scared. She was going downhill fast. The heaters were doing their work but she needed physical contact with her drake. Valera hoped she'd be capable of walking as far as the flight deck when the time came.

'I don't get it, Skipper,' said Grim. 'It came on like someone flicked a switch.'

Kullani was sitting up in bed, her face grey and with a tic in her left eye. To the casual observer, it probably looked like a bad cold.

'How's the head, Risa?'

Kullani's eyes swam towards her. 'I can barely hear you, the roaring inside is so loud. It's full of fluid, sloshing like a tank too full of sludge. I can't focus. I need my drake.'

Valera put her hand on Risa's clammy one.

'You've got to hang on. They can't keep us in lockdown forever… The *Maputo* attack is imminent and we're the arrowhead.'

'I thought the heaters would stop this,' said Kullani. 'Would make me feel normal.'

'Yeah, but flying your drake's the other half of the equation, right? We all get more and more grouchy the longer we're away from our drakes but it's worse for you. Reach out, see if you can touch minds. But do it carefully.'

'I'm not sure I can project through the sludge,' said Kullani, smiling feebly. 'I'll give it a shot.'

'None of us is an expert,' said Valera gently. 'We all have to find our own way. Remember I-X is with you the whole time, okay?'

Kullani gripped Valera's hand and squeezed it, then jerked back at the sound of a huge cheer from the squad rec. Valera heard wild whoops and the slap of high fives and Max's name was trumpeted loud and long. Footsteps pounded towards Kullani's door and it was thrust open.

'You have GOT to see this.' Monteith pointed at Kullani. 'Want a lift?'

'If you're asking if I'd like to arrive in a style befitting a woman of my importance, then yes, a lift would be lovely.'

Monteith flashed that awesome, melting smile of his. 'That is, of course, precisely what I am asking. May I?'

'You may.'

Monteith knelt by the bed, put his arms beneath her knees and shoulders and lifted her in one easy motion. The squad rec had gone quiet and Valera led the way out to find them all staring at her, the anticipation burning them like kids at Christmas.

There was an image of flight deck alpha on the big screen with a pause symbol across it. Monteith sat Kullani front and centre and the squad grouped around her, Valera and Grim sandwiching her.

'What happened? Did Kirby fall off the gantry or something?' asked Valera. 'Because that would be such a shame.'

'Oh, it's much, much better than that,' said Stepanek. 'Tap it, Reds.'

The pause symbol disappeared and Valera watched with increasing excitement and a very comforting sense of validation as Max's escape played out on the screen. The sequence ended to more whoops, cheers and high fives. Beside her, Kullani had tears rolling down her cheeks but her eyes were clearer. Grim was sobbing through the broadest smile Valera had seen in days.

'Did you ever doubt he'd do it?' Monteith's face was huge in Valera's vision when he bellowed the question.

She laughed and pushed him away. 'It's so good to see him actually do it, though. Tell me, is this ship-only or has it gone wide?'

'It's on every newsnet across UE,' said Calder. 'Can't believe there wasn't a blackout in place.'

'I'm sure there is,' said Valera. 'This is going to cause some serious ripples.'

She pushed herself from her seat and headed for her usual place.

'Okay, I-X,' said Stepanek. 'Looks like the skipper's got a few things to say.'

The squad moved quickly to their seats, still buzzing from the video. Stepanek ordered quiet.

'We have to plan fast, before Kirby's puppets are banging on our door,' said Valera. 'Can they break the encryption on our coms?'

'Not a chance,' said Gurney. 'We bounced every word around more parts of the central core than Max has notches on his bed post. And we've put in that hide and seek subroutine the Blammers sold me that sends the messages further into the murk if a trace is put out. It's really bloody clever.'

'So what happens when they break the regs and take our p-palms away for analysis?'

Gurney shrugged. 'It'll get them nothing. Every encrypted message is on auto-delete, every p-palm scrambles each screen tap to defeat keystroke analysis. I'll check everyone's kit to make sure but there's really nothing to worry about.'

'Good.' Valera felt a little better. 'And all of you... plausible deniability. We were all in lockdown so we couldn't communicate with anyone, all right? Don't go getting pissed and mouthing off. Moving on: Calder, we need to set up contact with Max if we can. He'll have dumped his locators or they'd have caught him by now. How do we tight-beam him?'

Calder pushed her hands through her hair. 'I've got some coms kit stripped out of an old suit of mine somewhere. Think if we can patch it into the ship's coms via the old wall buttons we might be able to piggyback the array.'

'Detectability?'

'Minuscule chance. So many coms in and out, it'd be virtually impossible to strip out one.'

'How long will it take?'

Calder shrugged. 'I don't even know it's possible yet.'

Valera smiled. 'Fair enough. Best get to it, we don't know how much time we've got before Kirby comes a-calling or we get put back on flight duty.'

'What's going to happen to him?'

Grim's question bled the euphoria from the squad room like a knife to the throat and every eye turned to Valera, searching for hope. She wanted to give it to them but she wasn't a bullshitter, never had been.

'Without help, you know he's got little chance out there,' she said. 'But there was no other choice. We don't know much about Max's condition barring how fit he is and how strong his spirit is. But he's going to be living with Martha twenty-four seven. We can all do the maths.'

'That bastard better not beat me into the Fall,' said Kullani. Laughter fled around the squad room, easing the pain of knowledge. 'Can't he leave me to be better at *one* thing than him?'

'Wouldn't really be him, would it?' said Monteith.

'Got no chance, has he?' said Gurney.

'But this is Max,' said Valera, wishing greater strength on him than even he possessed. 'He might even survive it. That's why I want contact. Then at least we can be with him on whatever journey he takes. It's the best we can hope for.'

It was mid-morning on the second day of the hunt for Max Halloran and the bridge was starting to smell. Nothing overpowering or nauseating but for those who worked there day by day, it was a warning that shouldn't be ignored. It was the smell that signified a behemoth operating beyond its safe working parameters; that the *Heart of Granite* should be making best speed to the Vermelho Sea for a regeneration cycle. Not running combat sorties.

Commander Avery paused by the brain and laid a hand gently on the shoulder of one of the bread-heads. Lieutenant Sally Hall started, her hands still making their delicate adjustments, a faraway look in her eyes.

'Just a quick one, I can see you're wired in right now,' she said. 'How's the texture?'

'Dry,' she said. 'Synaptic connection is slow... slower. You'll have to check with bio-systems integration but she feels proper creaky, like she's been on an all-nighter, you know? How long are we staying here?'

Avery pursed her lips. 'Just be gentle with her, all right?'

'Yes, ma'am.'

Avery strode to the command screens, seeing the buckets positioned on the floor to catch the odd drip of visceral fluid plopping down from the bone-metal interfaces. She took in the active drake cams relaying the hunt for Halloran. Flamehawk-G and Firestorm-E were grid-searching. Avery's eye was caught by two stationary cameras. She noted the call signs under the cams and patched herself into the squad com.

'Jas-G, Kal-G, this is Avery.'

'Copy, ma'am,' they replied.

'Why are you on the ground?'

'This is the farthest north confirmed landing point,' said Jas-G. 'He was here. Footprints of man and drake. Evidence of flame on the ground... Hold on, ma'am. Kally, hold that up to my cam?'

Avery sighed. It was a fused black mass, small and melted, almost unrecognisable from its original form.

'You reading that, Commander?' asked Jasmine.

'Copy, Jas-G. Now we know it didn't fail...'

'Never very likely,' said Kally.

'No indeed. He must have found a blade. Complete your sweep and come back. We've got some poor weather coming in from the east at dusk.'

'Copy, ma'am.'

Avery put her headset down on the tac-table and looked across the command consoles to Moeller. Since learning the truth, the man had aged ten years.

'Gerhard?'

Moeller straightened and told whoever he was talking to out in the field to stand by. 'Hammerclaws are on approach. I need to get back to Flight Command.'

Avery nodded. 'He can't just have vanished and there's nowhere to hide. Why haven't we found him? The cams should have picked up something.'

'We only know his position until he went dark. It was another hour before we got there and in that time he could have gone *anywhere*. We've covered three hundred square klicks and we haven't scratched the surface.'

'Think he's hiding?'

'Where? I think he'll fly east or west as far as he can and then he'll try to find shelter.'

'Then what?' asked Avery.

'Unless he finds sanctuary, he'll die.'

'Commander?' Avery swung round sharply. 'Bio-systems and integrated systems update. It's ugly stuff, want a précis?'

'Yes,' she said, relaxing. 'Go ahead, Doctor Rosenbach.'

'Sitting here all night has accelerated the existing problems. Being stationary has played havoc with her digestive system, blood pressure and musculoskeletal linkages. We've got tension in ligaments and cramps in major muscle groups. If we sit here another two days, we'll have to drag her to the Vermelho Sea.'

'What about life systems?'

'That depends on how long we're staying here and whether we still plan to hunt the *Maputo* or not.'

'Assume that we are.'

'Then it's going to get uncomfortable. To keep ground and air assets in combat condition, we'll have to divert power from the core life systems. Even so, we'll struggle to deliver peak nutrition levels to any of our assets. The *HoG* is already on reduced absorption. Combine that with her digestive inefficiency – she's been excreting undigested proteins for some days now – and we'll be in emergency conditions within forty-eight hours.'

'You're lucky I'm not one to shoot the messenger.'

'It's not that... Well, it is... It's that, well, while we can do the standing exercise routines with the *Heart*...'

'Yes, we've all enjoyed her gyrating on the spot and the rotational leg lift boogie.'

Rosenbach grimaced. 'It's not enough. Standing still places stress on the spine, and allows lactic acid to build up in the key joints. That affects the forty-mils and the spin-up of the rocket sheds. We're talking artillery jams already.'

Avery scratched her forehead. 'Anything else?'

Rosenbach tapped her p-palm and Avery's pinged as it received the report file. 'You said there was bad weather on the way?'

'An almighty sandstorm is hitting us just after dusk, winds in excess of a hundred and ten. We'll be locked tight for tonight and well into tomorrow. Satellite coms will be degraded or non-existent.'

'If the sandstorm lasts more than twelve hours, battery charge will be so low we'll have to head east immediately.'

She knew it shouldn't have but the news actually cheered Avery. Something to force Solomon's hand perhaps. Then again, she'd probably have the crew attach ropes to the *Heart* and pull her into battle.

'Thank you. I'll take your findings and recommendations to the marshal general.'

'Thank you, Commander.'

'Is Professor Markov back on board?'

'Arrived about three hours ago from the *Steelback*. She's briefed and, well, you know, irritable.'

Avery laughed. 'I wouldn't have it any other way. Perhaps you'd like to direct her ire towards Kirby or the marshal gen in the first instance. Up here, we're just trying to sweep up their mess.'

CHAPTER 30

> To guide a subject successfully through the Fall would move the course of human evolution in a new and exciting direction that would benefit us all. To say it would move us further from God is arrant nonsense based on groundless fears and a slavish adherence to ancient writings of dubious provenance.
>
> PROFESSOR HELENA MARKOV, ERC LECTURE PROGRAMME

Corsini was at his desk and it looked as if he hadn't slept. Crumpled suit, unshaven, unkempt hair, and his eyes were red-rimmed but bright.

'Been on the DoubleOs again, Gilles?' asked Solomon, settling down at her desk in her quarters and facing him through a desktop screen. She'd taken the precaution of appearing a little ragged herself. No point in pumping up his self-righteous indignation further than it was already bound to be. 'I'm guessing you've either found a new intern to screw or the crowds have got a little large on the front lawn.'

Corsini said nothing but his face flushed a deeper shade of absolutely furious. He picked up his screen and Solomon was treated to a jumble of jittering office imagery before he pointed it through his large bay window at the crowd below. Actually, it was less a crowd at the gates of the presidential residence, more of a howling mob, in front of whom a group of security personnel stood filming everyone and everything that they did.

Corsini held the screen there until the mob noticed him and began hurling abuse and missiles in his direction. A couple of half-bricks bounced from the windows. Corsini didn't flinch. Solomon assumed he must be used to it. He walked back to his desk and replaced the screen in its cradle before sitting down.

'All right, so people are unhappy,' said Solomon. 'Just for context, how many demonstrators are out there on a normal day?'

Corsini shrugged. 'Thirty to forty, usually religious nuts, a few peace protestors and the Luddite brigade.'

'I see.' There had to be five hundred people out there today. 'I'll never ever say this again but I'm sorry the events on the *Heart of Granite* have affected you in this way.'

Corsini gave a harsh laugh. 'If it was just them, I wouldn't care. Unfortunately, the newsnets are running outrageous conspiracy theories twenty-four seven, so I'm having to host a series of meetings to convince them we are not actually running a Fall research programme despite its proscription. They aren't buying the rogue drake thing. No one is.'

Solomon didn't reply at once. This was at the upper end of her PR fears and the acceleration of the situation was spectacular. If this got any worse, Corsini would shut them down, forcing him into inevitably disastrous diplomatic moves.

'The truth is that Halloran was in Landfill after exhibiting the early stages of the Fall. He broke out, escaped, and will be recaptured within the next twenty-four hours.'

Corsini stared straight down the barrel of the screen. 'No one, but no one, gives a shit about any of that. You're telling me the story I specifically said no one was buying.'

'You asked for the truth,' said Solomon, feeling an unusual sensation of discomfort.

'And I'm still waiting for it. I also speak regularly to Professor Markov because, for very obvious reasons, I have to keep a forensic watch on Project Cerberus. We are playing a very dangerous game here.'

Solomon made to speak but Corsini raised a hand.

'Let's assume I'm not a total idiot. Although I invited you to run the latest upgrade, I do not recall sanctioning live Fall-survival testing. So, let's try the truth again, shall we?'

Corsini was enjoying himself despite his situation.

'Halloran found out more than he should and had to be silenced. No one has sanctioned Cerberus survival-testing.'

'Well, congratulations on a monumental screw-up then, because it's starting to look like Halloran did it for himself. Promise me you're about to recapture him.'

'I can't do that. His locators are gone, his cams are gone; he's disappeared.'

Corsini leaned right into the screen. 'It's a fucking desert, Alex! And he's flying a thirty-metre-long firedrake. How hard can it be?'

'It's a fucking big desert and he could have gone anywhere. Now there's a major storm on the way. Even if he's survived this long, a sandstorm will finish him off.'

'You'd better pray you're right because if he Falls and survives and word gets out, I'll lose the election, if I last in office that long.'

'I'm aware of the risks,' said Solomon, feeling an unwelcome flush in her face.

'You know, Alex, I really don't think you are.'

The silence was growing ever more agonising. And as much as they told themselves contact was extremely unlikely, the spectre of hope was within each one of them and the longer they were denied what they wanted, the harder it got. Valera almost wished she hadn't asked Calder to put the coms package together in the first place.

The rig was in her pod and wires trailed out of the door, where they hooked into the old ship's com through which Calder had managed to access the main wide-beam com system and hide their signal amid the mass of traffic in and out of the behemoth.

Valera took a breath and tried again.

'Hal-X, Val-X. If you copy, please respond. Max, there's bad weather racing in from the east. Gale force winds have kicked up a sandstorm. You need to find shelter urgently.' Tears suddenly threatened and her voice wobbled. 'Please, Max, respond. We need to know you're alive. We want to help you. Hang in there, Hal-X.'

Nothing. Not even static clicks or wind rush.

Valera looked up at Stepanek, expecting to see denial, but he shrugged. 'He's a little bastard but he gets to you, doesn't he? Got to respect what he tried to do and I hate it that I can't help.'

'We have to believe we still can,' said Valera, wiping her eyes with the heels of her palms.

'How?' asked Stepanek. 'He's got nowhere to go.'

'Footsteps!' warned Redfearn from outside. 'Multiple, approaching fast.'

'Calder!' Valera snapped her fingers. 'Reds, get clear. Grim, get out of sight and stay in here.'

Calder yanked on the wires, pulling them from the behemoth's com. She bundled them up with the old suit com unit and was stuffing them into Valera's cupboard when the squad door opened, slapping against the bone wall.

'Don't you people ever knock?' asked Redfearn from outside, just before Valera opened her pod door to confront the intruders.

'I don't need your permission,' said Kirby. 'Get your squad into the rec right now.'

Valera stepped out into the corridor coming uncomfortably close to the ExO.

'You're rather in my way, sir,' she said, her mind full of the joy she'd take from kicking him straight in his balls. 'Reds, get the squad all neat and tidy, would you? I'd hate to disappoint the ExO.'

Kirby was forced to move back, close to Hewitt and Andersen.

Valera smiled sweetly and led Kullani and the others out of her pod.

'What were you doing in there?' demanded Kirby, walking close behind them.

'Group sex, sir,' said Valera. 'What else is there to do?'

Valera sat in her usual place, smiling at her squad, all standing to attention like they were about to meet the new teacher at school. Kirby would know it was a hair from an insult but that he could do nothing about it.

'Have a seat, sir.'

Stepanek was smiling at Andersen. 'Dental work going okay?'

'You will hold your tongue,' snapped Kirby. He didn't sit down. 'The fact is I need your help. Halloran is going to die out there and the coming storm means we have little time. He's weak and sick and so is his drake. We can save his life so let's put aside who did what to help who. Tell me where he's hiding and we'll go get them both. Squad's like family, right? So do the right thing by him.'

Kirby stared squarely at Valera and she met his gaze while she tried to unpick how she was feeling.

'How can we know where he's gone, sir?' she said, keeping her voice deliberately calm and even. 'We've had no way of contacting him since you threw him in Landfill.'

Kirby spread his hands. 'I just don't believe you. It's preposterous to think that none of you helped Halloran. Plainly, Grimaldi had her orders and I presume she's here somewhere. Perhaps I'll take her in for more detailed questioning in advance of her official hearing. She or one of the pilots from Landfill will talk and then I'll have what I want. So, last chance, Inferno-X. Speak up, save Max.'

Kullani twitched but said nothing. Kirby smiled horribly and turned his focus on her.

'And then there's you, Pilot Risa Kullani. A couple of things were brought to my attention ... A little note Moeller made about your condition in what he thinks is a private log, a bit of footage from the flight deck that came my way. Makes me wonder if you aren't hiding something rather more serious than a bang on the head.'

'I'm fine, sir. And I've had a brain pattern scan since.'

'Still, as ExO, I wonder if a couple of days under test in Landfill would show that you're Falling. But, you know, I'm not without heart. None of these things *has* to happen so long as I get enough intel to lead me to Halloran. You know how things are. I'm a busy man, prone to forgetting trivialities.'

Kullani stood up immediately and gave Valera a hug, speaking softly into her ear at the same time.

'Get Max. He can save me.'

Valera froze, realising what Kullani intended and not seeing a better option.

'Best you take me for testing. Better to be safe, right?'

Kirby was plainly off balance. 'What?'

Kullani smiled. 'Oh dear, no other bargaining chip? What's your next play, sir? Thing is, even if we knew anything, none of us would talk. And you know, the only people tougher than drake pilots are the flight crew.'

Kirby stared at her. 'You're making the biggest mistake of your short life.'

Kullani shrugged and pointed. 'Landfill's up in the skull. Want me to show you the way?'

CHAPTER 31

There is no chat-up line in the world that can beat: 'I'm Max, I'm a firedrake pilot.' MAXIMUS HALLORAN

They'd all been looking in the wrong place. Every pilot knew where they'd go if they went rogue and none of them would ever tell command. So the squadrons searched the ground for every likely hiding place, just as they'd been ordered, and none were surprised they didn't find him.

The ground-bound always thought in two dimensions and were arrogant enough to think a pilot would do the same. So while ground and air lizards were tasked with searching every centimetre of sand and the few areas of cover it contained, Max and Martha were flying very high, floating on the upper thermals, their energy use minimal, their peace complete though sadly temporary.

They had slept on the ground that first night. It was safe enough, though it had been cold and Max had spent most of his time in Martha's pouch, feeling her shiver and her yearning for the heated pen that had been her home all her life. Yet he didn't sense any anger or regret and he tried not to think too hard about why.

Waking this morning had been an anxious affair. Max had half-expected to be changed. To have Fallen. But he wasn't and didn't even feel weird... not cold or hot, no blurred eyesight or seeing visions of blood and fire everywhere.

But it wouldn't last. Not unless he could figure a way out of the mess he was in and that didn't seem too likely. He'd ignored it all day while they rode the glorious high skies far to the east but then Martha had begun to get edgy because she could sense something. It wasn't just that they were both getting tired again, and hungry... Bloody hell, Max was famished... It was more than that.

Valera's voice over the com had startled him after the day of static and he'd listened while the yearning to be back among them grew. His family were still with him and still hoping. He'd been desperate to respond but knew that he could not. Not if there was the slightest chance of being tracked. So he listened and kept the memories of her voice to remind him who he was fighting for.

Martha moaned a soft sound in her throat, half growl, half wail, and it hit him right in his heart. He wondered what she'd felt. Maybe a tensing in his muscles or something in his mind that he'd projected unconsciously. Whatever it was, it made him feel better. Less alone.

'We've got bigger problems than feeling sorry for ourselves, princess,' said Max. 'We need a place to shelter. You can feel the change in the air, can't you?'

It was a stupid question. Way up here, Max could feel it through her wings and in the occasional gentle buffeting of her sleek body. The outriders of the oncoming gale were reaching out, prodding them, warning them to get clear.

He turned Martha west away from the storm, heading back in the direction of the *Heart of Granite*, feeling the tremor in her muscles and the tiredness in his making the turn a little jerky. He wondered what would happen if she reached her limit of exhaustion, whether she'd fall from the sky or choose to take over and land before both of them were killed. Best not to find out.

The afternoon was on the wane and Max estimated the sandstorm was about two hours behind him. By the time he was in the vicinity of the *HoG*, she'd be locked down waiting for it to hit. They'd be scanning the radar for anything running in front of the storm so he had to stay high and well to the north of her to stay in neutral territory. The *Steelback* and the *Ironclaw* would be moving up to take flank duties if the attack on the *Maputo* was still going ahead once the storm had blown itself out. It wouldn't do to stray into their search grids.

The camel herd's shack came to mind, above which Anna-Beth had met him during that fateful skytime. It was a ruin but must have survived worse than what was coming. It had survived a war. And of course that's where all this had started. Where Anna-Beth had told him what was really going on. Part of him, a big part, wanted to take it all back and live in blissful ignorance. What he should have done was persuade her to land and take her to the old mattress he'd seen through holes in the roof. Surely there'd have been some spring left in it. It would have been beautiful: alone in the desert, sex to the echoes of drake calls and the whip of the wind around the corners of the building. Her scent, the feel of her wrapped around him, the sounds she made and the rippling of her body. There'd have been no need for words, no need for all the pain.

Max's eyes snapped open and for a moment he was disoriented. His limbs jerked reflexively with the shock of sudden consciousness and Martha squawked, her wings flaring and her legs jerking down. Max shuddered. He looked about him, using Martha's senses to assess his position.

He'd been asleep. He knew that, but not for how long. The desert was largely featureless, he was high in the sky and it all looked the same. He scanned for dust clouds to the north, anything to signify the movement of the *Heart*'s sister behemoths, and there they were, moving up before the storm forced them to a stop.

Max bit his lip. In his estimation, they should have been further away and at his eleven o'clock but they were a good deal closer and coming round to his ten. He felt a chill; he'd been asleep for ages, an hour at least. That was a lifetime in the pouch.

Martha had flown on, his head-up display confirming she'd maintained height and direction. Whether she had assumed control directly was impossible to say but the inevitable relaxation of his body hadn't altered her flight.

'So is this how it starts?'

Max was half-expecting to hear some stereotypical gravelly dragon voice say *yes,* but of course there was nothing. Martha responded to his arms trimming her attitude, beginning a long, slow descent. Max focused back on the ground far below, hoping to pick out a less obvious hiding place; a west-facing rocky outcrop would do.

'Thanks for keeping us in the air,' he said, sending thoughts of affection and happiness and feeling Martha's warmth spread across his mind in response. 'You must tell me how you did it one day.'

Martha gave her wings an extra beat. She shouldn't have been able to change her orders as set by his posture, the feel of his fingers or the positions of his arms and legs and the twitch of his muscles. If this was what the Fall felt like, then there was nothing to fear.

Max sobered. Of course that wasn't how it felt. The briefest thought of Risa Kullani, or the unfortunates in Landfill told him that. But *was* this the start? The merest change in the relationship easily glossed over by an involuntary movement or a stray thought. And Max was exhausted; there were bound to be consequences. It would be all right once he'd had a rest.

No lasting damage, Max, nothing a good night's sleep won't fix. That's what you always say, Dad. That's because it's nearly always true. And what about when it isn't? I dunno really, two good nights' sleep?

'Dammit!' roared Max, trying to clear his head, angry he'd dozed off again so quickly. 'We've got to get down on the deck, princess. Don't think I can stay awake much longer.'

Fatigue was only part of the problem. Max's body ached all over; most of his muscles were stiff and his breathing felt a little constricted. He'd been in the pouch and flying for ten hours straight, and that followed a night where he had only emerged at dawn to stretch out and take a piss. Never mind the disastrous implications for his mental state, he was seizing up physically. His head was pounding again. And he was hungry and the hunger was making him weak in mind and body. And the thirst? Don't even start with how thirsty he was.

'Hey, princess, can you hear me?' Martha rocked her head from side to side in response to the images he sent as much as to the sound of his voice. 'Might not make the old camel shack.'

If she understood him, she didn't indicate it. Their gentle descent continued and now Max had admitted his discomfort, it grew at a hyperbolic rate and he feared his body wouldn't react the way he needed it to next time. They would soon be crossing the *Heart of Granite*'s wake. He could see the gouges in the sand. The *HoG* herself must be about four hours south.

Martha's body rippled and she rocked her head again from side to side. Max felt a freezing cold rush across his body, leaving his head feeling like it was encased in ice. He wanted to cry out but there was nothing inside him to make a sound. On the back of the cold came fear, because this had to be the start of the Fall, but it was washed away by the warmth in his mind despite the ice stuck in his veins. At the last there were images and his subconscious mind decoded them and provided him with a single word that blazed in his head.

Trust.

Max found his voice and screamed.

'Don't do it, Martha, you don't have to do it.'

The feelings of cold had gone but the following rush of heat caused brief, extreme agony. He'd screamed for the second time and terror had rolled over him. He tried to push her away, shut her out of his mind. It was like trying to push sunlight. Max spoke to her; tried to persuade her to free him to fly like they always had, but there was nothing in return.

'Haven't I always treated you well, princess? We're friends, a team. We're in balance. Don't change it.'

But she had changed it and it had left him a passenger... a prisoner. She'd frozen the pouch and no longer did his movements drive her. No longer did his thoughts influence her.

'Not yet not yet not yet.' He'd been a pilot so short a time and it wasn't like he'd been with her *that* long since his escape. He didn't understand it. Perhaps this wasn't the Fall, but some precursor, some early symptom that would disappear as suddenly as it had come on. It didn't explain why Martha was in control, although maybe if he was having difficulties, something within her kicked in to keep them going. He clung on to the thought; it was all he had.

Max felt abandoned, forgotten even. No, he felt betrayed and he sent the emotion out as strongly as he could. Ice poured into his head again. He gasped, feeling the cold surge down his spine. The flood of emotions and images came again, coalescing in the repetition of the single word. *Trust.*

'So you do know I'm still here,' he said. Martha purred. 'Let me back in. I can help.'

She merely steepened their descent, flying in tight circles as if searching for something on the ground directly below her. Max looked too, seeing that they were above the *HoG*'s wake. The storm was closing faster, or that's how it felt. He could feel the gusts on Martha's flanks and wings.

Max tried to move his arms. He splayed his fingers and tensed muscles, tiny twitches made large by the fatigue clouding him. Of course none of it made any difference; Martha had already made the adjustments.

'Nothing down there but sand and shit,' said Max. 'We need a place to hole up, remember?'

In response, Martha barked. It was a sound of satisfaction and she dived. The desert floor was barren but for mounds of behemoth faeces; easily the most repulsive smell on the Holy Father's ruined Earth.

'I'm not sure I can build a sandcastle large enough in time,' said Max, trying to quell his fear, trying to believe Martha's solitary word.

Martha rattled phlegm along the length of her throat, the vibrations funnelling into the pouch. She levelled out at about fifty and swept south along the tail trough. She had something in mind.

Correction: Max *hoped* she had something in mind so they could ride out the storm.

Max looked left and right, trying to work out what she wanted to do. Martha barked once more, dived down until she was almost touching the deck, backed her wings in front of a pile of dung larger than she was and flew directly up to a couple of metres above it.

'Don't even think about it,' said Max. He clenched everything, praying she was just trying to find something to eat or track a scent or something, but it was more than that. 'Have you any idea what going in there would do to my sex life?'

Max's mind was bathed very briefly with thoughts of sustenance. A heartbeat later, a sheath slid over his face, sealing him in the pouch and Martha dropped tail-first straight into the dung. There was a disgusting squelching sound, the sensations of Martha working her way ever deeper into the mound and using her wings to gather more about her and finally plunging her head into the filthy mid-green sludge.

Max's last thought was how he was going to breathe in the sealed pouch, but a sharp impact at the base of his spine and a second one at the base of his neck were followed very swiftly by a floating, nightmare-fuelled oblivion.

Professor Helena Markov was irritable. Incompetence had that effect on her and this particular instance was uniquely piquing. Because having got here, on a bloody gecko of all things, and reviewed the whole sorry saga it was clear that no one was actually to blame, just some amorphous 'them' that had organised the whole thing and outwitted the internal security might of the flag-carrying behemoth.

So they sat around a table and she became increasingly frustrated at the bullet-dodging antics of Kirby and Moeller. In the end, she smoothed down her creased brown fatigues, pushed her long black hair back into a ponytail, and cleared her throat into a momentary pause to ensure that the two of them were paying her the correct level of attention.

'I get it. You don't know where Halloran is. What exactly are you expecting of me?'

'We felt you needed context in order to bring your skills to bear most effectively,' said Kirby.

Markov sighed. 'You sound like a role player in a training vid, Robert. It's me, Helena. Just talk to me like we've known each other for the last five years, why don't you?'

Kirby smiled for the first time since they'd sat down over their 'informal' drinks in the otherwise deserted Bridge Bar, as the afternoon waned towards dusk and the winds grew in strength.

'Sorry, guilty.'

'I'm not smiling. My signature's been forged on an upgrade approval. I'll bring anyone else down I can if it comes to it,' said Markov. Their reactions were enlightening. 'You didn't know.'

Kirby shook his head. 'Why would we?'

Markov didn't know whether to believe him or not. 'That makes this the most senior of crimes, then.'

'How far was the upgrade from being ready?' asked Moeller. 'How much risk is there to my pilots? Robert told me it was designed as a precursor to Fall testing.'

'He's right, and it depends on your definition of risk.'

Moeller frowned. '*Definition*? You need me to spell it out?'

'I can't stop pilots going through the Fall,' said Markov. 'It's only ever a question of time so there's no way to mitigate the risk you're talking about, that's the problem. My primary role is to develop the conditions that allow pilots to survive the Fall. What else can it be?'

Moeller gaped and it would have been comical if it weren't so sad. 'You're cold. What about methods to ensure they never hit the Fall in the first place?'

'Can't be done. That's something we have managed to prove. We can't even delay it but we can hide the symptoms and, perhaps most usefully, accelerate it.'

'And that's why you want him back? For analysis?'

'I never wanted him to go in the first place,' replied Markov. 'He isn't ready yet.'

Moeller's contempt was embarrassing to behold. 'And when will he be *ready*?' He even made the quote marks gesture with his fingers.

Markov tensed and decided to take a sip of her warm and uninviting synthesised white wine before speaking.

'Let me tell you a little tale,' she said sweetly. 'It's about a man who sat on the conflict budget committee four years ago and made an impassioned speech about the risks to drake pilots and how further research could only lead to more risks as scientists sought to make drakes ever more effective. That the current level of drake sentience was entirely adequate to win the war and that current treatments of early symptoms of the Fall would evolve organically through medical analysis.

'As a direct result, seventy-five per cent of the ERC's research budget was diverted to materials, training and medical care.

'But the clamour for Fall drugs didn't diminish, did it? It simply went underground and all the best research on drugs to mitigate Fall symptoms is now done on the black market. It also effectively halted research into surviving the Fall and we were left with a grand data gathering exercise in the hope suitable subjects might suggest themselves.

'But you knew all that, didn't you, Gerhard?'

'I know that there is a limit to how far mixed DNA experimentation can be allowed to go and I stopped you going over that line.'

But there was no real conviction in his voice.

'Right, your paternal side is happier to see them subside into madness than potentially become something far greater.'

'I know where you were heading with it so please don't take the holier-than-thou route with me,' said Moeller. 'The number of young souls you were willing to sacrifice on the altar of your research was staggering. And I wasn't alone, was I? How many of your precious team walked away even before the funding was cut?'

Markov shrugged. 'Being a scientist, particularly in pressurised military research, requires courage and some people don't have it. I have to make decisions that might affect one life but prolong or save a thousand others. I feel no guilt, but yours eats you, doesn't it? You condemned all of your precious pilots to the Fall, one after another.'

Markov could see the fight leave him and almost felt sorry for him. He swallowed the rest of his gin and signalled for another round.

'No one thought the war would go on so long,' he said quietly.

Markov gave a brief smile. 'So, now that we've established that I'm always right and you two are always wrong, let's move on to how I can help.'

The *Heart*'s PA announced the sealing of the behemoth in advance of the imminent arrival of the sandstorm. Soon, she'd shuffle round to keep her head away from the winds.

'Can he survive this?' asked Moeller. 'Assuming shelter, of course?'

'I've reviewed the data, well, what little data you have, and it's by no means certain he's survived so far. We have to assume that Halloran is smart enough to have selected a low expenditure environment, so either he's under a rock or he's been on the upper thermals during daylight.'

Both men reacted and Markov pursed her lips.

'Upper thermals it is, then,' she said, noting another victory with the slightest of smiles. 'That would indicate he's been in the pouch a considerable number of consecutive hours – and probably at night too, because his drake will need to share his body heat or be sluggish at dawn...'

Markov did some quick calculations.

'Halloran's only been flying combat for nine months so we can discount any effects from that. However, he's now been in-pouch for large parts of two days and, come morning, two nights in a drake with an unshielded upgrade. Factoring in the exponentially increasing risks of consecutive hours in the pouch, plus the upgrade and his helpful daily named pill mix, I'd say he is roughly eighty-five per cent likely to be in stage three Fall twenty-four hours from now.

'He and his drake must be returned here for analysis, alive or dead. I mean, this is beyond the wildest dreams of any ERC scientist. It's like ten years of data in a sparkly wrapper given to me on my birthday. I sincerely hope you can find him now I've told you where to look.'

'You're actually happy he's out there, aren't you?'

'I'd have liked it done under more controlled circumstances, Gerhard, but I'd be lying if I said I'm not excited about what might come back from the desert. Hal-X is our most likely candidate to survive the Fall.'

A fly landed on the table top to drink from a spilled drop. With impressive speed, Moeller swatted it with an open palm. He lifted his hand to flick away the carcass. It sparked once, faintly. They froze and stared at each other to confirm what each of them had seen.

'Oh fuck,' said Kirby.

'My lab,' said Markov. 'Now.'

CHAPTER 32

Anyone who thinks they've taken a lungful of the worst stink in the world has never been within a klick of behemoth shit.

MAXIMUS HALLORAN

Max thought he could hear voices. They were just out of reach, like claws appearing briefly from darkness to beckon him on, but it was too dim to follow. The voices would fade and he would shout after them but the sound was so muffled that they probably couldn't hear him.

He opened his eyes and was immediately reminded that it was better to keep them closed. For starters, there was nothing to see, and for another thing his eyes ached whenever he opened them. The only problem with keeping them closed was the vivid images that played across his eyelids; there were worlds aflame and lands stained red.

Max knew what was happening. He'd fought it at first, tried to get Martha to fly out of the filthy sludge and let him go but in his heart he knew she couldn't. Though he couldn't properly keep track of time, he was aware of its passage and marked it by the images that Martha sent to him as if she was trying to keep him informed of progress. *Progress*. Towards what end, he wondered. His death, most likely.

There was strength in Martha that hadn't been there before they'd landed in the behemoth sludge and she fed it into him somehow; presumably it was connected with the stabbing pains at the base of his neck and spine. He tried not to think too hard about the source of the nutrition but he did know he was no longer half as hungry or thirsty.

Max hadn't expected to be so calm. He could feel everything: the buffeting of the wind on the faeces in which they hid; the gentle massaging of his body to ease away fatigue in his muscles; the touch of Martha's mind on the periphery of his own – persistent but not intrusive; the vague anxiety that she tried to soothe away with images of calm; and the curious sense of inner peace that came over him whenever he was awake.

Max had the impression it was dark outside. He was tired but that was hardly a surprise. He had a headache too. It had been nagging at him since he awoke a while ago and it was slowly but surely growing in intensity. And now he came to examine himself, his extremities were cold too, almost numb. Max took in a breath and opened his eyes. Like before, it was dark. The hood Martha had encased him in was opaque. He could see shapes beyond it, like the after-images of a flash photo straight in the eyes, but he couldn't make them out.

That aside, if this was the Fall, then it didn't measure up to the rumours and scaremongering. Frankly, Risa taking heaters was worse than anything he was suffering now, despite the brief early pain in his back and neck and the disturbing imagery he was seeing.

So perhaps it wasn't the Fall. Perhaps this was just the consequences of the latest upgrade. He certainly didn't feel changed, he didn't feel different or better or worse or as if his brain was wired up in a new way.

'It's even quite comfortable in here,' said Max. 'If a little dull at times.'

Brace.

The word sat in his head, clear as drake sight, the voice familiar, the tone a warning.

Strength.

It echoed away into what Valera would have been delighted to call the caverns of his unoccupied mind.

'Um … Martha, is that you?' Warmth washed over him. 'Oh.'

Max wasn't sure what to think. All he did know was that his anxiety spiked and not even Martha's care could stop the sweats, the palpitations and the shivering.

'Why *strength*? And what's this about bracing myself?'

Pain.

'I can take some pain,' said Max, feeling nowhere near as brave as he hoped he was sounding.

Much.

Everything that the voice said was accompanied by imagery across his eyelids … A mouth open and screaming, fists clenched and a contorted face, eyes open and begging for mercy. All very comforting.

'When do we start?'

Now.

For the first time in his life, Max found that he was scared of dying. He opened his mouth to beg her to reconsider but before he could frame the words, it began.

It was impossible to say how many times his body was pierced. His back took the brunt but the stabbing pains were in his arms, legs, buttocks, chest and neck too. He'd have likened it to walking into a hail of metal shards but it was far, far worse than that. Every single point of entry was slow, deliberate and deep, as if Martha's primary intention was torture.

Max would have writhed with the agony but her pouch muscles had firmed to steel and from scalp to heel he had no movement whatsoever. He could just about move his toes and he did so vigorously, if only to convince himself he was still alive.

The cold that came with the piercings was shocking, leaving

him gasping for air – what little he could drag in with his torso mostly immobilised. Crawling tendrils issued from every sharp point, some of which felt like needles and others more like stilettos. He could trace some of them as they invaded his body, note them creeping to his heart, his lungs and into his abdominal cavity where they spread like cloying, freezing hands, gripping hard and beginning to squeeze.

Max screamed, the sound emerging like tortured whispers.

Toes. Toes, think about your toes. See how they still move and you can still move them. Holy God fuck... toes toes. She doesn't want to kill you she needs you if she wanted to kill you you'd be dead already so you're all right. Am I fuck all right what is she doing? How should I know it must be the alien part maybe I'm being improved or maybe harvested or some other such shit. Fuck me sideways I need this to stop I need this to stop please Holy Father let it stop let it stop.

Max's head was hot. Blood was thundering around inside his skull, looking for a way out. It was washing against the insides of his skull, pressing onto his brain from the outside and swelling it from the inside. Any moment, he expected blood to shoot from his eyes, nose, mouth, ears... anywhere to relieve the pressure.

He tried to open his eyes to let the blood out but his eyelids wouldn't respond. Instead, they showed him cascades of red with tumbling dark shadows within, all blown on a flame so hot it could turn bone to ash in a moment. He was nothing but a pile of ash supported by the pouch muscles. As soon as Martha let go, he'd crumble and be dust on the wind.

Every nerve was raw and screaming. Every tooth was being wrenched out by the root, every toe- and fingernail ripped from its berth, every piece of his skin stripped layer by layer, millions of pairs of miniature claws grabbing with precision to peel him away one molecule at a time.

He had no control of his mouth or he'd have opened it to scream. He made the sound within him instead, an endless hum dragged from lungs exhausted of air and collapsing while the noise went on and on.

Holy God, what now?

Inside his body, his muscles started to spasm. It began in his arms, a quivering sensation combining horribly with the cold and the piercings, spreading like an all-consuming virus to the rest of his body. He ground his teeth together while he tried to shake himself apart inside his skin. Every pierce point ricocheted with new pain.

'Please,' he forced out through a mouth caught in the net of palsy that ran through every muscle in his face. 'Please.'

Visions of the open sky wiped across his mind: vivid blues and whites followed by slate-grey and star-strewn black. They were glorious vistas of freedom and domain and he yearned to be there in the limitless space. Inside his cocoon he almost smiled but a shattering torment scythed into his brain and all he could see as he tumbled down, unable to resist any more, was a blazing white.

Gerhard Moeller ran into the ERC labs in the footsteps of Markov and a satisfying few metres ahead of Kirby. Childish, given the serious situation they could be in, but what the hell? He was still stung by the attitudes of both his colleagues towards his pilots and shocked by Markov's belief that drake pilots were mere tools to advance her knowledge. But she was still UE's most brilliant scientist so when she wanted to run, you ran.

'Get me Eleanor,' Markov ordered the nearest tech beyond the doors. She didn't break stride as she made for one of the analysis rooms. 'And fire up electron one and the DNA identware. I need a match almost before I've placed the sample.'

'I'm on it, Helena.'

The tech scurried away. Markov walked quickly into the room and fetched a glass holder for the spyfly. She opened it and nodded to Moeller who dropped the remains inside. Markov examined it briefly before snapping the lid shut and dropping it into electron one's receptor. She sat in the operator's chair and tapped up some feeds. Data, graphs and images popped up. The spyfly rotated slowly.

'*Helena,* eh?' said Moeller.

Markov shrugged. 'Hierarchy is the bane of teamwork. We leave that to you lot and a right cock-up you make of it too.'

She leaned back in her chair, Moeller and Kirby coming to either side of her and leaning in, hands on the desk like a clichéd corporate shot.

'What are we looking at here?' asked Kirby. 'Barring the subject of course.'

Markov indicated the various charts and data flows in turn. 'Spectrographic analyses; compound ratios; radio frequency range and function; memory analysis and DNA composition. This definitely isn't one of ours.'

'Helena?'

Markov turned a beaming smile on Rosenbach, who had entered the room looking harassed and unhappy.

'Ah, Eleanor. Got a spyfly here. I need to know any time the smart screens in the flight deck, on the turrets, launchers, hydroponics, solar arrays glitched even momentarily while you've been prioritising systems in the last three days.'

Rosenbach nodded. 'Where did you find this?'

'Bridge Bar,' said Kirby.

'Wow. Got a long way, then.'

'Quite,' said Markov. 'How long do you need?'

'Just a few minutes. I'll need to scribble a quick capture algorithm. I'll ping you the report as soon as.'

'Perfect. What's wrong, by the way?'

'Let's just say the sandstorm needs to be kind but I've just seen the wind speed and duration forecast and the projected volume of grit that'll hit us and, well... We're likely to have some issues.'

'With what?' asked Moeller.

'Pretty much everything concerned with our defensive capabilities.' Rosenbach flicked out her p-palm and sat in a chair away from the rest of them. 'More in a minute. Let me just get this seeker on its way.'

'How long have we got to wait for the bad news?' asked Kirby.

'Collating now,' said Markov. She entered a few values into the screen. 'Okay, okay... Oh dear.'

'What am I looking at?' asked Moeller, feeling his heart sink. The analysis screen was covered in lines of data, plus three graphs and a graphic of the reconstituted spyfly. There were some red figures but some green ones too. He didn't know why that comforted him and the look on Markov's face suggested it shouldn't.

Markov pointed at this and that on the screen as she spoke.

'It's a grade one *Maputo* spyfly, which suggests they have resource to burn as opposed to being on their last legs, so to speak. It was geared for electromagnetic, physiological and audio data and has probably transmitted whatever data it collected already. Worst: it's three days old. Even if it took a day to get here, it's collected a massive amount of data'

'Can you download its memory?'

'It's an in-out feed with a volatile buffer. Nothing stays in there for long. Our only hope is of interference, then the Mafs would lose the data in transmission.'

'We need to know what it might have leaked,' said Kirby.

'Knowing where it came in will at least let us plot likely routes,' said Markov. 'But three days... Wow, frankly, our darkest secrets could have been exposed.'

'Umm,' said Rosenbach, and she had their immediate attention. 'It might be worse than that. Three days ago our screening would have blocked it so how on earth did it get in?'

'Halloran probably opened his great big mouth and swallowed it,' said Kirby. 'What?'

Rosenbach was staring at him. 'Hitched a ride... Hmmm.'

'You've lost me,' said Kirby.

'I need to check something, Helena. Okay if I head off?'

'What is it?'

'I'm just wondering if it hitched a ride on one of the drake carcasses we brought back on board.'

Markov nodded. 'Good thought... Go ahead.'

Rosenbach hurried out of the room. Moeller turned back to Kirby. 'Not sure it really matters how the damn thing got in here, Avery needs to know we've been compromised.'

Kirby nodded. 'I'll ping her now. She'll want us round the tac-tables for a worst case scenario brainstorm. See you in Command and Control, I've got to sort something first.'

'No problem.'

'I'll ping you with any useful data,' said Markov. 'Don't expect too much good news.'

'These days good news feels like propaganda,' said Kirby.

'Talk to you later.'

There was never a time when forward recon was anything other than the biggest craphole duty for any squad. First to see drake fire close up before it toasted your arse; first to get targeted by enemy ground units and harried by fucking basilisks if you were unlucky enough to get caught off-lizard; and first to see a behemoth forty-mil muzzle flash.

'Good of Avery to commit significant forces to the mission,' muttered Horvald, the gecko jockey. His voice over the com was muffled by the sensory mask, and because his face was stuffed into the back of the gecko's neck.

'Perhaps she didn't feel like sacrificing anyone crucial,' said Ganeef, her voice whining and unhappy.

'Less moaning,' said Meyer. 'Job's the job and the Exterminators never shirk, never complain, just kick the shit out of whatever we find.'

There were days Meyer wished he was a private not a captain. He only got to moan to himself. And to be fair, this duty was worth moaning about. The gecko moved south in low profile across the undulating dunes while the sandstorm blasted all around them. Despite the buffeting, Horvald was keeping the ride relatively smooth and at a decent pace. Exterminators, two platoon, rode five across each flank of the gecko, strapped into bio-engineered outward-facing seats formed of bone, a layer of fat and rough skin.

Horvald lay flat in a body-socket engineered into the gecko's back, his senses directly connected to the gecko's. His hands were in sheaths on each side of its neck, allowing him to direct its movement and limited weapons suite. His mind was far more powerful than the dull beast's and directed its speed, sensory focus and direction. The gecko was an augmented version of the common little lizard, unlike the hundred per cent alien drake.

Not for Horvald, then, the inevitable slide towards the Fall, but on the other hand, lying face-down in slime for a job was just fucking sick. Meyer growled. Fucking Halloran. He was the reason they were out here now, not tucked up in bed while the *Heart* headed for some downtime after tearing the hide off the *Maputo*.

Meyer stared down into his lap, trying to ignore the maddening, intensifying, itching. He scratched ineffectually at his crotch, his fingers feeling like sausages in his gloves. He was sweating in his combats, his head slick under his sand hood and his goggles steamed up. Sand rattled in his mask filter and against his helmet; it blew in waves across his body, seeking out the most uncomfortable places in which to nestle. It was torture. Fucking Halloran.

Meyer growled again. He should have let the Mips catch the bastard when he ran through the Exterminator rack the other morning. That was a moment of mercy never to be repeated. Then he could have done his Fall in Landfill with all the other porridge brains.

But here they were, heading out into the desert to set up thermal imagery and radar on a fifteen klick spread a hundred klicks south and west of the *HoG*'s position. Not that they'd spot dick-all in this mess. The *HoG*'s radar and motion sensors were just so much fuzz at the moment, so the panic inspired by the spyfly incursion had led Avery and the exec to send platoons out to all points of the compass to set up an early warning grid for the moment the storm lifted.

Total pisser.

'Think the Mafs'll move in this soup?' asked Sidhu.

'Why would they?' said Meyer. The wind howled across the gecko, which shifted a little to the right to compensate. 'On the other hand, if I heard how creaky the *HoG* was, I might take a risk.'

'Reckon it'll be remote artillery and booby traps if anything,' said Reynolds.

'I'm with Reynolds,' said Kapetic, in her Slavic roll.

'Reluctant though I am to admit it, he's probably on the money this time,' said Meyer.

'That's 'cos I'm a thinker, a tactician,' said Reynolds. 'Primed for great things.'

'Hey, Reynolds, is "tactician" a synonym for "twat"?' asked Sidhu.

There was a brief silence.

'You might have to define "synonym", Sid,' said Kapetic.

'Fuck the lot of you,' said Reynolds. 'Call yourself a buddy, Sid—'

Ribald laughter bounced across the com. A dense gust of sand rattled against Meyer's goggles and hissed around his hood. He looked out into the pitch darkness, glad that the gecko had inner transparent eyelids and rudimentary night vision. Not to mention extremely sensitive heel pads that tested the ground with every step.

'Yeah, but do you know what a synonym is?' drawled McCarthy, a heavy northern Irish accent lacing his words.

'It's the name of the fist that knocks out your teeth,' said Reynolds.

'That was close to a smart retort,' said Sidhu.

'You might have to define "ret—" '

'Don't make me come over there,' said Reynolds.

'Now that would be a thing to see,' said Ganeef. 'Twenty says he's blown off our ride inside five seconds.'

'Okay, kids, let's focus,' said Meyer, cutting across Reynolds's next words. 'Horvo, what's our position?'

Horvald clicked his tongue. 'Coming up on position one in about three minutes, boss.'

'You heard our tour guide. Get prepped. Boots on the ground the moment we stop. Sidhu, Reynolds, you've got the lookout gig so fire up your thermals for distance. Squad two, set up the radar relays, squad one, we're on thermal imagery. Visibility is almost zero so all of you stay close, take a bead on the gecko and use the heat pads on her flanks to find your way back if you get detached. Any questions?'

They rode on in silence for the final few hundred metres. The gecko slowed and stopped and immediately turned its head downwind, though the swirling storm and the sand clogging the air made that almost pointless. Meyer unclipped and jumped to the ground, flicking on thermal imagers and seeing the heat signatures of his platoon glow and then settle. The gecko was picked out as a solid, comforting line of pale yellow.

'We've got five of these sites to assemble so let's not dawdle.'

Squad members hurried to the storage bins strapped to the lizard's rear flanks, pulling out canvas bags full of kit and weapons that were quickly and efficiently distributed around the platoon. Meyer turned a three-sixty, acutely aware that in the pitch-black, sand-filled night, no one was coming to help them if they got in trouble.

He set his shoulders and walked to the first setup point. 'Sid, Reynolds, you set?'

'In position, sir,' said Sidhu. 'Nothing on forward scope.'

'Copy that. All right, let's get planting. I want us back on the gecko in ten, max.'

Forty-five minutes later, the inadequacy of their kit was clear. Meyer stood over the thermal imaging equipment and cursed Halloran again. A gust of wind rocked him, blowing more sand across the gear. It would not stand. It wouldn't even lie down. There wasn't enough weight to keep it stable, the windbreaks had torn, fallen down or blown away, and the shifting sand beneath it undermined it still further.

'Wind speeds topping a hundred and thirty in the gusts, boss,' said Horvald from his suddenly attractive position lying sheltered on his gecko.

'Remind me how long it's going to blow?' asked Meyer.

'When we left, best case was twelve hours,' replied Horvald.

'Got a bead on the *HoG*?'

'You're joking. No satellite access, no line of sight.'

Meyer called a halt to efforts for the moment. It was surreal. He could only see his people as shifting heat signatures, making this more like some VR nightmare than an infantry recon duty. Beyond the scope of his platoon's position, there was nothing to see whatever. An unending darkness blown so hard it would have changed the landscape come daylight. And right in the middle of it all, cut off from the welcoming bulk of the *Heart of Granite*, Exterminator platoons were trying to throw a security net around their mother ship.

Meyer sighed. There was sand inside his combats, in his mouth, sand fucking everywhere, and the original plan was plainly unworkable and the backup was going to mean a whole lot more sand.

'All right, kids, this is where we really earn the pittance they pay us. Ten of us, five sets of kit, that's two to a set, and we're going to have to stay out here and physically hold them all upright. Horvald, once we've dropped everyone off, I need you to patrol the zone. Coms are going to be flaky so if you hear anything from anyone, relay it, don't assume it's already platoon-wide. Everyone buddy up and get back on the gecko... All but Sid and Reynolds. You can stay here. One last thing. I'm not losing anyone so don't go wandering off from your position.

'Any questions?'

'Can I trade in my mission bonus for a crack at bloody Halloran?' asked Ganeef.

Meyer chuckled. 'Get in line, Neef. Come on, saddle up... The night can only last so long, right?'

CHAPTER 33

When we look back on the *Heart of Granite*'s life, will we celebrate the many victories, lament those lost in combat and hold her up as a worthy flag carrier? Or will her history be forever tainted by the 'Halloran Incident'. I fear the media have already made up their minds.

NICOLA AVERY, COMMANDER, HEART OF GRANITE

'How long have we been out here?' asked Sidhu.

'Hours,' said Reynolds.

'Right, glad I asked because I really wasn't sure. Can you be more specific?'

'Something wrong with your mission timer?'

'No, I just wanted to hear your voice.'

Both men were lying down flat with their fists clamped around the imagers' legs, trying to keep them steady. They'd changed position a dozen times already as cramp, sand and the wind caused varying levels of discomfort. There was a sense of worth in it though, thought Sidhu. The screens on both the radar and thermal imager remained happily devoid of the signs of enemy advancement. While that might have been because the storm blocked everything out, it was marginally more likely to be because there was nothing out there.

'I need to take a shit,' said Reynolds.

'You smell like you already took it.'

'Funny.'

'No, really, not even the filters and gale force winds can wholly mask the odours you're pumping out.'

'Really?'

'Of course not, idiot. So go squat. Just not so far away you get lost or so close I can see the steam rising.'

Reynolds stood up and brushed himself down, pointlessly. He braced himself against the storm and at least had the sense to move off downwind.

'Keep the TI upright, will you?' said Reynolds, his voice crackling in the gale.

'I'm sure I can temporarily spare a limb.' Sidhu rolled over and sat up in between the two pieces of woefully unstable equipment, feeling the full force of the wind beat around his head. He set a firm hand on the top of each. From the darkness, Reynolds cleared his throat. 'Hey, dump-boy, go off-com. I don't need to hear your straining.'

'Copy that.'

The com went quiet and Sidhu took a long and relaxing breath. He focused on the roaring and whistling of the wind, the thrash of sand on his helmet and goggles and the forces across his body. It was amazing. He didn't want the night to end. He was cold, sore and tired but, Holy Father, he was *alive* out here at the mercy of nature; unlike their miserable, parasitic existence inside the *HoG*.

Sidhu's com crackled.

'Com check delta.' The voice was faint, swam in and out a bit but it was good enough. 'This is Meyer at station three, sound off in turn.'

'Sidhu, station one. You're a bit quiet but you're there.'

'Copy, Sid. Station two, come in.'

'Station two, Ganeef hearing you L and C.'

'Copy, Ganeef. Station four, you out there?' asked Meyer. The com washed and hissed in Sidhu's ear. 'Copy, Patel, hearing you L and C too. Station five, let's hear you.' More static. 'You're really soft, Kapetic. You need to boost.

'Now listen up: Horvald is on tour, currently between three and two and heading your way, Sid. When he gets to you, take five in the lee and get some fluids and solids in.'

Sidhu laughed. 'Sorry, boss, couldn't help it. Schoolboy humour...'

'What, exactly?'

'Just that Reynolds is downwind making room, so to speak.'

'Well, I hope he's finished before the *Maputo* steps on his sandy ass. Sunrise in three hours and ten minutes. Technically. But don't get your hopes up.'

'When are we going home, boss?' asked Ganeef.

'When the wind drops enough for us to weigh the kit down. Simple, eh?'

Sidhu's radar came alive. Pulsing, glowing points of green light. Six at least... no, eight.

'Shit,' he said. 'I have incoming on a bearing of one-nine-seven. Multiple contacts, I'm counting eight so far. Distance, three klicks and closing at speed... Basilisks. Basilisks on the ground.'

'Copy, Sid. Hold position, low profile. Station two, can you confirm?'

'Negative, Captain,' said McCarthy, who was partnering Ganeef. 'I'll ping as soon as we get a contact.'

'That goes for all stations,' said Meyer. 'Horvald, best speed to station one and stand by to extract. Go in dark, weapons free.'

'Copy, Captain,' said Horvald. 'I'll be coming up on your six, Sid. Hang tight.'

'Don't be too quick,' said Sid. 'I fancy nailing some big game... Just polishing the carbine now.'

'That better not be a euphemism,' said Ganeef, her com crackling badly.

'Come over here and find out,' said Sid.

'Stow the shit, Sid,' said Meyer. 'Status update.'

Sidhu hadn't taken his eyes off the radar. The basilisks were at two klicks and moving in a tight, two-column formation, presumably suffering the same contact issues.

'Still heading in like they've got sand-piercing headlights on. At two K and closing.'

'Copy that, Sid,' said Meyer. 'Keep on open com. Are you jamming reciprocals?'

'Technically,' said Sidhu, seeing the enable light blinking comfortingly. 'Mother only knows if it's actually working. Stand by...'

Sidhu frowned and looked at the radar. Still the TI screen showed nothing, meaning the basilisks were running dark. Their formation was shifting. It was so hard to be sure on this ancient piece of kit but if he was reading it right...

'We're acquired. Station two, you should have them in a few moments. I've got to go and get Reynolds.'

'Copy, Sid,' said Meyer. 'Horvald, step on it. All stations, eyes and ears, we have incoming on station one. Hold your positions, you're too far away to help anyway. Be careful, Sid.'

'You know me, chief,' said Sidhu, already moving in Reynolds's direction and bringing his rifle bag from his back to across his chest.

'Well, quite,' said Meyer. 'All stations, weapons free. Let's be ready.'

Sidhu switched to his private com.

'Reynolds, do you copy.' Nothing but static. 'Idiot.'

At least Reynolds wasn't far. His heat signature swam into view after a few paces. He was still squatting.

'Holy Mother, that must be some dump,' said Sidhu. 'Or serious constipation.'

Sidhu laughed into his breathing mask at the image of Reynolds straining away while the basilisks closed in, probably by scent. He had his rifle out and pushed the bag back over his shoulder. The

Shavek SA-GL8 assault rifle had a sixty round clip, quick slap drop and reload and an eight pill micro-grenade launcher under the barrel. Bullets were armour-piercing and the grenades were AP-fragmentation types; very nasty and just the ticket for hunting Maf lizards. Shame the opposition had much the same kit, really.

Sidhu shook his head and forced himself to focus. The basilisks would be on them in a couple of minutes. He and Reynolds needed to clear out past their sensor equipment and hope to blend into the storm noise if they could. Big if. He moved up fast, running around so he was approaching Reynolds from the front. Three paces from Reynolds, the squatting man leapt up and began to scramble backwards. Sidhu's com sprang to life.

'Contact, contact!' yelled Reynolds. 'Fuck me, it's come from nowhere. Do you copy, Sid?'

'Yeah, buddy. It's me. Calm down.' Sidhu moved after Reynolds, stepping over the cooling signature of his mess. 'Pull your strides up, get your Shavek handy and do it fast. We've got basilisks.'

'Fuck,' spat Reynolds. 'You scared the shit out of me.'

'Someone had to hurry you up.' Sidhu ran round behind Reynolds while he fumbled with his trousers. 'I'll sort your gun. You did grease it and seal it, didn't you?'

'No, I dipped it in cement before we left.'

'Touchy.'

Sidhu pulled the rifle clear and gave it a cursory check. It felt as if the trigger and grenade mechanisms were well gunked and the bio-plastic casing around the magazine housing felt in reasonable nick. Not that he could be certain of much through his gloves and anyway, no weapon could be entirely sealed against weather like this.

He slapped the gun into Reynolds's midriff. 'Let's go. Back to the imagers and beyond.'

With Reynolds's hand on his shoulder, they made best pace across the shifting sands into the teeth of the gale. It was almost dreamlike. The open com triggered.

'Sidhu, Meyer, status report.'

'I've got Reynolds, sir. Heading to station one now. How far is Horvald?'

'With you imminently. Take a bearing on station two and you'll find him.'

'Copy, sir.' Sidhu shivered as if someone had walked over his grave. 'Come on, Reynolds, let's pick up the p—'

A basilisk sprinted out of the mire of sand and night and Sidhu only saw it at the last second. The lizard's jaws, full of needle-sharp teeth, lunged forwards, its head swinging left and right. Sidhu had time to register that he couldn't hear a damn thing over the wind, the sand and the helmet tight to his head.

He pushed Reynolds away hard, hoping at least one of them would escape the jaws, pounding feet and thrashing tail. He dived to the ground, meaning to roll to safety, but the basilisk's head caught him flush on the back of his right shoulder and tossed him into the air, almost certainly saving his life.

Over the com, he heard Reynolds call out then make a noise like he'd been winded. Sidhu landed on his bruised shoulder and tumbled over and over. He couldn't help but cry out before he slithered to a stop and pushed himself back to his feet, rifle still clutched in both gloved hands.

'Meyer, Sidhu,' he said over the open com. 'We've been attacked. Single basilisk. No idea where it's gone.'

'I've got contacts on scope, Sid,' said Ganeef from station two. 'Incoming hard and spreading across our sensor arc towards you, Captain.'

'Understood. Sid, condition?'

Sidhu checked his compass and began to head back towards station one where Reynolds might be. He thumbed the launcher and the enable light flashed under his forefinger. His shoulder hurt like buggery but he didn't think it was broken. What he cared about now was his buddy.

'Reynolds, do you copy?'

The open com was full of noise. 'Incoming at one klick and closing fast,' said Ganeef. 'I have three contacts on our bead. Two more moving towards you, sir. They've either got our radar signature or can see our heat trace.'

'Got to be the radar,' said Meyer. 'Kill the imagers, people, retreat to rally point alpha and regroup. Sidhu?'

'Can't find Reynolds, sir. He's off com, no thermal. Still looking, sir.'

On a reflex, Sidhu dropped to the ground and rolled down a shallow decline. A basilisk, presumably the same one, sprinted past, its tail whipping over his head. He saw its shape in full this time, slate-grey against the dark and picked out a little by the sand hammering against its hide. They were bastards. Single-seater killing machines the Tweakers had reckoned were only good for fast recon. There it stood: fifteen metres of sleek reptilian athlete, smooth skinned and ridiculously fast.

'Reynolds!' shouted Sidhu down his private com, just about remembering to trigger the broadcast mute though he still had their chatter in his ear.

'They're right on us,' said Ganeef. 'McCarthy, watch our nine. I can feel them.'

A reptilian barking roar fed through the com alongside McCarthy screaming. There was gunfire and Sidhu fancied he could see muzzle flashes through the storm.

'McCarthy is down!' shouted Ganeef. 'Fucking thing took him in half. It's gone into the night.'

'Focus, Neef,' said Meyer. 'Get yourself clear.'

'They've beaded us, sir,' said Sidhu. 'I've got one circling me.'

'Those still clear, bug out now.' Meyer's voice was incredibly calm and measured, speaking into the blackness, trying to keep them together. 'Sid, Neef, you're trained for this. I'm coming to you. Horvald, pick up Sid. Get stuck in if you can. Provide the barrier.'

'Negative, sir, permission to find Reynolds first,' said Sidhu, watching the basilisk sprint off into the darkness but not believing for one second it was gone for good. He hoped it wasn't; he wanted it.

'Copy, Sid. Don't you dare fucking die. That's an order. Right, Ganeef, I'm coming to you. Horvald, meet us at station two.'

'Quicker if I pick you up, sir,' said Horvald.

'Negative. Protect Ganeef.'

Sidhu tuned down the open com, pushing his tongue against the centre stud in the com controls clipped behind his front teeth. It would reactivate when Meyer signalled him. Sidhu stayed in his fortunate dip in the sand, enjoying the relative calm as the gale blasted overhead, sending eddies and swirls of loose sand across his hiding place.

He gathered himself, checked his bearing, the waypoints and indicators set out on his head-up display and moved out at a crouch, aware the basilisk and its rider could be watching him from behind the cloak of the storm. He moved steadily on the bearing, his eyes straying to his right from where he felt any attack might come.

Mercifully, he came upon station one quickly and took a quick glance at the radar screen to check the position of the enemy basilisks. The breath caught in his throat. Those basilisks weren't scouting; they were the vanguard. Something much bigger was lumbering through the storm against all sense and reason.

Sidhu turned and retraced the few paces he and Reynolds had taken before the attack, flicking to open com.

'Captain Meyer, Sidhu, say you're hearing me, boss.'

'Easy, Sid, you're sounding stressed. What's up?'

'We're in trouble. I've just checked my radar. Basilisks are circling and heading back in to take us out. They're clearing a path. There's a behemoth on the way.'

'What? In this?' Meyer betrayed a mote of anxiety for the first time. 'Neef, can you confirm?'

'I'm not at the station, sir. Stand by.'

Even through the storm and the crackle of the com, Sidhu felt the shock and relative silence.

'It can't be anything else. Major contact, slow moving. Got to be the *Maputo*. No other Maf behemoth moving in this sector, the others are still way east and west, right?' Sidhu was still moving. Away to his right about half a dozen paces, a still heat signature. 'Damn.'

'Confirmed contact, sir,' came Ganeef's voice, wavering slightly. 'Definitely a behemoth.'

Over the open com, Meyer was relaying the message to the rest of the platoon, ordering them to maintain their move to the rally point. He was still intent on joining Ganeef, who was exposed and vulnerable, but there was more and it wasn't good news for any of them, though it was the right decision.

'Horvald, do you copy?' Meyer was breathing heavily, running as he spoke.

'Yes, sir.'

'Best speed to the *Heart of Granite*. Ping them the whole way. Only return when you've relayed the information.'

'Copy, sir,' said Horvald, his voice heavy. 'Hang in there, Exterminators. I'll be as quick as I can.'

'We're scattered,' said Meyer. 'And we're in trouble, let's not hide it. But we're Exterminators and we do what we do. No one gets lost, no one gets left behind.'

'Understood, sir,' said Sidhu, finding his heart pounding away, his body registering their dire position though his mind was still clear. 'I've got Reynolds, sir.'

'What's his situation?'

Sidhu knelt by his buddy. Reynolds was still and his heat signature was confusing but it looked like he was still alive. Sidhu stripped off a glove and felt for a pulse in Reynolds's neck. It was there but it was average at best. He put an ear to Reynolds's face, pulling his helmet aside and trying to get an idea of the state of the stricken soldier's breathing. Impossible. The wind and the muffling effects of Reynolds's mask conspired against him.

'He's still alive, sir, but I can't confirm injury. He's unconscious, I think. So hard to tell with the thermals. I'm switching to torch-light.'

'It'll be a beacon, Sid,' warned Meyer. 'Your call.'

'No choice, sir,' said Sidhu. 'Come on, Reynolds, give me a sign here.'

Sidhu switched his thermal imaging off and thumbed the studs on the side of his helmet. They had to be depressed simultaneously to switch on the quartet of bright halogen beams.

'Oh, no,' whispered Sidhu. 'Stay with me, Reynolds. Don't make a crap the last meaningful thing you did. Not a good epitaph for the headstone, buddy.'

Reynolds was still alive. His eyes were open and he was lying on his side, staring into the torch beams that Sid tried to keep from his face. Sid enabled his personal com and jacked the volume right up. He could hear Reynolds's breathing now; ragged gasps, short and agonised.

Reynolds's hands were clamped to his midriff. Somehow he'd managed to jam some sterile med packing into the wound and he was still holding it tight, his arms shaking with the effort. Blood had soaked right through the pack and was dripping into the sand.

'Captain Meyer, Sidhu. Reynolds has a serious gut injury. Bleeding heavily. I have to try and stem it and stabilise him.'

'Copy, Sid, do your best.'

Sidhu placed his hands over Reynolds's gloves and pushed with the slightest of pressure. 'Got to roll you over, Reynolds. I have to see the injury, gel it and stabilise you for evac.'

Reynolds rasped in a breath. 'Been listening to the com,' he said very softly and between gasps. 'Not sure I can walk out of here.'

'Horvald's coming back and I'm going nowhere. I'll keep you safe.'

'Top man.'

'It should have been my surname, buddy. Let's roll you. I won't lie to you. This is going to really, really hurt.'

Reynolds coughed a laugh. 'Thank you, doctor.'

Sidhu put one hand on Reynolds's shoulder, the other on his hip.

'On three...' he said. 'One, two...'

He rolled the soldier on to his back, dragging a long low growl of pain from him.

'What happened to "three"?' gasped Reynolds.

'Never could count,' said Sidhu. 'Okay, take your hands away, man. I need to see what I'm working with.'

Sidhu reached behind him and pulled his med supplies from the long pouch on his belt. Reynolds moved his hands and the pressure pack fell away. Whether it had been claws or teeth didn't matter, but Reynolds was slashed multiple times from the centre of his ribs to the base of his gut and the only things keeping his intestines in were the strips of skin in between the gashes. Reynolds was silent. He knew what Sidhu was seeing and they both knew the likely outcome.

'Let's get patching.'

Sidhu tore open the suture strip pack, aware that every moment more sand was blowing into the wound. He tried to shield it as best he could but the sand was bloody everywhere. Each suture strip was ten centimetres long and one wide and adhered to the skin brilliantly, allowing Sidhu to fix one end and pull a part of the wound closed as far as possible before setting the other end. Fuck knew how the medics got them off.

He had ten strips and cursed himself for not getting Reynolds's packs out too but there was no point in worrying about it. Sidhu worked as fast as he could with the wind threatening to whip away the strips and blowing sand on to the adhesive. He worked methodically, from the outside of the wound in, trying to knit the flayed skin as best he could, but there were still going to be ugly gaps.

He'd just about finished when the open com sparked up, making both of them jump.

'Basilisks incoming. One klick and closing hard. I've got three contacts beading on stations four and five, two heading for s-three and three more beading on s-one and s-two.'

It was Jen Picolet from station three, and the next voice was Meyer's and he was furious.

'How the fuck would you know, Pico? Are you still on station?'

'Yes, sir,' she said, voice rock-steady and determined. 'Someone has to relate and I'm the only one still in com range of everyone.'

'I gave you a direct order.'

'I'll be happy to go on report back on the *HoG*, sir.'

Meyer cursed. 'Your call, Pico. Leave whenever you want but if you stay, shout the numbers. You're our eyes. Good luck. You're more batshit than Sid.'

'Copy, sir,' said Picolet. 'I'll take that as a compliment.'

Sid chuckled and even Reynolds had a go at laughing but fell to a fit of coughing instead. Sid watched the suture strips, seeing them move and settle, remaining secure. He picked up the canister of gel skin, sobering quickly with Pico's voice in his ear, telling him how close the basilisks were getting.

'Sid, half a klick. Ganeef, seven fifty. Patel, Kapetic, two klicks.'

Sidhu aimed it at the top of the wound and pushed the top stud. A foamy white substance flowed out, spreading on contact. With a few quick swipes he'd covered the wound and he smoothed the foam down a little, feeling it begin to solidify, providing a sterile barrier.

'How much pain med have you taken?' he asked.

'All of it,' said Reynolds. 'Get your gun, Sid.'

'Sid, two-fifty and fast. Ganeef, six hundred, Patel, Kapetic, one point seven and fast.'

Sidhu pulled a hypo out of the kit and jabbed it into the wound at the side of the gel skin.

'Sid,' said Reynolds. 'Gun.'

Sidhu dropped the hypo and pulled his gun round. He flicked off his beams and switched to thermals, not that it did any good except make everything a whole lot darker. He thought to move from Reynolds but decided against it, instead moving to his other side so that he was facing station one, his weapon trained out over Reynolds's legs.

'Stay still,' said Sid.

'Oh, damn,' croaked Reynolds, voice a little slurred as the pain meds kicked in hard. 'And I was just dusting myself off for a run.'

'Shut up, I can't aim straight.'

'Don't burn my legs,' said Reynolds.

'You're on meds, you won't even notice till later.'

Picolet's voice rang out again, scared now. 'Sid, one on you now. Ganeef, same for you. Kapetic, Patel, one K and closing. Two on me. Duck and weave ... Oh shit.'

'Picolet!' shouted Meyer. 'Pico, do you copy!'

A woman screamed and gurgled, the horrible sound fed right into Sid's ears. It had to be either Picolet or Ganeef. Right in front of him, a basilisk sprinted out of the blackness. Just paces away and moving straight for them. It opened its mouth. Sidhu pulled the trigger and heard two dull pops; micro-grenades pumping out of the underslung barrel.

'Fuck,' he said.

The micros flew like a dream. Little flares in the night, straight into the basilisk's open mouth. The detonations were muted but their effect was devastating. The first blew the basilisk's neck to shreds, taking the jockey with it, electronics flashing and flaring in the mess of blood and skin and flesh scattering in all directions. The second micro destroyed the remains of the lizard's skull, sending bone fragments across the desert in an expanding sphere of razor-sharp hail.

Sidhu had put his head down the moment he'd fired grenades but it made little difference. He was aware of the basilisk's headless body plunging into the sand and ploughing right at them in the instant before the shock wave picked them both up and hurled them backwards.

He felt shards of bone ripping into his combats and flailing at his helmet. One caught his goggles with a glancing blow and shattered the left lens. And then he was on the ground again, tumbling out of control before sliding to a stop. Sidhu didn't care if he was badly hurt or not. He pushed himself to his feet, and ran to Reynolds, lying in the sand.

He dropped to his knees by him and switched to his beams. Of course, Reynolds was dead. His body was torn up. Bone fragments were lodged in his back and helmet and one leg had been all but torn off at the knee. At least his eyes were closed and the meds would have dulled the pain.

'Sorry, buddy, I'm so sorry.' Sidhu pounded the ground. 'Fuck, fuck, FUCK!'

He turned and sat with his back to Reynolds's crumpled body as the open com sparked up again.

'They went straight past me,' said Picolet. 'Kapetic, Patel and the others too. Ganeef's is still travelling north. I think Sid took his out.'

'Good to hear you, Pico,' said Meyer, still apparently charging across the sand. 'I'm closing on Ganeef. Great work, Sid.'

'Reynolds is dead,' said Sidhu. 'I fucked up, boss.'

There was a short silence across the com.

'Stay with him, Sid. What's the heading of the remaining basilisks?' asked Meyer, flat-voiced.

'If they carry on converging as they are, they'll all be on bearing three-four-zero.'

It didn't take a genius to work out what they were after.

'Horvald? Horvald, do you copy?' asked Meyer. 'You have incoming. I repeat, you have incoming.'

CHAPTER 34

Technically, the basilisk is only a one-jock lizard. But if you really want to, you can strap yourself halfway down its back. Now THAT is a ride... CORPORAL RAJ SIDHU, TWO COMPANY, THE EXTERMINATORS

'Do I copy?' muttered Horvald. 'Sadly, I do.'

The gecko was at a dead sprint and he could feel the lizard's anxiety in every fibre. It radiated from her in waves and filled his head with primal fear. She knew what was after her and she knew she wasn't fast enough. Horvald triggered his open com.

'Copy, Captain. We're at top speed and seventy-five short of the *Heart*. I'm transmitting the emergency signal plus the broadcast warning every couple of minutes. Nothing yet, sir.'

'They'll be on you in maybe fifteen minutes, mate. How long can you hold them off?'

'We've got a couple of tricks up our sleeves,' said Horvald. *Oh no we haven't.* 'I'll keep you posted. Stay safe out there.'

'Meyer out.'

Horvald closed his com. He wasn't sure who was in the worse position. Them out there, sitting among their dead and waiting to be picked off by whatever came out of the storm next, or him, shortly to be breakfast for basilisks.

'Right, let's see if we can shorten this trip any.'

Horvald brought up the terrain scanner with a gentle tick of his right little finger. It was mostly crocked by the sandstorm but it gave him reasonable readouts up to a hundred metres ahead.

'Okay, let's run by image here,' he said, trying to keep back the fear of the inevitable.

He resettled his face, feeling the sensory mask push air bubbles out of the receptor mucus that covered the gecko's neural interface. He could direct its head and eyes from here, issue orders to attack or flee by thought alone.

Horvald overlaid the terrain scanner on the gecko's optics. Using his legs and eyes, he steered the lizard along the most level course he could find, minimising climbs up even the most gentle slopes so long as he kept to his general heading. It made a difference, probably in the order of a metre per second but it was nowhere near enough. The fact was, the gecko was too big and heavy compared to the basilisk – a creature that would take as direct a line as possible, feet barely kissing the sand as it ran.

'*Heart of Granite* Flight Command, this is Lieutenant Jorge Horvald, please respond.' Nothing. He had no choice but to continue anyway and pray they picked up the emergency carrier wave, if not his voice. 'We have seven basilisks inbound as vanguard for an enemy behemoth. Repeat. A behemoth is moving towards your position, bearing two-zero-zero. Do you copy?' *Come on come on come on.*

'Shit, this storm needs to let up.'

But it wasn't letting up. If anything, it was intensifying.

Despite its low profile, the gecko was being buffeted by some major gusts and Horvald could hear the sand like hard rain on its skin. Horvald tracked the strength of the gusts for a few minutes while he moved the lizard as smoothly as he could across the shifting terrain. He tried the message another four times without a response.

Below him the gecko shuddered and tried to find more speed.

It squawked a warning that no one but him would hear. And he already knew the enemy were closing because the radar had just come alive. Horvald's stomach knotted with fear that he immediately transmitted to the gecko, which chittered and ducked its head. He tried to force calm into his voice.

'Meyer, Horvald, do you copy?' Static hiss. 'Dammit, well, just in case… I am sixty-three klicks out from the *Heart*. No confirmed contact with Flight Command. Am still signalling. Enemy on my six at two klicks and closing hard. Horvald out.'

Horvald tried to focus but his breath was coming too short and he could feel his hands shaking in the gloves and it was making his fine control difficult.

'Come on, Jorge, you're a gecko jock, get a bloody grip.'

But this wasn't how it was supposed to go. Not for him. An Exterminator jockey at the top of his game. If only there was a voice in his ear but he was alone; just him and his ride in the middle of a fucking desert in the pitch dark, eating sand and soon cooling in pools of their own blood. Horvald sighed and looked at the radar, seeing the basilisks in an arc a klick from his gecko's tail and closing.

'*Heart of Granite* Flight Command, this is Lieutenant Jorge Horvald, please respond.' *Guess what?* 'For the final time: I'm about to be taken down by seven Maf basilisks, this is an emergency warning. A Maf behemoth is heading your way now. You'll see it when the storm clears tomorrow. Trouble is, they'll be ready and you won't, because you didn't think anyone would be fool enough to move a behemoth in a storm. I'll take down as many of these bastards as I can before they spread my innards on the sand. Once again, you are under attack, *Heart of Granite*. Meyer's platoon is dying out here and now it's my turn. Horvald out.'

He scanned the terrain ahead and moved onto a direct trajectory to the *Heart*, skittering across the tops of dunes, down slopes and across scoured flat areas. The basilisks were on his tail now.

'Flight Com, Horvald. Maf behemoth moving on your position, bearing two-zero-zero. Basilisk outriders on me, Meyer lost.'

A pair came up on his flanks. He moved the gecko's head left and right, trying to keep them off. His radar was alive with signals around him. A third darted in to nip at the right rear leg. The jaws closed briefly and Horvald felt a sharp tug. The gecko stumbled right, sagging down into its hip. He pushed his right leg back hard, driving the gecko back to balance.

'Repeat: Flight Com, Horvald. Maf behemoth moving on your position, bearing two-zero-zero. Basilisk outriders on me, Meyer lost.'

The two flankers attacked together before Horvald had regained full speed. He felt the impact of their bodies and saw open mouths flash in, striking for his ride's neck. The gecko lunged forwards at his command, ducking low, jaws scraping the sand. Through the neural net, he felt the rake of teeth slicing into skin as if the pain was his own.

He gasped. 'Flight Com, Horvald. Maf behemoth moving on your position, bearing two-zero-zero. Basilisk outriders on me, Meyer lost.'

Horvald swiped the tail from side to side, feeling one satisfying contact. The gecko's jaws snapped left and right too, not scoring a hit but forcing their enemies to drop away. He had at least four around him now, trying to trip or bite him. He found perfect calm now the fight was on; and he was going to take at least one of them with him.

He began to repeat his message again but an impact high on the gecko's back shook him from his words.

'Shit.'

The basilisk, only about a quarter the size of the gecko, dug its claws into its back and used the seats for grip to begin moving up the spine. Horvald felt horribly vulnerable, his own back exposed, the armour protecting him inadequate for an attack from above.

Other basilisks drove close to box him in, and stop him shaking it free.

Horvald moved the gecko's head sharply right. The lizard bit out, catching a basilisk on the top of its head. Horvald ground his teeth together. He heard the enemy shriek and felt the gecko's jaws find flesh and bone beneath the skin and clamp almost shut. The satisfaction was enormous.

The basilisk slewed away and normally Horvald would have let go, but this time, he needed the momentum. He clung on. He could taste the flesh and feel the blood pouring from the wound. The basilisk's legs crumpled and it tumbled to the side. Horvald bit harder, feeling the gecko's body slewing round. He pushed his right foot down hard, forcing the gecko to drive its right legs into the sand, and rolled, crushing the basilisk on his back beneath him. He bounced and bumped in the moulded sheath. The gecko squealed, a wholly involuntary sound, as was the flailing of its legs and tail as it panicked in the search for balance.

'Flight Com *Heart*, Horvald. Maf behemoth moving on your position, bearing two-zero-zero. Basilisk outriders on me, Meyer lost.'

After what felt an age, Horvald forced some order on the gecko and had it back on its feet. Two down, or properly injured anyway. He stared out through those reptilian eyes. Both the radar and terrain scanner were down, lost in the tumble. He couldn't pick anything up. The gecko's tongue licked out but the air was too full of the scents of blood and sand to discern the position of their remaining enemies.

Horvald moved back towards the *HoG*. His gecko was hurt. Its left rear had damage at the knee, seriously depleting speed, and there were cuts on its back and flanks. He didn't think he could repel another concerted attack. Without the electronic aids, their isolation was acute. His shoulders hunched and he shivered, anticipating the inevitable.

Even so, the violence of the attack took him by surprise. He saw the basilisk tearing in at right angles at the last moment, jaws grabbing the gecko's neck right behind its skull and driving him to the right and onto his side. The gecko flailed but the basilisk held on. Another sprinted in unnoticed until he felt the awful sensation of teeth tearing at his ride's belly. The gecko struggled briefly but its life was pouring onto the sand.

'Flight Com *Heart*, Horvald. Maf behemoth moving on your position, bear—'

A claw swiped down on Horvald's barely protected back. He grunted, the sensation of pain mercifully brief because of the teeth shattering his skull.

'Try harder,' snapped Avery. 'I need it clean. I know it's a transmission. What is it saying?'

'Trying, Commander.'

The operator bent to his task, his ears reddening. Avery stalked away back to the tac-tables staffed by increasingly hollow-eyed staff. It was as busy as a daytime mission schedule but with Moeller in Flight Command, it was left to Kirby to spread some encouragement and calm a few nerves. Where the hell Solomon was, was anyone's guess. Actually, it wasn't. She was sleeping, as only the truly deluded can sleep, safe in the knowledge that she'd still be the all-powerful super-bitch in charge when she woke.

Avery stared at the screens ranged around the front of the C and C, seeing vague washing images of what was pretty much right outside the front door. The *HoG* was as good as blind. There were atmospherics out there that defied physics as far as she was concerned. At her disposal, she had the full spectrum of light and radio wave technology and not one of them, not one, could pierce more than eight kilometres of the storm.

As a result, every specialist worth the name had been turfed out of bed to try and squeeze the systems. So she also had Rosenbach in her ear telling her how everything she was doing was depleting the scant resources left to her by this or that fraction of a degree. If she believed everything the Tweaker said, the creaky old behemoth would probably keel over just after dawn.

Worse than all that, the platoons she'd sent out to place a forward sensor grid had disappeared into the storm and none had been heard from since. She supposed she shouldn't be surprised by that, but of course Moeller wanted to send out a whole load more to play hide and seek.

And now they had confirmation that someone, from somewhere, was attempting repeated contact. It couldn't possibly be good news. How bad... Well, that was the question.

'A free night in the Bridge Bar to anyone who can give me an accurate weather forecast.' Avery saw a line of heads drop a little lower and focus harder on their screens. 'All right, what was the last best forecast? Still claiming this'll blow over by midday?'

'Yes, ma'am,' came a voice. 'Weather radar and associated sensors are down. We're trying to gauge changes in the storm using traditional methods.'

'Like sticking your head out of the door and seeing how much sand you get in your hair?' said Lieutenant Edney from her tac-table.

Tired laughter ran around the room.

'Something like that,' said the forecaster. 'But also anemometers and a good old hydrometer.'

'What are they telling you?' asked Avery.

'Honestly? Almost nothing that you couldn't work out by sticking your head out of the door,' she replied to more laughter.

Avery nodded, happy to let the humour break the tension. 'ExO, Rosenbach, my office, please. Contingencies, contingencies...'

Avery led them into her office, which was a deliberately small affair comprising just a desk with three screens, a couple of chairs in front of it for occasions such as this, and three beautiful shots of the *Heart of Granite* on the two solid walls. The other two were glass and looked out over the C and C, specifically the tac-tables and front screens.

Avery sat in her straight-backed swivel chair and waved the others to seats.

'We're about two hours from dawn, we have no idea how long we'll be blind and we can assume the *Maputo* knows our position. What's our move?'

Kirby almost laughed but settled for a half smile, half frown.

'You think the *Maputo* might move on us?'

'I think so.'

'She's on her last legs, though. More likely the *Virunga* or the *Mombasa* to give her the chance to escape to the sea.'

'They're too far away to be a danger with an overnight march. The spyfly was *Maputo*'s,' said Avery. 'And we're on our last legs too but we're still intending to attack.'

Rosenbach shifted in her seat and Avery gestured her to speak.

'I've studied the footage of the *Maputo*'s tail-up from a few days back and there is clear and significant degradation of central musculature and core strength, hence the vibrations playing into the legs. I find it hard to believe they would choose to advance in a sandstorm, even though it's physically possible.'

'Chimes with my thinking,' said Kirby

'Assume they know the *HoG*'s condition and are planning to attack as a result.'

'The potential for the *Maputo* to accrue damage is huge, Commander,' said Rosenbach. She shrugged. 'We're all well versed with the issues of sand versus behemoth. That's why we seal up when there's a sandstorm and why I advised against launching geckos, even from the emergency port.

'Even with the blowers and vacuums going full blast, a behemoth on the march in a desert storm is taking on sand in massive quantities across its body, all blown in deep at a hundred K an hour. It'll get into the armour plate joints; the spin-up mechanisms for weapons and solars; retractable joint covers; directional coms linkage; even ammo boxes and missile loaders, auto-feed and tracking systems. And let's not forget the *Maputo*'s lungs, throat and mouth. Even with debris filtering, you cannot keep it all out.'

'All right... let's focus.' said Avery. 'It's great the *Maputo* will be itchy if she's marching. What does it mean in practical terms?'

'Our best case: all sorts of stuff starts grinding, slowing down or seizing up. It could expose weaknesses for attack as well as compromise defence. For me, if they are moving up, they're taking a huge gamble.'

Kirby raised his eyebrows. 'Only one reason why they'd be doing it.'

Avery locked gaze with him and they both spoke together. 'Wyverns.'

Wyverns were short-range, heavy, armour-depleting, burrowing missiles. The sort of ordnance every behemoth carried for the day two of them came into close contact. Missiles that, if fired from long range, would be taken out of the sky on a whim but when fired close and flat, gave the defenders little chance to deploy effective countermeasures.

'I'll wake the crew, put Moeller's emergency deployment into effect and write the audio and p-palm bulletin,' said Kirby. 'Not long till dawn and depending on how close they want to get, they may not wait for the storm to blow out.'

'Thanks, Robert. Eleanor, get hold of Markov, calculate how much you can divert to our EMP net and armour harmonics while keeping the air flowing and the drakes fully prepped. Everything else can pause for the time being.'

'Yes, Commander.'

'Are you all right?'

Across the table, Rosenbach had gone a little pale. 'Do you really think they're moving in to attack, hand-to-hand?'

Avery raised her eyebrows. 'I would.'

CHAPTER 35

> I don't suppose any drake pilot believes they're going to Fall. They all have faith the war will end before they do. And that's fine but when it does, how will we walk away from the biggest high of our lives?
> MAXIMUS HALLORAN

Meyer screamed at the fractionally brightening sky. Ganeef, McCarthy and Reynolds were all gone. He'd heard gunfire, explosions, shouting and screaming from the group converging on the rally point and then nothing. Horvald was surely a victim too. At least Picolet was still alive and was shouting the odds from station three. But Sid had gone quiet, so Meyer was running to station one to find him and trying to ignore the memory of his dismembered platoon members at station two.

'Behemoth still oncoming,' said Picolet. 'Approaching station one, speed fifteen klicks.'

'Copy that, Pico,' said Meyer. 'I can feel her through the ground.'

'You okay now, sir?'

'No, and I reserve the right to scream some more until I am.'

'I'll tweak my volume accordingly.'

'Good call.' Meyer checked his tracking system, which told him he was four hundred metres from station one. The vibrations through the ground were the familiar rumble of a behemoth on the march, though the equally familiar rolling thunder sounds were denied him by the endless, howling gale which showed no signs of abating. 'Sid! Sid, do you copy? I refuse to believe you're dead. I need you, man. Come back...' Nothing.

'...Sid! Where are you, Goddammit, answer me! Even if you're dead, respond via spectral coms, you bastard. That is an order.'

Meyer knew Sid was out there. It was daft but if he'd been dead, the world would have been truly altered and he'd have felt it. He heard what might have been static hiss but might also have been someone shushing him. Meyer raised a grim smile.

'That's "shh, sir",' said Meyer. 'Where are you?'

Meyer reached station one and glanced down at the sensor equipment. He could just make out the radar's outline as it vibrated gently across the sand to the ripple of the advancing behemoth's march.

Meyer stared out into the gloom, able to see sand driving east to west in the odd and faint glow of pre-dawn desert. The behemoth was close, probably no more than a klick away now. He moved forwards, sensing the ground rising slightly, imagining what he'd do in Sid's position then sprinkling it with batshit madness.

After about fifty metres, having moved nearer the path of the *Maputo* and up a shallow rise, Meyer dropped prone. He nudged Sidhu in the ribs.

'As clandestine meeting points go this is right up there,' he said.

Sidhu turned. This close, Meyer could make out the hollowness of his eyes.

'It's beautiful, isn't it?' said Sidhu, his voice flat and empty. 'Peace and majesty amidst the sand and wind. Makes you realise just how small you are. I would lie here forever if I didn't have to do some damage to someone. Lots of someones.'

'Got to rein yourself in, Sid. No vengeance shit.'

Sid looked forwards again. The *Maputo* was lumbering out of the gloom. She was mostly dark but picked out by the thin heat signatures where her tail dragged and from the warmth of her exhaust.

The *Maputo* was enormous. They all were, of course, but Meyer had never seen an enemy this close and it was, well... Majestic was right. Over a kilometre long, a little less than two hundred metres high at the apex of the spine and over two hundred and eighty metres wide, all carried on thirty-four pairs of legs. She was a little squatter than the *Heart* but that just made her silhouette all the more malevolent. Live exercises outside the *Heart* were one thing, this was wholly different. No one expected a soldier to get this close to an enemy behemoth and it was an opportunity they couldn't pass up.

'She's a beauty, isn't she?' said Sidhu.

'They all are,' said Meyer.

'Question is: how do we issue some corrective punishment?'

Meyer chuckled. 'I've got a better idea.'

'Oh yes?'

'Yeah. Fancy the ride of your life?'

'Are you suggesting...?'

'We carry spikes and lines for the specific purpose.'

'Most useless kit ever,' growled Sid.

'Not today, my friend.'

Sidhu pushed Meyer hard in the shoulder. Meyer laughed. 'I like your thinking, boss.'

'Of course. Let's do it.'

The *Maputo* was confirmed inbound. Horvald's final communication had been cleaned up enough to be understood and the general quarters autocom had sounded before dawn.

By now, the outer armour would be charged to deliver ECMs by the sack load; the forty-mils would be cleaned, oiled and coiled; the flank guns the same; and the missile batteries and anti-missile systems loaded and tracking. Elsewhere, programs would be running to simulate the likely effect of successful EMP strikes and the time it would take to bring back critical systems. Every soldier was on standby, every drake pilot was in the locker room and every drake, gecko and basilisk was taking on extra nutrition before being brought to ready.

Well, nearly every drake pilot. With her squad already on the flight deck and suiting up, Valera had gone to medical, not prepared to miss her early day visits to her recovering pilots – Roberts, Nugent, Holmes and Kane – but more importantly, her first ticket to see her pilot in Landfill. Her demand to have visiting rights breached Landfill protocol but Kirby had agreed readily enough. No doubt the video of their conversation would be scrutinised for clues as to Max's whereabouts.

'You should go,' said Kullani.

The ward was quiet. Every other patient was still asleep, aided by drugs for the most part, and wouldn't be woken with the *HoG* under threat of attack. No one wanted to test the effects of a full scale engagement on a patient well into the Fall. It was different for Kullani, so early into the Fall.

Valera was sitting on the side of her bed and Kullani was propped up with pillows looking comfortable but terminally bored, her mind distracted by thoughts of her drake and the inevitable loss of the beast beginning to consume her, slowly but surely. Valera squeezed her hand, wishing that they could reverse protocol and let her out to fly. Impossible, sadly.

'Bugger that,' she said. 'Moeller knows where I am. There's no rush. Anyway, there's a gale blowing out there and it's all very sandy . . . No place for a drake, eh?'

'No, I guess not.' Kullani gave a deep sigh.

'Yeah, we wish you were with us too. Squad room's become a hollow place without you and Max. You made it live, you know?'

A tear rolled down Kullani's face and she wiped it away quickly.

'Sorry, I'm not helping, am I?'

Kullani shook her head. 'No, the reverse. I've been desperate for a friendly face. I've hardly been here a moment but I feel so… removed. It's hard, Skipper, but at least I've got drugs to take away the craving for my drake. And the rest of you are out of lockdown so that's a plus.'

'Yeah, but only so we can fly to our deaths.'

Kullani grinned. 'How I would love to be doing that.'

'Flying or dying?'

'Both.'

There was no hint of humour in Kullani's voice and Valera was briefly taken aback.

'Maybe—'

'Maybe, what? No one's going to let me out, Skipper. There's one path and soon enough I'll be like Ella J over there, barely ever conscious and when I am, screaming in fear and agony. What a marvellous future lies ahead.'

'There's always hope,' said Valera.

Kullani met her gaze squarely. 'No there isn't. Not in here.'

Valera let her head drop and nodded. 'Sorry.'

'Not your fault.' It was Kullani's turn to squeeze her hand and Valera couldn't help but smile at the irony of it all. 'Anyway, it's not all bad. I've made some friends and I've even been reading a book for the first time in years.'

'Oh yes, what friends exactly?'

Kullani pointed at two beds. 'Diana and Dylan. Hard to believe they're both so young when they look so old and frail. It's tragic, really. But they look after me in their own way and I try to do the same to them… Sit with them and talk if they want.'

'And what did they make of Max?'

Kullani rolled her eyes. 'Holy Mother, don't get them started on Max. To hear them you'd think he was some saviour sent from heaven. I had it time after time yesterday… They'd be chatting or something and then catch sight of me and then one of them would strike a great theatrical pose and shout: "I'm Max fucking Halloran!" It's, well, it's just weird but he did have that effect on people, didn't he?'

Valera nodded and glanced up the ward so Kullani wouldn't see the tears welling up. Her com crackled.

'Valera, we need you on the flight deck.'

'Yes, sir,' she said.

She looked back to Kullani who shrugged and the two of them hugged hard. Valera felt Kullani's heart tripping away and her breath getting shorter as she tried to keep her sobs back.

'Come back and see me.'

'Try and stop me.'

They pushed back and Valera stood up and brushed herself down.

'How's Grim?' asked Risa.

'Remember I told you it was a mistake to fall in love with her?' said Valera. Kullani nodded. 'What a sack of shit piece of advice that was. She's amazing, she's there for all of us, she's buddied up with Paul to look after your drake and we're pushing hard to get her in to see you.'

'You'd better go. I need to cry now.'

'You got it, Risa. And believe me, there's always hope.'

Valera ran for the flight deck, fighting back her own tears but finding herself on the verge of laughter too at the thought of Dylan's and Diana's impersonation of Max. The whole thing had a surreal quality.

She had almost made it when the attack sirens sounded their haunting flat notes, alternating every few seconds with ship-wide orders. Valera sprinted the rest of the way, bursting on to the flight deck to find it teaming with people, ground lizards, drakes and more supply carts than she knew the *HoG* had on its roster.

The noise was extraordinary, energising and unnerving. The Hammerclaws were racing from the locker room towards their pens, with Whiteheat and Firestorm hot on their heels. Entire companies of marines were boarding geckos. Basilisks were screeching and swinging their heads, their whole bodies vibrating with the imminence of the hunt. The deck itself was still lowering into position, the *HoG*'s tail still arcing up and sand was blowing in. Valera wasn't at all comforted by the shuddering that accompanied the dual movements.

Moeller was blaring orders over the PA, every com channel she switched to was alive with chatter and she settled on the Flight Com's as she moved quickly across the busy deck, picking out this and that from the multiple voices on the channel.

'... EMP net active for incoming traffic... forty-mil firing solution delta-four active. Take-off angles of thirty-four degrees or less. *Maputo*'s position confirmed at fifty, five-oh, kilometres distance on bearing one-nine-seven... multiple missiles inbound... ECM full spread launched... Hammerclaws, await clearance when you stand on the runway. The air's a little crowded right now... Whiteheat, too slow, step it up. I need three squadrons sky-high on my go... Incoming, incoming...'

Detonations echoed across the flight deck, enemy missiles striking the EMP net or meeting the *Heart*'s anti-missile system. The *Heart of Granite* shuddered under the multiple waves of sound and shrapnel rattled against her scales, harmless and spent. Valera pushed open the locker room door and the sounds of chatter had died away before the bone and metal had thunked back into its frame.

Seventy-five pilots made a whole lot of silence and from every rank of lockers, eyes followed her as she moved to her own and opened it to pull out her suit.

'She's fine,' announced Valera, loud enough to carry the whole locker room. 'Or as fine as you can get when you're a Landfill resident.'

She began to strip off her fatigues, aware that pilots from all three squadrons were closing in to hear more. She paused and held up her hands.

'Thank you all for your concern. Risa sends her love and there's nothing left to do but get out there and fight. I'm not doing a "this is for Risa" speech, because it isn't. This is for the *HoG* and it's for United Europa and for all those undeserving rats we serve back in Paris and Berlin and London and wherever the fuck your old cap city is. Now bugger off, I want to talk to my squad in private.'

While the pilots from Flamehawk and Lavaflow beat a retreat to a respectful distance, Valera carried on suiting up, Redfearn and Gurney jumping into help. She took out her mobile earpiece before pulling her hood over her head and connecting into the suit's com net. It felt good to be wearing it again, despite the tightness.

'I'm going to make this quick. Risa needs a light. She's only been there half a second but she's already desperate. We need to give her hope if we can.'

'You're talking about Max,' said Stepanek.

Valera shrugged. 'If any of you have any inkling, any sense of him out there... anything at all, however small, tell me. If he's out there, we're bringing him home.'

'You think he might have *survived*?' asked Gurney.

'Can't fault a skipper for hoping,' she said.

'And this is Max we're talking about,' said Monteith.

'Yeah,' said Valera, warming to the thought. 'Max-fucking-Halloran!'

She would have explained but for a massive impact shaking the *Heart* from spine to claw, shaking locker doors open. The behemoth bellowed with a pain that chilled them all and sent thrumming vibrations through the floor. A sound none of them had ever heard before, would never had thought to. Outside, ERCs of every class chittered, screeched or roared in fear and confusion.

Valera led the stampede towards the door but they hadn't quite reached it before the lights went out.

'Bring the defence grid back online!' ordered Avery. 'Where's fire control? Rosenbach, get us back up. I need eyes!'

There was uproar. In the dim lights offered by the backup generators, orders were flying across ranks of consoles and tac-tables. The two hundred metre arc of screens across the front of the C and C was blank and dark. No radar, no thermals, even the feed from the *Heart*'s eyes was down. They were deaf, blind and defenceless.

'It's not an EMP strike,' shouted Rosenbach, running towards Avery. 'Wyvern, I think. Something's got through the armour at a dry spot, just like I feared. We haven't lost any systems independent of the *HoG*'s core generator. Backups have already brought key environmental systems online. We still have the EMP net but we don't have weapon systems or any powered musculature systems beyond vital functions.'

Avery's head snapped round. 'What?'

'Incoming missiles will not be targeted.'

'Yes, I heard,' said Avery. 'We can take a few hits. Can't we?'

'Armour has been prioritised but it won't keep everything out.'

'I'll take what I can get. What systems are disabled?'

'My best guess is the core power supply has been interrupted. Explains why no system with automatic redundancy has come back online.'

'Make a better guess.'

Rosenbach's cheeks reddened. 'Elements of the central electrical control systems have been compromised. The *HoG* is paralysed.'

Avery felt her first flush of real anxiety for about ten years. She flicked out her p-palm and pinged Moeller on his private com.

'Nic, we're in a real pickle here,' said Moeller.

Avery could hardly hear him above the din of voices yelling for something, anything, to happen and the sounds of what might have been destruction echoing up from the flight deck.

'Us too, Gerry. Tell me the flight deck is open.'

'Not all the way.'

'Shit. Can you launch drakes?'

'Yes, but it'll be a challenge. Wind speed is dropping rapidly, but there's still plenty of sand in the air.'

'The *Maputo* is going to give it a go, trust me. Get the drakes up, get them defending us from the spine out.'

'What's going on, Nic?'

'We're paralysed. You have to buy us some time.'

'Understood, I'll get the drakes busy. Moeller out.'

Avery looked up from her p-palm to see Rosenbach staring at her. Multiple strikes impacted the *HoG*. Warnings flashed on a few screens, unnaturally bright amid the dominating gloom. Dust was shaken from the metal and bone roof. The *Heart* moaned in pain again, a hideous mournful sound.

'Hang on, old thing,' said Avery. 'How long before we're back up and running?'

'I don't even know what the core problem is,' she said. 'I'm locked out of eighty per cent of systems. We're existing on work-arounds.'

'Get me back in control fast. Right now our only line of defence is a few drakes flying half-blind in a gale. Prioritise: I need my guns and my missiles.'

'I understand, ma'am.'

And Avery knew that she did; because if the enemy got the drop on them, and the paralysis stunt was planned not fortune, they could lose the *HoG* altogether.

CHAPTER 36

One thing you don't get to do as a behemoth commander is give your ride a rub down or a scratch under the chin to let it know you care. Part of me wishes I could. But I suppose if I really want to get close to my behemoth, I can put my hands in her brain instead. COMMANDER NICOLA AVERY

'Firedrake squadrons, Flight Command. Hammerclaw-K; Whiteheat-M; Lavaflow-A; Firestorm-E; Flamehawk-G; Inferno-X. Stack up, for take-off. You have your flight plans, your departure vectors and your defence zones. Wind speeds are peaking at one hundred and three kph. Space is tight on exit, and there are some vicious vortices out there, so get the power on, get clear and hunt well.'

Valera nudged her drake onto the crowded deck. 'Flight Com, Val-X, Inferno-X copies all.'

Down towards the partially open ramp, the runway was a slowly clearing mess. The crippling strike had caused panic among the ground lizards. Riderless geckos and basilisks had scattered across the deck, sending ground crew and infantry running for cover.

There were people down on the ground among fallen crates. Medics in carts with blue and green lights flashing whirred out to perform triage. Orders rang out from the com and a well-rehearsed procedure moved into action. Jockeyed basilisks began rounding up the stray lizards; teams of ground crew and infantry moved in with lines and prods to push and pull the errant beasts back towards their pens; and where they could, jockeys mounted subdued rides.

And all that in the jumping shadows of emergency lighting. Valera, once she was safely in the pouch, watched it through her drake's eyes. The clearing of the lizards was performed with admirable swiftness but merely served to put the plight of injured infantry and crew in the spotlight. Valera counted over thirty lying amid the debris caused by the missile strikes. She saw neck braces, drips and splints; blood on the bone floor; and three shrouds spread over fatalities.

She pursed her lips and waited, the drake com quiet, waiting for the signal, which came after an age and a further slam of incoming ordnance that shook spars from the roof, brought down lights and drew renewed screeches from already tense ground lizards. Her drake, like all of them, radiated the desire to be free, to fly and wreak revenge.

'All squadrons, Flight Command, runway is clear. Clear enough. Good luck out there. Hammerclaws, you are cleared to run.'

Valera sat her drake back and stretched her neck so she could see them go. It remained a glorious sight. Her drake's eyes were good and the gloom coalesced into sharp greyscale images, giving her clear sight of the last few strides and take-off. The Hammer's skipper cleared first and Valera sucked in a breath as she saw the drake blown hard to the right before it steadied and drove straight on under the tail, picking its moment to power away.

And so they launched. Every now and again, an anxious shifting of drake claws from the watchers signified a tricky take-off or a particularly robust blast from the gale. The worst was a Whiteheat drake, blown onto its back as it picked up its claws to fly. The drake disappeared below the jammed ramp and com silence fell barring calls to the unfortunate pilot. The whoops that accompanied the reappearance of the drake as she rose up to the left of the tail and swept out of the narrow gap and away bore testament to the tension running through them all.

It felt like an age before Valera was front and centre, her depleted squad, just ten out of the original twenty-four, lined up behind her.

'Flight Com, Val-X, we are good to go.'

'Copy that,' said Moeller. 'Strike hard and all come back. Inferno-X, you are clear to run.'

'Acknowledged,' said Valera.

She rolled her shoulders and splayed her fingers. Her drake shook herself at the wing roots then snapped her wings out and back. They rocked into take-off position and raced down the runway. Ahead, where she was used to the wide-open space of a fully deployed ramp and tail, there was a narrow slit, beyond which dawn was struggling to make an impression.

Missiles still ripped into the *HoG*'s outer armour and the behemoth shuddered at each impact. An EMP strike made the defensive net shiver. Nothing gave but neither hide nor polarised shield could maintain integrity forever.

Valera reached minimum velocity well before the hatched zone and focused her drake on more speed. She could already feel the fingers of the gale trying to push her off course. Her drake accelerated harder, stamped the last five long steps and took to the air.

Immediately, eddies and vortices whipping around the ramp, the tail and from the paralysed behemoth legs below struck her. She corrected, using tiny movements of her arms and legs and reaching out with her mind to suggest balanced flight. Freed of the minute delays of purely physical direction, the drake dipped a wing, flared the other and adjusted its attitude, allowing Valera to find the space to get them clear.

Beyond the shelter of the *HoG*, she was exposed to the full force of the storm. She pushed into the lightening sky as hard as she could, the gusting, sand-filled winds buffeting her with each wingbeat. Sand fizzed across scales and drove into her face, forcing her to seal the pouch completely and rely on filtered air.

The knowledge that Max couldn't possibly have survived the night in conditions far worse bled into her mind and though she tried to cling on to hope, there was none.

'Inferno-X, Val-X, it's cruel on exit, give your drakes their heads, let them fly out. Rendezvous on me and let's gather in a rotation. Visibility is no more than a hundred metres at best—' Detonations bloomed against the *Heart*, sending plumes of flame and debris into the sky. 'That's got to hurt. Flight Com, Val-X, got a bead on those last impacts. Let me get closer. I-X, in my wake.'

'Copy, Val-X. Remaining squadrons are moving into position. No contacts as yet.'

She listened to the acknowledgements of her squad as she ducked back towards the *Heart*, levelling out at a hundred, and flying from tail to nose before angling up again, her squad in her wing whirls.

'Flight Com, Val-X. Significant damage along the right flank between the fourth and twentieth vertebrae. Multiple impacts, none appears to have caused a rupture but there is some smouldering and minor cracking. I have a single large impact to the *Heart*'s head right on the bridge of her nose. Fires are burning, can't confirm intrusive strike but it's a focused attack, no other skull strikes.'

'Copy, Val-X. Get back on station. Flight Com out.'

Passing over the skull damage, her drake shuddered and barked. A confusion of emotions and half-grabbed images ran through Valera, none of which she could make out.

Valera shook her head to clear it but the after-images left her feeling a little anxious. She ascended to a thousand metres and moved into a wide circle on station, seeing her squad drop in to make the rotation.

'Any problems, report in now,' she said over the squad com. No one reported in. 'Squad, we'll take this in chevrons. Stepanek and C-Three, cover the left flank and respond to calls from the Hammers. Monteith, you've got C-Two. Cover the right flank, Whiteheat and Lavaflow. I'll take the head, Firestorm and Flamehawk. Keep me posted. Trust yourselves, trust the squad, we are I-X.'

They all joined the chorus. Valera noted the sky growing brighter. Vision was increasing; up to a hundred and fifty by now. The gale was finally blowing itself out and she knew that as fast as it had come on them, it would be gone and most of the sand would drop from the sky. She hoped the enemy would launch before then... I-X was good in the dust.

'All squadrons, Flight Command. Missile barrage ended. Expect drake contacts. Flight Com out.'

'They want the *HoG* alive,' said Valera. 'Now she's immobilised they won't so much as scratch her again.'

'Contacts, contacts.' It was O'Regan. 'Whiteheat has contacts. We have... one hundred plus inbound. Gonna need assistance here on a bearing of one-six-five.'

'Regan-M, Val-X, can you be more specific?'

'My pleasure, Val,' said O'Regan. 'I'm at a thousand and flying below... now... Five squadrons, repeat, five squadrons in wide front formation. They are at a height of two hundred, air speed one fifty, bearing zero-four-zero.'

'Subtle. Flight Com, can you confirm contacts?'

'Negative, Val-X, you're beyond current radar range,' said Moeller. 'All squadrons, orders: engage enemies on bearing one-six-five. Regan-M will assign targets. I-X to remain on support and second strike. Hit them hard.'

'Copy, Flight Com,' said O'Regan. 'All squads, ascend to a thousand and come on to one-six-five. Match speed with the enemy and make it snappy, this dust won't last long. Targets as follows...'

The UE drakes moved into attack positions, Valera bringing her chevron up a hundred metres adrift of Firestorm and Flamehawk. She didn't much like the idea of I-X as backup but despite the upgrade their depleted number made them the obvious second strike team. Shame though; a full-strength I-X could have practically destroyed a Maf squad in one pass.

Valera listened while the confirmations rolled in. The *HoG* drakes were on station. Below them, picked out as shadows in the remaining dust, the *Maputo*'s drakes closed on the stricken behemoth.

'Flight Com, Regan-M, all squadrons standing by.'

'Copy,' said Moeller. 'We have you and your targets on scope. Five klicks out and closing. You are cleared to attack.'

'Copy, Flight Com. All squads, strike is a go.'

The *HoG*'s squadrons attacked with I-X drakes tracking them, looking for their moment. A dark mass ahead and below about three hundred metres resolved itself into a broad formation of sand brown drakes. The five squadrons, in near perfect sphere formations, were spread across a klick of sky.

'Very pretty,' said Gurney. 'Even prettier when we set it on fire.'

'Reckon they're all upgraded?' asked Monteith.

'Reckon they're not,' said Gurney. 'They aren't coming in fast enough.'

The ferocity of the attack was breathtaking and Valera winced as Whiteheat battered into the central sphere. Brutal impacts bent Maf drakes in two. Claws ripped great rents in drake flesh or sought holds for close fighting. Maf and *HoG* drakes twisted and turned, bit and struck while they dropped towards the deck; each looking for the killing hold, or the heartbeat in which to breathe superheated flame. Under the assault, the enemy sphere dissolved into disarray.

The sheer violence was repeated across the enemy formation. Valera was tuned into the I-X squad com while her people reported on dozens of enemy drakes taken from the sky. Below her, the Firestormers had smashed into the enemy's left flank. They'd split into two, the first section crashing into the rear of the enemy formation, shattering the sphere, shunting enemies off balance, biting, ripping, killing.

The second section came in right behind, pouring fire over struggling enemies, heads angled back to play their flame downwind and sending multiple bodies tumbling and smoking from the sky. Valera counted seven down to one Firestorm drake with wings shredded, spiralling into the sand.

'Our turn,' said Valera. 'In your wing pairs, I-X, engage at will.'

The *Maputo*'s drakes fought for cohesion but with *HoG* squadrons all over them, they had been forced to break away to reform in smaller defensive units.

'Skipper?' asked Gurney.

'Drop off me twenty metres, Gur-X. I'll pick the target, you sweep up the collateral.'

'Copy, Skipper.'

Valera flexed her toes and her drake's claws mimicked her move. She flew on a few beats before diving vertically on the remains of the left-hand sphere of Maf flyers. Valera backed her drake's wings and slammed into her target. The force of impact broke its neck right behind its skull and the two of them rolled right and down, clipping a second, knocking it out of balance.

Gurney swooped by a wing beat later, overflying the clipped drake and toasting the enemy from snout to tail at very close range before angling upwards steeply to join her.

'Nice work,' she said 'Keep it going while they're off guard. Stay among them.'

Valera drove into a tight, upward right-hand curve. The air was charged with flame and anger as drakes collided, bodies rippling and spinning. Necks twined, fangs sought dominant hold, claws raked and tail spikes struck. Firestorm and Flamehawk came round for their second passes. Drakes surged in, blistering a corridor into the centre of the battle, their arrow formation devastatingly effective. At least four more enemies were taken from the fight, plummeting down to the sand to join the littering of corpses that had to number over forty now.

Sunlight bled over the horizon. Her drake locked its gaze on to a pair of Mafs whipping through the sky on the tail of two Firestormers.

'Watch my six, Gur-X. I'm on the hunt.'

'I'm on it, Skipper.'

Valera twitched her left arm down. Her drake barrel-rolled, taking her around a friendly drake. Ahead, she could see her targets through a confusion of sparring drakes and by the focus of their flying they were still tracking the Firestorm pair and maybe two hundred metres adrift of them and closing. The augmented enemy were fast and their slick movements were a contrast to those of the drakes they pursued. Not dramatic, but there all the same.

'Into my slipstream, Gur-X. Two targets, you take left.'

'Copy, Skipper.'

Valera opened her mind a fraction more, her drake sucking it in greedily, cajoling her for more. Valera twitched her arms and imagined speed. Her drake reacted, the connection sending a rush through her body and mind. Great beats of its wings powered it into the maelstrom of the fight.

A knot of sparring drakes dropped into her path. She snapped her drake's wings back and shot through the tiniest of gaps, feeling the brushing of bodies. Her drake fed her imagery of the dozens of individual battles in their zone that would cross their path. Valera felt the suggestions of direction from her ride, overlaid them with her own and plotted her route, switching left to drive around a tumbling pair locked by tooth and claw, and ducking under two enemies being chased by six Lavaflow flyers.

Valera closed fast, her upgraded drake allowing her to make the minute adjustments in the crowded battle zone to keep her right on them. Abruptly the two enemies split, abandoning their pursuit, and Valera and Gurney broke smoothly, a sharp turn and climb putting them into their targets' slipstreams.

'Skipper, you've got company.' said Nevant. 'Heading in on your seven.'

'I'll break off,' said Gurney.

'Negative,' said Valera. 'I've got these guys.'

She nicked left and right past drakes flying across her path, saw her target dive left to avoid a collision and calculated an intercept that her drake followed to perfection. She pulled in a wing, used the other as a drag and turned on a pebble, suggesting tight fire. The enemy raced below her, catching harsh flame across its wings. They blistered and tore, sending it hurtling out of control to smash into another drake, a *Heart* drake.

'Shit,' she spat. 'Gur-X, report.'

'Target down,' he said. 'Coming back to you.'

'You've still got two on your six,' said Nevant. 'Am in pursuit with Xav-X.'

Valera angled sharply up, turned on her tail and powered back down; the drakes hunting her emerged from a confusion of flyers. They had no chance to avoid her. She picked one and her drake's head snaked out and caught the oncoming drake on the top of the skull. Wings tight, Valera turned a sharp half-roll, dragging the enemy's head around to snap its neck. She imagined force and her drake crushed its skull before letting it drop.

Her drake exulted, spitting fragments from its mouth and they spun in the air, momentarily unbalanced as the Maf drake's weight dropped away, before powering upwards.

'Nev-X, report.'

'The other one's escap… Oh no it hasn't. Ouch! Hot pouch, courtesy of Gurney.'

Valera smiled. 'Good work, C-One. Reform at a thousand on my marker. Let's assess.'

She climbed past the battle and into clear air, seeing almost three hundred drakes still engaged in high velocity combat below her. The sand density was dropping rapidly. Light was flooding across the desert and she could see both the *Heart of Granite* close by and there, down to the south-south-west, the squatter *Maputo* fifty kilometres away.

Her emergency broadcast com crackled and fizzed and she caught snatches of a voice repeating a message.

'Unknown contact on channel alpha one alpha. Identify yourself.'

The voice spoke again. Different words this time and the odd one was clear enough. Valera swore, sure that she was understanding but hardly believing it.

'Captain Meyer, it's Valera Orin. Meyer, is that you?'

CHAPTER 37

> She stabbed me. She stabbed me a thousand times and poured ice into my veins. Apparently that's how a drake demonstrates affection.
>
> MAXIMUS HALLORAN

Max's eyes opened on the shifting dark of the pouch encasing him. He could feel some residual pain, echoes of agony. It still felt like he was pierced in more places than he had places but the icebound agony of it in his veins and the sheeting hot pain in his head had both faded.

'We're alive,' said Max.

His voice caused them to shift ... no, caused Martha to shift ... no. Max stilled completely while he decided whether to believe what had just happened. He had felt the sand beneath the tail when it moved. He had felt the dried faeces shift on drake scales.

Max rolled his shoulders, slowly and gently. Their wing shoulders brushed against the shifting dry matter, which felt like it was cracking and powdery.

'Whoa, that's ... weird.'

He pushed out with his mind but instantly knew he didn't have to. This wasn't yesterday or the day before and the old ways were obsolete. She was all around him ... just *there*. And where there should have been fear Max felt exhilaration and strength.

Martha wasn't at peace, though. Images began to tumble through his mind: the *HoG*, the flight deck, the pen, the food tubes.

We have to go home, said Max.

More imagery followed, some obviously borrowed from his memory: Kirby, Landfill, Dylan and Diana, Hewitt with his swollen face.

But we're dead if we don't go back, aren't we?

Martha shifted again and Max felt their hiding place cracking. Warmth suffused him and an image of Anna-Beth came to him. Then Kullani, the skipper, Grim, Monts...

We have to go home, princess. Now we're alive, we don't have a choice, do we?

Sensations of muscle tension and the building of power chased themselves through Max. The piercings across his body tingled, energy coursed his system and they exploded from the dried behemoth faeces and drove straight up, wings beating strongly, head stretched towards the blue.

They turned towards the rising sun, the air already hot, the growing warmth in their scales glorious. The wind across their body was cool and flecked with sand and dust, the faint rippling of membrane as it flowed around their wings and fled down their tail was an endless thrill.

They banked and rolled, dived and climbed; every move perfect, every tiny adjustment sheer delight. So pure, so effortless. Max felt the modulating pressure of the pierce points, sifted the images and decoded the thoughts, blending them with his own. He felt his body moving, knowing it was as much him as her. Not that that mattered any more... There *was* no him and her except where their minds meshed, there was only *they*.

'Waaaaaaaaa hoooooooo!' screamed Max. Martha exulted too, her bellow shuddering through her body. 'Fucking hell, what a RUSH!'

They played, explored, but always moved south. Max experimented, moving his arms, legs and torso as he always had, as he had been trained to do. Martha still responded but he felt her reluctance and it felt clumsy, slow. But now he'd tried the old way, he couldn't switch back.

A little help, he said.

Images tumbled into his mind and the pierce points tingled again. Max felt himself relax, decoding the imagery as best he could, understanding with it the desire for partnership. For a moment, he still couldn't work out how to get there, access that place where their movements came from shared stimuli, somewhere in a joint subconscious. When it came to him, it was so obvious he laughed, Martha responding with a rattling in her throat.

He stopped trying to fly, let all the tension leave his body and simply imagined it. They barrel-rolled, turned a long spiral climb and then powered away south.

That's more like it.

Martha barked her pleasure. The wind was glorious chill across their body. They adjusted their wing attitude to take advantage of a slow-rising thermal. The yearning grew with every wingbeat. Max felt it like he was an anchor being dragged from the ocean floor. Slowly at first, then gathering pace until it became an unstoppable pull. A pull he had no desire to halt.

It was the call home. The call to Mother.

Martha fed Max anxiety, which he felt as a rising nausea. It coalesced as anger and a growl rose in his throat. Martha roared and they accelerated harder. They could feel it like waves across the shore: Mother was hurt.

Images of the *HoG*, I-X, the flight deck full of drakes, and Anna-Beth flooded his mind. The message was clear enough that it crystallised into a single word that boomed about his skull: Protect.

What the fuck's happened?

They were afraid.

Max became aware of something else: a buzzing like a distant swarm of insects. Lights . . . mere pinpoints . . . sparked in his mind. They moved and shifted, pulsing, with the buzzing in sync somehow. Max tried to focus on it, force it into coherence, but he could make out nothing but an odd staccato shifting pattern.

Is this you or us doing that?

Martha didn't respond but sent out a chilling wail and they beat their wings still harder.

What is it? Is it anything?

Max's senses were ablaze... no... *their* senses were ablaze, it was just that he couldn't decode everything he was sensing, not yet anyway. The dominant feelings towards the *HoG* meshed uncomfortably with a growing familiarity he felt for the light swarm. Slowly, Max began to filter the chaos, pushing his mind out towards individual pinpoints, certain that Martha would be steering him gently, guiding and teaching.

Like pulling threads from a tangled ball of cotton, he began to tease sense from the mass of noise. Each thread had two distinct beats and wrapped about them were harmonious sounds, a little like sighing and cooing, chordal notes and faint bass rumbles. Max was so close to being able to name what they meant it made him twitch in frustration.

Martha pulled an image from his mind: a hand scribbling a name with a pen. Max gasped. The threads were signatures. Each one he teased out was subtly or dramatically different from the last. And so it became obvious what they represented.

Drakes... Holy Mother, that's a battle, isn't it?

Martha didn't need to confirm it. Max found his breathing short. Anna-Beth would be out there. So would the remnants of I-X.

Don't you dare die, any of you. I'm coming. But I've got to check on Mother first.'

'Say again, Captain, you're breaking up,' said Moeller.

By now, the whole of the Exec was in Flight Command. There had been no improvement in any situation barring the weather and right now, they all wished the storm was still blowing full force. Across the behemoth, teams strived to get systems back online and break the *HoG*'s paralysis, with very limited success. Up in the sky, the drake battle was increasing in ferocity. After the brilliant initial attack for his squads, the attrition rate was worrying and the only squad not to have lost people so far was Inferno-X.

The Mafs were running a classic strategy, continually breaking off by squadron and retreating a few hundred metres before heading back into the fight. The effect was to move the whole battle gently eastwards and leave the *HoG* exposed, but no counter-punch was forthcoming thus far.

But now the captain of an Exterminators platoon who should have returned hours ago was broadcasting from who knew where, saying something of great importance that none of them could decipher, and it was making Moeller nervous.

'... eat, am ... klicks to your ... *Maputo* has ... gro ... Six ... gec ... art ... on ... Pre ... they ... king fir ... tags ... age. Ove ...'

'Meyer, you are breaking up. Repeat, repeat, repeat.' Moeller slammed his palm on his desk and looked around at frustrated expressions that mirrored his own. He thumbed his p-palm. 'Yarif, I'm sending you all Meyer's coms. Get the voice-analysis and reconstruction software on it right now.'

'Apologies, sir,' came the reply from outside Moeller's office. 'I don't have access to any analytical systems. They're still down.'

'Get me Rosenbach.'

'Yes, sir.'

Moeller snapped his p-palm away. 'Any thoughts?'

Solomon', Avery' and Kirby's faces were tight with frustration.

'Do we know where he is?' asked Solomon.

'Not beyond his original mission co-ordinates and that he must have a visual on the *Maputo*,' said Moeller. 'He must be close; ground visibility is still awful.'

'Could Orin get a clearer signal?' asked Kirby.

'No,' said Moeller. 'That's why she passed him to me.'

'We have to know what he's saying,' said Kirby.

'Really?' snapped Moeller. 'I hadn't realised.'

'Cut that out right now,' said Avery. 'Find a solution or say nothing at all.'

It stank in the skull, it stank and it was not a place for claustrophobes. Eleanor Rosenbach hadn't thought she was one such but the journey up to the nerve ganglions in the centre of the skull, which carried messages to all major systems centres, had made her think again.

It was a long journey from the access points at the head of skull deck one, up the engineering and bio-systems flesh tunnels and into the bone-architectured space where key systems boards integrated electrical, mechanical and biological systems. A journey made necessary by the failure of the diagnostic systems in the ERC control centre. Arriving in the cramped space with nothing but a powerful splash light and her p-palm for company, Rosenbach sucked in a breath.

The impact from the wyvern, burrowing in before exploding, had caused fracturing all the way down here, some eight metres inside. The skull was supposed to be impregnable and she supposed it was, since the systems boards still had power from the emergency battery packs. But the shock had been sufficient to induce the widespread paralysis they were experiencing.

Visceral fluid was dripping through cracks in the bone and the cracked viewing panels revealed swelling and bruising on the flesh surrounding the nerve ganglion. She pinged the systems board with her p-palm and was relieved to get a ready prompt to begin a diagnostic.

'Finally you're talking to me,' she said.

While she waited for the diagnostic to run, she sat back against a curved bone wall and let her hands smooth across the floor, feeling the tackiness of leakage and, faintly, the warmth of the

HoG's life. She needed to find a solution, something to unlock the paralysis, or at least get some defence online. And until she did, every one of the ten thousand or so on board was vulnerable.

The weight of responsibility made her shudder and she shook her head to dispel the image at the same time as her p-palm bleeped to tell her the diagnostic was run and that Yarif wanted her to patch into Moeller and the Exec.

'Mister Moeller, this is Rosenbach. Are you reading me?'

'L and C. The marshal gen, ExO and Commander Avery are all in attendance. What have you got?'

'All data is streaming to the ERC staff p-palms for analysis and Helena is on call for clarification.' said Rosenbach. 'Poor old *HoG*, she's taken one hell of a kick. Systems boards are on batteries, there's nothing coming from the ganglion at junction seventeen alpha. Bruising and swelling may be impeding nerve impulses and the coolant system is offline. The diagnostic confirms a widespread system shock. Seventeen alpha controls the central spinal column, legs and ship-wide motor systems and none of that is online. I can see two possible solutions.'

'We're listening,' said Solomon.

Rosenbach felt a thrill of nerves. The marshal gen had never spoken to her before. Even though she was stuck up a stinking tunnel, it was still pretty cool.

'The first is a full reboot. If the ganglion is shocked, a systems reset should kick it back to life. Second, we get an ERC tech up to every junction and start to re-patch systems one by one. I need an all-clear to proceed one way or the other.'

'Why don't I have radar?' asked Avery. 'And why are coms so poor?'

'The *HoG*'s sensory functions are down. While she's blind, so are we. Our coms boosters and dishes can't align to get a strong bead. It's all linked to the same issue.'

'Which operation is the quicker?' asked Kirby.

'A reboot would take about an hour,' said Rosenbach. 'But if it doesn't work then we're back at square one. And we'll have zero systems for the first twenty minutes of the procedure.'

'Can't you fix seventeen alpha directly?' asked Solomon, her voice betraying her irritation.

'Not without surgery, ma'am. And if the swelling is acute, no number of reboots will work.'

'And what's the lead time for your re-patch?'

'We could have the first basic systems ... eyes and mouth, for instance, re-patched in a few minutes. The complication is linking back into the spine, with seventeen down. We'll have to assess the relative safe loads on the other junctions before I can give an estimate for defensive systems, radar and other imaging equipment.'

'So are we rolling the dice or going step by step?' asked Moeller.

'Why the hell does so much vital stuff get routed through this one junction?' asked Solomon. 'Pretty fucking convenient weak spot for our enemies to exploit.'

'It's an accident of biological design,' said Markov, chiming in for the first time. 'Go step by step. I'm dispatching techs to all junctions. Eyes in ten minutes, I'd say. Eleanor will update you as other systems come back online.'

'Okay, folks, let's get to it.' Avery clapped her hands. 'We're in your hands, Rosenbach.'

'Copy, Commander.' Rosenbach blew out her cheeks and began inputting re-patch options into her p-palm, using what few core systems she could access to aid her flow and load calculations. She got a ping from Markov. 'Hey, Helena.'

'Enjoying the stench up there?'

'It is uniquely awful.'

'Share me on your calcs and progress, will you? I'll leave you on point but I'll be plugged in, all right?'

'No problem.'

'What's up?'

'Nothing,' said Rosenbach. She patted the sticky wall. 'Being up here reminds you she's a living thing, that's all.'

'Something our Exec might want to remember from time to time. Good luck.'

Their fear deepened as they approached and overflew the ailing behemoth. Smoke was rising from the top of her skull and there were massive black streaks and impact points on her body. *Nothing* was moving. Her legs did not shift where they stood, none of the turrets or missile boxes were tracking, and her head was still when it should have been rocking gently, snout and tongue sampling the air.

Martha had continued keening; in fact it had intensified when they could see the damage close up, and now she was driving high up into the sky. Visibility was improving rapidly, heat was blooming as the sun rose and before long, only tiny dust particles would still be in suspension, like a fine mist.

A few klicks east, the drake battle raged on and the silence surrounding him when his ears should have been alive with com chatter was unnerving. He needed his coms back but didn't know how to activate them in his new environment, even though he still had the subvocal array on his throat.

But even through his frustrations and his anxiety over Mother's condition, he was still able to wonder at the extraordinary range of sensory information his pairing with Martha had opened up to him. Martha was using scent trails, heartbeats, brain activity, exhalations and even the eddies in the wake of wingbeats to build up a picture identifying each individual drake, ground lizard and behemoth, friend and enemy.

Decoding it was the problem; and like learning a new language, some of it was obvious, like the representations of the *HoG* and the *Maputo* because of their sheer scale. But much was confused and though he had an idea of how a friend and enemy drake sensed to him, he couldn't identify individuals and he so wanted to know which one was Anna-Beth.

He had sensory imagery of the paths of every drake in the battle while ahead, about fifty klicks, the enemy behemoth was stationary with a few drakes circling above it as dozens of ground lizards moved away from it and towards the *HoG*. There were others too, heading off in more tangential directions. He could see and monitor them all.

There's so much we don't know. Holy Mother, Martha, this is amazing. But I need coms. I need to be able to speak to my friends.

Abruptly, the incoming com feed activated and his head was full of chatter that made him well up. Back and forth between pilots, between Flight Com and the squadrons too. He grinned to hear Moeller's voice and a few others from the gantry. And there were Valera, Monteith and Redfearn among others, picking targets and toasting Mafs.

Of course... Just think it and it happens, right?

Martha purred her confirmation, more warmth in his mind.

Is Anna-Beth still out there?

Another confirmation but barbed this time.

Don't be jealous... it's a different thing, right? So what do we do, princess? Join the battle or stay in station?

Martha didn't respond but continued to ascend in a steep spiral. Max couldn't be certain but it seemed Martha was looking for, or waiting for, something. Something she couldn't or wouldn't share, and he was forced to listen to his friends fighting. It was plain from the chatter that the enemy had the upper hand.

We have to do something.

Max desperately wanted to speak, to announce his return, but he felt pressure from Martha to remain silent for now. He found his trust in her was complete so he bit his tongue. A familiar voice cut across the rest, carried on the emergency channel.

'This is Captain Meyer, two platoon, Exterminators. I am fifty klicks to your south-west. The *Maputo* has launched multiple ground lizards, all approaching your position. Six missile-carrying geckos are on an easterly heading seeking ideal firing positions. Missile tags indicate bio or chem agent. Over . . . Flight Com, please respond.'

They chilled and Martha squawked. Max searched his sensory map for the missile geckos that no one barring Meyer knew were out there because the *HoG's* arrays were down and ground visibility was only just beginning to improve.

Fuck fuck fuck. Bios . . . They want to kill Mother.

There they were . . . or he assumed it was them. A group of signatures represented by a series of mid-bass heartbeats, minimal brain activity and thermal trails left by feet and tails. It was no longer time for silence.

'Meyer, Hal-X, do you copy.'

'Meyer copies. Confirm your call sign.'

'You heard me, Meyer, it's Max.'

'Fuck off, Max.'

'Confirm your location and threat level to the *HoG*.'

Max heard Meyer say something to somebody else and then give a sigh. 'I'm strapped to a leg of the fucking *Maputo*, Halloran. And I'd say the Mafs are about to launch something lethal right down the *Heart*'s throat. And why aren't you dead, you bastard? I so wanted you to be dead.'

Martha barked a roar.

'Martha doesn't like you talking that way,' said Max, feeling their anger. 'I can help, Meyer. Personal shit later, all right?'

'You fucking owe me,' said Meyer.

'Whatever you want. The missile geckos, whatever they are. Confirm their direction.'

'Due east of our position. No escort, just snuck out when their drakes went off to fight ours.'

'Copy that, I'm tracking them.'

'Then take them out, Halloran. Do it for the nine of my platoon who died last night because of you.'

'Wow,' said Max. 'Sorry you lost people, Meyer. Hal-X out.'

'Fuck you, Halloran. And do something good for once in your life.'

Okay, princess, let's do some damage.

They came about on to a westerly heading and swept back over the *HoG* and into the empty desert. There were the enemy geckos, about twenty klicks from the *HoG*'s motionless head and sprinting hard. Meyer was wrong: they weren't going to launch down her throat, they were aiming for a free shot into the partially open flight deck. It would be a surer way to kill her.

They aren't going to get a chance to try.

They angled in to intercept across a clear sky. It was going to be a doddle. There were six of them, spread out across a few hundred metres of desert. Ten klicks and closing, and they were going to catch them broadside and helpless. Shared images tumbled through their consciousness representing a plan. Claws, fire, fangs and tail. And this time, Max was going to taste the blood himself.

A thousand metres out and flying at six hundred, they dropped into a staggering dive, their wings flat against their flanks. At five hundred out they were spotted; ordnance wound out of geckos' flanks and spun up, tracking them.

Shit, why don't we have those?

The air whistled past as they closed and they could see four missiles on the back of each one, squat and evil. They adjusted their flight slightly and saw the guns, forty-millimetres, nudge round and get a lock. They banked away hard, spreading their wings to drive into a steep climb. Forty-mil rounds thumped out of the twin guns. They spun and twisted, arched and dived, their movement fast enough, slick enough to beat the guns. This time. They steadied at fifteen hundred, turned and tracked the geckos.

For the briefest moment, Max paused to wonder how much

of that had been him, how much her and how much *them*. He'd relive the thrill later; when the job was done and Mother was saved.

We need help. Martha opened her mouth and roared long into the open sky. His com sparked up and he could hear the battle being played out. Max had to calm a rush of nerves before he spoke. He hadn't thought he'd ever do it again.

'Val-X, one-to-one, do you copy.'

'Val-X copies on one-to-one,' came the reply. 'Confirm call sign.'

'It's me, Skipper.'

'Holy fuck, Max!' screamed Valera. 'Is this for real?'

'Skipper, we have a bad situation. Kill missiles on geckos, preparing to target the *HoG*'s flight deck. I need I-X east about nine klicks. Can you break?'

'We're on our way.'

'Hurry. They're close and loaded with forty-mils. Tough lizards.'

Max checked the sensory trails. The enemy geckos were about fifteen klicks from their target, moving fast and in formation. There was a way into them avoiding the forty-mils' firing arcs but it would mean high-risk flying, low to the ground, particularly with the gusting uneven winds over the dunes.

'I-X, Val-X, orders orders. Break, break, new heading, zero nine zero. Ignore any company you bring. Fly hard in chevrons. Ground targets await. Val-X out.'

'Thanks, Skipper,' said Max as he felt the warmth of his family, a warmth to which Martha reacted with gentle pleasure. 'From what I could see, their payload is quads of short-range missiles. Meycr says they were tagged for chem or bio.'

'Copy that, Max.' She paused. 'I've got to call it in. They need to get defence hardware to the ramp.'

'Understood.'

'Max?'

'Yes, Skipper?'

'Did you Fall?'

'I think so,' said Max, and he felt no fear. 'It all feels different anyhow. Better.'

'Good that you're not insane or dead.'

'Both are positives.' A chill thought struck him. 'How's Risa? Is she flying with you?'

'Negative, Max. She's in Landfill.'

'Fuck,' spat Max and Martha responded with a deep grumble in her throat. 'They have to let her Fall.'

'Let's win this fight first, Hal-X.'

'Copy that.' Max focused back on the geckos, each of them trying to kill Risa and Grim and everyone else stuck on board.

That's not happening. They moved into a tight turn and lined up on the hindmost target. Max kept his counsel while the squad chat filled his ears, bringing them one step closer to being back with their family. But he dared not dream of life back on board. Not yet.

'C-Three clear,' said Stepanek. 'We're bringing a few friends.'

'Copy that, C-Three,' said Valera. 'C-Two, status?'

'We're low at two hundred,' said Monteith. 'Three bogeys on our tail.'

'Understood, Mont-X.' Valera was silent for a few moments and Max had time to imagine Stepanek's and Mont's faces. 'I-X, I'm calling this in to Flight Com on open com. Listen in and stay calm.'

Max tensed, wondering what she would disclose, and began a steep descent. They were still five klicks adrift of their target meaning Max could focus on the com for a while. It was worth every moment.

'Flight Com, Val-X, do you copy?'

'Confirmed, Val-X. Thanks for passing Meyer on to us. No joy yet,' said Moeller.

'I can help, sir. Captain Meyer has identified six missile-carrying geckos heading for the *Heart*. We believe them to be kill missiles, repeat, kill missiles. Inferno-X is heading due east in pursuit. We will overfly you shortly, and have company. Please assist.'

'Copy, Val-X. We cannot assist. All defensive capabilities are compromised.' There was a short pause. 'Confirm threat and contact with Meyer.'

'Six missile-carrying geckos closing on the *Heart of Granite*, specifically the flight deck. I have had no direct contact with Captain Meyer, sir.'

Max heard a definite click as the com cut out for a few moments.

'Please advise the intel source, Val-X.'

'Copy that, sir. Intel is credible. Call sign Hal-X spoke with Meyer.'

Pause. 'Say again, Val-X.'

'Call sign Hal-X, sir.'

CHAPTER 38

> Losing a pilot is the hardest thing. Even when you know the Fall would kill them anyway, it feels like personal failure. But losing Max was the worst. The moment he left my flight deck I was certain I would never see him again. His blood was on my hands. FLIGHT COMMANDER GERHARD MOELLER

Alexandra Solomon heard the words echo out of the speaker in Moeller's office and they were followed by her worst nightmare made real. Halloran. Not just alive but still flying and in the thick of the action. Out of her control, out of anyone's control.

Outside the office, the news spread through Flight Command like a frag missile detonation. There was a collective gasp followed by cheers and laughter and the buzz of excited conversation. Moeller, who was vainly attempting to suppress his delight, barked an order for calm and closed the door.

Solomon looked at Avery and Kirby, wanting their expressions to mirror her own, but neither came close. Avery's face held an air of healthy scepticism but her eyes betrayed her satisfaction. And Kirby's eyes were glinting as if he was calculating the value of the gift that had dropped into his lap. But his face held neither hate nor fear. Idiot.

'Suggest you move hardware to the ramp, sir,' came Valera's

voice, and Moeller tapped his p-palm, killing the feed to the control room if the disappointed faces turned their way were any guide. 'We'll do what we can, but they are heavily defended. You should prepare.'

'Copy, Val-X. Continue intercept. Flight Com out.'

Orin's com went quiet, leaving the other squadron leader feeds piping in. Inferno-X's sudden departure had shifted the battle dynamic. Maf and *HoG* drakes were streaming back towards the disabled behemoth, fighting as they came.

'This is a fucking calamity,' said Solomon. 'Get Rosenbach. She can't bring the main com feedback online until I give the order. I want this locked down tighter than a basilisk's arse.'

Avery stared at her and she was surprised by the contempt on the commander's face.

'By a stroke of the most astonishing fortune and due to the courage of one soldier, we know about a mortal threat to the *Heart*, and your primary concern is with *PR*?'

'You only think of the now. I always look to the future.'

'There won't *be* a future if we don't focus on the now.' Avery shook her head and turned to Moeller. 'Gerhard, get the duty company down to the ramp with the mobile missiles and the mounted heavy cals. Task all squads to support I-X and keep the Mafs away from them. Nothing else matters.'

Moeller smiled and began snapping out orders. Avery brought up her p-palm and tapped the small screen in the top left-hand corner.

'Helena, it's Avery. We've got incoming, ground and air. I need flank guns and I need forty-mil. Never mind the missiles. Tell me there's progress.'

'Of course there's progress but it can't be rushed.'

'This has to be,' said Avery. 'The ramp is exposed.'

'I hear you.'

'Thank you.'

Solomon turned away and waved Kirby over to her. She saw both Moeller and Avery clock them.

'We have to manage this very carefully,' she said. 'Corsini has been very specific about the consequences of Halloran's return.'

'And what if he performs exceptionally? What if he swings the battle in our favour? A way to win the war will have dropped into our laps.'

Solomon moved Kirby firmly out onto the balcony.

'Are you out of your mind? If it gets out that even one pilot survives the Fall and comes back changed, everything we're planning for is gone. Corsini loses the election, probably his life. The war ends. All contracts are void. We'll come away with nothing but the clothes on our backs and, if anything links us to this, not even those.'

Kirby nodded and there was an infuriating confidence in his expression. 'I understand all that. But with respect, you aren't thinking this through. Everyone involved in the Fall programme is on board. We welcome Max back here, Markov takes him for testing and reports that he is not a victim of the Fall. Therefore his survival poses questions about whether the common symptoms are really a prelude to the Fall or just an illness born of too much flying. Who is going to know? Who can challenge Markov on professional or intellectual grounds?'

Solomon saw the ragged ghost of a way out and she exhaled the breath she had been holding. 'Plausible deniability.'

Kirby shrugged. 'Absolutely. Want me to brief Markov?'

'Do it. But pick your moment. Let's see how this fight plays out – Avery's right, it could all be rendered irrelevant. Max might die out there. But if he makes it back on board, remember I'm not the only one Corsini will have spoken to. That pilot will have a target on his back.'

The ground was so close Max felt like he could touch it and it thrilled him. They were flying no more than five metres from the undulating desert terrain and often less than two, body ramrod straight, wings twitching more subtly than they ever could have managed before. She had deployed her second wings, ones the ERC had always thought useless, vestigial; a component of the alien DNA they had not identified. They were small, almost like a deployable tailplane, mounted just above her hips and it turned out they provided critical stability.

The gecko's jockey knew he was being pursued. His forty-mils were trained as far round as they could go and were peppering the air to either side of them but they didn't have the angle to get a hit. They were a hundred metres astern and closing fast.

They powered in. With a flick of wings and tail, they bumped up over the gecko's back and flamed out, the blue-hot beams of fire tearing into flesh, bone and missile housing, finally skewering the lizard's head before angling upwards almost vertically, wings beating hard to propel them away fast from enemy gunfire, twisting and curving all the way.

The gecko's missiles exploded, solid fuel detonating, obliterating the lizard, its jockey and spewing blood and body fragments across the sand.

'I-X, Hal-X, one down, repeat, one down.'

'Good job, Hal-X!' shouted Monteith. 'So good to hear you, man. Babysitting your chevron, want 'em back?'

The com was filled with the shouts of welcome and warmth of the return to the fold. Max felt wonderful... *they* felt wonderful. Martha barked her delight and they came about to join the squad flying in over the *HoG*.

'Later, Monts. Skipper, may I?'

'Be my guest, Hal-X.'

The geckos ahead were frighteningly close to a first potential firing position, only about eight klicks out now. That meant ten minutes to target zone plus however long it took them to prep the missiles. Not long, probably. Further west, he could see the mass of drakes moving closer. It was going to get very messy very quickly. Max leaned into the sensory map and reported on what he saw.

'I-X, you have twenty-three drakes in pursuit, steady at a thousand behind for now. Five enemy carriers below. Forty-mil flank defence, approximate one-six-five degree angle of fire. Your approach has got to be tight front or back and very, very low, five metres and less. Call it, Skipper.'

'How the hell are you clocking all the action?' asked Stepanek.

'New trick, buddy. Tell you later.'

'Thank you, Hal-X,' said Valera, as Inferno-X swept over the *HoG* and into the skirmish zone. Her guns remained still, the missiles locked out. 'With five targets, we'll take the rear three then the forward pair. Hal-X, take centre. Step-X, take right with Pal-X and Gar-X. I'll take left with Xav-X and Nev-X. C-Two, split for attack on the forward pair, attack on my go. The rest of you, spot for us and keep the Mafs off our backs.'

Max moved into his attack position. Martha called out, a new sound, a pulsing bark from the back of her throat, flat toned and piercing. The other drakes responded, mimicking her call.

'Holy Mother, Max, did you do that?' asked Redfearn.

'It was all Martha. I think she's happy to be home. So am I. Right, gang, we've got to get this right. Follow our lead, we'll be ground-hugging, so be careful. Let's go.'

Max dived, the two trios coming with him. He monitored them, noting the individual sensory signatures as they flew in mini-chevrons fifty metres either side of him.

'Level out at fifty and get used to the bumps. Don't drop below ten until they start firing. We'll go to five to be sure.'

Affirmations came through the com.

'I have incoming,' said Monteith. 'Twenty plus contacts, no formation. Looks like a multi-point attack. Speed it up down there.'

'Copy that,' said Valera.

'We see them too, Monts,' said Max. 'They'll try and cut us off before we reach our targets, and stay clear of the forty-mils themselves. Check the quad forming at four o'clock. They're on point.'

'Got 'em,' said Monteith. 'C-Two, let's take them before we do our run.'

'Levelling at fifty,' said Valera. 'It's rough down there. Nev, Xav let's drop to twenty. Get straight, get trimmed.'

Max and Martha cruised ahead of the others and descended to five metres. Her hip wings flicked out and they stabilised, closing fast on their target.

'Holy fuck, Max, how are you doing that?' asked Valera.

'Look, no hands!' Max laughed. 'Another new trick, Skipper. Stay in our tail wake. Low as you dare.'

Forty-mil weapons began to fire. Max focused forwards, hearing the whine of shells going past. All three targeted geckos were firing.

'Mind your flanks,' said Max. 'One's about to go down now. Fireworks a-coming.'

'Fucking show-off,' said Stepanek.

'You'll find I've hardly changed at all,' said Max.

'No surprise there,' said Stepanek.

'Max, the flankers are closing up fast,' said Xavier.

'Distract them, Xav,' said Max. 'I'm staying on target.'

Gunfire sounded right and left; the flanking geckos had slowed. Forty-mils swung back angling fire towards him. They pressed even lower for a few beats, gliding, their belly brushing the ground. Through Martha's eyes, Max kept focused on the gecko looming before them, dunes and lesser sand undulations whipping by either side, their wings making minute adjustments to keep them flying.

Shells ripped into the ground next to them, sending spats of sand against them. And then they were in the shadow of their target. They bumped up and their fire scorched great tracks in the gecko's spine as they passed by just a couple of metres above it. They spiralled hard into the air, long gone when the missiles exploded.

'Waaaaaaa hoooooooo!' yelled Max as they rolled and hovered.

Martha bled anxiety into his mind and Max checked his sensory map. 'Xavier. Xav-X, you're too wide. Pull away!'

They came hard about and dived on the left flank gecko.

'I'm in the slipstream,' said Xav-X. 'He can't track me.'

'Negative, negative,' said Max. 'It's a one-six-five flank angle.'

'Got to distract him from Valera.'

'You're too wide!' Max yelled. 'Go low!'

'Do it, Xav-X,' said Valera.

They flattened their wings against their flanks, diving almost vertically, hoping to get into position to strike before it was too late. Xavier was still tracking on his original course and hadn't corrected enough when the gecko had tucked into try and defend its mate.

Valera was still a hundred and fifty metres adrift and wouldn't be able to fire in time. Nevant was right with her, perfectly in position to distract or come in behind if something happened to her.

'Shit,' said Xavier, seeing the angles and his error.

Xavier veered sharply as the forty-mil fired. Shells tore into his right wing and flank, tearing great holes in the flesh and shredding wing membrane.

'Shiiiiiiiiiiiiit!' shouted Xavier as he fought for control and slewed down and right.

His dying drake was flailing with its one good wing, tail desperately trying to balance it when it collided with Valera's. She had seen it coming at the last moment and tucked in her wings but Xavier still sent her spinning, cutting across Nevant's line, forcing him to pull up sharply, then take desperate evasive action as both geckos' forty-mils spat into life.

Everything seemed to slow down. Beyond Valera, Xavier struck the sand, his drake tumbling over and over, the man himself silent in the pouch, his drake losing the damaged wing completely, smearing blood across the desert. Valera was out of control, spinning closer to the ground, impact seemed inevitable. But with a flick of her right wing, she killed the spin and a quick beat sent her forwards again. She cleared hard to the right, the attack run forgotten, gunfire chasing her skywards.

Max, about to become the focus of gecko fire himself, swooped out of his dive to the right as a great bloom of fire gouged at the sky on their right. Clouds of smoke billowed up as three drakes soared away.

'Good work, Step-X,' said Max.

'I can still teach you a thing or two, puppy,' said Stepanek.

'Focus, you two. I-X is one down,' snapped Valera.

Max checked in on the remainder of Inferno-X high above them. A Maf drake, engulfed in flame, tumbled down, trailing smoke. Elsewhere two Infernos were harrying another. One had a grip on its neck while it tried to get its head round to breathe fire. The other spun about them, looking for the gap to strike. A tail spike went in, tearing through a wing. The Maf drake shuddered and the Inferno scorched fire along its back. It was released to fall.

'Orders, Skipper.'

'You've got to get the last three. Stepanek's trio have holes from forty-mil. They won't manage another strike.'

'Tall order. Reckon I can get one before they reach their target zone.'

'Do it and let me think. We'll shadow you. The rest of I-X will keep the Mafs off you, best they can.'

'Copy that.' *You heard the skipper, princess.*

They turned into a shallow dive. Below, the three surviving geckos were racing towards the partially open ramp. They were just a couple of kilometres from the *Heart*'s nose and maybe fifteen hundred metres to her left, well out of range of small arms and handheld missile fire. Five minutes and they'd be in range of the flight deck.

They had changed formation, running in a flattened triangular pattern, each one able to rely on defensive fire from the other two. It gave them a new problem. Even flying ultra-low, they could be exposed by a rise in the ground, and bumping up to score the kill would paint a target on their back.

Any smart ideas?

Images cascaded into what Max was coming to realise was a shared consciousness. Allied and enemy positions, possible and preferred targets, flight plots and firing solutions. He added his own and their plan formed at the speed of thought.

They dropped to fifty metres and hurtled in, only three klicks from the rear left gecko and looking to stay in its left flank shadow to stop at least the lead lizard from firing. Max checked the organic map. The *HoG* loomed huge at its centre. Above him, Inferno-X battled and he could see Maf runners coming for him, pursued by the *HoG*'s finest.

'You don't have a prayer of getting to me.'

Just the other side of the *Heart* and closing fast was a mass of blips, like a cloud of flies. Drakes of both sides flooding into the combat zone.

'...Oh, but you might.'

Time for plan B. They dropped further and came round a tight curve to bead on their target's flank, seeing the forty-mil begin to track. Martha rattled phlegm in her throat and they flew low and fast into a twisting run of shallow dunes. Their combined senses went off the scale. Max could feel the pings in his pierce points, minute movements of his muscles in perfect sync with Martha's movements.

The sensory map blazed inside him, dunes flashed past, low walls of sand around which they flew. Their wing tips clipped sand from the ground, her belly, and almost the pouch brushed it too. Her hip wings – he had to think of a better name than that – flicked and ruffled, keeping her body level.

The signature of the gecko was huge and close, hidden by the desert. Max gasped, his face so close to the ground he could almost lick it. His whole body raced with energy, his limbs vibrated, their bodies were in total harmony, their minds locked together. It was, well, it was…

'Waaaaaaaaa hooooooooo!'

They were just a couple of hundred metres adrift now and still flying flank-on. They switched left and then right, and came out of the dunes no more than ten metres from the target's rear left leg. Great tongues of flame surged out and covered the gecko's body in yellow- and red-hot fire.

The lizard screamed and deviated sharply from its path. They beat their great wings and pulled above it. Just beyond it, the last two geckos' weapons were tracking. They breathed a cloud of flame downwards and turned their back to the enemies, climbing hard.

They howled at the impacts of forty-mil rounds, the pain exquisite and intense, burning into their reptilian body. They ached with the shock and it took Max a moment to realise that the move to turn their back on the enemy, natural as sunrise as it was, had been to save his life. *Their* life.

'Max! Are you okay?' came Valera's voice. 'Max?'

'We're still flying. We've taken one round through the left wing. Minor tear, nothing to seriously compromise agility. Three to the upper back, right opposite the pouch. Hurts like fuck, I can tell you.'

'I saw you spin over. Without that, they'd have taken you out, Max.' Valera's voice had a break in it. 'Another new trick?'

Max was going to reply but a host of drakes swept over the *HoG*'s motionless body and everything went completely insane.

CHAPTER 39

Sex used to be better than flying.

MAXIMUS HALLORAN

'No, Carlos! You can't patch the imaging that way, you'll compromise the central processing core. Love to see you explain that to Avery.'

'You're right, you're right,' said Carlos over the com. 'All right, if we reroute primary air flow systems via junction eight, that gives us space to jack in the radar at least.'

Rosenbach smiled and checked her route map.

'That works, Carlos. Who's on J-eight?'

'Who else would be in the sludge pits beneath leaky old hydroponics?'

'Hey, Asha. Did you bring a hat?'

'No,' she said. 'What do you want?'

'Carlos is going to pass you primary air flows. You've got the capacity. Then we can get radar up on nineteen and we're two steps from a few guns. And I understand guns will make everyone happy.'

'Yep. Nothing makes me smile more than a flank gun ripping someone's life away,' said Asha.

'I hear you.'

'Carlos, you ready?'

'Ready.'

'On three. I'll patch up behind you to make sure we don't close the loop prematurely. One, two, three.'

A few taps on interface screens and it was done. The amperage didn't spike and each system came back online in sequence.

'Commander Avery, Rosenbach. You should be seeing radar imagery.'

'Confirmed and well done... What the flying bastard is going on out there?'

'Sir?' asked Rosenbach.

'I'd say two behemoths' worth of drakes are in the sky right over us. Keep your head down...'

As if to make his point, there was a heavy impact to the *HoG*'s skull, audible even as deep as she was.

'What was that?' asked Carlos.

'Well, if I was a betting girl, I'd say it was a drake crashing into our head. Let's just hope it was one of theirs.'

'Rosenbach, Avery.'

'Commander.'

'Where are my guns?'

'Coming.'

'I need my guns,' said Avery. 'Still got two killers inbound. Drakes can't stop them both.'

'We're working on it, Commander.'

'Even releasing them for manual works. I've got people in position.'

'We're working on it, ma'am.'

'Avery out.'

'Do you enjoy pressure?' asked Asha.

'Can you guess why I sent you to the slime pit, Ash?'

They were like a fog over the remaining geckos. Swirling and clouding, obscuring the targets, alive to every move, and throwing sand back into the sky to further degrade visibility. The *HoG*'s drakes, warned by Valera, were clashing hard, trying to winnow the numbers down. But the *Maputo*'s drakes were tough opponents.

Max, with Redfearn and Monteith on his flanks, scorched in low about five klicks from the target gecko. Max called the incoming, the sensory map becoming easier to translate every wingbeat.

'I have three in line astern, coming in on our eight. Who's got them?'

'Ours,' said Stepanek.

'Four more on our three. Reckon that's your zone, Skipper.'

'I see them, Hal-X.'

'Okay, let's take this gecko down,' said Max.

'Copy that, Max,' said Redfearn.

'In your slipstream, Hal-X,' said Monteith.

No training could have prepared them for this fight. Maf drakes were using themselves as battering rams. Flying in from all corners, they smashed into escort drakes, blocking attackers out physically, running decoy, and flying obstruction formations, anything to keep the geckos on track.

The way ahead was a maze of drake bodies. *HoG* drakes were doing a fantastic job keeping the mass of Maf drakes away from the runs on the geckos. They'd had two aborted runs so far, leading to this last desperate attempt. One gecko had already reached its goal, with a fierce battle being fought in the sky above it.

Martha dropped to five metres, Max relaying the move to his flankers, who settled in at ten. Monteith suddenly pulled away right. Max saw him intercept an incoming drake, slapping it hard with his tail before his drake toasted the spinal scales with wide-angle fire. Nothing fatal but plenty of damage nonetheless.

'Good work, fella,' said Max.

'I do my best work within touching distance of the ground,' said Monteith.

'All right, we're a klick out. Break on my mark,' said Max.

They appeared from nowhere, or so it seemed. Even with the sensory map, Max missed them. They came out of the fog of pulsing signatures ahead of the gecko, five of them suddenly front and centre. Redfearn reacted beautifully, twitching out right and suggesting fire to her left which caught an enemy broadside and sent him ploughing the sand. Monteith took one full on, flaring back his wings and stabbing out with main talons, ripping into enemy wings. But three came on fast and low, or not, they were history if they held their course.

They held course for a split second more before twitching an h-wing and rolling just enough to release their electronic counter measures, naturally produced electrical discharges like balls of drake chaff, right into the face of their nearest attacker. They switched h-wings and snapped out their right wing too, turning ninety degrees on as close to a sixpence as a drake could get within the laws of physics.

Oh yeah. Their quad beams lit up the enemy pouch. *We are* soooo *good.*

The third had broken away, its job done, but they didn't give up. They dropped back on course as a fourth Maf drake barrelled into the space vacated by Redfearn, sideswiping her. They flashed over the gecko and breathed wide fire. Flame splashed across the gecko but their speed took them by too fast and they couldn't angle the strike properly to make the kill. The gecko sprinted on.

'Shit! Negative result,' said Max, as they twitched higher. 'We'll circle again.'

'They're reaching firing position,' said Monteith. 'We should get across the line of fire and chaff the fuck out of the whole area.'

'It's a plan,' said Valera. 'Who's in position? Max, you have to get in another run. Suggest you go vertical. They might be vulnerable as they set up.'

'Copy that, Skipper.'

'Val-X, Flight Com, do you have guns?'

'Negative, Val-X. Stand by.'

'Enemy carriers in position imminently. You need the flank guns.'

'Understood, Val-X. Stand by.'

'Dammit!' shouted Val-X.

'I'm in position,' said Calder. 'Got Reds with me, too.'

Max and Martha surged high. Ahead a Maf drake was running across their bow. They dragged round into a tight left, coming up right behind her and stamping their talons down, feeling the satisfying ripping of scales. The enemy juddered beneath them. They curled her neck down and breathed before dropping the carcass and surging back into the climb.

On sensory and in vision, they spotted the gecko through a crowd of drakes.

This is going to be some ride, princess.

'Get me my guns, Rosenbach!'

'I'm trying, Commander! If I give them to you now the *Heart* will stop breathing.'

'Manual flankers, it's all I ask.'

'I know. Give me a second.'

'I'm counting.'

'Carlos,' said Rosenbach. 'Or Ash, Rachel, Yuvraj, Charlie, Evie, any of you. We have to enable the flank weapons.'

'We can enable the lot for manual but you aren't going to like what gets turned off,' said Charlie from J-twelve.

'Hit me,' said Rosenbach, and Charlie did.

'That's complete systems failure. We can get it all back. Eventually,' said Charlie. 'Even the airflow pressure.'

'We *might* get it all back eventually,' said Ash. 'But you're talking about key bio-electrical systems going offline. No guarantee they'll spark up again.'

'Well, if we don't we're going down anyway,' said Charlie.

'Chemical warfare about to break out on the flight deck, you know? Not something you see every day.'

'Shit, but it's still a big call,' said Rosenbach, pressing her sweating palms together. 'Do it. Three stage downlink and enable. Let's go.'

Max and Martha screamed down the few hundred metres to his target. Enough enemies had seen him to make it difficult. Enough of his friends had seen him to give him a chance. A Maf came in from the left at ten o'clock. Martha twitched right and it missed by a hair. Another was closing from below. Max watched it come. He also watched as O'Regan hammered into its side, claws on its wing, and jaws around its throat. A third was on the dive. But it wasn't fast enough.

Below, the gecko was readying. Missiles were lifting on their beds. Around it, the evidence of their failed attacks was a grim reminder of the ultimate sacrifice drake pilots had made to save the *Heart*. Max was prepared to join them. Anything to save Mother. They shot past two Maf drakes trying to block them. They rolled their body right then left, reducing potentially damaging impacts to glancing blows. They held their course. Fifty metres.

They could see the missiles clearly now and the jockey in his shell just forward of them. They toyed briefly with the idea of fire but it would have been suicide. Instead they tipped their wings out and back to slow them and their body swept down. Their rear legs shot out from under them and their talons slammed into the gecko's back, missiles and all, and with a beat of their wings, pulled it over on to its side and back.

They let the broken body go, took two beats back and toasted its underside. They watched flames take hold. It was done. The jock could fire missiles all he wanted. They'd drill down into the sand and pulverise him on detonation.

Bright light flooded his vision.

'Missile launch, we have a missile launch.' Valera's voice was horribly calm. 'Confirm tracking towards the ramp. Entry in thirty seconds.'

Thirty. They had enough time. Just.

Martha roared and they twisted into a tight upward left-hand turn. They could see the missile flares to their right and calculated their trajectory. They beat their wings hard, trimmed their body for pace and made for the swiftly closing gap.

'I'm on it.' Gurney's voice was a sudden intrusion into Max's plans.

'Where are you?'

'Close enough. Calder and Redfearn are making a pass. I'm backup.'

Max spotted him on the organic map flying in from the north-east and a little too far away.

'Negative, Gurns. It's too tight. I'm faster.'

'Between us we'll stop them.'

Still flying hard, Max and Martha watched Calder and Red-fearn head in. The Maf drakes were standing off, circling high, waiting to call the hits. The two Inferno drakes shot across the line of the incoming missiles, dropping a dozen and more balls of electricity in their wake. Max held his breath. Two missiles chased the chaff, detonating in mid-air.

'Two flying,' said Valera.

Max could see gunfire from the ramp. 'They have to cease fire. Gur-X, we can take one each. Maintain course, increase speed if you can.'

'Copy that, Hal-X,' said Gurney.

'Good luck, buddy.'

'You too, freak.'

'Funny.'

They forced more beats from their wings. The smoke trail of the solid fuel rocket was mesmerising as it arced its path to the *HoG*. Ahead, Gurney was coming in on a perfect vector, his signature lit up by the electricity building in his drake's body as he prepared to release his chaff.

This has to work. This has to work.

Ten seconds. Five. Gurney shot across the bow of his missile, dumping multiple chaff balls that glared, fizzed and spat, confusing the missile – which deviated immediately, chasing away down to its doom.

Our turn.

Max felt a massive impact from below. They were shunted up and right by a Maf drake battering into them, having emerged from the confusing mass of signatures all around them.

'Shit!'

They released their chaff but they were too high, too wide. Dan Gurney saw it happen, twitched his drake down a fraction and caught the remaining missile square in the pouch. The detonation showered fragments of drake and pilot across Max's vision, which misted with tears for his friend that he couldn't wipe away.

'Avery, Rosenbach. You have everything on manual.'

'Confirmed, Eleanor. Your timing is impeccable.'

'All squads, Flight Com. Fly low, fly low. Tuck into the legs. Manual firing solution available and we cannot discriminate between Mafs and friendlies. Clear below fifty immediately.'

Confirmations rolled in as drakes flooded below the kill line, their abrupt break from combat catching all but the quickest-minded enemies on the hop.

'Flight Com copies all. Firing solution enabled in three, two, one... Guns guns guns.'

It was the most incredibly beautiful, comforting sound. The blatter and blast of flank machine guns and forty-mils filling the air with a dreadful density of lead, depleted uranium and armour-piercing mercury-centred rounds. It was the steady beat of hell's drums. The discordant echoes of drakes caught in the fire or shrieking warnings completed the ensemble.

The *HoG*'s drakes gathered in tight formation astern below the partially wound-up tail or flew beneath her belly – a unique opportunity with the ramp jammed half-open. Maf drakes streaked by, heading west to the *Maputo*, or scattered high, trying to get out of range. Max and Martha could hear the agonised cries of those caught in the gunfire.

Drakes were destroyed on the wing. Forty-mils ripped great lumps out of flesh or blew holes in skulls, flank guns tattooed wings and broke neck vertebrae. Bodies, dead and dying, fell from the sky, thumping to the sand to lie still or crawl away weakly in search of sanctuary. Wherever they could, the flank guns finished them off.

Their gambit had failed and the Maf drakes scattered back towards the *Maputo*, leaving carcasses littering the ground. And when the guns finally fell silent, Max heard the words he thought he'd longed for since the moment he'd flown out.

'All squadrons, Flight Com. Come on in. We'll see if we can get some lights on for you.'

But Martha growled and Max felt his mind flood with fury. They stormed back high into the dusty sky and turned towards the *Maputo* and the retreating drakes. For what they had already done to Mother, and what they had wanted to do, they would pay. All of them.

The sensory map showed him hundreds of signatures in the sky and on the ground. An overwhelming number, but his mind was full of the imagery of enemy drakes dropping from the sky one by one; and of ground units burning, drake fire immolating their sorry bodies, their screams brief and terrible.

More signatures closed on him from the rear. Some he could pick out and name. Inferno-X was in his slipstream.

'Hal-X, Val-X, what's going on?'

'We want revenge,' said Max. 'We're going after them.'

'Negative, Hal-X. Turn around and we'll see you home safe.'

'It's not that simple. We have to take her down now. Make them suffer.' Max felt some of their anger turn towards the *HoG*'s exec. 'Why haven't they ordered an attack on the *Maputo*?'

'Well, besides the fact that the *HoG* is paralysed and we cannot deploy ground forces to counter the considerable number of enemy grunts already out there setting up their defence nets, latest wisdom is that the *Maputo* was not as sick as she made out a few days ago.'

'She's just walked through a sandstorm,' said Max. 'This is the best chance we'll ever have.'

'Turn around, Hal-X,' said Valera. 'That's an order.'

'Val-X, Flight Com, control your squadron. You will bring them in immediately.'

'Copy, Flight Com. I'm on it.'

'Come on, Max.' It was Monteith. 'We want you back in the squad rack, man.'

'Yeah, Max, we've missed you, buddy,' said Calder.

'Even I've missed seeing your sorry arse,' said Stepanek.

'Max,' said Valera, her voice low. 'They'll declare you rogue and you know what that means. Come home. Trust me, trust the squad.'

'Once I-X, always I-X,' said Redfearn.

Max's heart was thumping. They were flying hard, gaining on the Maf drakes. The *Maputo* lay ahead, skin covered in sand, waiting. Their consciousness flooded with images and feelings of Mother, home and peace... the squad would protect them, they would get fixed, they would get food... but the *Maputo* was walking away unmolested, her drakes safe in her belly, waiting their chance... and Max was back in Landfill.

'Come on, Max, save yourselves for another day,' said Valera.

'They'll throw me away. Back into Landfill.'

'It's too late for that, don't you think?'

'They can't let me live, not like I am now. Can they?'

'They'll have to get through I-X first, Max. Turn around before you drop out of the sky. Look at you. You're a mess.'

And the fact was, they *were* exhausted. They were starving and they were bleeding, weakening with every wingbeat.

They flew on for a few seconds before roaring their defiance at the enemy and breathing a long blast of fire into the dust-filled sky. Max watched the particles ignite; embers falling from the heavens. They turned for home and felt the relief wash over them from the drakes watching over them.

'Hal-X, Flight Com, confirm status.'

'All good, Flight Com. Heading home as ordered.'

'Confirm you are in control, Hal-X.'

'Confirmed,' said Max. Martha grumbled. 'It's just words, princess.'

'Say again?' asked Moeller.

'Nothing,' said Max.

'Form up and await clearance to land, Inferno-X,' said Moeller. 'Good shift today, congratulations. Gurney is a hero. Xavier too. And you should know we've identified the missile agent as a human nerve toxin. They were trying to clean us out and leave the *HoG* for boarding. We got lucky today. Thank you. Flight Com out.'

CHAPTER 40

> It's a terrible thing to have to consider the mortality of your behemoth. But the fact is that the *Heart of Granite* came the closest of any behemoth to fall in the course of this ridiculous war.
>
> COMMANDER NICOLA AVERY

Rosenbach's expletive had echoed around Flight Command in the same instant the guns had fallen silent. Lights had dimmed, fan noise had faded and the few operational systems had snapped off like someone had flicked a switch. Lazily, the backup batteries had come to life and a faint whirr and hum indicated life systems running at minimum. Moeller and Avery shared a smile.

'Colourful language, Rosenbach,' said Avery. 'What just happened?'

'Well, you fired all the guns at once.'

'That is generally accepted practice when under attack.'

'A few junctions have fried as a result. Is everything down where you are?'

'Pretty much. We've still got coms and drake cam feed through the p-palm network but it's gloomy down here to say the least. We have emergency lighting on the flight deck so we're okay for landing.'

'We'll be down a while... Did we chase the Mafs off?'

'Yes, we did, so take your time, do what you need to get my lizard moving again.'

'Copy that, Commander.'

Avery turned to Moeller. 'Okay, let's bring the rest of them home.'

Inferno-X had flown back to the *HoG* in a small but perfectly formed sphere formation with Max and Martha at its centre. The coms might have been quiet, remembering Dan Gurney and Xavier Descontes, but the flying while they awaited clearance to land was anything but. They stormed back and forth along the *Heart of Granite*'s spine performing rolls and loops in formation, mostly out of respect for their fallen but also because they weren't going to miss a chance to show off.

Max felt the excitement mixed with sadness passed to him through the other drakes feeding off the emotions of their pilots. He could see it reflected in their signatures too, and he caught himself wondering how much else was still to be revealed to him.

'Very impressive, Inferno-X,' said Moeller. 'But unnecessary. You are clear to come aboard.'

'Copy, Flight Com,' said Valera. 'Sir, you know Meyer and Sidhu are still out there. Is someone picking them up?'

'Not imminently,' said Moeller. 'They are attached to the *Maputo*'s leg, surrounded by ground forces fifty klicks from here so they're on their own for now. Meyer's a resourceful man. They'll survive till we find a way to get him back.'

Valera led Inferno-X along the spine one final time before heading up to one fifty where they formed a holding ring. They were going to land in chevron order. Max and Martha lined up behind Monteith. They warmed themselves with images of Grim waiting for them and Max chuckled when he overlaid them with those of Anna-Beth and Martha responded with memories of Grim's loving care that actually made him feel jealous momentarily.

'All right, I-X, remember it's a narrow entry on to the flight deck. Keep the tail close above you to give you maximum landing angle. Max, be aware the ramp is only twenty per cent open, the deck is not fully deployed and the tail is at fifty per cent. Nothing you can't handle, just be aware of eddies and vortices playing around the walls.'

'Copy, Skipper. We can handle it,' said Max. 'Quick one-to-one, Skipper?'

'Go ahead, but make it snappy.'

'I want to see Kullani,' said Max. 'They can't keep her in Landfill. Not now.'

'I hear you, Max. But step lightly. Her drake's still emptying and they've done nothing to her yet. We have time.'

'Can I speak to Anna-Beth before we land?'

'Negative, Hal-X. We're still at work, here.'

'Then I'll have to go for the slow motion run to each other on the flight deck when our eyes meet.'

'Dodging the piles of puke from the unfortunate onlookers on the way.'

'Lovely image, thanks.'

'Always a pleasure.' There was a momentary pause. 'All right, I-X, let's get inside. Make it good.'

Max watched Inferno-X disappear under the tail, wincing at the tightness of the approach angle and seeing the gusting and eddies affecting balance.

Nothing we can't handle. Let's have some fun.

Monteith began his final approach. 'Hey, Max, I reckon you'll have quite an audience in there,' he said.

'There'd better be.'

They followed Monteith in very close, keeping in his slipstream, their h-wings keeping them perfectly balanced where he wobbled. Just inside the ramp, they flicked up a few metres, barrel-rolled and soared over the landing strip, heading straight for the packed Flight Command gallery.

Max watched people scattering as they closed, delighting at the open mouths and the shock on the faces of senior execs. In the beat before impact became inevitable, they deployed h-wings and turned hard right, showing the gallery their belly and the pouch, the downdraught of their wings ruining some smart hairstyles. They flicked up into a loop, talons walking across the bone roof of the flight deck before driving down towards the deck, executing a stall, tucking in their wings and dropping gently to the ground right outside their pen.

'Waaaaaaaa hooooooo!'

Martha roared and barked her pleasure. Max felt the thuds and vibrations of the remainder of Inferno-X coming on board. Safe home. Sort of.

The moment they landed, Grim rushed over, beaming through her tears. They bent their long neck down and Grim leapt up to hug them, stroking Martha's cheeks. Martha cooed and nuzzled back. Max wallowed in the emotions washing through him, but part of him felt awkward and wanted to leave them to it. This was still just between the two of them.

You're soft, princess.

He became aware of the weight of attention on them. Ground crew had abandoned their tasks, pilots were hurrying from their drakes, and the gallery was once again bursting with the staff of Flight Command.

Grim stood back to let them come to their seated rest position. Max was brought upright and all he could see was a mass of faces but not yet the one he wanted to see more than anything. Inferno-X was gathering at the front of the crowd and the sight of their faces brought a wonderful feeling across his body. Just to the right stood Moeller, Kirby, Avery, Markov and Solomon; stern expressions had replaced the shock. There were a couple of dozen Mips there too, some turning zapons over in their hands.

'That was some flying, Halloran,' said Moeller over the open com. 'Not sure it'll make the recommended landing protocol, though.'

'You're a damned liability,' said Solomon.

'And you're some welcoming committee,' said Max. 'Thanks for turning out.'

'Just come on out, Max,' said Moeller.

'Yes, sir.'

It was then Max caught sight of Anna-Beth and his heart flipped right over. She'd dragged her hood off her head but her suit showed off every line of her extraordinary body, yet it was her face he wanted to drink in. But she hardly dared look up at the pouch; her eyes were darting all over and she stood a fair way back, not quite lost in the crowd but not wanting to be too far forwards either. Yet she remained the most wonderful sight, hair slick with sweat and lubricant, face red with heat and her mouth... Oh, how he wanted to kiss that mouth.

The pouch released and Martha withdrew from every pierce point, making Max gasp.

Wow, that feels weird. Cold too, princess. Very cold.

Max levered himself out and slid down Martha's chest in a brief flood of lubricant. For a moment he looked back at Martha, feeling utterly lost. He almost climbed straight back in the pouch and had to force himself to turn away. He started to run across the flight deck towards Anna-Beth, the flapping remnants of his ruined suit providing him with little more than basic modesty. But two days in the pouch took their revenge and he stumbled repeatedly, almost falling, his stiff, aching, fatigued muscles betraying him. He slowed to an uncomfortable trot, wanting nothing more than to sag to the floor.

Anna-Beth began fighting her way through the crowd, which moved for her as realisation spread, while both Valera and Moeller gestured to stop anyone interfering. Max suppressed a laugh as Valera's words repeated in his head, and it might well have been like watching the end of a horrible slushy vid but he just didn't care.

He could feel Martha's disapproval, though it wasn't as

intense as within the pouch, and he pushed it back with feelings of warmth. Max almost broke down as he and Anna-Beth met, heaving in a breath when they touched and he felt the embrace he'd thought he'd never enjoy again. Anna-Beth clutched him hard and he felt her fingers brush against, ignore and then begin to probe the pierce points on his neck and down his back.

Max slowly became aware of the crowd's reaction. Some had cheered, some had applauded, but most had looked on in awkward silence and now a nervous, febrile chatter began to spread. Simultaneously, Anna-Beth tensed a little and he didn't try to stop her when she pulled back to take another look at him. He smiled through the chill sweeping his body.

'God, Max...'

'I'm still me,' he said, hoping he didn't sound desperate and willing the uncertainty to fade from her expression. 'Just a little, y'know... holey. Think "cheese" if it helps.'

She smiled and put a hand to his face. Max found he was anxious; he was losing the soul-deep connection to Martha, leaving him just plain 'Max' again and he didn't know what to do.

'You smell terrible,' said Anna-Beth.

'Like I said, still me.'

Anna-Beth clocked movement to his right.

'Uh-oh... Not sure everyone's as happy to see you as I am.' She put her mouth to his ear. 'I love you. Don't fuck up again.'

Max stepped away from her, turning back towards Martha and was greeted by multiple camera flashes from across the crowd.

'Enough of this nauseating homecoming,' said Solomon. 'Get that pilot under arrest and out of here now.'

Military Police raced in, zapons activated, but Inferno-X was faster, knowing what was likely to come. Max found himself completely surrounded by his squad but no one touched him, no one stood too close except Anna-Beth, who had her arms around him again. The Mips pulled up a couple of metres from them and Martha moved a step towards them, grumbling a warning in her throat.

The atmosphere, so briefly of welcome and celebration, became hostile and aggressive. Drakes barked and ground lizards squawked, picking up on the discomfort across the flight deck. Solomon marched up behind the Mips and thrust her way to the front.

'You will stand aside. Halloran will be taken into custody immediately.' She was staring square at Valera, who stared back. Max felt the eyes of some of the squad on him, unable to drag themselves from the sight of the pierce points covering his body. 'Stand aside.'

'I cannot do that without specific instruction from Commander Avery,' said Valera. 'I am concerned for the welfare of my pilot if he is placed in custody and under the terms of his contract—'

'Damn your fucking contract!' snapped Solomon, her eyes bulging, neck taut. She took a breath, remembering herself, but didn't take her eyes from Valera. 'Moeller, clear the flight deck. And someone get Halloran something to wear.'

Moeller spoke through the p-palm network, his voice sounding from hundreds of points at once. 'Clear the flight deck, repeat, clear the flight deck. All pilots to the squad room, flight crew to your pens and care for your drakes. All infantry and ground personnel exit immediately. Move it.'

People started to break away, some reluctantly, others apparently only too pleased to be released from the show. There were more flashes, more photography.

'Moeller, tell them any published photographs will result in serious individual sanctions,' said Solomon.

Moeller did so, his warning stark and bringing complaint and heightened volumes of conversation from the departing crew.

'What's the problem?' said Max into the void. 'It's not like I've grown another head, is it?'

Nobody laughed. Nobody even spoke and Max looked over

to Martha for comfort. She was still staring at the Mips and he could sense the tension within her.

'No, it's more the bloody hundreds of holes all over you that might have people a little spooked,' said Anna-Beth.

He trailed his fingers over a few of them, pulling away slightly as he felt their hard edges. They covered his torso and his limbs and he knew it was the same down his back.

'What are you going to do, eh?' he said.

Someone threw a set of flight crew overalls into the squad and he pulled them on over the remnants of his suit.

'All right,' said Solomon, and she was joined by Avery and Markov, the latter feasting her eyes on Max. 'Let's take a pace back. Squadron Leader Orin, you understand the delicacy of this situation. We cannot release Halloran into the general population.'

'Precisely why we're standing here,' said Valera. Max zipped up the overalls and focused his attention back on Solomon. 'You need to call your dogs off. They aren't taking him.'

Solomon's smile was thin but she waved away the Mips nonetheless. 'Very admirable. No one's going to hurt him but I want him out of sight right now. His drake's pen seems the ideal place.'

Valera nodded and Max cleared his throat. 'I'll be fine; I've got Martha as a minder, after all. But thanks for being there.'

'Once I-X, always I-X,' said Stepanek as Inferno-X began to move aside at a gesture from Valera. Stepanek held out a hand which Max took. 'Welcome back, freak. You look really fucking weird.'

Max chuckled and walked to Martha's pen, walking past her and into the warm interior. The overalls were itchy on his scars and it took everything he had not to scratch himself all over. As soon as he got inside, he was enveloped in a hug by Grim.

'Can't believe you're back.'

'Well, I am, and I'm going to get Risa back for you too.'

Grim hugged him harder then stepped back. 'You mean that?'

'You're family.' Grim smiled. 'Hey, give Martha a scrub, will you? Actually, maybe a bath. She stinks.'

'You smell worse.'

'Behemoth shit will do that.'

'I do not want to know,' said Grim.

Solomon coughed, and after a clasp of hands with Grim he turned round to see Solomon, Kirby, Avery and Markov joining him through the hole where the pen door had been and where the burn marks still scarred the floor.

'Can we make this quick? I need a shower and my pod.'

Solomon waved a hand. 'You can shower in the locker room but you aren't leaving the flight deck. There's a press pack outside that is hungry for meat. I can't let them get to you.'

'You mean Corsini can't allow it.'

Solomon shrugged. 'He's the boss.'

'So what now?' Max felt fidgety, tired, and very, very hungry.

'I won't lie to you, it's a delicate situation... Your death, missing in action, has been widely reported following a swathe of unhelpful stories and interviews.'

'So unreport it.'

The shrug was apologetic this time. 'It isn't quite that easy. There's going to have to be some unravelling. Actually a lot of unravelling. You're going to have to be patient, Max. Assuming you are still Max.'

'Well, of course I'm still bloody Max. Disappointed I'm not a drooling imbecile, are you?' He jabbed a finger at Kirby. 'And I bet you're gutted, aren't you?'

'Take it easy, Max,' said Avery.

'Why? What's this all about?'

'It's about what you represent. What you've become.'

Max stared at Solomon. 'None of you get it. I'm still me, only better. I've shown you how much better we are now. Unbreakable. I'm not the problem. I'm the solution. With us, more like us, we can win the war and go home.'

'I cannot take that risk,' said Solomon. 'I'm sorry.'

'So what, going to have me killed? Well, good luck with that and the grief-stricken drake that comes for you straight afterwards.'

Solomon's smile was condescending. 'And that means what, exactly?'

Max turned towards the flight deck. *Hey, princess, can you still hear me?*

There was swift movement without and Martha's broad muzzle appeared in the unrepaired doorway, scattering the quartet of senior executives left and right. Markov stared at Martha, then back at Max.

'Amazing,' she said, breathless with excitement. 'We are going to learn so much ... Everything. No one is having you killed, Max, believe me.'

'Are you threatening me?' asked Solomon, her eyes on Martha.

Max shrugged. 'If that's how you want to see it. I'm the future. You can't stop what other pilots will choose to do now they know the Fall is not the end but ... evolution; just like Diana and Dylan said it was. Embrace it, because you can't kill it. Martha won't let you.'

'It's easy to sedate a drake,' said Kirby.

'I'm sure you remember how well that worked last time. You don't understand, do you? The present is unwrapped, Marshal General. Best let the kids play with it.'

Solomon threw up her hands. 'You have no idea what this will do, do you? Back home the thought of a human symbiotically patched with alien and reptilian DNA is the surest way to trigger extremists into action and dump Corsini out of power. What then? What happens when the new president stops the war and decommissions every behemoth?'

Max shrugged. 'So what? We could all be dead tomorrow. Today you have to decide what you're going to do.'

Kirby sighed. 'We don't want you dead, Max. But we have to control this story. You understand that, don't you?'

'I understand a whole lot of things. One of them is not to believe anything you say.' He turned to Solomon. 'Or you. Ma'am.'

'Enough,' said Avery. 'We have a behemoth to fix and a regen cycle to run. There are no coms now and no coms while we're on the regen so all these questions can wait. No one on the outside is going to learn anything, are they? Meanwhile, Helena will have a thousand questions and tests for Max. Max *is* my pilot and we know none of the facts, so, there is no need to confine Max here . . . Please, Robert, Alex, would you leave.'

'Don't let him speak to anyone,' said Solomon.

Avery stared at them until they both made to go, and Martha withdrew her head to let them pass.

'Neat trick, eh?' he said to their backs. 'Thank you, ma'am.'

'Most of what the marshal general said was right. You do represent a massive problem on a huge scale. That's not a compliment.'

'Unusually, I'm not out to cause any trouble,' said Max.

'You never are. It just follows you around, doesn't it? Helena, how do you want to play this?'

Markov's face was alive with anticipation. 'Well, I'll need to conduct analysis on them both separately and together. I note the drake has gunshot wounds and needs ERC biotech intervention, so I'll start with you, Max, if that's okay?'

'Whatever you want. So long as you put Risa Kullani back in her drake and let them go through the Fall. She's strong, she can handle it. Don't let them pump drugs into her in Landfill.' Max felt hot all of a sudden. 'She's my wing, my friend. I'll co-operate, if you let her Fall.'

Markov nodded. 'Believe me, Max, nothing is happening to anyone in Neural Trauma until we understand everything about you. Risa is comfortable, her drake will be sustained and that's how it will remain, I promise you that.'

'Release her back to the squad, at least. She's only on heaters. We can deal with that.'

Markov's eyes flicked to Avery. 'I'll see what can be done. It's contingent on you, though, and what we find inside you. Assuming we feel we can control it, we'll let Kullani back to her drake and see her through the Fall. How does that sound?'

'Deal.'

'Good. You need rest and food, and then we'll begin. Solomon needs a story to tell, and me and you have a chance to write it for her.'

'Understood,' said Max.

Markov smiled. 'I cannot tell you how excited I am to get started so don't relax too much, will you? Right, I'll go and get the labs set up and brief the team.'

She began to walk away but stopped as main lights came on, and red lights began flashing as the flight deck and ramp began to complete their very belated deployment. A ripple ran through the *HoG*'s body and her legs began to sway gently as power was returned.

'She's good, that Eleanor of yours,' said Avery.

'Hands off. She stays with the ERC.' She looked at Max for a last time. 'You're a bona fide scientific miracle. Look after yourself.'

Max watched her go. 'Miracle, eh? I can live with that.'

Avery cleared her throat. 'Well, rein yourself in. You know there are going to be tests. A lot of tests. The professor is desperate to get her needles and probes into you.'

'Don't, ma'am, you're making me excited,' said Max.

Avery chuckled. 'What are we going to do with you, Max?'

'A nice warm bath and a cup of hot cocoa?'

'Now that is an order I am happy to make on your behalf.' She shouted through the door. 'Mister Moeller!'

'Yes, Commander.'

Moeller trotted over to the pen. Avery was on the move as she spoke.

'Halloran requires a bath and a cup of hot cocoa in bed. See he gets both, will you?'

She carried on walking. Max turned to Moeller and grinned.

'Good to see you, sir,' he said. 'I really mean that.'

'It's good to have you back, son,' said Moeller. A thought struck him and a broad smile grew on his face. 'You're going to give Solomon and Kirby a whole heap of grief, aren't you?'

'I think it's inevitable, sir.'

'Good,' said Moeller. 'Good lad.'

'How difficult would you like me to make it for them?' said Max, warming to the conversation.

'Well, as you know, I cannot sanction any action that would damage a fellow officer, but let's just say that your honest testimony and a supportive set of test results would be... beneficial. To us both.'

'I'll do what I can,' said Max. 'Do I get my bath and cocoa now?'

Moeller laughed. 'That you do, Hal-X. That you do.'

ACKNOWLEDGEMENTS

Thank you to Gillian Redfearn, whose unstinting attention, support, belief and friendship have helped me beyond measure; to Oscar who I joined in a game when he was three years old and the idea it inspired resulted in this book; and to my wife Clare whose gift of the time to pursue my dreams is so precious.